THE LAST DAYS OF
POMPEII

Edward George Earle Lytton Bulwer-Lytton, was born in London in 1803. He entered politics in 1831 and wrote THE LAST DAYS OF POMPEII in 1834. He was the author of many other books, plays, and poems during his life-time but this book was the most successful and remained the best known. He became a peer in 1855 and died in 1873.

THE LAST DAYS OF
POMPEII

A NOVEL BY
LORD LYTTON

Marshall Cavendish London

Published by Marshall Cavendish Publications Limited
58 Old Compton Street, London W1V 5PA.

Annotations and illustrations © 1976 by the Felix Gluck Press Limited,
Twickenham.
Illustrated by Harold T. King
Abridged text annotated and edited by Robin Wright, B.A. (Oxon.)
Historical Consultants: Dr. J. Ward-Perkins, former Director of the
British School in Rome, and Amanda Claridge

This volume first published in 1976
Printed by Sackville Smeets Ltd., London, typesetting by Ronset Ltd.,
Darwen, Lancs.

ISBN 0 85685 250 3

c.4

CONTENTS

LIST OF ILLUSTRATIONS

66 Some of the many types of gladiators from a stucco original in Pompeii.

67 Gladiator's leg irons – these were found in the gladiators' barracks at Pompeii; they were used to punish gladiators.

68 Doorway and hinge. Reconstruction of doorway. Doors were usually studded with ornamental nails.

69 Glass cup.

70 Cross-section of a tomb, showing the urns in the niches. Cross-section of an urn used to contain the ashes of the dead.

71 Cymbals. Pipe. Flutes.
Back and front view of a tombstone.

72 Roman lock.

73 Roman lock and key.

74 Money-changer's booth, often set up in the Forum.

75 Oil lamp and stand made of bronze. Glass bowl.

76 Money boxes. A metal money box which could be opened with a key, and two terra cotta ones which had to be smashed to retrieve the money.

78 Collapsable bronze table. The top would be inter-changeable. In the drawing the legs are not fully extended.

79 Gladiators' barracks.

81 Stilus. This was the instrument used for inscribing messages on wax tablets.

82 Gong made of bronze.

83 Gladiator's effects found in barracks at Pompeii. Helmet. Shield. Leg guard.

84 Fish hooks found at a blacksmith's at Pompeii.

85 Graffito of gladiators. The gladiator on the right carries a palm of victory whilst the one in the centre is probably being carried away. The inscription refers to the riot between the Nucerians and the Pompeians in AD 59.

86 Wall painting showing the amphitheatre at Pompeii. It commemorates the riot between the citizens of Pompeii and Nuceria (a town not far from Pompeii) in AD 59. The Pompeians slaughtered the opposition but the Emperor, who was a patron of Nuceria, closed the amphitheatre for ten years.

88 Gladiator's helmet found at the barracks at Pompeii.

90 Bed or couch found at Herculaneum. An animal head ornament was more usual than those on the bed.

93 Studded iron chest for storing valuable objects or money.

94 Portable lamp.

95, These are plaster casts of the hollows left by the bodies
97, of the people overwhelmed by the lava flow from Vesuvius.
100

96 Terra cotta pot. Glass jug. Bronze cooking pot.

99 Statue of Augustus depicted as Jupiter. Skull found at Pompeii by Lord Lytton on which it is said he based the character Arbaces.

101 Roman merchant ship. Reconstruction of one of the merchant ships of the kind that must have regularly visited the port of Pompeii.

CHARTS (Numbers indicate pages next to sets of charts)

18 Map of areas of Pompeii and Herculaneum, showing places linked to this book.
Reconstructed maps of Pompeii and Herculaneum.
Games and gaming in ancient Rome.

34 Inside a Temple.
Religions and their Gods.
Roman food.

66 A bakers' shop.
Transport in the Roman Empire.
Political and social organisation.

94 The Roman year.
Pompeian houses.
Volcanoes.

MIRROR

CHARACTERS

Apæcides	a young priest of Isis, intense brother of Ione
Arbaces	a sinister priest of Isis, prone to corrupting the young
Berbix	a gladiator
Burbo	a tavern-keeper and ex-gladiator, cousin of Calenus and husband of Stratonice
Calenus	an unprepossessing and grasping assistant to Arbaces, cousin of Burbo
Callias	a freedman in Arbaces' household
Clodius	a delicate young parasite, addicted to the dice
Davus	a slave of Ione
Diomed	a rich and pompous vulgarian, father of Julia
Eumolpus	a gladiator
Fulvia	a widow
Fulvius	a poet
Glaucus	our graceful hero, Athenian, generous and rich
Ione	our beautiful heroine, Athenian, orphan and sister of Apæcides
Julia	a rich, graceless, handsome girl, daughter of Diomed
Lydon	a young gladiator, son of Medon
Medon	a slave of Diomed, a Christian, father of Lydon
Nepimus	a gladiator
Niger	a gladiator
Nobilior	a gladiator
Nydia	a loving, blind slave-girl
Olinthus	a proselytizing Christian
Pansa	a self-important, ineffectual ædile
Sallust	a young poet, overfond of eating
Sosia	a foolish slave of Arbaces
Sporus	a gladiator
Staphyla	a former slave-girl of Stratonice
Stratonice	Amazonian wife of Burbo
Tetraides	a gladiator
Vespius	a warrior hero from Herculaneum
Witch of Vesuvius	a terrifying, deathlike hag

BOOK ONE

THE TWO GENTLEMEN OF POMPEII

'Ho, Diomed, well met! Do you sup with Glaucus to-night?' said a young man of small stature, who wore his tunic in those loose and effeminate folds which proved him to be a gentleman and a coxcomb.

'Alas, no! dear Clodius; he has not invited me,' replied Diomed, a man of portly frame and of middle age. 'By Pollux, a scurvy trick! for they say his suppers are the best in Pompeii.'

'Pretty well—though there is never enough of wine for me. It is not the old Greek blood that flows in his veins, for he pretends that wine makes him dull the next morning.'

'He is fond of the dice, too, I hear.'

'He is fond of every pleasure; and while he likes the pleasure of giving suppers, we are all fond of *him*.'

'Well, you must sup with me some evening; I have tolerable murænæ in my reservoir, and I will ask Pansa the ædile to meet you.'

'An ostentatious, bustling, ill-bred fellow,' muttered Clodius to himself, as he sauntered slowly away. 'He thinks with his feasts and his wine-cellars to make us forget that he is the son of a freedman;—and so we will, when we do him the honour of winning his money; these rich plebeians are a harvest for us spendthrift nobles.'

Thus soliloquising, Clodius arrived in the Via Domitiana, which was crowded with passengers and chariots, and exhibited all that gay and animated exuberance of life and motion which we find at this day in the streets of Naples.

The bells of the cars as they rapidly glided by each other jingled merrily on the ear, and Clodius with smiles or nods claimed familiar acquaintance with whatever equipage was most elegant or fantastic: in fact, no idler was better known in Pompeii.

'What, Clodius! and how have you slept on your good fortune?' cried, in a pleasant and musical voice, a young man, in a chariot of the most fastidious and graceful fashion. The owner himself was of that slender and beautiful symmetry from which the sculptors of Athens drew their models; his Grecian origin betrayed itself in his light but clustering locks, and the perfect harmony of his features. He wore no toga, which in the time of the emperors had indeed ceased to be the general distinction of the Romans, and was especially ridiculed by the pretenders to fashion; but his tunic glowed in the richest hues of the Tyrian dye, and the fibulæ, or buckles, by which it was fastened, sparkled with emeralds: around his neck was a chain of gold, which in the middle of his breast twisted itself into the form of a serpent's head, from the mouth of which hung pendent a large signet ring of elaborate and most exquisite workmanship; the sleeves of the tunic were loose, and fringed at the hand with gold: and across the waist a girdle wrought in arabesque designs, and of the same material as the fringe, served in lieu of pockets for the receptacle of the handkerchief and the purse, the stilus and the tablets.

'My dear Glaucus!' said Clodius, 'I rejoice to see that your losses have so little affected your mien. Why, you seem as if you had been inspired by Apollo, and your face shines with happiness like a glory; any one might take you for the winner, and me for the loser.'

'And what is there in the loss or gain of those dull pieces of metal that should change our spirit, my Clodius? You sup with me to-night, you know.'

'Who ever forgets the invitation of Glaucus!'

'But which way go you now?'

'Why, I thought of visiting the baths: but it wants yet an hour to the usual time.'

'Well, I will dismiss my chariot, and go with you. So, so, my Phylias,' stroking the horse nearest to him, which by a low neigh and with backward ears playfully acknowledged the courtesy: 'a holiday for you to-day. Is he not handsome, Clodius?'

'Worthy of Phœbus,' returned the noble parasite,—'or of Glaucus.'

BELLS

THE BLIND FLOWER-GIRL

DENARIUS OF CLAUDIUS   DENARIUS OF MARCUS ANTONIUS

DENARIUS OF TIBERIUS   DENARIUS OF AUGUSTUS

Talking lightly on a thousand matters, the two young men sauntered through the streets; they were now in that quarter which was filled with the gayest shops, their open interiors all and each radiant with the gaudy yet harmonious colours of frescoes, inconceivably varied in fancy and design. The sparkling fountains, that at every vista threw upwards their grateful spray in the summer air; the crowd of passengers, or rather loiterers, mostly clad in robes of the Tyrian dye; the gay groups collected round each more attractive shop; the slaves passing to and fro with buckets of bronze, cast in the most graceful shapes, and borne upon their heads; the country girls stationed at frequent intervals with baskets of blushing fruit, and flowers more alluring to the ancient Italians than to their descendants; the numerous haunts which fulfilled with that idle people the office of cafés and clubs at this day; the shops, where on shelves of marble were ranged the vases of wine and oil, and before whose thresholds, seats, protected from the sun by a purple awning, invited the weary to rest and the indolent to lounge—made a scene of such glowing and vivacious excitement, as might well give the Athenian spirit of Glaucus an excuse for its susceptibility to joy.

'Talk to me no more of Rome,' said he to Clodius. 'Pleasure is too stately and ponderous in those mighty walls: even in the precincts of the court—even in the Golden House of Nero, and the incipient glories of the palace of Titus, there is a certain dulness of magnificence—the eye aches—the spirit is wearied; besides, my Clodius, we are discontented when we compare the enormous luxury and wealth of others with the mediocrity of our own state.'

'It was from that feeling that you chose your summer retreat at Pompeii?'

'It was. I prefer it to Baiæ: I grant the charms of the latter, but I love not the pedants who resort there, and who seem to weigh out their pleasures by the drachm.'

'Yet you are fond of the learned, too; and as for poetry, why your house is literally eloquent with Æschylus and Homer, the epic and the drama.'

Thus conversing, their steps were arrested by a crowd gathered round an open space where three streets met; and, just where the porticoes of a light and graceful temple threw their shade, there stood a young girl, with a flower-basket on her right arm, and a small three-stringed instrument of music in the left hand, to whose low and soft tones she was modulating a wild and half-barbaric air. At every pause in the music she gracefully waved her flower-basket round, inviting the loiterers to buy; and many a sesterce was showered into the basket, either in compliment to the music or in compassion to the songstress—for she was blind.

'I must have yon bunch of violets, sweet Nydia,' said Glaucus, pressing through the crowd, and dropping a handful of small coins into the basket; 'your voice is more charming than ever.'

The blind girl started forward as she heard the Athenian's voice; then as suddenly paused, while the blood rushed violently over neck, cheek, and temples.

'So you are returned!' said she, in a low voice; and then repeated half to herself, 'Glaucus is returned!'

'Yes, child, I have not been at Pompeii above a few days. My garden wants your care, as before; you will visit it, I trust, to-morrow. And mind, no garlands at my house shall be woven by any hands but those of the pretty Nydia.'

Nydia smiled joyously, but did not answer; and Glaucus, placing in his breast the violets he had selected, turned gaily and carelessly from the crowd.

'So she is a sort of client of yours, this child?' said Clodius.

'Ay—does she not sing prettily? She interests me, the poor slave! Besides, she is from the land of the Gods' hill—Olympus frowned upon her cradle—she is of Thessaly.'

'The witches' country.'

'True: but for my part I find every woman a witch; and at Pompeii, by Venus! the very air seems to have taken a love-philtre, so handsome does every face without a beard seem in my eyes.'

'And lo! one of the handsomest in Pompeii, old Diomed's daughter, the rich Julia!' said Clodius, as a young lady, her face covered by her veil, and attended by two female slaves, approached them, in her way to the baths.'

'Fair Julia, we salute thee!' said Clodius.

Julia partly raised her veil, so as with some coquetry to display a bold Roman profile, a full dark bright eye, and a cheek over whose natural olive art shed a fairer and softer rose.

'And Glaucus, too, is returned!' said she, glancing meaningly at the Athenian. 'Has he forgotten,' she added, in a half-whisper, 'his friends of the last year?'

'Beautiful Julia! even Lethe itself, if it disappear in one part of the earth, rises again in another. Jupiter does not allow us ever to forget for more than a moment: but Venus, more harsh still, vouchsafes not even a moment's oblivion.'

'Glaucus is never at a loss for fair words.'

'Who is, when the object of them is so fair?'

'We shall see you both at my father's villa soon,' said Julia, turning to Clodius.

'We will mark the day in which we visit you with a white stone,' answered the gamester.

Julia dropped her veil, but slowly, so that her last glance rested on the Athenian with affected timidity and real boldness; the glance bespoke tenderness and reproach.

The friends passed on.

'Julia is certainly handsome,' said Glaucus.

'And last year you would have made that confession in a warmer tone.'

'True; I was dazzled at the first sight, and mistook for a gem that which was but an artful imitation.'

'Nay,' returned Clodius, 'all women are the same at heart. Happy he who weds a handsome face and a large dower. What more can he desire?'

Glaucus sighed.

They were now in a street less crowded than the rest.

Pompeii was the miniature of the civilisation of that age. Within the narrow compass of its walls was contained, as it were, a specimen of every gift which luxury offerred to power. In its minute but glittering shops, its tiny palaces, its baths, its forum, its theatre, its circus—in the energy yet corruption, in the refinement yet the vice, of its people, you beheld a model of the whole empire.

Crowded in the glassy bay were the vessels of commerce and the gilded galleys for the pleasures of the rich citizens. The boats of the fishermen glided rapidly to and fro; and afar off you saw the tall masts of the fleet under the command of Pliny. Upon the shore sat a Sicilian who, with vehement gestures and flexile features, was narrating to a group of fishermen and peasants a strange tale of shipwrecked mariners and friendly dolphins.

Drawing his comrade from the crowd, the Greek bent his steps towards a solitary part of the beach, and the two friends, seated on a small crag which rose amidst the smooth pebbles, inhaled the voluptuous and cooling breeze, which dancing over the waters, kept music with its invisible feet.

'Tell me, Clodius,' said the Greek at last, 'hast thou ever been in love?'

'Yes, very often.'

'He who has loved often,' answered Glaucus, 'has loved never. There is but one Eros, though there are many counterfeits of him. In fact, I am not in love; but I could be if there were but occasion to see the object. Eros would light his torch, but the priests have given him no oil.'

'Shall I guess the object?—Is it not Diomed's daughter? She adores you, and does not affect to conceal it; and, by Hercules, I say again and again, she is both handsome and rich. She will bind the door-posts of her husband with golden fillets.'

'No, I do not desire to sell myself. Diomed's daughter is handsome, I grant: and at one time, had she not been the grandchild of a freedman, I might have—— Yet no—she carries all her beauty in her face; her manners are not maiden-like, and her mind knows no culture save that of pleasure.'

'You are ungrateful. Tell me, then, who is the fortunate virgin?'

'You shall hear, my Clodius. Several months ago I was sojourning at Naples, a city utterly to my own heart, for it still retains the manners and stamp of its Grecian origin. One day I entered the temple of Minerva, to offer up my prayers, not for myself more than for the city on which Pallas smiles no longer. The temple was empty and deserted. I was startled in the midst of my devotions by a deep sigh; I turned suddenly round, and just behind me was a female. She had raised her veil also in prayer: and when our eyes met, methought a celestial ray shot from those dark and smiling orbs at once into my soul. Never, my Clodius, have I seen mortal face more exquisitely moulded: a certain melancholy softened and yet elevated its expression: that unutterable something which springs from the soul, and which our sculptors have imparted to the aspect of Psyche, gave her beauty I know not what of divine and noble; tears were rolling down her eyes. I guessed at once that she was also of Athenian lineage. I spoke to her, though with a faltering voice— "Art thou not, too, Athenian?" said I, "O beautiful virgin!" At the sound of my voice she blushed, and half drew her veil across her face,—"My birth is of Neapolis", said she, "but my heart, as my lineage, is Athenian."— "Let us, then," said I, "make our offerings together:" and, as the priest now appeared, we stood side by side, while we followed the priest in his ceremonial prayer; together we touched the knees of the goddess—together we laid our olive garlands on the altar. Silently we left the temple, and I was about to ask her where she dwelt, and if I might be permitted to visit her, when a youth, in whose features there was some kindred resemblance to her own, and who stood upon the steps of the fane, took her by the hand. She turned round and bade me farewell. The crowd separated us: I saw her no more. This is all

SILVER DRINKING CUP

my history. I do not love; but I remember and regret.'

As Clodius was about to reply, a slow and stately step approached them, and at the sound it made amongst the pebbles, each turned, and each recognised the new-comer.

It was a man who had scarcely reached his fortieth year, of tall stature, and of a thin but nervous and sinewy frame. His skin, dark and bronzed, betrayed his Eastern origin; and his features had something Greek in their outline (especially in the chin, the lip, and the brow), save that the nose was somewhat raised and aquiline; and the bones, hard and visible, forbade that fleshy and waving contour which, on the Grecian physiognomy preserved even in manhood the round and beautiful curves, of youth. His eyes, large and black as the deepest night, shone with no varying and uncertain lustre. A deep, thoughtful, and half-melancholy calm seemed unalterably fixed in their majestic and commanding gaze. His step and mien were peculiarly sedate and lofty, and something foreign in the fashion and the sober hues of his sweeping garments added to the impressive effect of his quiet countenance and stately form. Each of the young men, in saluting the new-comer, made mechanically, and with care to conceal it from him, a slight gesture or sign with their fingers; for Arbaces, the Egyptian, was supposed to possess the fatal gift of the evil eye.

'The scene must, indeed, be beautiful,' said Arbaces, with a cold though courteous smile, 'which draws the gay Clodius, and Glaucus the all-admired, from the crowded thoroughfares of the city.'

'Is Nature ordinarily so unattractive?' asked the Greek.

'To the dissipated—yes.'

Thus saying, he gathered his robe around him, and slowly swept away.

'I breathe more freely,' said Clodius. 'Imitating the Egyptians, we sometimes introduce a skeleton at our feasts. In truth, the presence of such an Egyptian as yon gliding shadow were spectre enough to sour the richest grape of the Falernian.'

'Strange man?' said Glaucus, musingly; 'yet dead though he seem to pleasure, and cold to the objects of the world, scandal belies him, or his house and his heart could tell a different tale.'

'Ah! there are whispers of other orgies than those of Osiris in his gloomy mansion. He is rich, too, they say. Can we not get him amongst us, and teach him the charms of dice? Pleasure of pleasures! hot fever of hope and fear! inexpressible unjaded passion! how fiercely beautiful thou art, O Gaming!'

'Inspired—inspired!' cried Glaucus, laughing; 'the oracle speaks poetry in Clodius. What miracle next!'

THE HOUSES OF POMPEII

Heaven had given to Glaucus every blessing but one: it had given him beauty, health, fortune, genius, illustrious descent, a heart of fire, a mind of poetry; but it had denied him the heritage of freedom. He was born in Athens, the subject of Rome. Succeeding early to an ample inheritance, he had indulged that inclination for travel so natural to the young, and had drunk deep of the intoxicating draught of pleasure amidst the gorgeous luxuries of the imperial court.

His retreat in Pompeii was at once one of the smallest, and yet one of the most adorned and finished of all the private mansions of Pompeii.

'Well, I must own,' said the ædile Pansa, 'that your house is a gem of its kind.'

'Praise from Pansa is indeed valuable on such subjects,' said Clodius, gravely.

'You flatter me, my Clodius; indeed you do,' quoth the ædile. 'You flatter me; but there is something pretty in the colours, to say nothing of the design;—and then for my kitchen, my friends—ah! that was all my fancy.'

'What is the design?' said Glaucus. 'I have not yet seen your kitchen, though I have often witnessed the excellence of its cheer.'

GLASS DRINKING HORN

'A cook, my Athenian—a cook sacrificing the trophies of his skill on the altar of Vesta, with a beautiful muræna (taken from the life) on a spit at a distance;—there is some invention there!'

At that instant the slaves appeared, bearing a tray covered with the first preparative initia of the feast. Amidst delicious figs, fresh herbs strewed with snow, anchovies, and eggs, were ranged small cups of diluted wine sparingly mixed with honey. As these were placed on the table, young slaves bore round to each of the five guests (for there were no more) the silver basin of perfumed water, and napkins edged with a purple fringe. But the ædile ostentatiously drew forth his own napkin, which was not, indeed, of so fine a linen, but in which the fringe was twice as broad, and wiped his hands with the parade of a man who felt he was calling for admiration.

'A splendid *mappa* that of yours,' said Clodius; 'why, the fringe is as broad as a girdle!'

'A trifle, my Clodius: a trifle! They tell me this stripe is the latest fashion at Rome; but Glaucus attends to these things more than I.'

'May this cup be my last!' said the young Sallust, as the table, cleared of its first stimulants, was now loaded with the substantial part of the entertainment, and the ministering slave poured forth to him a brimming cyathus—'May this cup be my last, but it is the best wine I have drunk at Pompeii!'

'When is our next wild-beast fight?' said Clodius to Pansa.

'It stands fixed for the ninth ide of August,' answered Pansa: 'on the day after the Vulcanalia;—we have a most lovely young lion for the occasion.'

'Whom shall we get for him to eat?' asked Clodius. 'Alas! there is a great scarcity of criminals. You must positively find some innocent or other to condemn to the lion, Pansa!'

'Indeed I have thought very seriously about it of late,' replied the ædile, gravely. 'It was a most infamous law that which forbade us to send our own slaves to the wild beasts. Not to let us do what we like with our own, that's what I call an infringement on property itself.'

'Well, thank Jupiter and the Fates! we have no Nero at present,' said Sallust.

'He was, indeed, a tyrant; he shut up our amphitheatre for ten years.'

'I wonder it did not create a rebellion,' said Sallust.

'It very nearly did,' returned Pansa, with his mouth full of wild boar.

Here the conversation was interrupted for a moment by a flourish of flutes, and two slaves entered with a single dish.

'Ah, what delicacy hast thou in store for us now, my Glaucus?' cried the young Sallust, with sparkling eyes.

Sallust was only twenty-four, but he had no pleasure in life like eating—perhaps he had exhausted all the others: yet had he some talent, and an excellent heart—as far as it went.

'I know its face, by Pollux!' cried Pansa. 'It is an Ambracian kid.'

'The kid is excellent,' said Sallust. The slave, whose duty it was to carve, and who valued himself on his science, had just performed that office on the kid to the sound of music, his knife keeping time, beginning with a low tenor and accomplishing the arduous feat amidst a magnificent diapason.

'Your cook is, of course, from Sicily?' said Pansa.

'Yes, of Syracuse.'

'I will play you for him,' said Clodius. 'We will have a game between the courses.'

The musicians, who were stationed in the portico without, had commenced their office with the kid; they now directed the melody into a more soft, a more gay, yet it may be a

POTTERY DRINKING HORN

more intellectual strain; and they chanted that song of Horace beginning 'Persicos odi,' &c., so impossible to translate, and which they imagined applicable to a feast that was simple enough for the gorgeous revelry of the time.

'Ah, good old Horace!' said Sallust, compassionately; 'he sang well of feats and girls, but not like our modern poets.'

'The immortal Fulvius, for instance,' said Clodius.

'Ah, Fulvius, the immortal!' said his umbra.

'And Spuræna; and Caius Mutius, who wrote three epics in a year—could Horace do that, or Virgil either?' said Lepidus.

'By the way,' said Sallust, 'have you seen the new ode by Spuræna, in honour of our Egyptian Isis? It is magnificent—the true religious fervour.'

'Isis seems a favourite divinity at Pompeii,' said Glaucus.

'Yes!' said Pansa, 'she is exceedingly in repute just at this moment; her statue has been uttering the most remarkable oracles. I am not superstitious, but I must confess that she has more than once assisted me materially in my magistracy with her advice. Her priests are so pious, too! none of your gay, none of your proud, ministers of Jupiter and Fortune: they walk barefoot, eat no meat, and pass the greater part of the night in solitary devotion!'

'An example to our other priesthoods, indeed!—Jupiter's temple wants reforming sadly,' said Lepidus, who was a great reformer for all but himself.

'They say that Arbaces the Egyptian has imparted some most solemn mysteries to the priests of Isis,' observed Sallust. 'He boasts his descent from the race of Rameses, and declares that in his family the secrets of remotest antiquity·are treasured.'

'He certainly possesses the gift of the evil eye,' said Clodius.

'If Arbaces were not so rich,' said Pansa, with a stately air, 'I should stretch my authority a little, and inquire into the truth of the report which calls him an astrologer and a sorcerer. Agrippa, when ædile of Rome, banished all such terrible citizens. But a rich man—it is the duty of an ædile to protect the rich!'

'What think you of this new sect, which I am told has even a few proselytes in Pompeii, these followers of the Hebrew God—Christus?'

'Oh, mere speculative visionaries,' said Clodius; 'they have not a single gentleman amongst them; their proselytes are poor, insignificant, ignorant people!'

'Who ought, however, to be crucified for their blasphemy,' said Pansa, with vehemence; 'they deny Venus and Jove! Nazarene is but another name for atheist. Let me catch them —that's all.'

The second course was gone—the feasters fell back on their couches—there was a pause while they listened to the soft voices of the South, and the music of the Arcadian reed. Glaucus was the most rapt and the least inclined to break the silence, but Clodius began already to think that they wasted time.

'*Bene vobis!* (your health!) my Glaucus,' said he, quaffing a cup to each letter of the Greek's name, with the ease of the practised drinker. 'Will you not be avenged on your ill-fortune of yesterday? See, the dice court us.'

'As you will,' said Glaucus.

'The dice in summer, and I an ædile!' said Pansa, magisterially; 'it is against all law.'

'Not in your presence, grave Pansa,' returned Clodius, rattling the dice in a long box; 'your presence restrains all license: it is not the thing, but the excess of the thing, that hurts.'

The third course, consisting of a variety of fruits, pistachio nuts, sweetmeats, tarts, and confectionery tortured into a thousand fantastic and airy shapes, was now placed upon the table; and the ministri, or attendants, also set there the wine (which had hitherto been handed round to the guests) in large jugs of glass, each bearing upon it the schedule of its age and quality.

'This cup to the Graces!' said Pansa, and he thrice emptied his calix. The guests followed his example.

'Companions,' said Clodius, 'I give you the beautiful Ione.'

'Ione!—the name is Greek,' said Glaucus, in a soft voice. 'I drink the health with delight. But who is Ione?'

'She is of the most rare beauty,' said Pansa; 'and what a voice!'

'She can feed only on nightingales' tongues,' said Clodius.

DICE

IMPERIAL DENARIUS OF AUGUSTUS

DENARIUS OF POMPEIUS RUFUS

'Nightingales' tongues!—beautiful thought!' sighed the umbra.

'Enlighten me, I beseech you,' said Glaucus.

'Know then, my Glaucus,' said Clodius, 'that Ione is a stranger who has but lately come to Pompeii. She sings like Sappho, and her songs are her own composing; and as for the tibia, and the cithara, and the lyre, I know not in which she must outdoes the Muses. Her beauty is most dazzling. Her house is perfect; such taste—such gems—such bronzes! She is rich, and generous.'

'Her lovers, of course,' said Glaucus, 'take care that she does not starve; and money lightly won is always lavishly spent.'

'Her lovers—ah, there is the enigma!— Ione has but one vice—she is chaste. She has all Pompeii at her feet, and she has no lovers: she will not even marry.'

'No lovers!' echoed Glaucus.

'No; she has the soul of Vesta, with the girdle of Venus.'

'A miracle!' cried Glaucus. 'Can we not see her?'

'I will take you there this evening,' said Clodius; 'meanwhile——,' added he, once more rattling the dice.

'By Pollux!' cried Glaucus, 'this is the second time I have thrown the caniculæ' (the lowest throw).

'Now Venus befriend me!' said Clodius, rattling the box for several moments. 'O Alma Venus—it is Venus herself!' as he threw the highest cast, named from that goddess,—whom he who wins money, indeed, usually propitiates!

'Venus is ungrateful to me,' said Glaucus, gaily; 'I have always sacrificed on her altar.'

The conversation now grew general and animated; the wine circulated more freely; and Ione once more became the subject of euology to the guests of Glaucus.

13

'Instead of watching the stars; let us visit one at whose beauty the stars grow pale,' said Lepidus.

They passed the jewellers' quarter, sparkling with lights, caught and reflected by the gems displayed in the shops, and arrived at last at the door of Ione. The vestibule blazed with rows of lamps; curtains of embroidered purple hung on either aperture of the tablinum, whose walls and mosaic pavement glowed with the richest colours of the artist; and under the portico which surrounded the odorous viridarium they found Ione, already surrounded by adoring and applauding guests!

'Did you say she was Athenian?' whispered Glaucus, ere he passed into the peristyle.

'No, she is from Naples.'

'Naples!' echoed Glaucus; and at that moment the group, dividing on either side of Ione, gave to his view that bright, that nymph-like beauty, which for months had shone down upon the waters of his memory.

GOLDEN ARM BAND

THE TEMPLE OF ISIS

The story returns to the Egyptian. We left Arbaces upon the shores of the noonday sea, after he had parted from Glaucus and his companion. As he approached to the more crowded part of the bay, he paused and gazed upon that animated scene with folded arms, and a bitter smile upon his dark features.

'Gulls, dupes, fools, that ye are!' muttered he to himself; 'whether business or pleasure, trade or religion, be your pursuit, you are equally cheated by the passions that ye should rule! How I could loathe you, if I did not hate—yes, hate! Greek or Roman, it is from us, from the dark lore of Egypt, that ye have stolen the fire that gives you souls. My soul, by the power of its wisdom, controls and chains you, though the fetters are unseen. So long as craft can master force, so long as religion has a cave from which oracles can dupe mankind, the wise hold an empire over earth. Even from your vices Arbaces distils his pleasures;—pleasures unprofaned by vulgar eyes—pleasures vast, wealthy, inexhaustible, of which your enervate minds, in their unimaginative sensuality, cannot conceive or dream!'

Thus saying, the Egyptian moved slowly on; and, entering the town, his tall figure towered above the crowded throng of the forum, and swept towards the small but graceful temple consecrated to Isis.

That edifice was then but of recent erection; the ancient temple had been thrown down in the earthquake sixteen years before, and the new building had become as much in vogue with the versatile Pompeians. As Arbaces now arrived at the rails which separated the profane from the sacred place, a crowd, composed of all classes, but especially of the commercial, collected, breathless and reverential, before the many altars which rose in the open court. In the walls of the cella, elevated on seven steps of Parian marble, various statues stood in niches, and those walls were ornamented with the pomegranate consecrated to Isis. An oblong pedestal occupied the interior building, on which stood two statues, one of Isis, and its companion represented the silent and mystic Orus. But the building contained many other deities to grace the court of the Egyptian deity: her kindred and many-titled Bacchus, and the Cyprian Venus, a Grecian disguise for herself, rising from her bath, and the dog-headed Anubis, and the ox Apis, and various Egyptian idols of uncouth form and unknown appellations.

Ranged now on either side the steps was the sacrificial crowd, arrayed in white garments, while at the summit stood two of the inferior priests, the one holding a palm-branch, the other a slender sheaf of corn. In the narrow passage in front thronged the bystanders.

'And what,' whispered Arbaces to one of the bystanders, who was a merchant engaged in the Alexandrian trade, which trade had probably first introduced in Pompeii the worship of the Egyptian goddess—'what occasion now assembles you before the altars of the venerable Isis? It seems, by the white robes of the group before me, that a sacrifice is to be rendered; and by the assembly of the priests, that ye are prepared for some oracle. To what question is it to vouchsafe a reply?'

'We are merchants,' replied the bystander (who was no other than Diomed) in the same voice, 'who seek to know the fate of our vessels, which sail for Alexandria to-morrow. We are about to offer up a sacrifice and implore an answer from the goddess. I am not one of those who have petitioned the priest to sacrifice, as you may see by my dress, but I have some interest in the success of the fleet;—by Jupiter! yes. I have a pretty trade, else how could I live in these hard times?'

The Egyptian replied gravely,—'That though Isis was properly the goddess of agriculture, she was no less the patron of commerce.' Then turning his head towards the east, Arbaces seemed absorbed in silent prayer.

And now in the centre of the steps appeared a priest robed in white from head to foot, the veil parting over the crown; two new priests relieved those hitherto stationed at either corner, being naked half-way down to the breast, and covered, for the rest, in white and loose robes. At the same time, seated at the bottom of the steps, a priest commenced a solemn air upon a long wind instrument of music. Half-way down the steps stood another flamen, holding in one hand the votive wreath, in the other a white wand; while, adding to the picturesque scene of that eastern ceremony, the stately ibis (bird sacred to the Egyptian worship) looked mutely down from the wall upon the rite, or stalked beside the altar at the base of the steps.

At that altar now stood the sacrificial flamen.

The countenance of Arbaces seemed to lose all its rigid calm while the aruspices inspected the entrails, and to be intent in pious anxiety. It was then that a dead silence fell over the whispering crowd, and the priests gathering round the cella, another priest, naked save by a cincture round the middle, rushed forward, and dancing with wild gestures, implored an answer from the goddess. He ceased at last in exhaustion, and a low murmuring noise was heard within the body of the statue: thrice the head moved, and the lips parted, and then a hollow voice uttered these mystic words:—

'There are waves like chargers that meet and glow,
There are graves ready wrought in the rocks below,
On the brow of the future the dangers lour,
But blest are your barks in the fearful hour.'

The voice ceased—the crowd breathed more freely—the merchants looked at each other. 'Nothing can be more plain,' murmured Diomed; 'there is to be a storm at sea, as there very often is at the beginning of autumn, but our vessels are to be saved. O beneficent Isis!'

'Lauded eternally be the goddess!' said the merchants: 'what can be less equivocal than her prediction?'

Raising one hand in sign of silence to the people, for the rites of Isis enjoined what to the lively Pompeians was an impossible suspense from the use of the vocal organs, the chief priest poured his libation on the altar, and after a short concluding prayer the ceremony was over, and the congregation dismissed. Still, however, as the crowd dispersed themselves here and there, the Egyptian lingered by the railing, and when the space became tolerably cleared, one of the priests, approaching it, saluted him with great appearance of friendly familiarity.

The countenance of the priest was remarkably unprepossessing. Around the brows the skin was puckered into a web of deep and intricate wrinkles—the eyes, dark and small, rolled in a muddy and yellow orbit—the nose, short yet coarse, was distended at the nostrils like a satyr's,—and the thick but pallid lips, the high cheek-bones, the livid and motley hues that struggled through the parchment skin, completed a countenance which none could behold without repugnance, and few without terror and distrust: whatever the wishes of the mind, the animal frame was well fitted to execute them; the wiry muscles of the throat, the broad chest, the nervous hands and lean gaunt arms, which were bared above the elbow, betokened a form capable alike of great active exertion and passive endurance.

'Calenus,' said the Egyptian to this fascinating flamen, 'you have improved the voice of the statue much by attending to my suggestion; and your verses are excellent. Always prophesy good fortune, unless there is an absolute impossibility of its fulfilment.'

'Assuredly,' replied the priest, leading the way to one of the small chambers which surrounded the open gate. Here they seated themselves before a small table spread with dishes containing fruit and eggs, and various cold meats, with vases of excellent wine, of which while the companions partook, a curtain, drawn across the entrance opening to the court, concealed them from view, but admonished them by the thinness of the partition to speak low, or to speak no secrets: they chose the former alternative.

'Thou knowest,' said Arbaces, in a voice that scarcely stirred the air, so soft and inward was its sound, 'that it has ever been my maxim to attach myself to the young. From their flexile and unformed minds I can carve out my fittest tools. I weave—I warp—I mould them at my will. Of the men I make merely followers or servants; of the women—'

'Mistresses,' said Calenus, as a livid grin distorted his ungainly features.

'Yes, I do not disguise it: woman is the main object, the great appetite, of my soul. I loathe your ready-made and ripened courtesans; it is in the soft and unconscious progress of innocence to desire that I find the true charm of love; it is thus that I defy satiety; and by contemplating the freshness of others, I sustain the freshness of my own sensations. From the young hearts of my victims I draw the ingredients of the caldron in which I re-youth myself. But enough of this: to the subject before us. You know, then, that in Neapolis some time since I encountered Ione and Apæcides, brother and sister, the children of Athenians who had settled at Neapolis. The death of their parents, who knew and esteemed me, constituted me their guardian. I was not unmindful of the trust. The youth, docile and mild, yielded readily to the impression I sought to stamp upon him. To Apæcides I taught the solemn faith of Isis. I unfolded to him something of those sublime allegories which are couched beneath her worship. I excited in a soul peculiarly alive to religious fervour that enthusiasm which imagination begets on faith. I have placed him amongst you: he is one of you.'

'He is so,' said Calenus: 'but in thus stimulating his faith, you have robbed him of wisdom. He is horror-struck that he is no longer duped: our sage delusions, our speaking statues and secret staircases dismay and revolt him; he pines; he wastes away; he mutters to himself; he refuses to share our ceremonies. He has been known to frequent the company of men suspected of adherence to that new and atheistical creed which denies all our gods, and terms our oracles the inspirations of that malevolent spirit of which eastern tradition speaks. Our oracles—alas! we know well whose inspirations *they* are!'

'This is what I feared,' said Arbaces, musingly, 'from various reproaches he made me when I last saw him. Of late he hath shunned my steps: I must find him: I must continue my lessons: I must lead him into the adytum of Wisdom. I must teach him that there are two stages of sanctity—the first, FAITH—the next, DELUSION; the one for the vulgar, the second for the sage.'

'I never passed through the first,' said Calenus; 'nor you either, I think, my Arbaces.'

'You err,' replied the Egyptian, gravely. 'I believe at this day (not indeed that which I teach, but that which I teach not). Nature has a sanctity against which I cannot (nor would I) steel conviction. I believe in mine own knowledge, and that has revealed to me,—but no matter. Now to earthlier and more inviting themes. If I thus fulfilled my object with Apæcides, what was my design for Ione? Thow knowest already I intend her for my queen—my bride—my heart's Isis. Never till I saw her knew I all the love of which my nature is capable.'

'She is not yours yet, then?' said the priest.

'No; she loves me—but as a friend:—she loves me with her mind only.'

'And hast thou no fear, then, of thy rivals? The gallants of Italy are skilled in the art to please.'

'None! Her Greek soul despises the barbarian Romans, and would scorn itself if it admitted a thought of love for one of that upstart race.'

'But thou art an Egyptian, not a Greek!'

'Egypt,' replied Arbaces, 'is the mother of Athens. It is time for me to begin my operations on her fancies and her heart: in the one case, to divert the source of love to me; in the other, in me to awaken it. It is for this that I have sought you.'

'And how can I assist you?'

'I am about to invite her to a feast in my house: I wish to dazzle—to bewilder—to inflame her senses. Our arts—the arts by which Egypt trained her young novitiates—must be employed; and, under veil of the mysteries of religion, I will open to her the secrets of love.'

'Ah! now I understand:—one of those voluptuous banquets that, despite our dull vows of mortified coldness, we, thy priests of Isis, have shared at thy house.'

'No, no! Thinkest thou her chaste eyes are ripe for such scenes? No; but first we must ensnare the brother—an easier task. Listen to me, while I give you my instructions.'

TEMPLE OF ISIS

1. TEMPLE OF ISIS
2. SHRINE OF HARPOCRATES
3. PURGATORIUM
   WITH STAIRS TO CELLAR
4. ALTAR
5. HALL OF INITIATION
6. HALL OF MYSTERIES
7. PIT FOR REFUSE OF
   SACRIFICES
   PRIESTS' QUARTERS
8. KITCHEN
9. DINING ROOM
10. BEDROOM

MORE OF THE FLOWER-GIRL

The sun shone gaily into the house of Glaucus. The morning rays entered through rows of small casements, and through the door which opened on the garden, that answered to the inhabitants of the southern cities the same purpose that a greenhouse or conservatory does to us. The size of the garden did not adapt it for exercise, but the various and fragrant plants with which it was filled gave a luxury to that indolence so dear to the dwellers in a sunny clime. Merrily the sunbeams played to and fro on the tessellated floor and the brilliant walls—far more happily came the rays of joy to the heart of the young Glaucus.

'I have seen her, then,' said he, as he paced that narrow chamber—'I have heard her—nay, I have spoken to her again.'

At that moment a shadow darkened the threshold of the chamber, and a young female, still half a child in years, broke upon his solitude. She was dressed simply in a white tunic, which reached from the neck to the ankles; under her arm she bore a basket of flowers, and in the other hand she held a bronze water-vase; her features were more formed than exactly became her years, yet they were soft and feminine in their outline, and, without being beautiful in themselves, they were almost made so by their beauty of expression; there was something ineffably gentle, and you would say patient, in her aspect. A look of resigned sorrow, of tranquil endurance, had banished the smile, but not the sweetness, from her lips; something timid and cautious in her step—something wandering in her eyes, led you to suspect the affliction which she had suffered from her birth:—she was blind; but in the orbs themselves there was no visible defect—their melancholy and subdued light was clear, cloudless, and serene. 'They tell me that Glaucus is here,' said she; 'may I come in?'

'Ah, my Nydia,' said the Greek, 'is that you? I knew you would not neglect my invitation.'

'I have brought you some flowers,' said she, and feeling about the room till she found the table that stood by Glaucus, she laid the basket upon it: 'they are poor, but they are fresh-gathered.'

'Poor Nydia,' thought Glaucus, gazing on her; 'thine is a hard doom! Thou seest not the earth—nor the sun—nor the ocean—nor the stars;—above all, thou canst not behold Ione.'

At that last thought his mind flew back to the past evening, and was a second time disturbed in its reveries by the entrance of Clodius. It was a proof how much a single evening had sufficed to increase and to refine the love of the Athenian for Ione, that whereas he had confided to Clodius the secret of his first interview with her, and the effect it had produced on him, he now felt an invincible aversion even to mention to him her name.

When Clodius therefore spoke to him in affected transports of the beauty of Ione,

GIRL WITH FLOWERS

Glaucus felt only resentment and disgust that such lips should dare to praise her; he answered coldly, and the Roman imagined that his passion was cured instead of heightened. Clodius scarcely regretted it, for he was anxious that Glaucus should marry an heiress yet more richly endowed—Julia, the daughter of the wealthy Diomed, whose gold the gamester imagined he could readily divert into his own coffers. Their conversation did not flow with its usual ease; and no sooner had Clodius left him than Glaucus bent his way to the house of Ione. In passing by the threshold he again encountered Nydia, who

had finished her graceful task. She knew his step on the instant.

'You are early abroad?' said she.

'Yes; for the skies of Campania rebuke the sluggard who neglects them.'

'Ah, would I could see them!' murmured the blind girl, but so low that Glaucus did not overhear the complaint.

The Thessalian lingered on the threshold a few moments, and then guiding her steps by a long staff, which she used with great dexterity, she took her way homeward. She soon turned from the more gaudy streets, and entered a quarter of the town but little loved by the decorous and the sober.

She knocked at the back-door of a sort of tavern; it opened, and a rude voice bade her give an account of the sesterces. Ere she could reply, another voice, less vulgarly accented, said,—

'Never mind those petty profits, my Burbo. The girl's voice will be wanted again soon at our rich friend's revels; and he pays, as thou knowest, pretty high for his nightingales' tongues.'

'Oh, I hope not—I trust not,' cried Nydia, trembling; 'I will beg from sunrise to sunset, but send me not there.'

'And why?' asked the same voice.

'Because—because I am young, and delicately born, and the female companions I meet there are not fit associates for one who—who——'

'Is a slave in the house of Burbo,' returned the voice ironically, and with a coarse laugh.

The Thessalian put down the flowers, and, leaning her face on her hands, wept silently.

Meanwhile, Glaucus sought the house of the beautiful Neapolitan. He found Ione sitting amidst her attendants, who were at work around her. Her harp stood at her side, for Ione herself was unusually idle, perhaps unusually thoughtful, that day. He thought her even more beautiful by the morning light, and in her simple robe, than amidst the blazing lamps, and decorated with the costly jewels of the previous night: not the less so from a certain paleness that overspread her transparent hues,—not the less so from the blush that mounted over them when he approached. Accustomed to flatter, flattery died upon his lips when he addressed Ione. He felt it beneath her to *utter* the homage which every *look* conveyed. They spoke of Greece; this was a theme on which Ione loved rather to listen than to converse: it was a theme on which the Greek could have been eloquent for ever. He described to her the silver olive groves that yet clad the banks of Ilyssus, and the temples, already despoiled of half their glories—but how beautiful in decay!

One evening, the fifth after their first meeting at Pompeii, Glaucus and Ione, with a small party of chosen friends, were returning from an excursion round the bay; their vessel skimmed lightly over the twilight waters, whose lucid mirror was only broken by the dripping oars. As the rest of the party conversed gaily with each other, Glaucus lay at the feet of Ione, and he would have looked up in her face, but he did not dare. Ione broke the pause between them.

'My poor brother,' said she, sighing, 'how once he would have enjoyed this hour!'

'Your brother!' said Glaucus; 'I have not seen him. Occupied with you, I have thought of nothing else, or I should have asked if that was not your brother for whose companionship you left me at the Temple of Minerva, in Neapolis?'

'It was.'

'And is he here?'

'He is.'

'At Pompeii! and not constantly with you? Impossible!'

'He has other duties,' answered Ione, sadly; 'he is a priest of Isis.'

'So young, too; and that priesthood, in its laws at least, so severe!' said the warm and bright-hearted Greek, in surprise and pity. 'And he does not repent his choice?—I trust he is happy.'

Ione sighed deeply, and lowered her veil over her eyes.

BRONZE VASE

'I wish,' said she, after a pause, 'that he had not been so hasty. Perhaps, like all who expect too much, he is revolted too easily!'

'Then he is not happy in his new condition. And this Egyptian, was he a priest himself? was he interested in recruits to the sacred band?'

'No. His main interest was in our happiness. He thought he promoted that of my brother. We were left orphans.'

'Like myself,' said Glaucus, with a deep meaning in his voice.

Ione cast down her eyes as she resumed,—

'And Arbaces sought to supply the place of our parent. You must know him. He loves genius.'

'Arbaces! I know him already; at least, we speak when we meet. But for your praise I would not seek to know more of him. My heart inclines readily to most of my kind. But that dark Egyptian, with his gloomy brow and icy smiles, seems to me to sadden the very sun. One would think that, like Epimenides, the Cretan, he had spent forty years in a cave, and had found something unnatural in the daylight ever afterwards.'

'His calm, his coldness,' said Ione, 'are perhaps but the exhaustion of past sufferings; as yonder mountain' (and she pointed to Vesuvius) 'which we see dark and tranquil in the distance, once nursed the fires for ever quenched.'

They both gazed on the mountain as Ione said these words; the rest of the sky was bathed in rosy and tender hues, but over that grey summit, rising amidst the woods and vineyards that then clomb half-way up the ascent, there hung a black and ominous cloud, the single frown of the landscape.

THE FOWLER SNARES THE BIRD AGAIN

Arbaces had not of late much frequented the house of Ione; and when he had visited her he had not encountered Glaucus, nor knew he, as yet, of that love which had so suddenly sprung up between himself and Glaucus. In his interest for the brother of Ione, he had been forced, too, a little while, to suspend his interest in Ione herself. His pride and his selfishness were aroused and alarmed at the sudden change which had come over the spirit of the youth. He trembled lest he himself should lose a docile pupil, and Isis an enthusiastic servant. Apæcides had ceased to seek or to consult him. He was rarely to be found; he turned sullenly from the Egyptian, —nay, he fled when he perceived him in the distance.

Arbaces passed through a thick grove in the city, which lay between his house and that of Ione, in his way to the latter; and there, leaning against a tree, and gazing on the ground, he came unawares on the young priest of Isis.

'Apæcides!' said he,—and he laid his hand affectionately on the young man's shoulder.

The priest started; and his first instinct seemed to be that of flight. 'My son,' said the Egyptian, 'what has chanced that you desire to shun me?'

Apæcides remained silent and sullen, looking down on the earth, as his lips quivered, and his breast heaved with emotion.

'Speak to me, my friend,' continued the Egyptian. 'Speak. Something burdens thy spirit. What hast thou to reveal?'

'To thee—nothing.'

'And why is it to me thou art thus unconfidential?'

'Because thou hast been my enemy.'

'Let us confer,' said Arbaces, in a low voice; and drawing the reluctant arm of the priest in his own, he led him to one of the seats which were scattered within the grove.

Apæcides was in the spring of his years, yet he seemed to have exhausted even more of life than the Egyptian; his delicate and regular features were worn and colourless; his eyes were hollow, and shone with a brilliant and feverish glare: his frame bowed prematurely, and in his hands the blue and swollen veins indicated the lassitude and weakness of the relaxed fibres. You saw in his face a strong resemblance to Ione, but the expression was altogether different from that majestic and spiritual calm which breathed so divine and classical a repose over his sister's beauty.

CAPUA

CAMPANIA

NOLA

MT VESUVIUS

CUMAE

PUTEOLI
(POZZUOLI)

BAIAE

NEAPOLIS
(NAPLES)

BOSCOREALE

MISENUM
(MISENO)

HERCULANEUM

POMPEII

R. SARNUS
(SARNO)

NUNCERIA

STABIAE

SINUS OF CUMANUS
(BAY OF NAPLES)

AENARIA
(ISCHIA)

SURENTUM
(SORRENTO)

MAIN ROADS ———

CAPREAE
(CAPRI)

AREA OF POMPEII
AND HERCULANEUM

ETRURIA

ROME

POMPEII

THESSALY

MT OLYMPUS

PHRYGIA

MARATHON

SICILY

THERMOPOLY

IONIA

MT ETNA

SYRACUSE

ATHENS

SYRIA

MEDITERRANEAN

SEA

ALEXANDRIA

PLACES MENTIONED IN BOOK

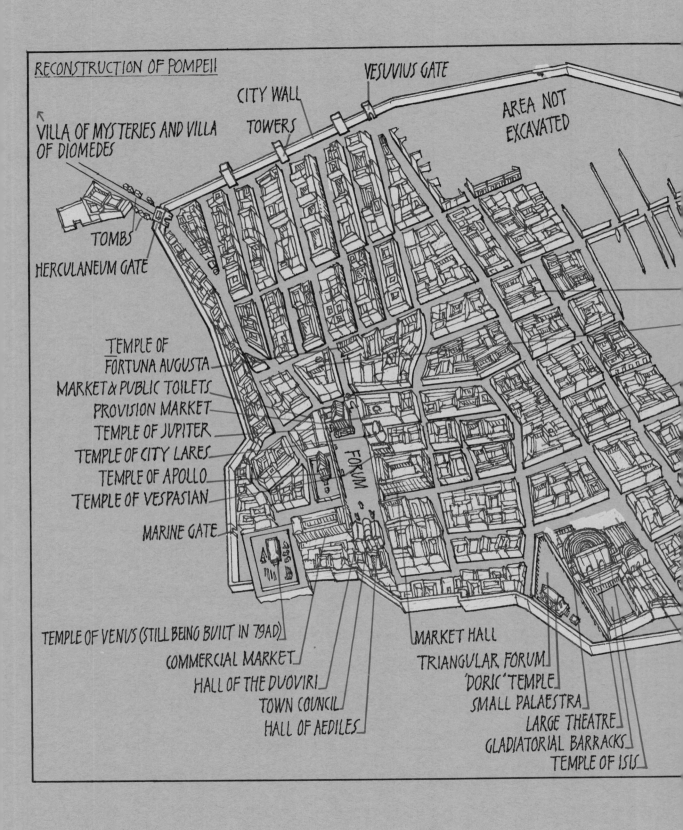

RECONSTRUCTION OF POMPEII

VESUVIUS GATE

CITY WALL

TOWERS

AREA NOT EXCAVATED

VILLA OF MYSTERIES AND VILLA OF DIOMEDES

TOMBS

HERCULANEUM GATE

TEMPLE OF FORTUNA AUGUSTA

MARKET & PUBLIC TOILETS

PROVISION MARKET

TEMPLE OF JUPITER

TEMPLE OF CITY LARES

TEMPLE OF APOLLO

TEMPLE OF VESPASIAN

MARINE GATE

FORUM

TEMPLE OF VENUS (STILL BEING BUILT IN 79AD)

COMMERCIAL MARKET

HALL OF THE DUOVIRI

TOWN COUNCIL

HALL OF AEDILES

MARKET HALL

TRIANGULAR FORUM

'DORIC' TEMPLE

SMALL PALAESTRA

LARGE THEATRE

GLADIATORIAL BARRACKS

TEMPLE OF ISIS

THE EXCAVATION OF POMPEII
OVER THE CENTURIES

1826

1890

1976

NOLAN GATE

SARNO GATE

AREA NOT EXCAVATED

CENTRAL BATHS
FORUM BATHS
STABIAN BATHS

AMPHITHEATRE

LARGE PALAESTRA

AREA NOT
EXCAVATED

NUCERIAN GATE

TOMBS

STABIAN GATE

TEMPLE OF JUPITER MILICHIUS
SMALL THEATRE

HERCULANEUM
ONLY A SMALL PART HAS SO FAR
BEEN EXCAVATED.

ARCH

HALL

BATHS

BATHS

HALL

PALAESTRA

THE FOUR SIDES OF A KNUCKLEBONE

ETRUSCAN DIE
(C. 900 B.C.)

DICE BOX

ROMAN DICE
MADE IN THE FORM OF PEOPLE

GIRL PLAYING WITH
KNUCKLEBONES, FROM
A PAINTING AT
HERCULANEUM

GAMES AND GAMING

The Romans were obsessed with games and gambling. They had a variety of board and dice games. Most of their rules have been lost, and evidence can only be gained from games found in excavations (throughout the Empire), especially from tombs, and contemporary allusions found in surviving writings.

Boards have been found scratched into the steps of public buildings in Rome, and wall paintings from Pompeii show gamblers playing dice. Gambling was illegal except during the Saturnalian festival, but its prosecution seems not to have been very strictly enforced.

Knucklebones

These were either natural (from the ankle joint of a cloven-hoofed animal), or made from stone or bronze.
Five bones were tossed up and they all had to be caught on the back of the hand. Any that fell had to be picked up without shaking off the ones already caught on the hand.

A variation of knucklebones.
The rules were comparatively simple. When the bones were thrown, they should fall with one of the flat sides uppermost. If one fell on its edge and rolled over on its side it did not count.
Each side had a number – 1, 3, 4, 6. Though these numbers were not marked, each side was different. Scoring was according to the surfaces uppermost. Four bones were thrown, and if different surfaces came up this was the top throw – the 'Venus'. If four aces turned up, it was the lowest throw – the 'dog'.
As the numbers were not inscribed, many other variations could be played.

Duodecima scripta ('twelve lines').

Two players started with a set of 15 pieces each – one set of counters black, one white. The board was divided into 24 sections, numbered 1 to 24. White played from 1 to 24; black from 24 to 1. Three dice were thrown, and each piece moved separately. If you landed on an opponent's piece you went back to the start; but if your opponent had two or more pieces on a space then you were not allowed to move to that space. The game was taken seriously (as with chess today). It had many devotees and books were written about the moves.

DUODECIMA SCRIPTA BOARD
WITH COUNTERS IN POSITION

PLAYING DICE, WALL PAINTING

IVORY PIECES
FROM VARIOUS GAMES

'You say I have been your enemy,' said Arbaces. 'I know the cause of that unjust accusation: I have placed you amidst the priests of Isis—you are revolted at their trickeries and imposture—you think that I too have deceived you—the purity of your mind is offended—you imagine that I am one of the deceitful——'

'You knew the jugglings of that impious craft,' answered Apæcides; 'why did you disguise them from me? Young as I was, rich, fervent, the sunny pleasures of earth before me, I resigned all without a sigh, nay, with happiness and exultation, in the thought that I resigned them for the abstruse mysteries of diviner wisdom, for the companionship of gods—for the revelations of Heaven—and now—now——'

Convulsive sobs checked the priest's voice; he covered his face with his hands, and large tears forced themselves through the wasted fingers, and ran profusely down his vest.

'What I promised to thee, that will I give, my friend, my pupil. I henceforth will be your priest, your guide, and you who now curse my friendship shall live to bless it.'

The young man lifted up his head, and gazed with a vacant and wondering stare upon the Egyptian.

'And what wilt thou teach me, O singular and fearful man? New cheats—new——'

'No—I have thrown thee into the abyss of disbelief; I will lead thee now to the eminence of faith. Thou hast seen the false types: thou shalt learn now the realities they represent. There is no shadow, Apæcides, without its substance. Come to me this night. Your hand.'

Impressed, excited, bewildered, Apæcides gave him his hand, and master and pupil parted.

It was true that for Apæcides there was no retreat. He had taken the vows of celibacy: he had devoted himself to a life that at present seemed to possess all the austerities of fanaticism, without any of the consolations of belief. It was natural that he should yet cling to a yearning desire to reconcile himself to an irrevocable career.

Meanwhile Arbaces pursued his slow and stately way to the house of Ione. As he entered the tablinum, he heard a voice from the porticoes of the peristyle beyond, which, musical as it was, sounded displeasingly on his ear—it was the voice of the young and beautiful Glaucus, and for the first time an involuntary thrill of jealousy shot through the breast of the Egyptian. On entering the peristyle, he found Glaucus seated by the side of Ione. The fountain in the odorous garden cast up its silver spray in the air, and kept a delicious coolness in the midst of the sultry noon. The handmaids, almost invariably attendant on Ione, who with her freedom of

LYRE

life preserved the most delicate modesty, sat at a little distance; by the feet of Glaucus lay the lyre on which he had been playing to Ione. The scene—the group before Arbaces, was stamped by that peculiar and refined ideality of poesy which we yet, not erroneously, imagine to be the distinction of the ancients,—the marble columns, the vases of flowers, the statue, white and tranquil, closing every vista; and, above all, the two living forms, from which a sculptor might have caught either inspiration or despair!

Arbaces, pausing for a moment, gazed on the pair with a brow from which all the usual stern serenity had fled; he recovered himself by an effort, and slowly approached them, but with a step so soft and echoless, that even the attendants heard him not; much less Ione and her lover.

'And yet,' said Glaucus, 'it is only before we love that we imagine that our poets have truly described the passion; the instant the sun rises, all the stars that had shone in his absence vanish into air. The poets exist only in the night of the heart; they are nothing to us when we feel the full glory of the god.'

'A gentle and most glowing image, noble Glaucus.'

Both started, and recognised behind the seat of Ione the cold and sarcastic face of the Egyptian.

'You are a sudden guest,' said Glaucus, rising, and with a forced smile.

'So ought all to be who know they are welcome,' returned Arbaces, seating himself, and motioning to Glaucus to do the same.

'I am glad,' said Ione, 'to see you at length together; for you are suited to each other, and you are formed to be friends.'

'Give me back some fifteen years of life,' replied the Egyptian, 'before you can place me on an equality with Glaucus. Happy should I be to receive his friendship; but what can I give him in return? Can I make to him the same confidences that he would repose in me—of banquets and garlands—of Parthian steeds, and the chances of the dice? these pleasures suit his age, his nature, his career: they are not for mine.'

So saying, the artful Egyptian looked down and sighed; but from the corner of his eye he stole a glance towards Ione, to see how she received these insinuations of the pursuits of her visitor. Her countenance did not satisfy him. Glaucus, slightly colouring, hastened gaily to reply. Nor was he, perhaps, without the wish in his turn to disconcert and abash the Egyptian.

'You are right, wise Arbaces,' said he; 'we can esteem each other, but we cannot be friends. My banquets lack the secret salt which, according to rumour, gives such zest to your own. And, by Hercules! when I have reached your age, if I, like you, may think it wise to pursue the pleasures of manhood, like you, I shall be doubtless sarcastic on the gallantries of youth.'

The Egyptian raised his eyes to Glaucus with a sudden and piercing glance.

'I do not understand you,' said he, coldly; 'but it is the custom to consider that wit lies in obscurity.' He turned from Glaucus as he spoke, with a scarcely perceptible sneer of contempt, and after a moment's pause addressed himself to Ione. 'I have not, beautiful Ione,' said he, 'been fortunate enough to find you within doors the last two or three times that I have visited your vestibule.'

'The smoothness of the sea has tempted me much from home,' replied Ione, with a little embarrassment.

The embarrassment did not escape Arbaces; but without seeming to heed it, he replied with a smile: 'You know the old poet says, that "Women should keep within doors, and there converse."'

'The poet was a cynic,' said Glaucus, 'and hated women.'

'He spake according to the customs of his country, and that country is your boasted Greece.'

'To different periods different customs. Had our forefathers known Ione, they had made a different law.'

'Did you learn these pretty gallantries at Rome?' said Arbaces, with ill-suppressed emotion.

'One certainly would not go for gallantries to Egypt,' retorted Glaucus, playing carelessly with his chain.

After a short conversation, Glaucus took his leave of Ione.

When he was gone, Arbaces, drawing his seat nearer to the fair Neapolitan's, said in those bland and subdued tones, in which he knew so well how to veil the mingled art and fierceness of his character,—

'Think not, my sweet pupil, if so I may call you, that I wish to shackle that liberty you adorn while you assume: but which, if not greater, as you rightly observe, than that possessed by the Roman women, must at least be accompanied by great circumspection, when arrogated by one unmarried. Continue to draw crowds of the gay, the brilliant, the wise themselves, to your feet but reflect, at least, on those censorious tongues which can so easily blight the tender reputation of a maiden; and while you provoke admiration, give, I beseech you, no victory to envy.'

'What mean you, Arbaces?' said Ione, in an alarmed and trembling voice: 'I know you are my friend, that you desire only my honour and my welfare. What is it you would say?'

'Your friend—ah, how sincerely! May I speak then as a friend, without reserve and without offence?'

'I beseech you do so.'

'This young profligate, this Glaucus, how didst thou know him? Hast thou seen him often?' And as Arbaces spoke, he fixed his gaze steadfastly upon Ione, as if he sought to penetrate into her soul.

Recoiling before that gaze, with a strange fear which she could not explain, the Nea-politan answered with confusion and hesi-tation,—'He was brought to my house as a countryman of my father's, and I may say of mine. I have known him only within this last week or so: but why these questions?'

'Forgive me,' said Arbaces; 'I thought you might have known him longer. Base insinu-ator that he is!'

'How! what mean you? Why that term?'

'It matters not: let me not rouse your indignation against one who does not deserve so grave an honour.'

'I implore you speak. What has Glaucus insinuated? or rather, in what do you *suppose* he has offended?'

Smothering his resentment at the last part of Ione's question, Arbaces continued,— 'You know his pursuits, his companions, his habits; the comissatio and the alea (the revel and the dice) make his occupation;—and amongst the associates of vice how can he dream of virtue?'

'Still you speak riddles. By the gods! I entreat you, say the worst at once.'

'Well, then, it must be so. Know, my Ione, that it was but yesterday that Glaucus boasted openly—yes, in the public baths—of your love to him. He said it amused him to take advantage of it. Nay, I will do him justice, he praised your beauty. Who could deny it? But he laughed scornfully when his

Clodius, or his Lepidus, asked him if he loved you enough for marriage, and when he purposed to adorn his door-posts with flowers?'

'Impossible! How heard you this base slander?'

'Nay, would you have me relate to you all the comments of the insolent coxcombs with which the story has circled through the town? Be assured that I myself disbelieved at first, and that I have now painfully been convinced by several ear-witnesses of the truth of what I have reluctantly told thee.'

Ione sank back, and her face was whiter than the pillar against which she leaned for support.

Most cunningly had the Egyptian appealed to Ione's ruling foible—most dexterously had he applied the poisoned dart to her pride. He fancied he had arrested what he hoped, from the shortness of the time she had known Glaucus, was, at most, but an incipient fancy; and hastening to change the subject, he now led her to talk of her brother. Their convers-ation did not last long. He left her, resolved not again to trust so much to absence, but to visit—to watch her—every day.

No sooner had his shadow glided from her presence, than woman's pride—her sex's dissimulation—deserted his intended victim, and the haughty Ione burst into passionate tears.

BEWARE OF THE DOG
(FROM A MOSAIC)

CAVE CANEM

A MINIATURE LIKENESS OF THE ROMAN BATHS

When Glaucus left Ione, he felt as if he trod upon air. In the interview with which he had just been blessed, he had for the first time gathered from her distinctly that his love was not unwelcome to, and would not be un-rewarded by, her. This hope filled him with a rapture for which earth and heaven seemed too narrow to afford a vent. Unconscious of the sudden enemy he had left behind, and forgetting not only his taunts but his very existence, Glaucus passed through the gay streets, repeating to himself, in the wanton-ness of joy, the music of the soft air to which Ione had listened with such intentness; and now he entered the Street of Fortune, with its raised footpath—its houses painted with-out, and the open doors admitting the view of the glowing frescoes within.

Sauntering through the crowd, Glaucus soon found himself amidst a group of his merry and dissipated friends.

'What news from Rome?' said Lepidus, as he languidly joined the group.

'The emperor has been giving a splendid supper to the senators,' answered Sallust.

'He is a good creature,' quoth Lepidus; 'they say he never sends a man away without granting his request.'

'Perhaps he would let me kill a slave for my reservoir of lampreys?' returned Sallust, eagerly.

'Not unlikely,' said Glaucus; 'for he who grants a favour to one Roman, must always do it at the expense of another. Be sure, that for every smile Titus has caused, a hundred eyes have wept.'

'Long live Titus!' cried Pansa, overhearing the emperor's name, as he swept patronis-ingly through the crowd; 'he has promised my brother a quæstorship, because he had run through his fortune.'

'Ah, Glaucus! how are you? gay as ever?' said Clodius, joining the group.

'Are you come to sacrifice to Fortune?' said Sallust.

'I sacrifice to her every night,' returned the gamester.

'I do not doubt it. No man has made more victims!'

'By Hercules, a biting speech!' cried Glaucus, laughing.

'The dog's letter is never out of your mouth, Sallust,' said Clodius, angrily: 'you are always snarling.'

'I may well have the dog's letter in my mouth, since, whenever I play with you, I have the dog's throw in my hand,' returned Sallust.

'Hist!' said Glaucus, taking a rose from a flower-girl, who stood beside.

'The rose is the token of silence,' replied Sallust, 'but I love only to see it at the supper-table.'

'Talking of that, Diomed gives a grand feast next week,' said Sallust: 'are you invited, Glaucus?'

'Yes, I received an invitation this morning.'

'And I, too,' said Sallust, drawing a square piece of papyrus from his girdle: 'I see that he asks us an hour earlier than usual: an earnest of something sumptuous.'

'Oh! he is rich as Crœsus,' said Clodius; 'and his bill of fare is as long as an epic.'

'Well, let us to the baths,' said Glaucus: 'this is the time when all the world is there; and Fulvius, whom you admire so much, is going to read us his last ode.'

The young men assented readily to the proposal, and they strolled to the baths.

Although the public thermæ, or baths, were instituted rather for the poorer citizens than the wealthy (for the last had baths in their own houses), yet, to the crowds of all ranks who resorted to them, it was a favourite place for conversation, and for that indolent lounging so dear to a gay and thoughtless

people. The general subject of conversation was, however, the spectacle announced in the amphitheatre; and each new-comer was fastened upon by a group eager to know if Pompeii had been so fortunate as to produce some monstrous criminal, some happy case of sacrilege or of murder, which would allow the ædiles to provide a man for the jaws of the lion: all other more common exhibitions seemed dull and tame, when compared with the possibility of this fortunate occurrence.

'For my part,' said one jolly-looking man, who was a goldsmith, 'I think the emperor, if he is as good as they say, might have sent us a Jew.'

'Why not take one of the new sect of Nazarenes?' said a philosopher. 'I am not cruel: but an atheist, one who denies Jupiter himself, deserves no mercy.'

'I care not how many gods a man likes to believe in,' said the goldsmith; 'but to deny all gods is something monstrous.'

'Yet I fancy,' said Glaucus, 'that these people are not absolutely atheists. I am told that they believe in a God—nay, in a future state.'

'Quite a mistake, my dear Glaucus,' said the philosopher. 'I have conferred with them —they laughed in my face when I talked of Pluto and Hades.'

'O ye gods!' exclaimed the goldsmith, in horror; 'are there any of these wretches in Pompeii?'

'I know there are a few: but they meet so privately that it is impossible to discover who they are.'

As Glaucus turned away, a sculptor, who was a great enthusiast in his art, looked after him admiringly.

'Ah!' said he, 'if we could get *him* on the arena—there would be a model for you! What limbs! what a head! he ought to have been a gladiator! A subject—a subject—worthy of our art! Why don't they give him to the lion?'

Meanwhile Fulvius, the Roman poet, whom his contemporaries declared immortal, and who, but for this history, would never have been heard of in our neglectful age, came eagerly up to Glaucus. 'Oh, my Athenian, my Glaucus, you have come to hear my ode!'

'Certainly; we lose time till we hear your poem.'

At this instant there was a rush of some twenty persons from the baths into the portico; and a slave stationed at the door of a small corridor now admitted the poet, Glaucus, Clodius, and a troop of the bard's other friends, into the passage.

STABIAN BATHS

CROSS SECTION OF WOMENS' HOT ROOM

1 MENS' DRESSING ROOM
2 WOMENS' DRESSING ROOM
3 MENS' COLD ROOM
4 MENS' TEPID ROOM
5 WOMENS' TEPID ROOM
6 MENS' HOT ROOM
7 WOMENS' HOT ROOM
8 PRIVATE BATHS
9 FURNACE AND WATER TANK
10 SWIMMING POOL
11 GAMES AREA

1 BATH BASIN
2 BRONZE HEATER
3 FURNACE
4 HOT AIR CHAMBER EXTENDING UNDER FLOOR BETWEEN WALLS
5 WATER HEATER

'A poor place this, compared with the Roman thermæ!' said Lepidus, disdainfully.

'Yet is there some taste in the ceiling,' said Glaucus, who was in a mood to be pleased with everything; pointing to the stars which studded the roof.

Lepidus shrugged his shoulders, but was too languid to reply.

They now entered a somewhat spacious chamber, which served for the purposes of the apodyterium (that is, a place where the bathers prepared themselves for their luxurious ablutions).

In this apartment Fulvius seated himself with a magisterial air, and his audience gathering round him, encouraged him to commence his recital.

The poet did not require much pressing. He drew forth from his vest a roll of papyrus, and after hemming three times, as much to command silence as to clear his voice, he began that wonderful ode, of which, to the great mortification of the author of this history, no single verse can be discovered.

By the plaudits he received, it was doubtless worthy of his fame; and Glaucus was the only listener who did not find it excel the best odes of Horace.

The poem concluded, those who took only the cold bath began to undress; they suspended their garments on hooks fastened in the wall, and receiving, according to their condition, either from their own slaves or those of the thermæ, loose robes in exchange, withdrew into that graceful circular building which yet exists, to shame the unlaving posterity of the south.

The more luxurious departed by another door to the tepidarium, a place which was heated to a voluptuous warmth, partly by a movable fireplace, principally by a suspended pavement, beneath which was conducted the caloric of the laconicum.

Here this portion of the intended bathers, after unrobing themselves, remained for some time enjoying the artificial warmth of the luxurious air. And this room, as befitted its important rank in the long process of ablution, was more richly and elaborately decorated than the rest; the arched roof was beautifully carved and painted; the windows above, of ground glass, admitted but wandering and uncertain rays; below the massive cornices were rows of figures in massive and bold relief; the walls glowed with crimson, the pavement was skilfully tessellated in white mosaics. Here the habituated bathers, men who bathed seven times a day, would remain in a state of enervate and speechless lassitude, either before or (mostly) after the water-bath; and many of these victims of the pursuit of health turned their listless eyes on the new-comers, recognising their friends with a nod, but dreading the fatigue of conversation.

From this place the party again diverged, according to their several fancies, some to the sudatorium, which answered the purpose of our vapour-baths, and thence to the warm-bath itself; those more accustomed to exercise, and capable of dispensing with so cheap a purchase of fatigue, resorted at once to the calidarium, or water-bath.

STRIGILS AND OIL FLASK

In order to complete this sketch, and give to the reader an adequate notion of this, the main luxury of the ancients, we will accompany Lepidus, who regularly underwent the whole process, save only the cold-bath, which had gone lately out of fashion. Being then gradually warmed in the tepidarium, which has just been described, the delicate steps of the Pompeian élégant were conducted to the sudatorium. Here let the reader depict to himself the gradual process of the vapour-bath, accompanied by an exhalation of spicy perfumes. After our bather had undergone this operation, he was seized by his slaves, who always awaited him at the baths, and the dews of heat were removed by a kind of scraper. Thence, somewhat cooled, he passed into the water-bath, over which fresh perfumes were profusely scattered, and on emerging from the opposite part of the room, a cooling shower played over his head and form. Then wrapping himself in a light robe, he returned once more to the tepidarium, where he found Glaucus, who had not encountered the sudatorium; and now, the main delight and extravagance of the bath commenced. Their slaves anointed the bathers from vials of gold, of alabaster, or of crystal, studded with profusest gems, and containing the rarest unguents gathered from all quarters of the world.

'But tell me,' said a corpulent citizen, who was groaning and wheezing under the operation of being rubbed down, 'tell me, O Glaucus!—evil chance to thy hands, O slave! why so rough?—tell me—ugh—ugh!—are the baths at Rome really so magnificent?' Glaucus turned, and recognised Diomed, though not without some difficulty, so red and so inflamed were the good man's cheeks by the scraping he had so lately undergone. 'I fancy they must be a great deal finer than these. Eh?' Suppressing a smile, Glaucus replied,—

'Imagine all Pompeii converted into baths, and you will then form a notion of the size of the imperial thermæ of Rome. But a notion of the *size* only. Imagine every entertainment for mind and body—enumerate all the gymnastic games our fathers invented—repeat all the books Italy and Greece have produced—suppose places for all these games, admirers for all these works—add to this, baths of the vastest size, the most complicated construction—intersperse the whole with gardens, with theatres, with porticoes, with schools—suppose, in one word, a city of the gods, composed but of palaces and public edifices, and you may form some faint idea of the glories of the great baths of Rome.'

While Glaucus was thus conversing, Lepidus, with closed eyes and scarce perceptible breath, was undergoing all the mystic operations, not one of which he ever suffered his attendants to omit. After the perfumes and the unguents, they scattered over him the luxurious powder which presented any further accession of heat: and this being rubbed away by the smooth surface of the pumice, he began to indue, not the garments he had put off, but those more festive ones termed 'the synthesis,' with which the Romans marked their respect for the coming ceremony of supper, if rather, from its hour (three o'clock in our measurement of time), it might not be more fitly denominated dinner. This done, he at length opened his eyes and gave signs of returning life.

At the same time, too, Sallust betokened by a long yawn the evidence of existence.

'It is supper time,' said the epicure; 'you, Glaucus and Lepidus, come and sup with me.'

'Recollect you are all three engaged to my house next week,' cried Diomed, who was mightily proud of the acquaintance of men of fashion.

'Ah, ah! we recollect,' said Sallust; 'the seat of memory, my Diomed, is certainly in the stomach.'

Passing now once again into the cooler air, and so into the street, our gallants of that day concluded the ceremony of a Pompeian bath.

ARBACES WINS THE GAME

The evening darkened over the restless city as Apæcides took his way to the house of the Egyptian. He avoided the more lighted and populous streets; and as he strode onward with his head buried in his bosom, and his arms folded within his robe, there was something startling in the contrast, which his solemn mien and wasted form presented to the thoughtless brows and animated air of those who occasionally crossed his path.

At length, however, a man of a more sober and staid demeanour, and who had twice passed him with a curious but doubting look, touched him on the shoulder.

'Apæcides!' said he, and he made a rapid sign with his hands: it was the sign of the cross.

'Well, Nazarene,' replied the priest, and his face grew paler; 'what wouldst thou?'

'Nay,' returned the stranger, 'I would not interrupt thy meditations; but the last time we met, I seemed not to be so unwelcome.'

'You are not unwelcome, Olinthus; but I am sad and weary: nor am I able this evening to discuss with you those themes which are most acceptable to you.'

'O backward of heart!' said Olinthus, with bitter fervour; 'and art thou sad and weary, and wilt thou turn from the very springs that refresh and heal?'

'O earth!' cried the young priest, striking his breast passionately, 'from what regions shall my eyes open to the true Olympus, where thy gods really dwell? Am I to believe with this man, that none whom for so many centuries my fathers worshipped have a being or a name? Am I to break down, as something blasphemous and profane, the very altars which I have deemed most sacred? or am I to think with Arbaces—what?'

He paused, and strode rapidly away in the impatience of a man who strives to get rid of himself.

Olinthus did not suffer Apæcides thus easily to escape him. He overtook and addressed him thus:—

'I do not wonder, Apæcides, that I distress you; that I shake all the elements of your mind: that you are lost in doubt; that you drift here and there in the vast ocean of uncertain and benighted thought. I wonder not at this, but bear with me a little; watch and pray—the darkness shall vanish, the storm sleep, and God Himself, as He came of yore on the seas of Samaria, shall walk over the lulled billows, to the delivery of your soul. Ours is a religion jealous in its demands,

TRIPOD TABLE

but how infinitely prodigal in its gifts! It troubles you for an hour, it repays you by immortality.'

But Apæcides, yet unprepared for the renunciation of that faith—that life, for which he had sacrificed so much, and still haunted by the promises of the Egyptian, gathered up his robes and fled away with a speed that defied pursuit.

Breathless and exhausted, he arrived at last in a remote and sequestered part of the city, and the lone house of the Egyptian stood before him. As he paused to recover himself, the moon emerged from a silver cloud, and shone full upon the walls of that mysterious habitation.

No other house was near—the darksome vines clustered far and wide in front of the building, and behind it rose a copse of lofty forest trees, sleeping in the melancholy moonlight; beyond stretched the dim outline of the distant hills, and amongst them the quiet crest of Vesuvius, not then so lofty as the traveller beholds it now.

Apæcides passed through the arching vines, and arrived at the broad and spacious portico. Before it, on either side of the steps, reposed the image of the Egyptian sphinx, and the moonlight gave an additional and yet more solemn calm to those large, and harmonious, and passionless features, in which the sculptors of that type of wisdom united so much of loveliness with awe; half way up the extremities of the steps darkened the green and massive foliage of the aloe, and the shadow of the eastern palm cast its long and unwaving boughs partially over the marble surface of the stairs.

Something there was in the stillness of the place, and the strange aspect of the sculptured sphinxes, which thrilled the blood of the priest with a nameless and ghostly fear, and

he longed even for an echo to his noiseless steps as he ascended to the threshold.

He knocked at the door, over which was wrought an inscription in characters unfamiliar to his eyes; it opened without a sound, and a tall Ethiopian slave, without question or salutation, motioned to him to proceed.

The wide hall was lighted by lofty candelabra of elaborate bronze, and round the walls were wrought vast hieroglyphics, in dark and solemn colours, which contrasted strangely with the bright hues and graceful shapes with which the inhabitants of Italy decorated their abodes. At the extremity of the hall, a slave, whose countenance, though not African, was darker by many shades than the usual colour of the south, advanced to meet him.

'I seek Arbaces,' said the priest; but his voice trembled even in his own ear. The slave bowed his head in silence, and leading Apæcides to a wing without the hall, conducted him up a narrow staircase, and then traversing several rooms, in which the stern and thoughtful beauty of the sphinx still made the chief and most impressive object of the priest's notice, Apæcides found himself in a dim and half-lighted chamber, in the presence of the Egyptian.

Arbaces was seated before a small table, on which lay unfolded several scrolls of papyrus, impressed with the same character as that on the threshold of the mansion. A small tripod stood at a little distance, from the incense in which the smoke slowly rose. Near this was a vast globe, depicting the signs of heaven; and upon another table lay several instruments, of curious and quaint shape, whose uses were unknown to Apæcides. The farther extremity of the room was concealed by a curtain, and the oblong window in the roof admitted the rays of the moon, mingling sadly with the single lamp which burned in the apartment.

'Seat yourself, Apæcides,' said the Egyptian, without rising.

The young man obeyed.

'You ask me,' resumed Arbaces, after a short pause, in which he seemed absorbed in thought,—'You ask me, or would do so, the mightiest secrets which the soul of man is fitted to receive; it is the enigma of life itself that you desire me to solve. Placed like children in the dark, and but for a little while, in this dim and confined existence, we shape our spectres in the obscurity; our thoughts now sink back into ourselves in terror, now wildly plunge themselves into the guideless gloom, guessing what it may contain;—stretching our helpless hands here and there, lest, blindly, we stumble upon some hidden danger; not knowing the limits of our boundary, now feeling them suffocate us with compression, now seeing them extend far away till they vanish into eternity. In this state all wisdom consists necessarily in the solution of two questions—"What are we to believe? and What are we to reject?" These questions you desire me to decide?'

Apæcides bowed his head in assent.

'Man *must* have some belief,' continued the Egyptian, in a tone of sadness. 'He must fasten his hope to something? it is our common nature that you inherit when, aghast and terrified to see that in which you have been taught to place your faith swept away, you float over a dreary and shoreless sea of incertitude, you cry for help, you ask for some plank to cling to, some land, however dim and distant, to attain. Well, then, listen.'

For some time the Egyptian discoursed on the mysteries of life and on nature and religion.

At last he ceased and there rose about, around, beneath, the softest music that Lydia ever taught, or Iona ever perfected. It came like a stream of sound, bathing the senses unawares; enervating, subduing with delight. It seemed the melodies of invisible spirits, such as the shepherd might have heard in the golden age, floating through the vales of Thessaly, or in the noontide glades of Paphos. The words which had rushed to the lip of Apæcides, in answer to the sophistries of the Egyptian, died tremblingly away. He felt it as a profanation to break upon that enchanted strain—the susceptibility of his excited nature, the Greek softness and ardour of his secret soul, were swayed and captured by surprise. He sank on the seat with parted lips and thirsting ear; while in a chorus of voices rose a melting song.

As the voices died away, the Egyptian seized the hand of Apæcides, and led him, wandering, intoxicated, yet half-reluctant, across the chamber towards the curtain at the far end; and now, from behind that curtain, there seemed to burst a thousand sparkling stars; the veil itself, hitherto dark, was now lighted by these fires behind into the tenderest blue of heaven.

'Oh! what miracle is this, Arbaces?' said Apæcides in faltering accents. 'After having denied the gods, art thou about to reveal to me——'

'Their pleasures!' interrupted Arbaces, in a tone so different from its usual cold and tranquil harmony that Apæcides started, and thought the Egyptian himself transformed; and now, as they neared the curtain, a wild— a loud—an exulting melody burst from behind its concealment. With that sound the veil was rent in twain—it parted—it seemed to vanish into air: and a scene, which no Sybarite ever more than rivalled, broke upon the dazzled gaze of the youthful priest. A vast banquet-room stretched beyond, blazing with countless lights, which filled the warm air with the scents of frankincense, of jasmine, of violets, of myrrh; all that the most odorous flowers, all that the most costly spices could distil, seemed gathered into one ineffable and ambrosial essence: from the light columns that sprang upwards to the airy roof, hung draperies of white, studded with golden stars. At the extremities of the room two fountains cast up a spray, which, catching the rays of the roseate light, glittered like countless diamonds. In the centre of the room as they entered there rose slowly from the floor, to the sound of unseen minstrelsy, a table spread with all the viands which sense ever devoted to fancy, and vases crowned with the exotics of the East. The couches, to which this table was the centre, were covered with tapestries of azure and gold; and from invisible tubes in the vaulted roof descended showers of fragrant waters, that cooled the delicious air, and contended with the lamps, as if the spirits of wave and fire disputed which element could furnish forth the most delicious odours. And now, from behind the snowy draperies, trooped such forms as Adonis beheld when he lay on the lap of Venus. They came, some with garlands, others with lyres; they surrounded the youth, they led his steps to the banquet. They flung the chaplets round him in rosy chains. The earth—the thought of earth, vanished from his soul. He imagined himself in a dream, and suppressed his breath lest he should wake too soon; the senses, to which he had never yielded as yet, beat in his burning pulse, and confused his dizzy and reeling sight.

A group of three maidens, entwined with a chain of starred flowers, and who, while they imitated, might have shamed the Graces, advanced towards him in the gliding measures of the Ionian dance.

Now approaching, they wreathed their chaplet round his head; now kneeling, the youngest of the three proffered him the bowl, from which the wine of Lesbos foamed and sparkled. The youth resisted no more, he grasped the intoxicating cup, the blood mantled fiercely through his veins. He sank upon the breast of the nymph who sat beside him, and turning with swimming eyes to seek for Arbaces, whom he had lost in the whirl of his emotions, he beheld him seated beneath a canopy at the upper end of the table, and gazing upon him with a smile that encouraged him to pleasure. He beheld him, but not as he had hitherto seen, with dark and sable garments, with a brooding and solemn brow: a robe that dazzled the sight, so studded was its whitest surface with gold and gems, blazed upon his majestic form; white roses, alternated with the emerald and the ruby, and shaped tiara-like, crowned his raven locks. He appeared, like Ulysses, to have gained the glory of a second youth—his features seemed to have exchanged thought for beauty, and he towered amidst the loveliness that surrounded him, in all the beaming and relaxing benignity of the Olympian god.

'Drink, feast, love, my pupil!' said he; 'blush not that thou art passionate and young. That which thou art, thou feelest in thy veins: that which thou shalt be, survey!'

With this he pointed to a recess, and the eyes of Apæcides, following the gesture, beheld on a pedestal, placed between the statues of Bacchus and Idalia, the form of a skeleton.

'Start not,' resumed the Egyptian; 'that friendly guest admonishes us but of the shortness of life. From its jaws I hear a voice that summons us to ENJOY.'

As he spoke, a group of nymphs surrounded the statue; they laid chaplets on its pedestal, and, while the cups were emptied and refilled at that glowing board, they sang hymns to the image of Death.

Then she who sat beside Apæcides suddenly took up the song:

'Happy is yet our doom,
  The earth and the sun are ours!
And far from the dreary tomb
  Speed the wings of the rosy Hours—
Sweet is for thee the bowl,
  Sweet are thy looks, my love;
I fly to thy tender soul,
  As the bird to its mated dove!
    Take me, ah, take!
Clasp'd to thy guardian breast,
Soft let me sink to rest:
    But wake me—ah, wake!
And tell me with words and sighs,
But more with thy melting eyes,
    That my sun is not set—
That the Torch is not quench'd at the Urn
That we love, and we breathe, and burn,
  Tell me—thou lov'st me yet!'

ASTRONOMICAL GLOBE WITH SIGNS OF THE ZODIAC

BOOK TWO

A FLASH HOUSE IN POMPEII

In one of those parts of Pompeii, which were tenanted not by the lords of pleasure, but by its minions and its victims, the haunt of gladiators and prize-fighters, of the vicious and the penniless, of the savage and the obscene, was a large room, that opened at once on a confined and crowded lane. Before the threshold was a group of men, whose iron and well-strung muscles, whose short and Herculean necks, whose hardy and reckless countenances, indicated the champions of the arena. On a shelf, without the shop, were ranged jars of wine and oil; and right over

where they neglected the mind, was typified by the gaudy colours which decorated the walls, and the shapes, fantastic but not inelegant, in which the lamps, the drinking-cups, the commonest household utensils, were wrought.

'By Pollux!' said one of the gladiators, as he leaned against the wall of the threshold, 'the wine thou sellest us, old Silenus,'—and as he spoke he slapped a portly personage on the back,—'is enough to thin the best blood in one's veins.'

The man thus caressingly saluted, and whose bared arms, white apron, and keys and napkin tucked carelessly within his girdle, indicated him to be the host of the tavern, was already passed into the autumn of his years; but his form was still so robust and athletic, that he might have shamed even the sinewy shapes beside him, save that the muscles had seeded, as it were, into flesh, that the cheeks

AMPHORAE FOR HOLDING OIL AND FOOD

this was inserted in the wall a coarse painting, which exhibited gladiators drinking. Within the room were placed several small tables, arranged somewhat in the modern fashion of 'boxes,' and round these were seated several knots of men, some drinking, some playing at dice, some at that more skilful game called 'duodecim scriptæ'. The hour was in the early forenoon, and nothing better, perhaps, than that unseasonable time itself denoted the habitual indolence of these tavern loungers. The gay disposition of all the Pompeians, who sought, at least, to gratify the sense even

were swelled and bloated, and the increasing stomach threw into shade the vast and massive chest which rose above it.

'None of thy scurrilous blusterings with me,' growled the gigantic landlord, in the gentle semi-roar of an insulted tiger; 'my wine is good enough for a carcase which shall so soon soak the dust of the spoliarium.'

'Croakest thou thus, old raven!' returned the gladiator, laughing scornfully; 'thou shalt live to hang thyself with despite when thou seest me win the palm crown; and when I get the purse at the amphitheatre, as I certainly shall, my first vow to Hercules shall be to forswear thee and thy vile potations evermore.'

'Hear to him,' cried the host. 'Sporus, Niger, Tetraides, he declares he shall win the purse from you. Why, by the gods! each of your muscles is strong enough to stifle all his body, or I know nothing of the arena!'

'Ha!' said the gladiator, colouring with rising fury, 'our lanista would tell a different story.'

'What story could he tell against me, vain Lydon?' said Tetraides, frowning.

'Or me, who have conquered in fifteen fights?' said the gigantic Niger, stalking up to the gladiator.

'Or me?' grunted Sporus, with eyes of fire.

'Tush!' said Lydon, folding his arms, and regarding his rivals with a reckless air of defiance. 'The time of trial will soon come; keep your valour till then.'

'Ay, do,' said the surly host; 'and if I press down my thumb to save you, may the Fates cut my thread!'

'Your rope, you mean,' said Lydon, sneeringly: 'here is a sesterce to buy one.'

The wine-vender seized the hand extended to him, and griped it in so stern a vice that the blood spirted from the fingers' ends over the garments of the bystanders.

They set up a savage laugh.

'I will teach thee, young braggart, to play the Macedonian with me! I am no puny Persian, I warrant thee! What, man! have I not fought twenty years in the ring, and never lowered my arms once? And have I not received the rod from the editor's own hand as a sign of victory, and as a grace to retirement on my laurels? And am I now to be lectured by a boy?' So saying, he flung the hand from him in scorn.

Without changing a muscle, but with the same smiling face with which he had previously taunted mine host, did the gladiator brave the painful grasp he had undergone. But no sooner was his hand released, than, crouching for one moment as a wild cat crouches, you might see his hair bristle on his head and beard, and with a fierce and shrill yell he sprang on the throat of the giant, with an impetus that threw him, vast and sturdy as he was, from his balance;—and down, with the crash of a falling rock, he fell;—while over him fell also his ferocious foe.

Our host, perhaps, had had no need of the rope so kindly recommended to him by Lydon, had he remained three minutes longer in that position. But, summoned to his assistance by the noise of his fall, a woman, who had hitherto kept in an inner apartment, rushed to the scene of battle. This new ally was in herself a match for the gladiator; she was tall, lean, and with arms that could give other than soft embraces. In fact, the gentle helpmate of Burbo the wine-seller had, like himself, fought in the lists—nay, under the emperor's eye. And Burbo himself—Burbo, the unconquered in the field, according to report, now and then yielded the palm to his soft Stratonice. This sweet creature no sooner saw the imminent peril that awaited her worse half, than without other weapons than those with which Nature had provided her, she darted upon the incumbent gladiator, and, clasping him round the waist with her long and snakelike arms, lifted him by a sudden wrench from the body of her husband, leaving only his hands still clinging to the throat of his foe. Meanwhile, the gladiators, lapped, and pampered, and glutted upon blood, crowded delightedly round the combatants— their nostrils distended—their lips grinning— their eyes gloatingly fixed on the bloody throat of the one and the indented talons of the other.

'*Habet!* (he has got it!) *habet!*' cried they, with a sort of yell, rubbing their nervous hands.

'*Non* habeo, ye liars; I have not *got* it!' shouted the host, as with a mighty effort he wrenched himself from those deadly hands, and rose to his feet, breathless, panting, lacerated, bloody; and fronting, with reeling eyes, the glaring look and grinning teeth of his baffled foe, now struggling (but struggling with disdain) in the gripe of the sturdy amazon.

'Fair play!' cried the gladiators: 'one to one;' and, crowding round Lydon and the woman, they separated our pleasing host from his courteous guest.

GRAFFITO OF GLADIATOR

But Lydon, feeling ashamed at his present position, and endeavouring in vain to shake off the grasp of the virago, slipped his hand into his girdle, and drew forth a short knife. So menacing was his look, so brightly gleamed the blade, that Stratonice, who was used only to that fashion of battle which we moderns call the pugilistic, started back in alarm.

'O gods!' cried she, 'the ruffian!—he has concealed weapons! Is that fair? Is that like a gentleman and a gladiator? No, indeed, I scorn such fellows.' With that she contemptuously turned her back on the gladiator, and hastened to examine the condition of her husband.

But he had already recovered himself. The purple hues receded from the crimson surface of his cheek, the veins of the forehead retired into their wonted size. He shook himself with a complacent grunt, satisfied that he was still alive, and then looking at his foe from head to foot with an air of more approbation than he had ever bestowed upon him before,—

'By Castor!' said he, 'thou art a stronger fellow than I took thee for! I see thou art a man of merit and virtue; give me thy hand, my hero!'

'Jolly old Burbo!' cried the gladiators, applauding, 'staunch to the backbone. Give him thy hand, Lydon.'

'Oh, to be sure,' said the gladiator: 'but now I have tasted his blood, I long to lap the whole.'

'By Hercules!' returned the host, quite unmoved, 'that is the true gladiator feeling. Pollux! to think what good training may make a man; why, a beast could not be fiercer!'

'A beast! O dullard! we beat the beasts hollow!' cried Tetraides.

'Well, well,' said Stratonice, who was now employed in smoothing her hair and adjusting her dress, 'if ye are all good friends again, I recommend you to be quiet and orderly; for some young noblemen, your patrons and backers, have sent to say they will come here to pay you a visit: they wish to see you more at their ease than at the schools, before they make up their bets on the great fight at the amphitheatre. So they always come to my house for that purpose: they know we only receive the best gladiators in Pompeii—our society is very select—praised be the gods!'

'Yes,' continued Burbo, drinking off a bowl, or rather a pail of wine, 'a man who has won my laurels can only encourage the brave. Lydon, drink, my boy; may you have an honourable old age like mine!'

'Come here,' said Stratonice, drawing her husband to her affectionately by the ears, in that caress which Tibullus has so prettily described—'Come here!'

'Not so hard, she-wolf! thou art worse than

26

the gladiator,' murmured the huge jaws of Burbo.

'Hist!' said she, whispering him; 'Calenus has just stole in, disguised, by the back way. I hope he has brought the sesterces.'

'Ho! ho! I will join him,' said Burbo; 'meanwhile, I say, keep a sharp eye on the cups—attend to the score. Let them not cheat thee, wife; they are heroes, to be sure, but then they are arrant rogues: Cacus was nothing to them.'

'Never fear me, fool!' was the conjugal reply; and Burbo, satisfied with the dear assurance, strode through the apartment, and sought the penetralia of his house.

'So those soft patrons are coming to look at our muscles,' said Niger. 'Who sent to previse thee of it, my mistress?'

'Lepidus. He brings with him Clodius, the surest better in Pompeii, and the young Greek, Glaucus.'

'A wager on a wager,' cried Tetraides; 'Clodius bets on me, for twenty sesterces! What say you, Lydon?'

'He bets on *me!*' said Lydon.

'No, on *me!*' grunted Sporus.

'Dolts! do you think he would prefer any of you to Niger?' said the athletic, thus modestly naming himself.

'Well, well,' said Stratonice, as she pierced a huge amphora for her guests, who had now seated themselves before one of the tables, 'great men and brave, as ye all think yourselves, which of you will fight the Numidian lion in case no malefactor should be found to deprive you of the option?'

'I who have escaped your arms, stout Stratonice,' said Lydon, 'might safely, I think, encounter the lion.'

TAVERN

1. COUNTERS WITH JARS SUNK INTO TOP AND FOOD ON PLATES
2. KETTLE WITH STOVE
3. OVEN FOR WARMING DRINKS
4. DRINKING CUPS BREAD AND LADLES
5. AMPHORAE
6. SCREEN TO BACK ROOMS

'But tell me,' said Tetraides, 'where is that pretty young slave of yours—the blind girl, with bright eyes? I have not seen her a long time.'

'Oh! she is too delicate for you, my son of Neptune,' said the hostess, 'and too nice even for us, I think. We send her into the town to sell flowers and sing to the ladies: she makes us more money so than she would by waiting on you. Besides, she has often other employments which lie under the rose.'

'Other employments!' said Niger; 'why, she is too young for them.'

'Silence, beast!' said Stratonice; 'you think there is no play but the Corinthian. If Nydia were twice the age she is at present, she would be equally fit for Vesta—poor girl!'

'But, hark ye, Stratonice,' said Lydon; 'how didst thou come by so gentle and delicate a slave? She were more meet for the handmaid of some rich matron of Rome than for thee.'

'That is true,' returned Stratonice; 'and some day or other I shall make my fortune by selling her. How came I by Nydia, thou askest.'

'Ay!'

'Why, thou seest, my slave Staphyla—thou rememberest Staphyla, Niger?'

'Ay, a large-handed wench, with a face like a comic mask. How should I forget her, by Pluto, whose hand-maid she doubtless is at this moment!'

'Tush, brute!—Well, Staphyla died one day, and a great loss she was to me, and I went into the market to buy me another slave. But, by the gods! they were all grown so dear since I had bought poor Staphyla, and money was so scarce, that I was about to leave the place in despair, when a merchant plucked me by the robe. "Mistress," said he, "dost thou want a slave cheap? I have a child to sell—a bargain. She is but little, and almost an infant, it is true; but she is quick and quiet, docile and clever, sings well, and is of good blood, I assure you." "Of what country?" said I. "Thessalian." Now I knew the Thessalians were acute and gentle; so I said I would see the girl. I found her just as you see her now, scarcely smaller and scarcely younger in appearance. She looked patient and resigned enough, with her hands crossed on her bosom, and her eyes downcast. I asked the merchant his price: it was moderate, and I bought her at once. The merchant brought her to my house, and disappeared in an instant. Well, my friends, guess my astonishment when I found she was blind! Ha! ha! a clever fellow that merchant! I ran at once to the magistrates, but the rogue was already gone from Pompeii. So I was forced to go home in a very ill humour, I assure you; and the poor girl felt the effects of it too. But it was not her fault that she was blind, for she had been so from her birth. By degrees, we got reconciled to our purchase. True, she had not the strength of Staphyla, and was of very little use in the house, but she could soon find her way about the town, as well as if she had the eyes of Argus; and when one morning she brought us home a handful of sesterces, which she said she had got from selling some flowers she had gathered in our poor little garden, we thought the gods had sent her to us. So from that time we let her go out as she likes, filling her basket with flowers, which she wreathes into garlands after the Thessalian fashion, which pleases the gallants; and the great people seem to take a fancy to her, for they always pay her more than they do any other flower-girl, and she brings all of it home to us, which is more than any other slave would do. So I work for myself, but I shall soon afford from her earnings to buy me a second Staphyla; doubtless, the Thessalian kidnapper had stolen the blind girl from gentle parents. Besides her skill in the garlands, she sings and plays on the cithara, which also brings money, and lately—but *that* is a secret.'

'*That* is a secret! What!' cried Lydon, 'art thou turned sphinx?'

'Sphinx, no!—why sphinx!'

'Cease thy gabble, good mistress, and bring us our meat—I am hungry,' said Sporus, impatiently.

'And I, too,' echoed the grim Niger, whetting his knife on the palm of his hand.

The amazon stalked away to the kitchen, and soon returned with a tray laden with large pieces of meat half-raw: they drew round the table with the eyes of famished wolves—the meat vanished, the wine flowed. So leave we those important personages of classic life to follow the steps of Burbo.

TWO WORTHIES

In the earlier times of Rome the priesthood was a profession, not of lucre but of honour. It was embraced by the noblest citizens—it was forbidden to the plebeians. Afterwards, and long previous to the present date, it was equally open to all ranks; at least, that part of the profession which embraced the flamens, or priests,—not of religion generally, but of peculiar gods. Even the priest of Jupiter (the Flamen Dialis) preceded by a lictor, and entitled by his office to the entrance of the senate, at first the especial dignitary of the patricians, was subsequently the choice of the people. The less national and less honoured deities were usually served by plebeian ministers; and many embraced the profession less from the impulse of devotion than the suggestions of a calculating poverty. Thus Calenus, the priest of Isis, was of the lowest origin. His relations, though not his parents, were freedmen. He had received from them a liberal education, and from his father a small patrimony, which he had soon exhausted. He embraced the priesthood as a last resource from distress.

Calenus had but one surviving relative at Pompeii, and that was Burbo. Various dark and disreputable ties, stronger than those of blood, united together their hearts and interests; and often the minister of Isis stole disguised and furtively from the supposed austerity of his devotions;—and gliding through the back door of the retired gladiator rejoiced to throw off the last rag of hypocrisy.

Wrapped in a large mantle Calenus now sat in the small and private chamber of the wine-cellar, whence a small passage ran at once to that back entrance, with which nearly all the houses of Pompeii were furnished.

Opposite to him sat the sturdy Burbo, carefully counting on a table between them a little pile of coins which the priest had just poured from his purse—for purses were as common then as now, with this difference—they were usually better furnished!

'You see,' said Calenus, 'that we pay you handsomely, and you ought to thank me for recommending you to so advantageous a market.'

'I do, my cousin, I do,' replied Burbo, affectionately, as he swept the coins into a leathern receptacle, which he then deposited in his girdle. 'And by Isis, Pisis, and Nisis, or whatever other gods there may be in Egypt, my little Nydia is a very Hesperides—a garden of gold to me.'

PURSE

'She sings well, and plays like a muse,' returned Calenus; 'those are virtues that he who employs me always pays liberally.'

'He is a god,' cried Burbo, enthusiastically; 'every rich man who is generous deserves to be worshipped. But come, a cup of wine, old friend: tell me more about it. What does she do? she is frightened, talks of her oath, and reveals nothing.'

'Nor will I, by my right hand! I, too, have taken that terrible oath of secrecy.'

'Oath! what are oaths to men like us?'

'True oaths of a common fashion; but this!' —and the stalwart priest shuddered as he spoke. 'Yet,' he continued, in emptying a huge cup of unmixed wine, 'I will own to thee, that it is not so much the oath that I dread as the vengeance of him who proposed it.'

At this moment they heard a slight noise at the door, as of one feeling the handle. The priest lowered the hood over his head.

'Tush!' whispered the host, 'it is but the blind girl,' as Nydia opened the door, and entered the apartment.

'Ho! girl, and how durst thou? thou lookest pale,—thou hast kept late revels! No matter, the young must be always young,' said Burbo, encouragingly.

The girl made no answer, but she dropped on one of the seats with an air of lassitude. Her colour went and came rapidly: she beat the floor impatiently with her small feet, then she suddenly raised her face, and said with a determined voice,—

'Master, you may starve me if you will,— you may beat me,—you may threaten me with death,—but I will go no more to that unholy place!'

'How, fool!' said Burbo, in a savage voice, and his heavy brows met darkly over his fierce and bloodshot eyes; 'how, rebellious! Take care.'

'I have said it,' said the poor girl, crossing her hands on her breast.

'What! my modest one, sweet vestal, thou wilt go no more! Very well, thou shalt be carried.'

'I will raise the city with my cries,' said she, passionately; and the colour mounted to her brow.

'We will take care of that too; thou shalt go gagged.'

'Then may the gods help me!' said Nydia, rising; 'I will appeal to the magistrates.'

'*Thine oath remember!*' said a hollow voice, as for the first time Calenus joined in the dialogue.

At these words a trembling shook the frame of the unfortunate girl; she clasped her hands imploringly. 'Wretch that I am!' she cried, and burst violently into sobs.

Whether or not it was the sound of that vehement sorrow which brought the gentle Stratonice to the spot, her grisly form at this moment appeared in the chamber.

'How now? what hast thou been doing with my slave, brute?' said she, angrily, to Burbo.

'Be quiet, wife,' said he, in a tone half-sullen, half-timid; 'you want new girdles and fine clothes, do you? Well then, take care of your slave, or you may want them long. *Væ capiti tuo*—vengeance on thy head, wretched one!'

'What is this?' said the hag, looking from one to the other.

Nydia started as by a sudden impulse from the wall against which she had leaned: she threw herself at the feet of Stratonice; she embraced her knees, and looking up at her with those sightless but touching eyes,—

'O my mistress!' sobbed she, 'you are a woman—you have had sisters,—you have been young like me,—feel for me,—save me! I will go to those horrible feasts no more!'

'Stuff!' said the hag, dragging her up rudely by one of those delicate hands, fit for no harsher labour than that of weaving the flowers which made her pleasure or her trade; —'stuff! these fine scruples are not for slaves.'

'Hark ye,' said Burbo, drawing forth his purse, and chinking its contents: 'you hear this music, wife; by Pollux! if you do not break in yon colt with a tight rein, you will hear it no more.'

'The girl is tired,' said Stratonice, nodding to Calenus; 'she will be more docile when you next want her.'

'*You! you!* who is here?' cried Nydia, casting her keen eyes round the apartment with so fearful and straining a survey, that Calenus rose in alarm from his seat.

'She *must* see with those eyes!' muttered he.

'Who is here! Speak, in heaven's name! Ah, if you were blind like me, you would be less cruel,' said she; and she again burst into tears.

'Take her away,' said Burbo, impatiently; 'I hate these whimperings.'

'Come!' said Stratonice, pushing the poor child by the shoulders.

Nydia drew herself aside, with an air to which resolution gave dignity.

'Hear me,' she said; 'I have served you faithfully,—I, who was brought up—Ah! my mother, my poor mother! didst thou dream I should come to this!' She dashed the tear from her eyes, and proceeded:—'Command me in aught else, and I will obey; but I tell you now, hard, stern, inexorable as you are,— I tell you that I will go there no more; or, if I am forced there, that I will implore the mercy of the prætor himself—I have said it. Hear me, ye gods, I swear!'

The hag's eyes glowed with fire; she seized the child by the hair with one hand, and raised on high the other—that formidable right hand, the least blow of which seemed capable to crush the frail and delicate form that trembled in her grasp. That thought itself appeared to strike her, for she suspended the blow, changed her purpose, and dragging Nydia to the wall, seized from a hook a rope, often, alas! applied to a similar purpose, and the next moment the shrill, the agonised shrieks of the blind girl, rang piercingly through the house.

GLAUCUS MAKES A PURCHASE

'Holla, my brave fellows!' said Lepidus, stooping his head as he entered the low door-way of the house of Burbo. 'We have come to see which of you most honours your lanista.' The gladiators rose from the table in respect to three gallants known to be among the gayest and richest youths of Pompeii.

'What fine animals!' said Clodius to Glaucus: 'worthy to be gladiators!'

'It is a pity they are not warriors,' returned Glaucus.

A singular thing it was to see the dainty and fastidious Lepidus, whom in a banquet a ray of daylight seemed to blind,—whom in the bath a breeze of air seemed to blast,—in whom Nature seemed twisted and perverted from every natural impulse, and curdled into one dubious thing of effeminacy and art;—a singular thing was it to see this Lepidus, now all eagerness, and energy, and life, patting the vast shoulders of the gladiators with a blanched and girlish hand, feeling with a mincing gripe their great brawn and iron muscles, all lost in calculating admiration at that manhood which he had spent his life in carefully banishing from himself.

'Ha! Niger, how will you fight?' said Lepidus: 'and with whom?'

'Sporus challenges me,' said the grim giant; 'we shall fight to the death, I hope.'

'Ah! to be sure,' grunted Sporus, with a twinkle of his small eye.

'He takes the sword, I the net and the trident: it will be rare sport. I hope the survivor will have enough to keep up the dignity of the crown.'

'Never fear, we'll fill the purse, my Hector,' said Clodius: 'let me see,—you fight against Niger? Glaucus, a bet—I back Niger.'

'I told you so,' cried Niger exultingly. 'The noble Clodius knows me; count yourself dead already, my Sporus.'

Clodius took out his tablet.—'A bet,—ten sestertia. What say you?'

'So be it,' said Glaucus. 'But whom have we here? I never saw this hero before;' and he glanced at Lydon, whose limbs were slighter than those of his companions, and who had something of grace, and something even of nobleness, in his face, which his profession had not yet wholly destroyed.

'It is Lydon, a youngster, practised only with the wooden sword as yet,' answered Niger, condescendingly. 'But he has the true blood in him, and has challenged Tetraides.'

'*He* challenged *me*,' said Lydon: 'I accept the offer.'

'And how do you fight?' asked Lepidus. 'Chut, my boy, wait a while before you contend with Tetraides.' Lydon smiled disdainfully.

'Is he a citizen or a slave?' said Clodius.

'A citizen;—we are all citizens here,' quoth Niger.

'Stretch out your arm, my Lydon,' said Lepidus, with the air of a connoisseur.

The gladiator, with a significant glance at his companions, extended an arm which, if not so huge in its girth as those of his comrades, was so firm in its muscles, so beautifully symmetrical in its proportions, that the three visitors uttered simultaneously an admiring exclamation.

'Well, man, what is your weapon?' said Clodius, tablet in hand.

'We are to fight first with the cestus; afterwards, if both survive, with swords,' returned Tetraides, sharply.

'With the cestus!' cried Glaucus; 'there you are wrong, Lydon; the cestus is the Greek fashion: I know it well. You should have encouraged flesh for that contest; you are far too thin for it—avoid the cestus.'

GLADIATOR'S
SWORD SHEATH
AND LANCE

'I cannot,' said Lydon.

'And why?'

'I have said—because he has challenged me.'

'But he will not hold you to the precise weapon.'

'My honour holds me!' returned Lydon, proudly.

'I bet on Tetraides, two to one, at the cestus,' said Clodius; 'shall it be, Lepidus?—even betting, with swords.'

'If you give me three to one, I will not take the odds,' said Lepidus: 'Lydon will never come to the swords. You are mighty courteous.'

'What say you, Glaucus?' said Clodius.

'I will take the odds three to one.'

'Ten sestertia to thirty.'

'Yes.'

Clodius wrote the bet in his book.

'Pardon me, noble sponsor mine,' said Lydon, in a low voice to Glaucus: 'but how much think you the victor will gain?'

'How much? why, perhaps seven sestertia.'

'You are sure it will be as much?'

'At least. But out on you!—a Greek would have thought of the honour, and not the money. O Italians! everywhere ye are Italians!'

A blush mantled over the bronzed cheek of the gladiator.

'Do not wrong me, noble Glaucus; I think of both, but I should never have been a gladiator but for the money.'

'Base! mayest thou fall! A miser never was a hero.'

'I am not a miser,' said Lydon, haughtily, and he withdrew to the other end of the room.

'But I don't see Burbo; where is Burbo? I must talk with Burbo,' cried Clodius.

'He is within,' said Niger, pointing to the door at the extremity of the room.

'And Stratonice, the brave old lass, where is she?' quoth Lepidus.

'Why, she was here just before you entered; but she heard something that displeased her yonder, and vanished. Pollux! old Burbo had perhaps caught hold of some girl in the back room. I heard a female's voice crying out; the old dame is as jealous as Juno.'

'Ho! excellent!' cried Lepidus, laughing. 'Come, Clodius, let us go shares with Jupiter; perhaps he has caught a Leda.'

At this moment a loud cry of pain and terror startled the group.

'Oh, spare me! spare me! I am but a child, I am blind—is not *that* punishment enough?'

'O Pallas! I know that voice, it is my poor flower-girl!' exclaimed Glaucus, and he darted at once into the quarter whence the cry rose.

He burst the door; he beheld Nydia writhing in the grasp of the infuriate hag; the cord, already dabbled with blood, was raised in the air,—it was suddenly arrested.

'Fury!' said Glaucus, and with his left hand he caught Nydia from her grasp; 'how dare you use thus a girl,—one of your own sex, a child! My Nydia, my poor infant!'

'Oh? is that you—is that Glaucus?' exclaimed the flower-girl, in a tone almost of transport; the tears stood arrested on her cheek; she smiled, she clung to his breast, she kissed his robe as she clung.

'And how dare you, pert stranger! interfere between a free woman and her slave. By the gods! despite your fine tunic and your filthy perfumes, I doubt whether you are even a Roman citizen, my mannikin.'

'Fair words, mistress,—fair words!' said Clodius, now entering with Lepidus. 'This is my friend and sworn brother; he must be put under shelter of your tongue, sweet one; it rains stones!'

'Give me my slave!' shrieked the virago, placing her mighty grasp on the breast of the Greek.

'Not if all your sister Furies could help you,' answered Glaucus. 'Fear not, sweet Nydia; an Athenian never forsook distress!'

GLADIATOR'S GOOD LUCK CHARM

'Holla!' said Burbo, rising reluctantly, 'what turmoil is all this about a slave? Let go the young gentleman, wife,—let him go: for his sake the pert thing shall be spared this once.' So saying, he drew, or rather dragged off, his ferocious helpmate.

'Methought when we entered,' said Clodius, 'there was another man present?'

'He is gone.'

For the priest of Isis had indeed thought it high time to vanish.

'Oh, a friend of mine! a brother cupman, a quiet dog, who does not love these snarlings,' said Burbo, carelessly. 'But go, child, you will tear the gentleman's tunic if you cling to him so tight; go, you are pardoned.'

'Oh, do not—do not forsake me!' cried Nydia, clinging yet closer to the Athenian.

Moved by her forlorn situation, her appeal to him, her own innumerable and touching graces, the Greek seated himself on one of the rude chairs. He held her on his knees,—he wiped the blood from her shoulders with his long hair,—he kissed the tears from her cheeks,—he whispered to her a thousand of those soothing words with which we calm the grief of a child;—and so beautiful did he seem in his gentle and consoling task, that even the fierce heart of Stratonice was touched. His presence seemed to shed light over that base and obscene haunt,—young, beautiful, glorious, he was the emblem of all that earth made most happy, comforting one that earth had abandoned!

'Well, who could have thought our blind Nydia had been so honoured!' said the virago, wiping her heated brow.

Glaucus looked up at Burbo.

'My good man,' said he, 'this is your slave; she sings well, she is accustomed to the care of flowers,—I wish to make a present of such a slave to a lady. Will you sell her to me?' As he spoke he felt the whole frame of the poor girl tremble with delight; she started up, she put her dishevelled hair from her eyes, she looked around, as if, alas, she had the power to *see!*

'Sell our Nydia! no, indeed,' said Stratonice, gruffly.

Nydia sank back with a long sigh, and again clasped the robe of her protector.

'Nonsense!' said Clodius, imperiously: 'you must oblige me. What, man! what, old dame! offend me, and your trade is ruined. Is not Burbo my kinsman Pansa's client?

Am I not the oracle of the amphitheatre and its heroes? If I say the word, Break up your wine-jars,—you sell no more. Glaucus, the slave is yours.'

Burbo scratched his huge head, in evident embarrassment.

'The girl is worth her weight in gold to me.'

'Name your price, I am rich,' said Glaucus.

The ancient Italians were like the modern, there was nothing they would not sell, much less a poor blind girl.

'I paid six sestertia for her, she is worth twelve now,' muttered Stratonice.

'You shall have twenty; come to the magistrates at once, and then to my house for your money.'

'I would not have sold the dear girl for a hundred but to oblige noble Clodius,' said Burbo, whiningly. 'And you will speak to Pansa about the place of *designator* at the amphitheatre, noble Clodius? it would just suit me.'

'Thou shalt have it,' said Clodius; adding in a whisper to Burbo, "Yon Greek can make your fortune; money runs through him like a sieve: mark to-day with white chalk, my Priam.'

'*An dabis?*' said Glaucus, in the formal question of sale and barter.

'*Dabitur,*' answered Burbo.

'Then, then, I am to go with you,—with you? O happiness!' murmured Nydia.

'Pretty one, yes; and thy hardest task henceforth shall be to sing thy Grecian hymns to the loveliest lady in Pompeii.'

The girl sprang from his clasp; a change came over her whole face, so bright the instant before; she sighed heavily, and then once more taking his hand, she said,—

'I thought I was to go to *your* house?'

'And so thou shalt for the present; come, we lose time.'

BRONZE SCALES

THE RIVAL OF GLAUCUS PRESSES ONWARD IN THE RACE

Ione was one of those brilliant characters which, but once or twice, flash across our career. She united in the highest perfection the rarest of earthly gifts,—Genius and Beauty.

It was no wonder that she had completely chained and subdued the mysterious but burning soul of the Egyptian, a man in whom dwelt the fiercest passions. Her beauty and her soul alike enthralled him.

Set apart himself from the common world, he loved that daringness of character which also made itself, among common things, aloof and alone. He did not, or he would not see, that that very isolation put her yet more from him than from the vulgar. Far as the poles—far as the night from day, his solitude was divided from hers. He was solitary from his dark and solemn vices—she from her beautiful fancies and her purity of virtue.

If it was not strange that Ione thus enthralled the Egyptian, far less strange was it that she had captured, as suddenly as irrevocably, the bright and sunny heart of the Athenian. The gladness of a temperament which seemed woven from the beams of light had led Glaucus into pleasure. He obeyed no more vicious dictates when he wandered into the dissipations of his time, than the exhilarating voices of youth and health. He threw the brightness of his nature over every abyss and cavern through which he strayed. His imagination dazzled him, but his heart never was corrupted. Of far more penetration than his companions deemed, he saw that they sought to prey upon his riches and his youth: but he despised wealth save as the means of enjoyment, and youth was the great sympathy that united him to them.

But all that was best and brightest in his soul woke at once when he knew Ione. His ideas glowed more brightly, his soul seemed more awake and more visible, in Ione's presence. If natural to love her, it was natural that she should return the passion. It was as if the poetry of life gathered and fed itself in them, and in their hearts were concentrated the last rays of the sun of Delos and of Greece.

But if Ione was independent in her choice of life, so was her modest pride proportionably vigilant and easily alarmed. The falsehood of the Egyptian was invented by a deep knowledge of her nature. The story of coarseness, of indelicacy, in Glaucus, stung her to the quick. She felt it a reproach upon her character and her career, a punishment above

all to her love; she felt, for the first time, how suddenly she had yielded to that love; she blushed with shame at a weakness, the extent of which she was startled to perceive: she imagined it was that weakness which had incurred the contempt of Glaucus; she endured the bitterest curse of noble natures—*humiliation!* Yet her love, perhaps, was no less alarmed than her pride. If one moment she murmured reproaches upon Glaucus—if one moment she renounced, she almost hated him—at the next she burst into passionate tears, her heart yielded to its softness, and she said in the bitterness of anguish, 'He despises me—he does not love me.'

From the hour the Egyptian had left her she had retired to her most secluded chamber, she had shut out her hand-maids, she had denied herself to the crowds that besieged her door. Glaucus was excluded with the rest; he wondered, but he guessed not why! He was troubled, but his hopes were not dimmed, for he knew already that he loved and was beloved; what more could he desire as an amulet against fear?

At deepest night, then, when the streets were hushed, and the high moon only beheld his devotions, he stole to that temple of his heart—her home; and wooed her after the beautiful fashion of his country. He covered her threshold with the richest garlands, in which every flower was a volume of sweet passion; and he charmed the long summer night with the sound of the Lydian lute: and verses, which the inspiration of the moment sufficed to weave.

But the window above opened not; no smile made yet more holy the shining air of night. All was still and dark. He knew not if his verse was welcome and his suit was heard.

Yet Ione slept not, nor disdained to hear. Those soft strains ascended to her chamber; they soothed, they subdued her. While she listened, she believed nothing against her lover; but when they were stilled at last, and his step departed, the spell ceased; and, in the bitterness of her soul, she almost conceived in that delicate flattery a new affront.

I said she was denied to all; but there was one exception, there was one person who would not be denied, assuming over her actions and her house something like the authority of a parent; Arbaces, for himself, claimed an exemption from all the ceremonies observed by others. He entered the threshold with the license of one who feels that he is privileged and at home. Utterly unaware of his real character or his hidden love, she felt for him the reverence which genius feels for wisdom, and virtue for sanctity. She regarded him as one of those mighty sages of old, who attained to the mysteries of knowledge by an exemption from the passions of their kind. She scarcely considered him as a being, like herself, of the earth, but as an oracle at once dark and sacred. She did not love him, but she feared. His presence was unwelcome to her; it dimmed her spirit even in its brightest mood; he seemed, with his chilling and lofty aspect, like some eminence which casts a shadow over the sun. But she never thought of forbidding his visits.

Arbaces himself now resolved to exert all his arts to possess himself of that treasure he so burningly coveted. He was cheered and elated by his conquests over her brother. From the hour in which Apæcides fell beneath the voluptuous sorcery of that fête which we have described, he felt his empire over the young priest triumphant and insured. He knew that there is no victim so thoroughly subdued as a young and fervent man for the first time delivered to the thraldom of the senses.

When Apæcides recovered, with the morning light, from the profound sleep which succeeded to the delirium of wonder and of pleasure, he was, it is true, ashamed—terrified—appalled. His vows of austerity and celibacy echoed in his ear; his thirst after holiness—had it been quenched at so unhallowed a stream? But Arbaces knew well the means by which to confirm his conquest. From the arts of pleasure he led the young priest at once to those of his mysterious wisdom. He bared to his amazed eyes the initiatory secrets of the sombre philosophy of the Nile—those secrets plucked from the stars, and the wild chemistry, which, in those days, when Reason herself was but the creature of Imagination, might well pass for the lore of a diviner magic.

It was necessary to him, as to all, to believe in something; and undivided and, at last, unreluctant, he surrendered himself to that belief which Arbaces inculcated, and which all that was human in passion—all that was flattering in vanity—all that was alluring in pleasure, served to invite to, and contributed to confirm.

This conquest, thus easily made, the Egyptian could now give himself wholly up to the pursuit of a far dearer and mightier object; and he hailed, in his success with the brother, an omen of his triumph over the sister.

He had seen Ione on the day following the revel we have witnessed; and which was also the day after he had poisoned her mind against her rival. The next day, and the next, he saw her also: and each time he laid himself out with consummate art, partly to confirm her impression against Glaucus, and principally to prepare her for the impressions he desired her to receive.

It was on the fourth day from the date of the close of the previous book, that Arbaces and Ione sat together.

'You wear your veil at home,' said the Egyptian; 'that is not fair to those whom you honour with your friendship.'

'But to Arbaces,' answered Ione, who, indeed, had cast the veil over her features to conceal eyes red with weeping,—'to Arbaces, who looks only to the mind, what matters it that the face is concealed?'

'I do look only to the mind,' replied the Egyptian: 'show me then your face—for there I shall see it.'

'You grow gallant in the air of Pompeii,' said Ione, with a forced tone of gaiety.

'Do you think, fair Ione, that it is only at Pompeii that I have learned to value you?' The Egyptian's voice trembled—he paused for a moment, and then resumed.

'There is a love, beautiful Greek, which is not the love only of the thoughtless and the young—there is a love which sees not with the eyes, which hears not with the ears; but in which soul is enamoured of soul.'

'And its name is friendship!' replied Ione: her answer was innocent, yet it sounded like the reproof of one conscious of the design of the speaker.

'Friendship!' said Arbaces, vehemently. 'No; that is a word too often profaned to apply to a sentiment so sacred. Friendship! it is a tie that binds fools and profligates! Friendship! it is the bond that unites the frivolous hearts of a Glaucus and a Clodius!

ROMAN
YOUNG MAN

Friendship! no, *that* is an affection of earth, of vulgar habits and sordid sympathies. No; it is not love, and it is not friendship, that Arbaces feels for Ione. Give it no name—earth has no name for it—it is not of earth—why debase it with earthly epithets and earthly associations?'

Never before had Arbaces ventured so far, yet he felt his ground step by step: he knew that he uttered a language which was strange and unfamiliar, to which no precise idea could be attached, from which he could imperceptibly advance or recede, as occasion suited, as hope encouraged or fear deterred. Ione trembled, though she knew not why; her veil hid her features, and masked an expression, which, if seen by the Egyptian, would have at once damped and enraged him; in fact, his never was more displeasing to her—the harmonious modulation of the most suasive voice that ever disguised unhallowed thought fell discordantly on her ear. She thought that he, in truth, spoke only of the affection and sympathy of the soul; but was it not precisely that affection and that sympathy which had made a part of those emotions she felt for Glaucus; and could any other footstep than his approach the haunted adytus of her heart?

Anxious at once to change the conversation, she replied, therefore, with a cold and indifferent voice, 'Whomsoever Arbaces honours with the sentiment of esteem, it is natural that his elevated wisdom should colour that sentiment with its own hues; it is natural that his friendship should be purer than that of others, whose pursuits and errors he does not deign to share. But tell me, Arbaces, hast thou seen my brother of late? He has not visited me for several days; and when I last saw him his manner disturbed and alarmed me much. I fear lest he was too precipitate in the severe choice that he has adopted, and that he repents an irrevocable step.'

'Be cheered, Ione,' replied the Egyptian. 'It is true, that some little time since he was troubled and sad of spirit; those doubts beset him which were likely to haunt one of that fervent temperament, which ever ebbs and flows, and vibrates between excitement and exhaustion. But *he*, Ione, *he* came to me in his anxieties and his distress; he sought one who pitied and loved him; I have calmed his mind—I have removed his doubts—I have taken him from the threshold of Wisdom into its temple; and before the majesty of the goddess his soul is hushed and soothed. Fear not, he will repent no more; they who trust themselves to Arbaces never repent but for a moment.'

'You rejoice me,' answered Ione. 'My dear brother! in his contentment I am happy.'

The conversation then turned upon lighter subjects; the Egyptian exerted himself to please, he condescended even to entertain; the vast variety of his knowledge enabled him to adorn and light up every subject on which he touched; and Ione, forgetting the displeasing effect of his former words, was carried away, despite her sadness, by the magic of his intellect. Her manner became unrestrained and her language fluent; and Arbaces, who had waited his opportunity, now hastened to seize it.

'You have never seen,' said he, 'the interior of my home; it may amuse you to do so: it contains some rooms that may explain to you what you have often asked me to describe—the fashion of an Egyptian house. Devote, then, to the austere friend of your youth, one of these bright summer evenings, and let me boast that my gloomy mansion has been honoured with the presence of the admired Ione.'

Unconscious of the pollutions of the mansion, of the danger that awaited her, Ione readily assented to the proposal. The next evening was fixed for the visit; and the Egyptian, with a serene countenance, and a heart beating with fierce and unholy joy, departed. Scarce had he gone, when another visitor claimed admission.——But now we return to Glaucus.

THE POOR TORTOISE – NEW CHANGES FOR NYDIA

The morning sun shone over the small and odorous garden enclosed within the peristyle of the house of the Athenian. He lay reclined, sad and listlessly, on the smooth grass which intersected the viridarium; and a slight canopy stretched above, broke the fierce rays of the summer sun.

Glaucus was interrupted by the entrance of Nydia. She came with her light, though cautious step, along the marble tablinum. She passed the portico, and paused at the flowers which bordered the garden. She had her water-vase in her hand, and she sprinkled the thirsting plants, which seemed to brighten at her approach. She bent to inhale their odour. She touched them timidly and caressingly. She felt, along their stems, if any withered leaf or creeping insect marred their beauty. And as she hovered from flower to flower, with her earnest and youthful countenance and graceful motions, you could not have imagined a fitter handmaid for the goddess of the garden.

BRONZE JUG

'Nydia, my child!' said Glaucus.

At the sound of his voice she paused at once—listening, blushing, breathless; with her lips parted, her face upturned to catch the direction of the sound, she laid down the vase—she hastened to him; and wonderful it was to see how unerringly she threaded her dark way through the flowers, and came by the shortest path to the side of her new lord.

'Nydia,' said Glaucus, tenderly stroking back her long and beautiful hair, 'it is now three days since thou hast been under the protection of my household gods. Have they smiled on thee? Art thou happy?'

'Ah! so happy!' sighed the slave.

'And now,' continued Glaucus, 'that thou hast recovered somewhat from the hateful recollections of thy former state,—and now that they have fitted thee [touching her broidered tunic] with garments more meet for thy delicate shape,—and now, sweet child, that thou hast accustomed thyself to a happiness, which may the gods grant thee ever! I am about to pray at thy hands a boon.'

'Oh! what can I do for thee?' said Nydia, clasping her hands.

'Listen,' said Glaucus, 'and young as thou art, thou shalt be my confidant. Hast thou ever heard the name of Ione?'

The blind girl gasped for breath, and turning pale as one of the statues which shone upon them from the peristyle, she answered with an effort, and after a moment's pause,—

'Yes! I have heard that she is of Neapolis, and beautiful.'

'Beautiful! her beauty is a thing to dazzle the day! Neapolis! nay, she is Greek by origin; Greece only could furnish forth such shapes. Nydia, I love her!'

'I thought so,' replied Nydia, calmly.

'I love, and thou shalt tell her so. I am about to send thee to her. Happy Nydia, thou

wilt be in her chamber—thou wilt drink the music of her voice—thou wilt bask in the sunny air of her presence!'

'What! what! wilt thou send me from thee?'

'Thou wilt go to Ione,' answered Glaucus, in a tone that said, 'What more canst thou desire?'

Nydia burst into tears.

Glaucus, raising himself, drew her towards him with the soothing caresses of a brother.

'My child, my Nydia, thou weepest in ignorance of the happiness I bestow on thee. She is gentle, and kind, and soft as the breeze of spring. She will be a sister to thy youth—she will appreciate thy winning talents—she will love thy simple graces as none other could, for they are like her own. Weepest thou still, fond fool? I will not force thee, sweet. Wilt thou not do for me this kindness?'

'Well, if I can serve thee, command. See, I weep no longer—I am calm.'

'That is my own Nydia,' continued Glaucus, kissing her hand. 'Go, then, to her: if thou art disappointed in her kindness—if I have deceived thee, return when thou wilt. I do not *give* thee to another; I but lend. My home ever be thy refuge, sweet one. Ah! would it could shelter all the friendless and distressed! But if my heart whispers truly, I shall claim thee again soon, my child. My home and Ione's will become the same, and thou shalt dwell with both.'

A shiver passed through the slight frame of the blind girl, but she wept no more—she was resigned.

'Go, then, my Nydia, to Ione's house—they shall show thee the way. Take her the fairest flowers thou canst pluck; the vase which contains them I will give thee: thou must excuse its unworthiness. Thou shalt take, too, with thee the lute that I gave thee yesterday, and from which thou knowest so well to awaken the charming spirit. Thou shalt give her, also, this letter, in which, after a hundred efforts, I have embodied something of my thoughts. Let thine ear catch every accent, every modulation of her voice, and tell me, when we meet again, if its music should flatter me or discourage. It is now, Nydia, some days since I have been admitted to Ione; there is something mysterious in this exclusion. I am distracted with doubts and fears; learn—for thou art quick, and thy care for me will sharpen tenfold thy acuteness—learn the cause of this unkindness; speak of me as often as thou canst; let my name come ever to thy lips: *insinuate* how I love rather than *proclaim* it; watch if she sighs whilst thou speakest, if she answer thee; or, if she reproves, in what accents she reproves. Be my friend, plead for me: and oh! how vastly wilt thou overpay the little I have done for thee!'

THE HAPPY BEAUTY
AND THE BLIND SLAVE

A slave entered the chamber of Ione. A messenger from Glaucus desired to be admitted.

Ione hesitated an instant.

'She is blind, that messenger,' said the slave; 'she will do her commission to none but thee.'

Base is that heart which does not respect affliction! The moment she heard the messenger was blind, Ione felt the impossibility of returning a chilling reply. Glaucus had chosen a herald that was indeed sacred—a herald that could not be denied.

'What can he want with me? what message can he send?' and the heart of Ione beat quick. The curtain across the door was withdrawn; a soft and echoless step fell upon the marble; and Nydia, led by one of the attendants, entered with her precious gift.

She stood still a moment, as if listening for some sound that might direct her.

'Will the noble Ione,' said she, in a soft and low voice, 'deign to speak, that I may know whither to steer these benighted steps, and that I may lay my offerings at her feet?'

'Fair child,' said Ione, touched and soothingly, 'give not thyself the pain to cross these slippery floors; my attendant will bring to me what thou hast to present;' and she motioned to the handmaid to take the vase.

'I may give these flowers to none but thee,' answered Nydia; and, guided by her ear, she walked slowly to the place where Ione sat, and kneeling when she came before her, proffered the vase.

Ione took it from her hand, and placed it on the table at her side. She then raised her gently, and would have seated her on the couch, but the girl modestly resisted.

'I have not yet discharged my office,' said she; and she drew the letter of Glaucus from her vest. 'This will, perhaps, explain why he who sent me chose so unworthy a messenger to Ione.'

The Neapolitan took the letter with a hand, the trembling of which Nydia at once felt and sighed to feel. With folded arms, and downcast looks, she stood before the proud and stately form of Ione;—no less proud, perhaps, in her attitude of submission. Ione waved her hand, and the attendants withdrew; she gazed again upon the form of the young slave in surprise and beautiful compassion; then, retiring a little from her, she opened and read the following letter:—

'Glaucus to Ione sends more than he dares to utter. Is Ione ill? thy slaves tell me "No," and that assurance comforts me. Has Glaucus offended Ione?—ah! that question I may not ask from *them*. For five days I have been banished from thy presence. Has the sun shone?—I know it not. Has the sky smiled?—it has had no smile for me. My sun and my sky are Ione. Do I offend thee? Am I too bold? Do I say that on the tablet which my tongue has hesitated to breathe? Alas! it is in thine absence that I feel most the spells by which thou hast subdued me. And absence, that deprives me of joy, brings me courage. Thou wilt not see me; thou hast banished also the common flatterers that flock around thee. Canst thou confound me with them? It is not possible! Thou knowest too well that I am not of them—that their clay is not mine. For even were I of the humblest mould, the fragrance of the rose has penetrated me, and the spirit of thy nature hath passed within me, to embalm, to sanctify, to inspire. Have they slandered me to thee, Ione? Thou wilt not believe them. Did the Delphic oracle itself tell me thou wert unworthy, I would not believe it; and am I less incredulous than thou? I think of the last time we met—of the song which I sang to thee—of the look that thou gavest me in return. Disguise it as thou wilt, Ione, there is something kindred between us, and our eyes acknowledged it, though our lips were silent. Deign to see me, to listen to me, and after that exclude me if thou wilt. I meant not so soon to say I loved. But those words rush to my heart—they will have way. Accept, then, my homage and my vows. We met first at the shrine of Pallas; shall we not meet before a softer and a more ancient altar?

'Beautiful! adored Ione! If my hot youth and my Athenian blood have misguided and allured me, they have but taught my wanderings to appreciate the rest—the haven they have attained. I hang up my dripping robes on the Sea-god's shrine. I have escaped shipwreck. I have found THEE. Ione, deign to see me; thou art gentle to strangers, wilt thou be less merciful to those of thine own land? I await thy reply. Accept the flowers which I send—their sweet breath has a language more eloquent than words. They take from the sun the odours they return—they are the emblem of the love that receives and repays tenfold—the emblem of the heart that drunk thy rays, and owes to thee the germ of the treasures that it proffers to thy smile. I send these by one whom thou wilt receive for her own sake, if not for mine. She, like us, is a stranger; her fathers' ashes lie under brighter skies: but, less happy than we, she is blind and a slave. Poor Nydia! I seek as much as possible to repair to her the cruelties of Nature and of Fate, in asking permission to place her with thee. She is gentle, quick, and docile. She is skilled in music and the song; and she is a very Chloris to the flowers. She thinks Ione, that thou wilt love her: if thou dost not, send her back to me.

'One word more,—let me be bold, Ione. Why thinkest thou so highly of yon dark Egyptian? he hath not about him the air of honest men. We Greeks learn mankind from our cradle; we are not the less profound, in that we affect no sombre mien; our lips smile, but our eyes are grave—they observe—they note—they study. Arbaces is not one to be credulously trusted: can it be that he hath wronged me to thee? I think it, for I left him with thee; thou sawest how my presence stung him; since then thou hast not admitted me. Believe nothing that he can say to my disfavour; if thou dost, tell me so at once; for this Ione owes to Glaucus. Farewell! this letter touches thy hand; these characters meet thine eyes—shall they be more blessed than he who is their author. Once more, farewell!'

It seemed to Ione, as she read this letter, as if a mist had fallen from her eyes. What had been the supposed offence of Glaucus?—that he had not really loved! And now, plainly, and in no dubious terms, he confessed that love. From that moment his power was fully restored. At every tender word in that letter, so full of romantic and trustful passion, her heart smote her. And had she doubted his faith, and had she believed another? and had she not, at least, allowed to him the culprit's right to know his crime, to plead in his defence?—the tears rolled down her cheeks —she kissed the letter—she placed it in her bosom: and, turning to Nydia, who stood in the same place and in the same posture,—

'Wilt thou sit, my child,' said she, 'while I write an answer to this letter?'

'You will answer it, then!' said Nydia, coldly. 'Well, the slave that accompanied me will take back your answer.'

'For you,' said Ione, 'stay with me—trust me, your service shall be light.'

Nydia bowed her head.

'What is your name, fair girl?'

'They call me Nydia.'

'Your country?'

'The land of Olympus—Thessaly.'

'Thou shalt be to me a friend,' said Ione, caressingly, 'as thou art already half a countrywoman. Meanwhile, I beseech thee, stand not on these cold and glassy marbles.—There! now that thou art seated, I can leave thee for an instant.'

'Ione to Glaucus greeting.—come to me, Glaucus,' wrote Ione,—'Come to me tomorrow. I may have been unjust to thee; but I will tell thee, at least, the fault that has been imputed to thy charge. Fear not, henceforth, the Egyptian—fear none. Thou sayest thou hast expressed too much—alas! in these hasty words I have already done so. Farewell.'

As Ione reappeared with the letter, which she did not dare to read after she had written

INSIDE A TEMPLE

PAINTING OF TEMPLE CEREMONY

STATUE OF ISIS

Isis was the Egyptian goddess of heaven. Osiris, the sun god, was her husband. Osiris was killed by the ruler of darkness, Set. Horus (Orus in *The Last Days of Pompeii*), born after his father's death, was the sun that arises each morning, avenging his father's death and conquering darkness.

The Roman state tried to abolish the cult of Isis after its introduction from Egypt (towards the end of the Republic). Temples built to Isis in Rome were pulled down, but the cult increased in popularity among the Romans during the Empire. Pompeii, on the main trade route to Egypt, was particularly enthusiastic about the cult of Isis. Worshippers of Isis believed that they were incarnations of the goddess and that if her judgment after death were favourable that they would expect happiness in the afterlife.

The worshippers used to fast, and abstained from earthly things. They were regular attenders at the temple ceremonies. This was unusual, for most other deities at that time were only worshipped on their particular festival days. What was also unusual was that the cult was served by full-time priests. These were necessary because each day there were two main ceremonies, and there were also special initiation ceremonies and festivities.

The priests were renowned for their knowledge of astrology, the meaning of dreams and the conjuring up of spirits. The day of a priest started before daybreak. His first duty was to enter the temple and open the great main door, which was then covered by a curtain. As the worshippers were admitted to the temple area, and approached the steps of the temple, the curtain was pulled back and the image of Isis was revealed.

The worshippers offered up prayers and silently contemplated the divinity. At the same time they shook their sistra, the mystical musical instrument of the worship of Isis, in their right hands. One hour after sunrise, the priests offered up a prayer and the service ended.

The next service was at 2.00 p.m. It was the act of blessing the sacred Nile water (kept in a tank on the temple precincts).

Offerings and sacrifices were made, and prayers said.

On great festival days the myth of Isis and Osiris was acted out for the worshippers. There were also secret ceremonies – probably carried out at night. These were undoubtedly connected with the initiation of converts, but sadly little is known of these ceremonies. It seems that they included visions of Isis appearing before the worshippers.

INCENSE VESSEL

PRIEST WITH DOGS HEAD

STONE BASIN

SISTRUM

RELIGIONS AND THEIR GODS

The ancient Romans had only minor gods, mostly concerned with the family and agriculture – the only exceptions were Juno and Jupiter. Most of the major State gods were borrowed from Greece, while the later 'mystery' gods were imported from Egypt and the East. The Romans renamed them and made them their own. Religious practice was formal and not generally deeply felt. It was more an observance, an outward sign of glorification of the State deities. With no strong belief in any particular god, the Roman only called on him or her in times of trouble. Priests were elected by the people for a term of office. They did not work full time and they usually had other duties. Nor did they serve in a particular temple; they helped in and supervised the rites in all the State temples.

MINERVA

JUNO

VENUS FROM A POMPEIAN INLAID MARBLE DECORATION.

TEMPLE OF JUPITER: OUTSIDE, SPEAKERS PLATFORM (BY THE STAIRS) INSIDE, SMALL SHRINES TO JUNO AND MINERVA.

PLAN OF THE FORUM IN POMPEII, SHOWING HOW CLOSELY PUBLIC BUILDINGS AND STATE TEMPLES WERE RELATED

TEMPLES OF 1 JUPITER 2 APOLLO 3 VESPASIAN 4 CITY LARES PUBLIC BUILDINGS 5 MARKETS 6 TREASURY 7 MUNICIPAL BUILDINGS 8 VOTING ROOMS 9 MEETING PLACE 10 ARCH OF TIBERIUS

VENUS
GODDESS OF LOVE AND NATURE – THE GREEK APHRODITE. HER IMAGE WAS PAINTED AND SCRATCHED EVERYWHERE IN POMPEII, ON SHOPS, HOUSES AND TAVERNS. PATRON SAINT OF POMPEII.

JUPITER
BRINGER OF STORMS AND THUNDER CHIEF GOD OF ROMAN WORSHIP. LINKED WITH JUNO AND MINERVA AS PROTECTOR OF THE STATE.

BUST OF JUPITER FROM POMPEII

INCENSE
PAN

FLESH HOOK

ENTRAIL BOWL

STATUE OF APOLLO

ALTAR OF
THE TEMPLE
OF VESPASIAN

TEMPLE OF VESPASIAN
THE CULT OF THE EMPERORS STARTED
AT THE DEATH OF AUGUSTUS (AD14).
AUGUSTUS ALSO COUPLED HIS NAME
WITH AN ANCIENT FERTILITY DEITY,
FORTUNA, AND A TEMPLE DEDICATED
TO HER STOOD NOT FAR FROM THE FORUM.

APOLLO
FIRST ASSOCIATED WITH THE ORACLES
AUGUSTUS TRANSFORMED HIM
INTO THE GOD OF PEACE AND
ENLIGHTENMENT.

BACCHUS
GREEK DIONYSUS, GOD OF WINE AND
ABANDON. CENTRE OF A MYSTERY CULT
ASSOCIATED WITH THE PLEASURES AND
ECSTASIES OF THE FLESH.
HIS FOLLOWERS WERE SAVED FROM
THE UNDERWORLD AND THEY INHER-
ITED HAPPINESS IN THE AFTERLIFE.
HIS TEMPLE WAS SET OUTSIDE THE
CITY WALL.

SILENUS SAID TO BE BACCHUS' TEACHER. ASTRIDE
A WINE SKIN. BRONZE FROM HERCULANEUM

LARES
GUARDIAN SPIRITS OF THE HOUSE TO
WHOM SIMPLE OFFERINGS WERE MADE.
FRUIT, SPECIAL CAKES & A PORTION OF
EVERY MEAL EATEN WERE ACCEPTABLE.
PORTRAYED AS DANCING FIGURES WITH
DRINKING HORNS. THE GENIUS, OR
PROTECTING SPIRIT OF THE MASTER
OF THE HOUSE, IS SHOWN WITH WITH
A TOGA DRAWN OVER HIS HEAD.
THE SERPENTS WERE PROBABLY
SYMBOLS OF FERTILITY AND THE
BOUNTY OF NATURE.

CAPITAL FROM TEMPLE
OF ZEUS MILICHIUS
AN AGRICULTURAL GOD.

LARE   GENIUS   SERPENT

TYPICAL HOUSE ALTAR. SOME
ALTARS ALSO HAD LITTLE STATUES.

ROMAN RECIPES BASED ON THE COOKERY BOOK OF APICIUS

EXACT QUANTITIES OF INGREDIENTS WERE RARELY GIVEN THESE WERE LEFT TO THE COOK'S INDIVIDUAL TASTES.

LIQUAMEN (FISH SAUCE)

A WELL KNOWN POMPEIAN RECIPE, USED INSTEAD OF SALT TO FLAVOUR FOOD.
PLACE SPRATS OR MACKEREL IN CASSEROLE POUR SALTED WATER OVER FISH. ADD ORIGAN, GRAPE JUICE (BOILED). BOIL MIXTURE RAPIDLY UNTIL REDUCED, COOL, STRAIN TILL CLEAR.

MUSSELS

BOIL MUSSELS IN A LIQUID MADE AS FOLLOWS: CUT UP LEEKS, ADD FISH SAUCE, MINT & CUMIN, STIR IN WINE (VERY SWEET) AND WATER.

HAM

BOIL LEAN PIECE OF HAM WITH PLENTY OF DRIED FIGS. ENJOY WITH ROLLS AND SPICED WINE.

TASTY DESSERT

SHELL SOME NUTS, ADD PINE KERNELS, TOAST LIGHTLY, POUND TOGETHER THOUROUGHLY WITH MILK, EGGS, HONEY, FISH SAUCE, AND PEPPER AND A LITTLE WINE AND OIL. COOK CAREFULLY IN A SHALLOW DISH, STIRRING WELL, AND SERVE.

SWEETS

COOK SOME WHOLEMEAL FLOUR IN HOT WATER UNTIL IT FORMS A HARD PASTE. COVER DISH WITH MIXTURE AND LEAVE TO COOL. CUT INTO SMALL SQUARES, FRY IN OLIVE OIL, PLACE IN A DISH, POUR HONEY OVER THE SWEETS AND SPRINKLE WITH PEPPER.

SPOONS

DIPPER

KNIVES

MOULD

PORTABLE STOVE

COOKING RANGE, CHARCOAL PLACED IN BOTTOM, POTS PLACED IN CONTAINERS AT BACK

TRICLINIUM. BENCHES MADE OF STONE SMALL SEATS FOR CHILDREN.

(Ah! common rashness, common timidity of love!)—Nydia started from her seat.

'You have written to Glaucus?'

'I have.'

'And will he thank the messenger who gives to him thy letter?'

Ione forgot that her companion was blind; she blushed from the brow to the neck, and remained silent.

'I mean this,' added Nydia, in a calmer tone; 'the lightest word of coldness from thee will sadden him—the lightest kindness will rejoice. If it be the first, let the slave take back thine answer; if it be the last, let me—I will return this evening.'

'And why, Nydia,' asked Ione, evasively, 'wouldst thou be the bearer of my letter?'

'It is so, then!' said Nydia. 'Ah! how could it be otherwise; who could be unkind to Glaucus?'

'My child,' said Ione, a little more reservedly than before, 'thou speakest warmly— Glaucus, then, is amiable in thine eyes?'

'Noble Ione! Glaucus has been that to me which neither fortune nor the gods have been —a friend!'

The sadness mingled with dignity with which Nydia uttered these simple words, affected the beautiful Ione: she bent down and kissed her. 'Thou art grateful, and deservedly so; why should I blush to say that Glaucus is worthy of thy gratitude? Go, my Nydia—take to him thyself this letter—but return again. If I am from home when thou returnest—as this evening, perhaps, I shall be—thy chamber shall be prepared next my own. Nydia, I have no sister—wilt thou be one to me?'

The Thessalian kissed the hand of Ione, and then said, with some embarrassment,—

'One favour, fair Ione—may I dare to ask it?'

'Thou canst not ask what I will not grant,' replied the Neapolitan.

'They tell me,' said Nydia, 'that thou art beautiful beyond the loveliness of earth. Alas! I cannot see that which gladdens the world! Wilt thou suffer me, then, to pass my hand over thy face?—that is my sole criterion of beauty, and I usually guess aright.'

She did not wait for the answer of Ione, but, as she spoke, gently and slowly passed her hand over the bending and half-averted features of the Greek.

Her touch lingered over the braided hair and polished brow—over the downy and damask cheek—over the dimpled lip—the swan-like and whitish neck. 'I know now, that thou art beautiful,' she said: 'and I can picture thee to my darkness henceforth, and for ever!'

When Nydia left her, Ione sank into a deep but delicious reverie. Glaucus then loved her; he owned it—yes, he loved her. She drew forth again that dear confession; she paused over every word, she kissed every line; she did not ask why he had been maligned, she only felt assured that he had been so. She wondered how she had ever believed a syllable against him; she wondered how the Egyptian had been enabled to exercise a power against Glaucus; she felt a chill creep over her as she again turned to his warning against Arbaces, and her secret fear of that gloomy being darkened into awe. She was awakened from these thoughts by her maidens, who came to announce to her that the hour appointed to visit Arbaces was arrived; she started, she had forgotten the promise. Her first impression was to renounce it; her second, was to laugh at her own fears of her eldest surviving friend. She hastened to add the usual ornaments to her dress, and doubtful whether she should yet question the Egyptian more closely with respect to his accusation of Glaucus, or whether she should wait till, without citing the authority, she should insinuate to Glaucus the accusation itself, she took her way to the gloomy mansion of Arbaces.

STILUS

PEN

PAPYRUS SCROLLS

INK WELLS

WAX TABLETS

IONE ENTRAPPED

'O dearest Nydia!' exclaimed Glaucus as he read the letter of Ione, 'whitest robed messenger that ever passed between earth and heaven—how, how shall I thank thee?'

'I am rewarded,' said the poor Thessalian.

'To-morrow—to-morrow! how shall I while the hours till then?'

The enamoured Greek would not let Nydia escape him, though she sought several times to leave the chamber; he made her recite to him over and over again every syllable of the brief conversation that had taken place between her and Ione. The hours thus painful to Nydia passed rapidly and delightfully to him, and the twilight had already darkened ere he once more dismissed her to Ione with a fresh letter and with new flowers. Scarcely had she gone, than Clodius and several of his gay companions broke in upon him; they rallied him on his seclusion during the whole day, and his absence from his customary haunts; they invited him to accompany them to the various resorts in that lively city, which night and day proffered diversity to pleasure. He willingly accepted the proposal of his comrades, and laughingly they sallied out together down the populous and glittering streets.

In the meantime Nydia once more gained the house of Ione, who had long left it; she inquired indifferently whither Ione had gone.

The answer arrested and appalled her.

'To the house of Arbaces—of the Egyptian? Impossible!'

'It is true, my little one,' said the slave, who had replied to her question. 'She has known the Egyptian long.'

'Long! ye gods, yet Glaucus loves her!' murmured Nydia to herself.

'And has,' asked she aloud,—'has she often visited him before?'

'Never till now,' answered the slave. 'If all the rumoured scandal of Pompeii be true, it would be better, perhaps, if she had not ventured there at present. But she, poor mistress mine, hears nothing of that which reaches us; the talk of the vestibulum reaches not to the peristyle.'

'Never till now!' repeated Nydia. 'Art thou sure?'

'Sure, pretty one: but what is that to thee or to us?'

Nydia hesitated a moment, and then, putting down the flowers with which she had been charged, she called to the slave who had accompanied her, and left the house without saying another word.

When she arrived at the house of the Athenian, she learnt that he had gone out with a party of his friends, and none knew whither. He probably would not be home before midnight.

The Thessalian groaned; she sank upon a seat in the hall, and covered her face with her hands as if to collect her thoughts. 'There is no time to be lost,' thought she, starting up. She turned to the slave who had accompanied her.

'Knowest thou,' said she, 'if Ione has any relative, any intimate friend at Pompeii?'

'Why, by Jupiter!' answered the slave, 'art thou silly enough to ask the question? Every one in Pompeii knows that Ione has a brother who, young and rich, has been—under the rose I speak—so foolish as to become a priest of Isis.'

'A priest of Isis! O Gods! his name?'

'Apaecides.'

'I know it all,' muttered Nydia: 'brother and sister, then, are to be both victims! Apaecides! yes, that was the name I heard in—— Ha! he well, then, knows the peril that surrounds his sister; I will go to him.'

She sprang up at that thought, and taking the staff which always guided her steps, she hastened to the neighbouring shrine of Isis. Till she had been under the guardianship of the kindly Greek, that staff had sufficed to conduct the poor blind girl from corner to corner of Pompeii. But since she had been under the roof of Glaucus, he had ordered a slave to accompany her always; and the poor devil thus appointed, who was somewhat of the fattest, and who, after having twice performed the journey to Ione's house, now saw himself condemned to a third excursion (whither the gods only knew), hastened after her, deploring his fate.

Nydia, however, required but little of his assistance to find her way to the popular temple of Isis: the space before it was now deserted, and she won without obstacle to the sacred rail.

'There is no one here,' said the fat slave. 'What dost thou want, or whom? Knowest thou not that the priests do not live in the temple?'

'Call out,' said she, impatiently; 'night and day there is always one flamen, at least, watching in the shrines of Isis.'

The slave called,—no one appeared.

'Seest thou no one?'

'No one.'

'Thou mistakest; I hear a sigh: look again.'

The slave, wondering and grumbling, cast round his heavy eyes, and before one of the altars, whose remains still crowd the narrow space, he beheld a form bending as in meditation.

PRIEST OF ISIS

'I see a figure,' said he; 'and by the white garments, it is a priest.'

'O flamen of Isis!' cried Nydia; 'servant of the Most Ancient, hear me!'

'Who calls?' said a low and melancholy voice.

'Methinks I know thy voice? thou art he whom I seek; yet I have heard thee speak but once before. Art thou not the priest Apaecides?'

'I am that man,' replied the priest, emerging from the altar, and approaching the rail.

'Hush!' said she, speaking quick and low; 'art thou indeed Apaecides?'

'If thou knowest me, canst thou not recall my features?'

'I am blind,' answered Nydia; 'my eyes are in my ear, and *that* recognises thee: yet swear thee thou art he.'

'By the gods I swear it, by my right hand, and by the moon! Who art thou, whence comest thou, pale maiden?' said Apaecides, fearfully: 'I know thee not; I have never seen thee before.'

'But thou hast heard my voice: no matter, those recollections it should shame us both to recall. Listen, thou hast a sister.'

'Speak! speak! what of her?'

'Thou knowest the banquets of the dead, stranger,—it pleases thee, perhaps, to share them—would it please thee to have thy sister a partaker? Would it please thee that Arbaces was her host?'

'O gods, he dare not! Girl, if thou mockest me, tremble! I will tear thee limb from limb!'

'I speak the truth; and while I speak, Ione is in the halls of Arbaces—for the first time his guest. Thou knowest if there be peril in that first time! Farewell! I have fulfilled my charge.'

'Stay! stay!' cried the priest, passing his wan hand over his brow. 'If this be true, what—what can be done to save her? They may not admit me. I know not all the mazes of that intricate mansion.'

'I will dismiss yon slave, be thou my guide and comrade; I will lead thee to the private door of the house: I will whisper to thee the word which admits. Take some weapon: it may be needful!'

'Wait an instant,' said Apæcides, retiring into one of the cells that flank the temple, and reappearing in a few moments wrapped in a large cloak, which was then much worn by all classes, and which concealed his sacred dress. 'Now,' he said, grinding his teeth, 'if Arbaces hath dared to—but he dare not! he dare not! Why should I suspect him? Is he so base a villain? O gods protect—hush! are there gods? Yes, there is one goddess, at least, whose voice I can command; and that is—Vengeance!'

Muttering these disconnected thoughts, Apæcides, followed by his silent and sightless companion, hastened through the most solitary paths to the house of the Egyptian.

The slave, abruptly dismissed by Nydia, shrugged his shoulders, muttered an adjuration, and, nothing loath, rolled off to his cubiculum.

IONE IN THE HOUSE OF ARBACES

When Ione entered the spacious hall of the Egyptian, the same awe which had crept over her brother impressed itself also upon her: there seemed to her as to him something ominous and warning in the still and mournful faces of those dread Theban monsters, whose majestic and passionless features the marble so well portrayed.

The tall Æthiopian slave grinned as he admitted her, and motioned to her to proceed. Half-way up the hall she was met by Arbaces himself, in festive robes, which glittered with jewels. Although it was broad day without, the mansion, according to the practice of the luxurious, was artificially darkened, and the lamps cast their still and odour-giving light over the rich floors and ivory roofs.

'Beautiful Ione,' said Arbaces, as he bent to touch her hand, 'it is you that have eclipsed the day—it is your eyes that light up the halls —it is your breath which fills them with perfumes.'

'You must not talk to me thus,' said Ione, smiling, 'you forget that your lore has sufficiently instructed my mind to render these graceful flatteries to my person unwelcome. It was you who taught me to disdain adulation: will you unteach your pupil?'

ORGAN

There was something so frank and charming in the manner of Ione, as she thus spoke, that the Egyptian was more than ever enamoured, and more than ever disposed to renew the offence he had committed; he, however, answered quickly and gaily, and hastened to renew the conversation.

He led her through the various chambers of a house, which seemed to contain to her eyes, inexperienced to other splendour than the minute elegance of Campanian cities, the treasures of the world.

'I have often heard,' said she, wonderingly, 'that you were rich; but I never dreamed of the amount of your wealth.'

'Would I could coin it all,' replied the Egyptian, 'into one crown, which I might place upon that snowy brow!'

The Egyptian was intoxicated and subdued by her grace even more than by her beauty: it was with difficulty that he suppressed his emotions.

Suddenly, as they stood in one hall, which was surrounded by draperies of silver and white, the Egyptian clapped his hands, and, as if by enchantment, a banquet rose from the floor—a couch or throne, with a crimson canopy, ascended simultaneously at the feet of Ione—and at the same instant from behind he curtains swelled the softest music.

Arbaces placed himself at the feet of Ione, —and children, young and beautiful as Loves, ministered to the feast.

The feast was over, the music sank into a low and subdued strain, and Arbaces thus addressed his beautiful guest:—

'Hast thou never in this dark and uncertain world—hast thou never aspired, my pupil, to look beyond—hast thou never wished to put aside the veil of futurity, and to behold on the shores of Fate the shadowy images of things to be? For it is not the past alone that has its ghosts: each event *to come* has also its spectrum—its shade; when the hour arrives, life enters it, the shadow becomes corporeal, and walks the world. Thus, in the land beyond the grave, are ever two impalpable and spiritual hosts—the things to be, the things that have been! If by our wisdom we can penetrate that land, we see the one as the other, and learn, as *I* have learned, not alone the mysteries of the dead, but also the destiny of the living.'

'As thou hast learned!—Can wisdom attain so far?'

'Wilt thou prove my knowledge, Ione, and behold the representation of thine own fate?'

The Neapolitan trembled; she thought of Glaucus, and sighed as well as trembled: were their destinies to be united? Half incredulous, half believing, half awed, half alarmed by the words of her strange host, she remained for some moments silent, and then answered,—

'It may revolt—it may terrify; the knowledge of the future will perhaps only embitter the present!'

The Egyptian rose, and taking her by the hand, he led her across the banquet-room—the curtains withdrew as by magic hands, and the music broke forth in a louder and gladder strain; they passed a row of columns, on either side of which fountains cast aloft their fragrant waters; they descended by broad and easy steps into a garden. The eve had commenced; the moon was already high in heaven, and those sweet flowers that sleep by day, and fill, with ineffable odours, the airs of night, were thickly scattered amidst alleys cut through the star-lit foliage; or, gathered in baskets, lay like offerings at the feet of the frequent statues that gleamed along their path.

'Whither wouldst thou lead me, Arbaces?' said Ione, wonderingly.

'But yonder,' said he, pointing to a small building which stood at the end of the vista. 'It is a temple consecrated to the Fates—our rites require such holy ground.'

They passed into a narrow hall, at the end of which hung a sable curtain. Arbaces lifted it; Ione entered, and found herself in total darkness.

'Be not alarmed,' said the Egyptian, 'the light will rise instantly.' While he so spoke, a soft, and warm, and gradual light diffused itself around; as it spread over each object, Ione perceived that she was in an apartment of moderate size, hung everywhere with black; a couch with draperies of the same hue was beside her. In the centre of the room was a small altar, on which stood a tripod of bronze.

At one side, upon a lofty column of granite, was a colossal head of the blackest marble, which she perceived, by the crown of wheat-ears that encircled the brow, represented the great Egyptian goddess. Arbaces stood before the altar: he had laid his garland on the shrine, and seemed occupied with pouring into the tripod the contents of a brazen vase; suddenly from that tripod leaped into life a blue, quick, darting, irregular flame; the Egyptian drew back to the side of Ione, and muttered some words in a language unfamiliar to her ear; the curtain at the back of the altar waved tremulously to and fro—it parted slowly, and in the aperture which was thus made, Ione beheld an indistinct and pale landscape, which gradually grew brighter and clearer as she gazed; at length she discovered plainly trees, and rivers, and meadows, and all the beautiful diversity of the richest earth. At length, before the landscape, a dim shadow glided; it rested opposite to Ione; slowly the same charm seemed to operate upon it as over the rest of the scene; it took form and shape, and lo!—in its feature and in its form Ione beheld herself!

Then the scene behind the spectre faded away, and was succeeded by the representation of a gorgeous palace; a throne was raised in the centre of its hall, the dim forms of slaves and guards were ranged around it, and a pale hand held over the throne the likeness of a diadem.

A new actor now appeared; he was clothed from head to foot in a dark robe—his face was concealed—he knelt at the feet of the shadowy Ione—he clasped her hand—he pointed to the throne, as if to invite her to ascend it.

The Neapolitan's heart beat violently. 'Shall the shadow disclose itself?' whispered a voice beside her—the voice of Arbaces.

'Ah, yes!' answered Ione, softly.

Arbaces raised his hand—the spectre seemed to drop the mantle that concealed its form—and Ione shrieked—it was Arbaces himself that thus knelt before her.

'This is, indeed, thy fate!' whispered again the Egyptian's voice in her ear. 'And thou art destined to be the bride of Arbaces.'

Ione started—the black curtain closed over the phantasmagoria: and Arbaces himself—the real, the living Arbaces—was at her feet.

'Oh, Ione!' said he, passionately gazing upon her, 'listen to one who has long struggled vainly with his love. I adore thee! The Fates do not lie—thou art destined to be mine—I have sought the world around, and found none like thee. Ione, turn upon me those eyes—shed upon me thy smile. Dark is my soul when thy face is hid from it:—shine over me, my sun—my heaven—my daylight!—Ione, Ione—do not reject my love!'

Alone, and in the power of this singular and fearful man, Ione was not yet terrified; the respect of his language, the softness of his voice, reassured her; and, in her own purity, she felt protection. But she was confused—astonished: it was some moments before she could recover the power of reply.

'*I love another!*' said Ione, blushingly, but in a firm voice.

'By the gods—by hell!' shouted Arbaces, rising to his fullest height; 'dare not tell me that—dare not mock me:—it is impossible!—Whom hast thou seen—whom known? Oh, Ione, it is thy woman's invention, thy woman's art that speaks—thou wouldst gain time; I have surprised—I have terrified thee. Do with me as thou wilt—say that thou lovest not me; but say not that thou lovest another!'

'Alas!' began Ione; and then, appalled before his sudden and unlooked-for violence, she burst into tears.

Arbaces came nearer to her—his breath glowed fiercely on her cheek; he wound his arms round her—she sprang from his embrace. In the struggle a tablet fell from her bosom on the ground: Arbaces perceived, and seized it—it was the letter that morning received from Glaucus. Ione sank upon the couch, half dead with terror.

Rapidly the eyes of Arbaces ran over the writing. He read it to the end, and then, as the letter fell from his hand, he said, in a voice of deceitful calmness,—

'Is the writer of this the man thou lovest?'

Ione sobbed, but answered not.

'Speak!' he rather shrieked than said.

'It is—it is!'

'And his name—it is written here—his name is Glaucus!'

WINE WARMER

1 LID
2 CHARCOAL CONTAINER
3 WINE POURED IN HERE
4 WARM WINE
5 TAP TO POUR WINE
6 PIPE TO LET OFF STEAM

Ione, clasping her hands, looked round as for succour or escape.

'Then hear me,' said Arbaces, sinking his voice into a whisper; 'thou shalt go to thy tomb rather than to his arms! What! thinkest thou Arbaces will brook a rival such as this puny Greek? What! thinkest thou that he has watched the fruit ripen, to yield it to another! Pretty fool—no! Thou art mine—all—only mine: and thus—thus I seize and claim thee!' As he spoke, he caught Ione in his arms; and, in that ferocious grasp, was all the energy—less of love than of revenge.

But to Ione despair gave supernatural strength: she again tore herself from him—she rushed to that part of the room by which she had entered—she half withdrew the curtain—he had seized her—again she broke away from him—and fell, exhausted, and with a loud shriek, at the base of the column which supported the head of the Egyptian goddess. Arbaces paused for a moment, as if to regain his breath; and thence once more darted upon his prey.

At that instant the curtain was rudely torn aside, the Egyptian felt a fierce and strong grasp upon his shoulder. He turned—he beheld before him the flashing eyes of Glaucus, and the pale, worn, but menacing, countenance of Apæcides. 'Ah,' he muttered, as he glared from one to the other, 'what Fury hath sent ye hither?'

'Até,' answered Glaucus; and he closed at once with the Egyptian. Meanwhile, Apæcides raised his sister, now lifeless, from the ground; his strength, exhausted by a mind long over-wrought, did not suffice to bear her away, light and delicate though her shape: he placed her, therefore, on the couch, and stood over her with a brandishing knife, watching the contest between Glaucus and the Egyptian, and ready to plunge his weapon in the bosom of Arbaces should he be victorious in the struggle. Both the antagonists were now locked in each other's grasp—the hand of each seeking the throat of the other—the face drawn back—the fierce eyes flashing—the muscles strained—the veins swelled—the lips apart—the teeth set;—both were strong beyond the ordinary power of men, both animated by relentless wrath; they coiled, they wound, around each other; they rocked to and fro—they swayed from end to end of their confined arena:—they uttered cries of ire and revenge;—they were now before the altar—now at the base of the column where the struggle had commenced: they drew back for breath—Arbaces leaning against the column—Glaucus a few paces apart.

'O ancient goddess!' exclaimed Arbaces, clasping the column, and raising his eyes toward the sacred image it supported, 'protect thy chosen,—proclaim thy vengeance against this thing of an upstart creed, who

with sacrilegious violence profanes thy resting-place and assails thy servant.'

As he spoke, the still and vast features of the goddess seemed suddenly to glow with life; through the black marble, as through a transparent veil, flushed luminously a crimson and burning hue; around the head played and darted coruscations of livid lightning; the eyes became like balls of lurid fire, and seemed fixed in withering and intolerable wrath upon the countenance of the Greek. Awed and appalled by this sudden and mystic answer to the prayer of his foe, and not free from the hereditary superstitions of his race, the cheeks of Glaucus paled before that strange and ghastly animation of the marble, —his knees knocked together,—he stood, seized with a divine panic, dismayed, aghast, half unmanned before his foe! Arbaces gave him not breathing time to recover his stupor: 'Die, wretch!' he shouted, in a voice of thunder, as he sprang upon the Greek; 'the Mighty Mother claims thee as a living sacrifice!' Taken thus by surprise in the first consternation of his superstitious fears, the

IRON KNIFE

Greek lost his footing—the marble floor was as smooth as glass—he slid—he fell. Arbaces planted his foot on the breast of his fallen foe. Apæcides, taught by his sacred profession, as well as by his knowledge of Arbaces, to distrust all miraculous interpositions, had not shared the dismay of his companion; he rushed forward,—his knife gleamed in the air,—the watchful Egyptian caught his arm as it descended,—one wrench of his powerful hand tore the weapon from the weak grasp of the priest,—one sweeping blow stretched him to the earth—with a loud and exulting yell Arbaces brandished the knife on high. Glaucus gazed upon his impending fate with unwinking eyes, and in the stern and scornful resignation of a fallen gladiator, when, at that awful instant, the floor shook under them with a rapid and convulsive throe,—a mightier spirit than that of the Egyptian was abroad!— a giant and crushing power, before which sunk into sudden impotence his passion and his arts. It woke—it stirred—that Dread Demon of the Earthquake—laughing to scorn alike the magic of human guile and the malice of human wrath. As a Titan, on whom the mountains are piled, it roused itself from the sleep of years,—it moved on its tortured couch,—the caverns below groaned and trembled beneath the motion of its limbs. In

the moment of his vengeance and his power, the self-prized demigod was humbled to his real clay. Far and wide along the soil went a hoarse and rumbling sound,—the curtains of the chamber shook as at the blast of a storm, —the altar rocked—the tripod reeled, and high over the place of contest, the column trembled and waved from side to side,—the sable head of the goddess tottered and fell from its pedestal;—and as the Egyptian stooped above his intended victim, right upon his bended form, right between the shoulder and the neck, struck the marble mass! the shock stretched him like the blow of death, at once, suddenly, without sound or motion, or semblance of life, upon the floor, apparently crushed by the very divinity he had impiously animated and invoked!

'The Earth has preserved her children,' said Glaucus, staggering to his feet. 'Blessed be the dread convulsion! Let us worship the providence of the gods!' He assisted Apæcides to rise, and then turned upward the face of Arbaces; it seemed locked as in death; blood gushed from the Egyptian's lips over his glittering robes; he fell heavily from the arms of Glaucus, and the red stream trickled slowly along the marble. Again the earth shook beneath their feet; they were forced to cling to each other; the convulsion ceased as suddenly as it came; they tarried no longer; Glaucus bore Ione lightly in his arms, and they fled from the unhallowed spot. But scarce had they entered the garden than they were met on all sides by flying and disordered groups of women and slaves, whose festive and glittering garments contrasted in mockery the solemn terror of the hour; they did not appear to heed the strangers,—they were occupied only with their own fears. After the tranquillity of sixteen years, that burning and treacherous soil again menaced destruction; they uttered but one cry, 'THE EARTHQUAKE! THE EARTHQUAKE!' and passing unmolested from the midst of them, Apæcides and his companions, without entering the house, hastened down one of the alleys, passed a small open gate, and there, sitting on a little mound over which spread the gloom of the dark green aloes, the moonlight fell on the bended figure of the blind girl,—she was weeping bitterly.

BOOK THREE

THE FORUM OF THE POMPEIANS

It was early noon, and the forum was crowded alike with the busy and the idle. Along its broad pavement, composed of large flags of marble, were assembled various groups, conversing in that energetic fashion which appropriates a gesture to every word, and which is still the characteristic of the people of the south. Here, in seven stalls on one side the colonnade, sat the money-changers, with their glittering heaps before them, and merchants and seamen in various costumes crowding round their stalls. On one side, several men in long togas were seen bustling rapidly up to a stately edifice, where the magistrates administered justice;—these were the lawyers, active, chattering, joking, and punning. In the centre of the space, pedestals supported various statues, of which the most remarkable was the stately form of Cicero. Around the court ran a regular and symmetrical colonnade of Doric architecture; and there several, whose business drew them early to the place, were taking the slight morning repast which made an Italian breakfast, talking vehemently on the earthquake of the preceding night as they dipped pieces of bread in their cups of diluted wine. In the open space, too, you might perceive various petty traders exercising the arts of their calling. Here one man was holding out ribands to a fair dame from the country; another man was vaunting to a stout farmer the excellence of his shoes;

STOPCOCK

1 PIPE FROM MAIN RESERVOIR
2 WATER TANK
3 HOUSE SUPPLY
4 PUBLIC FOUNTAIN

a third, a kind of stall-restaurateur, still so common in the Italian cities, was supplying many a hungry mouth with hot messes from his small and itinerant stove, while—contrast strongly typical of the mingled bustle and intellect of the time—close by, a schoolmaster was expounding to his puzzled pupils the elements of the Latin grammar. A gallery above the portico, which was ascended by small wooden staircases, had also its throng; though, as here the immediate business of the place was mainly carried on, its groups wore a more quiet and serious air.

Every now and then the crowd below respectfully gave way as some senator swept along the Temple of Jupiter (which filled up one side of the forum, and was the senators' hall of meeting), nodding with ostentatious condescension to such of his friends or clients as he distinguished amongst the throng.

Facing the steps of the Temple of Jupiter, with folded arms, and a knit and contemptuous brow, stood a man of about fifty years of age. His dress was remarkably plain,—not so much from its material, as from the absence of all those ornaments which were worn by the Pompeians of every rank. His forehead was high and bald; the few locks that remained at the back of the head were concealed by a sort of cowl, which made a part of his cloak, to be raised or lowered at pleasure, and was now drawn half-way over the head, as a protection from the rays of the sun. The colour of his garments was brown, no popular hue with the Pompeians; all the usual admixtures of scarlet or purple seemed carefully excluded. His belt, or girdle, contained a small receptable for ink, which hooked on to the girdle, a stilus (or implement of writing), and tablets of no ordinary size. What was rather remarkable, the cincture held no purse, which was the almost indispensable appurtenance of the girdle, even when that purse had the misfortune to be empty!

It was not often that the gay and egotistical Pompeians busied themselves with observing the countenances and actions of their neighbours; but there was that in the lip and eye of this bystander so remarkably bitter and disdainful, as he surveyed the religious procession sweeping up the stairs of the temple, that it could not fail to arrest the notice of many.

'Who is yon cynic?' asked a merchant of his companion, a jeweller.

'It is Olinthus,' replied the jeweller; 'a reputed Nazarene.'

The merchant shuddered. 'A dread sect!' said he, in a whispered and fearful voice. 'It is said, that when they meet at nights they always commence their ceremonies by the murder of a new-born babe; they profess a community of goods, too,—the wretches! A community of goods! What would become of merchants, or jewellers either, if such notions were in fashion?'

'That is very true,' said the jeweller; 'besides, they wear no jewels,—they mutter imprecations when they see a serpent; and at Pompeii all our ornaments are serpentine.'

'Do but observe,' said a third, who was a fabricant of bronze, 'how yon Nazarene scowls at the piety of the sacrificial procession. He is murmuring curses on the temple, be sure. Do you know, my friend, that this fellow, passing by my shop the other day, and seeing me employed on a statue of Minerva, told me with a frown that, had it been marble, he would have broken it; but the bronze was too strong for him. "Break a goddess!" said I. "A goddess!" answered the atheist; "it is a demon,—an evil spirit!" Then he passed on his way cursing. Are such things to be borne? What marvel that the earth heaved so fearfully last night, anxious to reject the atheist from her bosom?—An atheist, do I say? worse still—a scorner of the Fine Arts! Woe to us fabricants of bronze, if such fellows as this give the law to society!'

'These are the incendiaries that burnt Rome under Nero,' groaned the jeweller.

While such were the friendly remarks provoked by the air and faith of the Nazarene, Olinthus himself became sensible of the effect he was producing; he turned his eyes round, and observed the intent faces of the accumulating throng, whispering as they gazed; and surveying them for a moment with an expression, first of defiance and afterwards of compassion, he gathered his cloak round him and passed on, muttering audibly, 'Deluded idolaters!—did not last night's convulsion warn ye? Alas! how will ye meet the last day?'

As Olinthus stalked through the crowd, and gained one of the more private places of egress from the forum, he perceived gazing upon him a pale and earnest countenance, which he was not slow to recognise.

Wrapped in a pallium that partially concealed his sacred robes, the young Apæcides surveyed the disciple of that new and mysterious creed, to which at one time he had been half a convert.

'Is *he*, too, an impostor? Does this man, so plain and simple in life, in garb, in mien— does he too, like Arbaces, make austerity the robe of the sensualist? Does the veil of Vesta hide the vices of the prostitute?'

Olinthus, accustomed to men of all classes, and combining with the enthusiasm of his faith a profound experience of his kind, guessed, perhaps, by the index of the countenance, something of what passed within the breast of the priest. He met the survey of Apæcides with a steady eye, and a brow of serene and open candour.

'Peace be with thee!' said he, saluting Apæcides.

'Peace!' echoed the priest, in so hollow a tone that it went at once to the heart of the Nazarene. He stopped short, and then added in a low tone—'We cannot converse here, I will follow thee to the banks of the river; there is a walk which at this time is usually deserted and solitary.'

Olinthus bowed assent. He passed through the streets with a hasty step, but a quick and observant eye. Every now and then he exchanged a significant glance, a slight sign, with some passenger, whose garb usually betokened the wearer to belong to the humbler classes; for Christianity was in this the type of all other and less mighty revolutions—the grain of mustard-seed was in the hearts of the lowly.

THE CONGREGATION

Followed by Apæcides, the Nazarene gained the side of the Sarnus;—that river, which now has shrunk into a petty stream, then rushed gaily into the sea, covered with countless vessels, and reflecting on its waves the gardens, the vines, the palaces, and the temples of Pompeii. From its more noisy and frequented banks, Olinthus directed his steps to a path which ran amidst a shady vista of trees, at the distance of a few paces from the river. This walk was in the evening a favourite resort of the Pompeians, but during the heat and business of the day was seldom visited, save by some groups of playful children, some meditative poet, or some disputative philosophers. At the side farthest from the river, frequent copses of box interspersed the more delicate and evanescent foliage, and these were cut into a thousand quaint shapes, sometimes into the forms of fauns and satyrs, sometimes into the mimicry of Egyptian pyramids, sometimes into the letters that composed the name of a popular or eminent citizen.

This walk now, as the noonday sun shone perpendicularly through the chequered leaves, was entirely deserted; at least no other forms than those of Olinthus and the priest infringed upon the solitude. They sat themselves on one of the benches, placed at intervals between the trees, and facing the faint breeze that came languidly from the river, whose waves danced and sparkled before them;—a singular and contrasted pair; the believer in the latest —the priest of the most ancient—worship of the world!

'Since thou leftst me so abruptly,' said Olinthus, 'hast thou been happy? has thy heart found contentment under these priestly

robes? hast thou, still yearning for the voice of God, heard it whisper comfort to thee from the oracles of Isis? That sigh, that averted countenance, give me the answer my soul predicted.'

And with all the earnestness of a man believing ardently himself, and zealous to convert, the Nazarene poured forth to Apæcides the assurances of Scriptural promise. He spoke first of the sufferings and miracles of Christ—he wept as he spoke: he turned next to the glories of the Saviour's Ascension—to the clear predictions of Revelation. He described that pure and unsensual heaven destined to the virtuous— those fires and torments that were the doom of guilt.

'Come,' said the Nazarene, as he perceived the effect he had produced, 'come to the humble hall in which we meet—a select and a chosen few; listen there to our prayers; note the sincerity of our repentant tears; mingle in our simple sacrifice—not of victims, nor of garlands, but offered by white-robed thoughts upon the altar of the heart. The flowers that we lay there are imperishable—they bloom over us when we are no more; nay, they accompany us beyond the grave, they spring up beneath our feet in heaven, they delight us with an eternal odour, for they are of the soul, they partake of its nature; these offerings are temptations overcome, and sins repented. Come, oh come! lose not another moment; prepare already for the great the awful journey, from darkness to light, from sorrow to bliss, from corruption to immortality! This is the day of the Lord the Son, a day that we have set apart for our devotions. Though we meet usually at night, yet some amongst us are gathered together even now. What joy, what triumph, will be with us all, if we can bring one stray lamb into the sacred fold!'

There seemed to Apæcides, so naturally pure of heart, something ineffably generous and benign in that spirit of conversation which animated Olinthus—a spirit that found its own bliss in the happiness of others—that sought in its wide sociality to make companions for eternity. He was touched, softened, and subdued. He was not in that mood which can bear to be left alone; curiosity, too, mingled with his purer stimulants—he was anxious to see those rites of which so many dark and contradictory rumours were afloat. He paused a moment, looked over his garb, thought of Arbaces, shuddered with horror, lifted his eyes to the broad brow of the Nazarene, intent, anxious, watchful—but for *his* benefits, for his salvation! He drew his cloak round him, so as wholly to conceal his robes, and said, 'Lead on, I follow thee.'

Olinthus pressed his hand joyfully, and then descending to the river side, hailed one of the boats that plied there constantly; they entered it; an awning overhead, while it sheltered them from the sun, screened also their persons from observation: they rapidly skimmed the wave. From one of the boats that passed them floated a soft music, and its prow was decorated with flowers—it was gliding towards the sea.

'So,' said Olinthus, sadly, 'unconscious and mirthful in their delusions, sail the votaries of luxury into the great ocean of storm and shipwreck! we pass them, silent and unnoticed, to gain the land.'

Apæcides, lifting his eyes, caught through the aperture in the awning a glimpse of the face of one of the inmates of that gay bark—it was the face of Ione. The priest sighed, and once more sunk back upon his seat. They reached the shore where, in the suburbs, an alley of small and mean houses stretched towards the bank; they dismissed the boat, landed, and Olinthus, preceding the priest, threaded the labyrinth of lanes, and arrived at last at the closed door of a habitation somewhat larger than its neighbours. He knocked thrice—the door was opened and closed again, as Apæcides followed his guide across the threshold.

They passed a deserted atrium, and gained an inner chamber of moderate size, which, when the door was closed, received its only light from a small window cut over the door itself. But, halting at the threshold of this chamber, and knocking at the door, Olinthus said, 'Peace be with you!' A voice from within returned, 'Peace with whom?' 'The Faithful!' answered Olinthus, and the door opened; twelve or fourteen persons were sitting in a semicircle, silent, and seemingly absorbed in thought, and opposite to a crucifix rudely carved in wood.

They lifted up their eyes when Olinthus entered, without speaking; the Nazarene himself, before he accosted them, knelt suddenly down, and by his moving lips, and his eyes fixed steadfastly on the crucifix, Apæcides saw that he prayed inly. This rite performed, Olinthus turned to the congregation—'Men and brethren,' said he, 'start not to behold amongst you a priest of Isis; he hath sojourned with the blind, but the Spirit hath fallen on him—he desires to see, to hear, and to understand.'

'Let him,' said one of the assembly; and Apæcides beheld in the speaker a man still younger than himself, of a countenance equally worn and pallid, of an eye which equally spoke of the restless and fiery operations of a working mind.

'Let him,' repeated a second voice, and he who thus spoke was in the prime of manhood;

his bronzed skin and Asiatic features bespoke him a son of Syria—he had been a robber in his youth.

'Let him,' said a third voice; and the priest, again turning to regard the speaker, saw an old man with a long grey beard, whom he recognised as a slave to the wealthy Diomed.

'Let him,' repeated simultaneously the rest —men who, with two exceptions, were evidently of the inferior ranks. In these exceptions, Apæcides noted an officer of the guard, and an Alexandrian merchant.

It was at this time that an inner door opened gently, and a very old man entered the chamber, leaning on a staff. At his presence, the whole congregation rose; there was an expression of deep, affectionate respect upon every countenance; and Apæcides, gazing on his countenance, felt attracted towards him by an irresistible sympathy. No man ever looked upon that face without love; for there had dwelt the smile of the Deity, the incarnation of divinest love;—and the glory of the smile had never passed away.

'My children, God be with you!' said the old man, stretching his arms; and as he spoke the infants ran to his knee. He sat down, and they nestled fondly to his bosom. It was beautiful to see that mingling of the extremes of life—the rivers gushing from their early source—the majestic stream gliding to the ocean of eternity! As the light of declining day seems to mingle earth and heaven, making the outline of each scarce visible, and blending the harsh mountain-tops with the sky, even so did the smile of that benign old age appear to hallow the aspect of those around, to blend together the strong distinctions of varying years, and to diffuse over infancy and manhood the light of that heaven into which it must so soon vanish and be lost.

'Father,' said Olinthus, 'thou on whose form the miracle of the Redeemer worked; thou who wert snatched from the grave to become the living witness of His mercy and His power; behold! a stranger in our meeting —a new lamb gathered to the fold!'

'Let me bless him,' said the old man: the throng gave way. Apæcides approached him as by an instinct: he fell on his knees before him—the old man laid his hand on the priest's head, and blessed him, but not aloud. As his lips moved, his eyes were upturned, and tears—those tears that good men only shed in the hope of happiness to another—flowed fast down his cheeks.

The children were on either side of the convert; his heart was theirs—he had become as one of them—to enter into the kingdom of Heaven.

THE SO CALLED CHRISTIAN ALTAR

A WEDDING DATE IS FIXED

Days are like years in the love of the young, when no bar, no obstacle, is between their hearts—when the sun shines, and the course runs smooth—when their love is prosperous and confessed. Ione no longer concealed from Glaucus the attachment she felt for him, and their talk now was only of their love. Over the rapture of the present the hopes of the future glowed like the heaven above the gardens of spring. They went in their trustful thoughts far down the stream of time: they laid out the chart of their destiny to come; they suffered the light of to-day to suffuse the morrow.

They had now advanced far into August—the next month their marriage was fixed, and the threshold of Glaucus was already wreathed with garlands; and nightly, by the door of Ione, he poured forth the rich libations. He existed no longer for his gay companions; he was ever with Ione. In the mornings they beguiled the sun with music: in the evenings they forsook the crowded haunts of the gay for excursions on the water, or along the fertile and vine-clad plains that lay beneath fatal mount of Vesuvius. The earth shook no more; the lively Pompeians forgot even that there had gone forth so terrible a warning of their approaching doom. Glaucus imagined that convulsion, in the vanity of his heathen religion, an especial interposition of the gods, less in behalf of his own safety than that of Ione. He offered up the sacrifices of gratitude at the temples of his faith; and even the altar of Isis was covered with his votive garlands;—as to the prodigy of the animated marble, he blushed at the effect it had produced on him. He believed it, indeed, to have been wrought by the magic of man; but the result convinced him that it betokened not the anger of a goddess.

Of Arbaces, they heard only that he stil lived; stretched on the bed of suffering, he recovered slowly from the effect of the shock he had sustained—he left the lovers un-molested—but it was only to brood over the hour and the method of revenge.

Alike in their mornings at the house of Ione, and in their evening excursions, Nydia was usually their constant, and often their sole companion. They did not guess the secret fires which consumed her:—the abrupt freedom with which she mingled in their conversation—her capricious and often her peevish moods found ready indulgence in the recollection of the service they owed her, and their compassion for her affliction. They felt an interest in her, perhaps the greater and more affectionate from the very strangeness

ROMAN LADY

and waywardness of her nature, her singular alternations of passion and softness—the mixture of ignorance and genius—of delicacy and rudeness—of the quick humours of the child, and the proud calmness of the woman. Although she refused to accept of freedom, she was constantly suffered to be free; she went where she listed; no curb was put either on her words or actions; they felt for one so darkly fated, and so susceptible of every wound, the same pitying and compliant indulgence the mother feels for a spoiled and sickly child,—dreading to impose authority, even where they imagined it for her benefit. But her chief delight was still in visiting the few feet of ground which made the garden of Glaucus;—in tending the flowers that at least repaid her love. Sometimes she entered the chamber where he sat, and sought a conversation, which she nearly always broke off abruptly—for conversation with Glaucus only tended to one subject—*Ione;* and that name from his lips inflicted agony upon her. Often she bitterly repented the service she had rendered to Ione: often she said inly, 'If she had fallen, Glaucus could have loved her no longer;' and then dark and fearful thoughts crept into her breast.

The friendless childhood of Nydia had hardened prematurely her character; perhaps the heated scenes of profligacy through which she had passed, seemingly unscathed, had ripened her passions, though they had not sullied her purity. The orgies of Burbo might only have disgusted, the banquets of the Egyptian might only have terrified, at the moment; but the winds that pass unheeded over the soil leave seeds behind them. As darkness, too, favours the imagination, so, perhaps, her very blindness contributed to feed with wild and delirious visions the love of the unfortunate girl. The voice of Glaucus had been the first that had sounded musically to her ear; his kindness made a deep impres-sion upon her mind; when he had left Pompeii in the former year, she had treasured up in her heart every word he had uttered; and when any one told her that this friend and patron of the poor flower-girl was the most brilliant and the most graceful of the young revellers of Pompeii, she had felt a pleasing pride in nursing his recollection.

One morning, when she repaired to her usual task in the garden of the Athenian, she found Glaucus under the columns of the peristyle, with a merchant of the town; he was selecting jewels for his destined bride. He had already fitted up her apartment; the jewels he bought that day were placed also within it—they were never fated to grace the fair form of Ione.

'Come hither, Nydia; put down thy vase, and come hither. Thou must take this chain from me—stay—there, I have put it on.—

RING

EAR RING

FIBULA

NYDIA ENCOUNTERS JULIA

'What happiness to Ione! what bliss to be ever by the side of Glaucus, to hear his voice!—And *she* too can see him!'

Such was the soliloquy of the blind girl, as she walked alone and at twilight to the house of her new mistress, whither Glaucus had already preceded her. Suddenly she was interrupted in her fond thoughts by a female voice.

'Blind flower-girl, whither goest thou? There is no pannier under thine arm; hast thou sold all thy flowers?'

The person thus accosting Nydia was a lady of a handsome but a bold and unmaidenly countenance: it was Julia, the daughter of Diomed. Her veil was half raised as she spoke; she was accompanied by Diomed himself, and by a slave carrying a lantern before them—the merchant and his daughter were returning home from a supper at one of their neighbours'.

'Dost thou not remember my voice?' continued Julia. 'I am the daughter of Diomed the wealthy.'

'Ah! forgive me; yes, I recall the tones of your voice. No, noble Julia, I have no flowers to sell.'

'I heard that thou wert purchased by the beautiful Greek Glaucus; is that true, pretty slave?' asked Julia.

'I serve the Neapolitan, Ione,' replied Nydia, evasively.

'Ah! and it is true, then——'

'Come, come!' interrupted Diomed, with his cloak up to his mouth, 'the night grows cold; I cannot stay here while you prate to that blind girl: come, let her follow you home, if you wish to speak to her.'

'Do child,' said Julia, with the air of one not accustomed to be refused; 'I have much to ask of thee: come.'

'I cannot this night, it grows late,' answered Nydia. 'I must be at home; I am not free, noble Julia.'

'What, the meek Ione will chide thee? But come, then, to-morrow: do—remember I have been thy friend of old.'

'I will obey thy wishes,' answered Nydia; and Diomed again impatiently summoned his daughter: she was obliged to proceed, with the main question she had desired to put to Nydia unasked.

Meanwhile we return to Ione. The interval of time that had elapsed that day between the first and second visit of Glaucus had not been too gaily spent: she had received a visit from her brother. Since the night he had assisted in saving her from the Egyptian, she had not before seen him.

There, Servilius, does it not become her?'

'Wonderfully!' answered the jeweller; for jewellers were well-bred and flattering men, even at that day. 'But when these ear-rings glitter in the ears of the noble Ione, *then*, by Bacchus! you will see whether my art adds anything to beauty.'

'Ione?' repeated Nydia, who had hitherto acknowledged by smiles and blushes the gift of Glaucus.

'Yes,' replied the Athenian, carelessly toying with the gems; 'I am choosing a present for Ione, but there are none worthy of her.'

He was startled as he spoke by an abrupt gesture of Nydia; she tore the chain violently from her neck, and dashed it on the ground.

'How is this? What, Nydia, dost thou not like the bauble? art thou offended?'

'You treat me ever as a slave and as a child,' replied the Thessalian, with a breast heaving with ill-suppressed sobs, and she turned hastily away to the opposite corner of the garden.

Glaucus did not attempt to follow, or to soothe; he was offended; he continued to examine the jewels and to comment on their fashion—to object to this and to praise that, and finally to be talked by the merchant into buying all; the safest plan for a lover, and a plan that any one will do right to adopt,—provided always that he can obtain an Ione!

When he had completed his purchase and dismissed the jeweller, he retired into his chamber, dressed, mounted his chariot, and went to Ione. He thought no more of the blind girl, or her offence; he had forgotten both the one and the other.

He spent the forenoon with his beautiful Neapolitan, repaired thence to the baths, supped (if, as we have said before, we can justly so translate the three o'clock *cœna* of the Romans) alone, and abroad, for Pompeii had its restaurateurs:—and returning home to change his dress ere he again repaired to the house of Ione, he passed the peristyle, but with the absorbed reverie and absent eyes of a man in love, and did not note the form of the poor blind girl, bending exactly in the same place where he had left her. He had scarcely entered his favourite chamber, which opened on the peristyle, and seated himself musingly on his couch, when he felt his robe timorously touched, and, turning, he beheld Nydia kneeling before him, and holding up to him a handful of flowers—a gentle and appropriate peace-offering;—her eyes, darkly upheld to his own, streamed with tears.

'I have offended thee,' said she, sobbing, 'and for the first time. I would die rather than cause thee a moment's pain—say that thou wilt forgive me. See! I have taken up the chain; I have put it on; I will never part from it—it is thy gift.'

'My dear Nydia,' returned Glaucus, and raising her, he kissed her forehead, 'think of it no more!'

BONE HAIR PINS

Occupied with his own thoughts,—thoughts of so serious and intense a nature,—the young priest had thought little of his sister; in truth, men, perhaps of that fervent order of mind which is ever aspiring *above* earth, are but little prone to the earthlier affections; and it had been long since Apæcides had sought those soft and friendly interchanges of thought, those sweet confidences, which in his earlier youth had bound him to Ione, and which are so natural to that endearing connection which existed between them.

Ione, however, had not ceased to regret his estrangement: she attributed it, at present, to the engrossing duties of his severe fraternity. And often, amidst all her bright hopes, and her new attachment to her betrothed—often, when she thought of her brother's brow prematurely furrowed, his unsmiling lip, and

SHOP SIGN OF DAIRY

bended frame, she sighed to think that the service of the gods could throw so deep a shadow over that earth which the gods created.

But this day when he visited her there was a strange calmness on his features, a more quiet and self-possessed expression in his sunken eyes, than she had marked for years. This apparent improvement was but momentary—it was a false calm, which the least breeze could ruffle.

'May the gods bless thee, my brother!' said she, embracing him.

'The gods! Speak not thus vaguely; perchance there is but *one* God!'

'My brother!'

'What if the sublime faith of the Nazarene be true? What if God be a monarch—One—Invisible—Alone? What if these numerous, countless deities, whose altars fill the earth, be but evil demons, seeking to wean us from the true creed? This may be the case, Ione!'

Ione answered as a believer in the poesy of the old mythology would answer. We may judge how obstinate and hard the contest which Christianity had to endure among the heathens.

Apæcides had not yet adopted formally the Christian faith, but he was already on the brink of it. He already participated the

doctrines of Olinthus—he already imagined that the lively imaginations of the heathen were the suggestions of the arch-enemy of mankind. He hastened to reply vehemently, and yet so confusedly, that Ione feared for his reason more than she dreaded his violence.

'Ah, my brother!' said she, 'these hard duties of thine have shattered thy very sense. Come to me, Apæcides, my brother, my own brother; give me thy hand, let me wipe the dew from thy brow;—chide me not now, I understand thee not; think only that Ione could not offend thee!'

'Ione,' said Apæcides, drawing her towards him, and regarding her tenderly, 'can I think that this beautiful form, this kind heart, may be destined to an eternity of torment?'

'Dii meliora! the gods forbid!' said Ione, in the customary form of words by which her contemporaries thought an omen might be averted.

The words, and still more the superstition they implied, wounded the ear of Apæcides. He rose, muttering to himself, turned from the chamber, then, stopping, half way, gazed wistfully on Ione, and extended his arms.

Ione flew to them in joy; he kissed her earnestly, and then he said,—

'Farewell, my sister! when we next meet, thou mayst be to me as nothing; take thou, then, this embrace—full yet of all the tender reminiscences of childhood, when faith and hope, creeds, customs, interests, objects, were the same to us. Now, the tie is to be broken!'

With these strange words he left the house.

SIGN OF WINE SHOP

SHOP SIGN OF BUILDERS

THE PORTER – THE GIRL – AND THE GLADIATOR

The door of Diomed's house stood open, and Medon, the old slave, sat at the bottom of the steps by which you ascended to the mansion. On the opposite side, but at some yards nearer the gate, was a spacious hostelry, at which those brought by business or by pleasure to Pompeii often stopped to refresh themselves. In the space before the entrance of the inn now stood wagons, and carts, and chariots, some just arrived, some just quitting, in all the bustle of an animated and popular resort of public entertainment. Before the door, some farmers, seated on a bench by a small circular table, were talking over their morning cups, on the affairs of their calling. By the roof of the inn stretched a terrace, on which some females, wives of the farmers above mentioned, were, some seated, some leaning over the railing, and conversing with their friends below. In a deep recess, at a little distance, was a covered seat, in which some two or three poorer travellers were resting themselves, and shaking the dust from their garments. On the other side stretched a wide space, originally the burial-ground of a more ancient race than the present denizens of Pompeii, and now converted into the Ustrinum, or place for the burning of the dead. Above this rose the terraces of a gay villa, half hid by trees. The tombs themselves, with their graceful and varied shapes, the flowers and the foliage that surrounded them, made no melancholy feature in the prospect. Hard by the gate of the city, in a small niche, stood the still form of the well-disciplined Roman sentry, the sun shining brightly on his polished crest, and the lance on which he leaned. The gate itself was divided into three arches, the centre one for vehicles, the others for the foot-passengers; and on either side rose the massive walls which girt the city, composed, patched, repaired at a thousand different epochs, according as war, time, or the earthquake had shattered that vain protection. At frequent intervals rose square towers, whose summits broke in picturesque rudeness the regular line of the wall, and contrasted well with the modern buildings gleaming whitely by.

The curving road, which in that direction leads from Pompeii to Herculaneum, wound out of sight amidst hanging vines, above which frowned the sullen majesty of Vesuvius.

'Hast thou heard the news, old Medon?' said a young woman, with a pitcher in her hand, as she paused by Diomed's door to gossip a moment with the slave, ere she repaired to the neighbouring inn to fill the vessel, and coquet with the travellers.

'The news! what news?' said the slave, raising his eyes moodily from the ground.

'Why, there passed through the gate this morning, no doubt ere thou wert well awake, such a visitor to Pompeii!'

'Ay,' said the slave, indifferently.

'Yes, a present from the noble Pomponianus.'

'A present! I thought thou saidst a visitor?'

'It is both visitor and present. Know, O dull and stupid! that it is a most beautiful young tiger, for our approaching games in the amphitheatre. Hear you that, Medon? Oh, what pleasure! I declare I shall not sleep a wink till I see it; they say it has such a roar!'

'Poor fool!' said Medon, sadly and cynically.

'Fool me no fool, old churl! It is a pretty thing, a tiger, especially if we could but find somebody for him to eat. We have now a lion and a tiger; only consider that, Medon! and for want of two good criminals perhaps we shall be forced to see them eat each other. By-the-by, your son is a gladiator, a handsome man and a strong, can you not persuade him to fight the tiger? Do now, you would oblige me mightily; nay, you would be a benefactor to the whole town.'

'Vah! vah!' said the slave, with great asperity; 'think of thine own danger ere thou thus pratest of my poor boy's death.'

'My own danger!' said the girl, frightened and looking hastily around—'Avert the omen! let thy words fall on thine own head!' And the girl, as she spoke, touched a talisman suspended round her neck. ' "Thine own danger!" what danger threatens me?'

'Had the earthquake but a few nights since no warning?' said Medon. 'Has it not a voice? Did it not say to us all, "Prepare for death; the end of all things is at hand?" '

'Bah, stuff!' said the young woman, settling the folds of her tunic. 'Now thou talkest as they say the Nazarenes talk—methinks thou art one of them. Well, I can prate with thee, grey croaker, no more: thou growest worse and worse—*Vale!* O Hercules, send us a man for the lion—and another for the tiger!'

Holding up her tunic from the dusty road, the young woman stepped lightly across to the crowded hostelry.

'My poor son!' said the slave, half aloud, 'is it for things like this thou art to be butchered? Oh! faith of Christ, I could worship thee in all sincerity, were it but for the horror which thou inspirest for these bloody lists.'

The old man's head sank dejectedly on his breast. He remained silent and absorbed, but every now and then with the corner of his sleeve he wiped his eyes. His heart was with his son; he did not see the figure that now approached from the gate with a quick step,

and a somewhat fierce and reckless gait and carriage. He did not lift his eyes till the figure paused opposite the place where he sat, and with a soft voice addressed him by the name of—

'Father!'

'My boy! my Lydon! is it indeed thou?' said the old man, joyfully. 'Ah, thou wert present to my thoughts.'

'I am glad to hear it, my father,' said the gladiator, respectfully touching the knees and beard of the slave; 'and soon may I be always present with thee, not in thought only.'

'Yes, my son—but not in this world,' replied the slave, mournfully.

'Talk not thus, O my sire! look cheerfully, for I feel so—I am sure that I shall win the day; and then, the gold I gain buys thy freedom. Oh! my father, it was but a few days since that I was taunted, by one, too, whom I would gladly have undeceived, for he is more generous than the rest of his equals. He is not Roman—he is of Athens—by him I was taunted with the lust of gain—when I demanded what sum was the prize of victory. Alas! he little knew the soul of Lydon!'

'My boy! my boy!' said the old slave, as, slowly ascending the steps, he conducted his son to his own little chamber, communicating with the entrance hall. 'Generous, affectionate, pious as are thy motives,' said Medon, when they were thus secured from observation,

'thy deed itself is guilt: thou art to risk thy blood for thy father's freedom—that might be forgiven; but the prize of victory is the blood of another. Oh, *that* is a deadly sin; no object can purify it. Forbear! forbear! rather would I be a slave for ever than purchase liberty on such terms!' sighed the old man .

'I will hear the whole world talk if thou wilt,' answered the gladiator, gaily; 'but not till thou art a slave no more. Beneath thy own roof, my father, thou shalt puzzle this dull brain all day long, ay, and all night too, if it give thee pleasure. Oh, such a spot as I have chalked out for thee!—it is one of the nine hundred and ninety-nine shops of old Julia Felix, in the sunny part of the city, where thou mayst bask before the door in the day—and I will sell the oil and the wine for thee, my father—and then, please Venus (or if it does not please her, since thou lovest not her name, it is all one to Lydon;)—then, I say, perhaps thou mayst have a daughter, too, to tend thy grey hairs, and hear shrill voices at thy knee, that shall call thee "Lydon's father!" Ah! we shall be so happy—the prize can purchase all. Cheer thee! cheer up, my sire!—And now I must away—day wears—the lanista waits me. Come! thy blessing!'

As Lydon thus spoke, he had already quitted the dark chamber of his father; and speaking eagerly, though in a whispered tone, they now stood at the same place in which we introduced the porter at his post.

'O bless thee! bless thee, my brave boy!' said Medon, fervently; 'and may the great Power that reads all hearts see the nobleness of thine, and forgive its error!'

The tall shape of the gladiator passed swiftly down the path; the eyes of the slave followed its light but stately steps, till the last

OLIVE PRESS

1 PRESS
2 OLIVES IN NET BAG
3 BOWL FOR SEDIMENTS
4 RUN OFF TO SETTLING TANK

glimpse was gone; and then, sinking once more on his seat, his eyes again fastened themselves on the ground. His form, mute and unmoving, as a thing of stone.

'May I enter?' said a sweet voice. 'Is thy mistress Julia within?'

The slave mechanically motioned to the visitor to enter, but she who addressed him could not see the gesture—she repeated her question timidly, but in a louder voice.

'Have I not told thee!' said the slave, peevishly: 'enter.'

'Thanks,' said the speaker, plaintively; and the slave, roused by the tone, looked up, and recognised the blind flower-girl. Sorrow can sympathise with affliction—he raised himself, and guided her steps to the head of the adjacent staircase (by which you descended to Julia's apartment), where, summoning a female slave, he consigned to her the charge of the blind girl.

THE DRESSING-ROOM OF A POMPEIAN BEAUTY

The elegant Julia sat in her chamber, with her slaves around her;—like the cubiculum which adjoined it, the room was small, but much larger than the usual apartments appropriated to sleep, which were so diminutive, that few who have not seen the bed-chambers, even in the gayest mansions, can form any notion of the petty pigeon-holes in which the citizens of Pompeii evidently thought it desirable to pass the night. The couch itself was more like a very narrow and small sofa, light enough to be transported easily, and by the occupant himself, from place to place; and it was, no doubt, constantly shifted from chamber to chamber, according to the caprices of the inmate, or the changes of the season; for that side of the house which was crowded in one month, might, perhaps, be carefully avoided in the next. There was also among the Italians of that period a singular and fastidious apprehension of too much daylight; their darkened chambers were the effect of the most elaborate study. In their porticoes and gardens they courted the sun whenever it so pleased their luxurious tastes. In the interior of their houses they sought rather the coolness and the shade.

Julia's apartment at that season was in the lower part of the house, immediately beneath the state rooms above, and looking upon the garden, with which it was on a level. The wide door, which was glazed, alone admitted the morning rays: yet her eye, accustomed to

a certain darkness, was sufficiently acute to perceive exactly what colours were the most becoming—what shade of the delicate rouge gave the brightest beam to her dark glance, and the most youthful freshness to her cheek.

On the table, before which she sat, was a small and circular mirror of the most polished steel: round which, in precise order, were ranged the cosmetics and the unguents—the perfumes and the paints—the jewels and the combs—the ribands and the gold pins, which were destined to add to the natural attractions of beauty the assistance of art and the capricious allurements of fashion. Through the dimness of the room glowed brightly the vivid and various colourings of the wall, in all the dazzling frescoes of Pompeian taste. Before the dressing-table, and under the feet of Julia, was spread a carpet, woven from the looms of the East. Near at hand; on another table, was a silver basin and ewer; an extinguished lamp, of most exquisite workmanship, in which the artist had represented a Cupid reposing under the spreading branches of a myrtle-tree; and a small roll of papyrus, containing the softest elegies of Tibullus. Before the door, which communicated with the cubiculum, hung a curtain richly broidered with gold flowers. Such was the dressing-room of a beauty eighteen centuries ago.

The fair Julia leaned indolently back on her seat, while the ornatrix (*i.e.* hairdresser) slowly piled, one above the other, a mass of small curls, dexterously weaving the false with the true, and carrying the whole fabric to a height that seemed to place the head rather at the centre than the summit of the human form.

Her tunic, of a deep amber, which well set off her dark hair and somewhat embrowned complexion, swept in ample folds to her feet,

BONE COMB

which were cased in slippers, fastened round the slender ankle by white thongs; while a profusion of pearls were embroidered in the slipper itself, which was of purple, and turned slightly upward, as do the Turkish slippers at this day. An old slave, skilled by long experience in all the arcana of the toilet, stood beside the hairdresser, with the broad and studded girdle of her mistress over her arm, and giving, from time to time (mingled with judicious flattery to the lady herself), instructions to the mason of the ascending pile.

The toilet was now arranged according to the last mode of Rome. The fair Julia regarded herself with a last gaze of complacent vanity, and reclining again upon her seat, she bade the youngest of her slaves, in a listless tone, read to her the enamoured couplets of Tibullus. This lecture was still proceeding, when a female slave admitted Nydia into the presence of the lady of the place.

'*Salve*, Julia!' said the flower-girl, arresting her steps within a few paces from the spot where Julia sat, and crossing her arms upon her breast. 'I have obeyed your commands.'

'You have done well, flower-girl,' answered the lady. 'Approach—you may take a seat.'

One of the slaves placed a stool by Julia, and Nydia seated herself.

Julia looked hard at the Thessalian for some moments in rather an embarrassed silence. She then motioned her attendants to withdraw, and to close the door. When they were alone, she said, looking mechanically from Nydia, and forgetful that she was with one who could not observe her countenance,—

'You serve the Neapolitan, Ione?'

'I am with her at present,' answered Nydia.

'Is she as handsome as they say?'

'I know not,' replied Nydia. 'How can *I* judge?'

'Ah! I should have remembered. But thou hast ears, if not eyes. Do thy fellow-slaves tell thee she is handsome? Slaves talking with one another forget to flatter even their mistress.'

'They tell me that she is beautiful.'

'Hem!—say they that she is tall?'

'Yes.'

'Why, so am I.—Dark haired?'

'I have heard so.'

'So am I. And doth Glaucus visit her much?'

'Daily,' returned Nydia, with a half-suppressed sigh.

'Daily, indeed! Does he find her handsome?'

'I should think so, since they are so soon to be wedded.'

'Wedded!' cried Julia, turning pale even through the false roses on her cheek, and starting from her couch. Nydia did not, of course, perceive the emotion she had caused. Julia remained a long time silent; but her heaving breast and flashing eyes would have betrayed, to one who *could* have seen, the wound her vanity had sustained.

'They tell me thou art a Thessalian,' said she, at last breaking silence.

'And truly!'

'Thessaly is the land of magic and of witches, of talismans and of love-philtres,' said Julia.

'It has ever been celebrated for its sorcerers,' returned Nydia, timidly.

'Knowest thou, then, blind Thessalian, of any love-charms?'

'I!' said the flower-girl, colouring; '*I!* how should I? No, assuredly not!'

'The worse for thee; I could have given thee gold enough to have purchased thy freedom hadst thou been more wise.'

'But what,' asked Nydia, 'can induce the beautiful and wealthy Julia to ask that question of her servant? Has she not money, and youth, and loveliness? Are *they* not love-charms enough to dispense with magic?'

'To all but one person in the world,' answered Julia, haughtily: 'but methinks thy blindness is infectious: and—— But no matter.'

'And that one person?' said Nydia, eagerly.

'Is *not* Glaucus,' replied Julia, with the customary deceit of her sex. 'Glaucus—no!'

Nydia drew her breath more freely, and and after a short pause Julia recommenced.

'But tell me,—thou hearest the gossip of slaves, always prone to these dim beliefs; always ready to apply to sorcery for their own low loves,—hast thou ever heard of any Eastern magician in this city, who possesses the art of which thou art ignorant? No vain chiromancer, no juggler of the market-place, but some more potent and mighty magician of India or of Egypt?'

'Of Egypt?—yes!' said Nydia, shuddering. 'What Pompeian has not heard of Arbaces?'

'Arbaces! true,' replied Julia, grasping at the recollection. 'They say he is a man above all the petty and false impostures of dull pretenders,—that he is versed in the learning of the stars, and the secrets of the ancient Nox; why not in the mysteries of love?'

'If there be one magician living whose art is above that of others, it is that dread man,' answered Nydia; and she felt her talisman while she spoke.

'He is too wealthy to divine for money?' continued Julia, 'Can I not visit him?'

'It is an evil mansion for the young and the beautiful,' replied Nydia. 'I have heard, too, that he languishes in——'

'An evil mansion!' said Julia, catching only the first sentence. 'Why so?'

'The orgies of his midnight leisure are impure and polluted—at least, so says rumour.'

'I will seek him this very day,' resumed Julia; 'nay why not this very hour?'

'At daylight, and in his present state, thou hast assuredly the less to fear,' answered Nydia, yielding to her own sudden and secret wish to learn if the dark Egyptian were indeed possessed of those spells to rivet and attract love, of which the Thessalian had so often heard.

'And who dare insult the rich daughter of Diomed?' said Julia, haughtily. 'I will go.'

'May I visit thee afterwards to learn the result?' asked Nydia, anxiously.

'Kiss me for thy interest in Julia's honour,' answered the lady. 'Yes, assuredly. This eve we sup abroad—come hither at the same hour to-morrow, and thou shalt know all: I may have to employ thee too; but enough for the present. Stay, take this bracelet for the new thought thou hast inspired me with; remember, if thou servest Julia, she is grateful and she is generous.'

'I cannot take thy present,' said Nydia, putting aside the bracelet; 'but young as I am, I can sympathise unbought with those who love—and love in vain.'

'Sayest thou so!' returned Julia. 'Thou speakest like a free woman—and thou shalt yet be free—farewell!'

GOLD NECKLACE

JULIA SEEKS ARBACES

Arbaces was seated in a chamber which opened on a kind of balcony or portico that fronted his garden. His cheek was pale and worn with the sufferings he had endured, but his iron frame had already recovered from the severest effects of that accident which had frustrated his fell designs in the moment of victory. The air that came fragrantly to his brow revived his languid senses, and the blood circulated more freely than it had done for days through his shrunken veins.

He changed his position restlessly, as he revolved scheme after scheme, which no sooner occurred than it was dismissed: several times he struck his breast and groaned aloud, with the desire of vengeance, and a sense of his impotence to accomplish it. While thus absorbed, a boy slave timidly entered the chamber.

A female, evidently of rank from her dress, and that of the single slave who attended her, waited below and sought an audience with Arbaces.

'A female!' his heart beat quick. 'Is she young?'

'Her face is concealed by her veil; but her form is slight, yet round, as that of youth.'

'Admit her,' said the Egyptian: for a moment his vain heart dreamed the stranger might be Ione.

The first glance of the visitor now entering the apartment sufficed to undeceive so erring a fancy. True, she was about the same height as Ione, and perhaps the same age—true, she was finely and richly formed—but where was that undulating and ineffable grace which accompanied every motion of the peerless Neapolitan—the chaste and decorous garb, so simple even in the care of its arrangement—the dignified yet bashful step—the majesty of womanhood and its modesty?

'Pardon me that I rise with pain,' said Arbaces, gazing on the stranger: 'I am still suffering from recent illness.'

'Do not disturb thyself, O great Egyptian!' returned Julia, seeking to disguise the fear she already experienced beneath the ready resort of flattery; 'and forgive an unfortunate female, who seeks consolation from thy wisdom.'

'And what,' said his low, deep voice, 'brings thee, O maiden! to the house of the Eastern stranger?'

'His fame,' replied Julia.

'In what?' said he, with a strange and slight smile.

'Canst thou ask, O wise Arbaces? Is not

CANDELABRA

thy knowledge the very gossip theme of Pompeii?'

'Thou comest to me for advice in unhappy love,' said he; 'well, turn that face on the ungrateful one: what other love-charm can I give thee?'

'Oh, cease these courtesies!' said Julia; 'it *is* a love-charm, indeed, that I would ask from thy skill!'

'Fair stranger!' replied Arbaces, somewhat scornfully, 'love-spells are not among the secrets I have wasted the midnight oil to attain.'

'Is it indeed so? Then pardon me, great Arbaces, and farewell!'

'Stay; although I confess that I have left the witchery of philtres and potions to those whose trade is in such knowledge, yet am I myself not so dull to beauty but that in earlier youth I may have employed them in my own behalf. I may give thee advice, at least, if thou wilt be candid with me. Tell me then, first, art thou unmarried, as thy dress betokens?'

'Yes,' said Julia.

'And, being unblest with fortune, wouldst thou allure some wealthy suitor?'

'I am richer than he who disdains me.'

'Strange and more strange! And thou lovest him who loves not thee?'

'I know not if I love him,' answered Julia, haughtily; 'but I know that I would see myself triumph over a rival—I would see him who rejected me my suitor—I would see her whom he has preferred, in her turn despised.'

'A natural ambition and a womanly,' said the Egyptian, in a tone too grave for irony. 'Yet more, fair maiden; wilt thou confide to me the name of thy lover? Can he be Pompeian, and despise wealth, even if blind to beauty?'

'He is of Athens,' answered Julia.

'Ha!' cried the Egyptian, impetuously, as the blood rushed to his cheek; 'there is but one Athenian, young and noble, in Pompeii. Can it be Glaucus of whom thou speakest!'

'Ah! betray me not—so indeed they call him.'

The Egyptian sank back, gazing vacantly on the averted face of the merchant's daughter, and muttering inly to himself: this conference, with which he had hitherto only trifled, amusing himself with the credulity and vanity of his visitor—might it not minister to his revenge?

'I see thou canst assist me not,' said Julia, offended by his continued silence; 'guard at least my secret. Once more, farewell!'

'Maiden,' said the Egyptian, in an earnest and serious tone, 'thy suit hath touched me—I will minister to thy will. Listen to me; I have not myself dabbled in these lesser mysteries, but I know one who hath. At the base of Vesuvius, less than a league from the city, there dwells a powerful witch; beneath the rank dews of the new moon, she has gathered the herbs which possess the virtue to chain Love in eternal fetters. Her art can bring thy lover to thy feet. Seek her, and mention to her the name of Arbaces: she fears that name, and will give thee her most potent philtres.'

'Alas!' answered Julia, 'I know not the road to the home of her whom thou speakest of: the way, short though it be, is long to traverse for a girl who leaves, unknown, the house of her father. The country is entangled with wild vines, and dangerous with precipitous caverns. I dare not trust to mere strangers to guide me; the reputation of women of my rank is easily tarnished—and though I care not who knows that I love Glaucus, I would not have it imagined that I obtained his love by a spell.'

'Were I but three days advanced in health,' said the Egyptian, rising and walking (as if to try his strength) across the chamber, but with irregular and feeble steps, 'I myself would accompany thee.—Well, thou must wait.'

'But Glaucus is soon to wed that hated Neapolitan.'

'Wed!'

'Yes; in the early part of next month.'

'So soon! Art thou well advised of this?'

'From the lips of her own slave.'

'It shall not be!' said the Egyptian, impetuously. 'Fear nothing, Glaucus shall be thine. Yet how, when thou obtainest it, canst thou administer to him this potion?'

'My father has invited him, and, I believe, the Neapolitan also, to a banquet, on the day following to-morrow: I shall then have the opportunity to administer it.'

'So be it!' said the Egyptian, with eyes

flashing such fierce joy, that Julia's gaze sank trembling beneath them. 'To-morrow eve, then, order thy litter.'

Left alone, Arbaces summoned one of his slaves, bade him hasten to track the steps of Julia, and acquaint himself with her name and condition. This done, he stepped forth into the portico. The skies were serene and clear; but he, deeply read in the signs of their various change, beheld in one mass of cloud, far on the horizon, which the wind began slowly to agitate, that a storm was brooding above.

'It is like my vengeance,' said he, as he gazed; 'the sky is clear, but the cloud moves on.'

THE WITCH'S CAVERN

It was when the heats of noon died gradually away from the earth, that Glaucus and Ione went forth to enjoy the cooled and grateful air. At that time, various carriages were in use among the Romans; the one most used by the richer citizens, when they required no companion in their excursions, was the *biga*, already described in the early portion of this work; that appropriated to the matrons, was termed *carpentum*, which had commonly two wheels; the ancients used also a sort of litter, a vast sedan-chair, more commodiously arranged than the modern, inasmuch as the occupant thereof could lie down at ease, instead of being perpendicularly and stiffly jostled up and down. There was another carriage, used both for travelling and for excursions in the country; it was commodious, containing three or four persons with ease, having a covering which could be raised at pleasure; and, in short, answering very much the purpose of (though very different in shape from) the modern britska. It was a vehicle of this description that the lovers, accompanied by one female slave of Ione, now used in their excursion. About ten miles from the city, there was at that day an old ruin, the remains of a temple, evidently Grecian; and as for Glaucus and Ione everything Grecian possessed an interest, they had agreed to visit these ruins: it was thither they were now bound.

They arrived at the ruins; they examined them with that fondness with which we trace the hallowed and household vestiges of our own ancestry—they lingered there till Hesperus appeared in the rosy heavens; and then returning homeward in the twilight, they were more silent than they had been; for in the shadow and beneath the stars they felt more oppressively their mutual love.

It was at this time that the storm began to creep visibly over them. At first, a low and distant thunder gave warning of the approaching conflict of the elements; and then rapidly rushed above the dark ranks of the serried clouds. The suddenness of storms in that climate is something almost preternatural, and might well suggest to early superstition the notion of a divine agency—a few large drops broke heavily among the boughs that half overhung their path, and then, swift and intolerably bright, the forked lightning darted across their very eyes, and was swallowed up by the increasing darkness.

'Swifter, good Carrucarius!' cried Glaucus to the driver; 'the tempest comes on apace.'

The slave urged on the mules—they went swift over the uneven and stony road—the clouds thickened, near and more near broke the thunder, and fast rushed the dashing rain.

'Dost thou fear?' whispered Glaucus, as he sought excuse in the storm to come nearer to Ione.

'Not with thee,' said she, softly.

At that instant, the carriage, fragile and ill-contrived (as, despite their graceful shapes, were, for practical uses, most of such inventions at that time), struck violently into a deep rut, over which lay a log of fallen wood; the driver, with a curse, stimulated his mules yet faster for the obstacle, the wheel was torn from the socket, and the carriage suddenly overset.

Glaucus, quickly extricating himself from the vehicle, hastened to assist Ione, who was fortunately unhurt; with some difficulty they raised the carruca (or carriage) and found that it ceased any longer even to afford them shelter; the springs that fastened the covering were snapped asunder, and the rain poured fast and fiercely into the interior.

In this dilemma, what was to be done? They were yet some distance from the city—no house, no aid, seemed near.

'There is,' said the slave, 'a smith about a mile off; I could seek him, and he might fasten at least the wheel to the carruca—but, Jupiter! how the rain beats; my mistress will be wet before I come back.'

'Run thither at least,' said Glaucus; 'we must find the best shelter we can till you return.'

The lane was overshadowed with trees, beneath the amplest of which Glaucus drew Ione. He endeavoured, by stripping his own cloak, to shield her yet more from the rapid rain; but it descended with a fury that broke through all puny obstacles: and suddenly, while Glaucus was yet whispering courage to his beautiful charge, the lightning struck one of the trees immediately before them, and split with a mighty crash its huge trunk in twain. This awful incident apprised them of the danger they braved in their present shelter, and Glaucus looked anxiously round for some less perilous place of refuge. 'We are now,' said he, 'half-way up the ascent of Vesuvius; there ought to be some cavern, or hollow in the vine-clad rocks, could we but find it, in which the deserting Nymphs have left a shelter.' While thus saying he moved from the trees, and, looking wistfully towards the mountain, discovered through the advancing gloom a red and tremulous light at no considerable distance. 'That must come,' said he, 'from the hearth of some shepherd or vine-dresser—it will guide us to some hospitable retreat. Wilt thou stay here, while I—yet no—that would be to leave thee to danger.'

'I will go with you cheerfully,' said Ione. 'Open as the space seems, it is better than the treacherous shelter of these boughs.'

Half leading, half carrying Ione, Glaucus, accompanied by the trembling female slave, advanced towards the light, which yet burned red and steadfastly. At length the space was no longer open; wild vines entangled their steps, and hid from them, save by imperfect intervals, the guiding beam. But faster and fiercer came the rain, and the lightning assumed its most deadly and blasting form; they were still, therefore, impelled onward, hoping, at last, if the light eluded them, to arrive at some cottage or some friendly cavern. The vines grew more and more intricate—the light was entirely snatched from them; but a narrow path, which they trod with labour and pain, guided only by the constant and long-lingering flashes of the storm, continued to lead them towards its direction. The rain ceased suddenly; precipitous and rough crags of scorched lava frowned before them, rendered more fearful by the lightning that illumined the dark and dangerous soil. Sometimes the blaze lingered over the iron-grey heaps of scoria, covered in part with ancient mosses or stunted trees, as if seeking in vain for some gentler product of earth, more worthy of its ire; and sometimes leaving the whole of that part of the scene in darkness, the lightning, broad and sheeted, hung redly over the ocean, tossing far below, until its waves seemed glowing into fire; and so intense was the blaze, that it brought vividly into view even the sharp outline of the more distant windings of the bay, from the eternal Misenum, with its lofty brow, to the beautiful Sorrentum and the giant hills behind.

Our lovers stopped in perplexity and doubt, when suddenly, as the darkness that gloomed between the fierce flashes of lightning once more wrapped them round, they saw near, but high, before them, the mysterious light. Another blaze, in which heaven and earth were reddened, made visible to them the whole expanse; no house was near, but just where they had beheld the light, they thought they saw in the recess of the cavern the outline of a human form. The darkness once more returned; the light, no longer paled beneath the fires of heaven, burned forth again: they resolved to ascend towards it; they had to wind their way among vast fragments of stone, here and there overhung with wild bushes; but they gained nearer and nearer to the light, and at length they stood opposite the mouth of a kind of cavern, apparently formed by huge splinters of rock that had fallen transversely athwart each other: and, looking into the gloom, each drew back involuntarily with a superstitious fear and chill.

A fire burned in the far recess of the cave; and over it was a small cauldron; on a tall and thin column of iron stood a rude lamp; over that part of the wall, at the base of which burned the fire, hung in many rows, as if to dry, a profusion of herbs and weeds. A fox, couched before the fire, gazed upon the strangers with its bright and red eye—its hair bristling—and a low growl stealing from between its teeth; in the centre of the cave was an earthen statue, which had three heads

of a singular and fantastic cast: they were formed by the real skulls of a dog, a horse, and a boar; a low tripod stood before this wild representation of the popular Hecate.

But it was not these appendages and appliances of the cave that thrilled the blood of those who gazed fearfully therein—it was the face of its inmate. Before the fire, with the light shining full upon her features, sat a woman of considerable age. Perhaps in no country are there seen so many hags as in Italy—in no country does beauty so awfully change, in age, to hideousness the most appalling and revolting. But the old woman now before them was not one of these specimens of the extreme of human ugliness; on the contrary, her countenance betrayed the remains of a regular but high and aquiline order of feature: with stony eyes turned upon them—with a look that met and fascinated theirs—they beheld in that fearful counten- ance the very image of a corpse!—the same,

the glazed and lustreless regard, the blue and shrunken lips, the drawn and hollow jaw— the dead, lank hair, of a pale grey—the livid, green, ghastly skin, which seemed all surely tinged and tainted by the grave!

'It is a dead thing,' said Glaucus.

'Nay—it stirs—it is a ghost or *larva*,' faltered Ione, as she clung to the Athenian's breast.

'Oh, away, away!' groaned the slave, 'it is the Witch of Vesuvius!'

'Who are ye?' said a hollow and ghostly voice. 'And what do ye here?'

The sound, terrible and deathlike as it was —suiting well the countenance of the speaker, and seeming rather the voice of some bodiless wanderer of the Styx than living mortal— would have made Ione shrink back into the pitiless fury of the storm, but Glaucus, though not without some misgiving, drew her into the cavern.

'We are storm-beaten wanderers from the neighbouring city,' said he, 'and decoyed hither by yon light; we crave shelter and the comfort of your hearth.'

As he spoke, the fox rose from the ground, and advanced towards the strangers, showing, from end to end, its white teeth, and deepen- ing in its menacing growl.

'Down, slave!' said the witch; and at the sound of her voice the beast dropped at once, covering its face with its brush, and keeping only its quick, vigilant eye fixed upon the invaders of its repose. 'Come to the fire if ye will!' said she, turning to Glaucus and his companions. 'I never welcome living thing— save the owl, the fox, the toad, and the viper —so I cannot welcome ye; but come to the fire without welcome—why stand upon form?'

The language in which the hag addressed them was a strange and barbarous Latin, interlarded with many words of some more rude and ancient dialect. She did not stir from her seat, but gazed stonily upon them as Glaucus now released Ione of her outer wrapping garments, and making her place herself on a log of wood, which was the only

other seat he perceived at hand, fanned with his breath the embers into a more glowing flame. The slave, encouraged by the boldness of her superiors, divested herself also of her long *palla*, and crept timorously to the opposite corner of the hearth.

'We disturb you, I fear,' said the silver voice of Ione, in conciliation.

The witch did not reply—she seemed like one who has awakened for a moment from the dead, and has then relapsed once more into the eternal slumber.

'Tell me,' said she, suddenly, and after a long pause, 'are ye brother and sister?'

'No,' said Ione, blushing.

'Are ye married?'

'Not so,' replied Glaucus.

'Ho, lovers!—ha!—ha!—ha!' and the witch laughed so loud and so long that the caverns rang again.

The heart of Ione stood still at that strange mirth. Glaucus muttered a rapid counterspell to the omen—and the slave turned as pale as the cheek of the witch herself.

'Why dost thou laugh, old crone?' said Glaucus, somewhat sternly, as he concluded his invocation.

'Did I laugh?' said the hag, absently.

'She is in her dotage,' whispered Glaucus: as he said this, he caught the eye of the hag fixed upon him with a malignant and vivid glare.

'Thou liest!' said she, abruptly.

'Thou art an uncourteous welcomer,' returned Glaucus.

'Hush! provoke her not, dear Glaucus!' whispered Ione.

'I will tell thee why I laughed when I discovered ye were lovers,' said the old woman. 'It was because it is a pleasure to the old and withered to look upon young hearts like yours—and to know the time will come when you will loathe each other—loathe— loathe—ha!—ha!—ha!'

It was now Ione's turn to pray against the unpleasing prophecy.

'The gods forbid!' said she. 'Yet, poor woman, thou knowest little of love, or thou wouldst know that it never changes.'

'Was I young once, think ye?' returned the hag, quickly; 'and am I old, and hideous, and deathly now? Such as is the form, so is the heart.' With these words she sank again into a stillness profound and fearful, as if the cessation of life itself.

'Hast thou dwelt here long?' said Glaucus, after a pause, feeling uncomfortably oppressed beneath a silence so appalling.

'Ah, long!—yes.'

'It is but a drear abode'.

'Ha! thou mayst well say that—Hell is beneath us!' replied the hag, pointing her bony finger to the earth. 'And I will tell thee a secret—the dim things below are preparing wrath for ye above—you, the young, and the thoughtless, and the beautiful.'

'Thou utterest but evil words, ill becoming the hospitable,' said Glaucus; 'and in future I will brave the tempest rather than thy welcome.'

'Thou wilt do well. None should ever seek me—save the wretched!'

'And why the wretched?' asked the Athenian.

'I am the witch of the mountain,' replied the sorceress, with a ghastly grin; 'my trade is to give hope to the hopeless: for the crossed in love I have philtres; for the avaricious, promises of treasure; for the malicious, potions of revenge; for the happy and the good, I have only what life has—curses! Trouble me no more.'

With this the grim tenant of the cave relapsed into a silence so obstinate and sullen, that Glaucus in vain endeavoured to draw her into farther conversation. She did not evince, by any alteration of her locked and rigid features, that she even heard him. Fortunately, however, the storm, which was brief as violent, began now to relax; the rain grew less and less fierce; and at last, as the clouds parted, the moon burst forth in the purple opening of heaven, and streamed clear and full into that desolate abode. Never had she shone, perhaps, on a group more worthy of the painter's art. The young, the all-beautiful Ione, seated by that rude fire—her lover already forgetful of the presence of the hag, at her feet, gazing upward to her face, and whispering sweet words—the pale and affrighted slave at a little distance—and the ghastly hag resting her deadly eyes upon them; yet seemingly serene and fearless (for the companionship of love hath such power) were these beautiful beings, things of another sphere, in that dark and unholy cavern, with its gloomy quaintness of appurtenance. The fox regarded them from his corner with his keen and fiery eye: and as Glaucus now turned towards the witch, he perceived for the first time, just under her seat, the bright gaze and crested head of a large snake: whether it was that the vivid colouring of the Athenian's cloak, thrown over the shoulders of Ione, attracted the reptile's anger—its crest began to glow and rise, as if menacing and preparing itself to spring upon the Neapolitan;—Glaucus caught quickly at one of the half-burned logs upon the hearth—and, as if enraged at the action, the snake came forth from its shelter, and with a loud hiss raised itself on end till its height nearly approached that of the Greek.

'Witch!' cried Glaucus, 'command thy creature, or thou wilt see it dead.'

'It has been despoiled of its venom!' said the witch, aroused at his threat; but ere the words had left her lip, the snake had sprung

GLASS JUGS

upon Glaucus; quick and watchful, the agile Greek leaped lightly aside, and struck so fell and dexterous a blow on the head of the snake, that it fell prostrate and writhing among the embers of the fire.

The hag sprung up, and stood confronting Glaucus with a face which would have befitted the fiercest of the Furies, so utterly dire and wrathful was its expression—yet even in horror and ghastliness preserving the outline and trace of beauty—and utterly free from that coarse grotesque at which the imaginations of the North have sought the source of terror.

'Thou hast,' said she, in a slow and steady voice—which belied the expression of her face, so much was it passionless and calm— 'thou hast had shelter under my roof, and warmth at my hearth; thou hast returned evil for good; thou hast smitten and haply slain the thing that loved me, and was mine: nay, more, the creature, above all others, conse-crated to gods and deemed venerable by man —now hear thy punishment. By the moon, who is the guardian of the sorceress—by Orcus, who is the treasurer of wrath—I curse thee! and thou art cursed! May thy love be blasted—may thy name be blackened—may the infernals mark thee—may thy heart wither and scorch—may thy last hour recall to thee the prophet voice of the Saga of Vesuvius! And thou,' she added, turning sharply towards Ione, and raising her right arm—when Glaucus burst impetuously on her speech:—

'Hag!' cried he, 'forbear! Me thou hast cursed, and I commit myself to the gods—I

defy and scorn thee! but breathe but one word against yon maiden, and I will convert the oath on thy foul lips to thy dying groan. Beware!'

'I have done,' replied the hag, laughing wildly; 'for in thy doom is she who loves thee accursed. And not the less, that I heard *her* lips breathe thy name, and know by what word to commend thee to the demons. *Glaucus*—thou art doomed!' So saying, the witch turned from the Athenian, and kneeling down beside her wounded favourite, which she dragged from the hearth, she turned to them her face no more.

'O Glaucus!' said Ione, greatly terrified, 'what have we done?—Let us hasten from this place; the storm has ceased. Good mistress, forgive him—recall thy words—he meant but to defend himself—accept this peace-offering to unsay the said:' and Ione, stooping, placed her purse on the hag's lap.

'Away!' said she, bitterly—'away! The oath once woven the Fates only can untie. Away!'

'Come, dearest!' said Glaucus, impatiently. 'Thinkest thou that the gods above us or below hear the impotent ravings of dotage? Come!'

Long and loud rang the echoes of the cavern with the dread laugh of the Saga—she deigned no further reply.

The lovers breathed more freely when they gained the open air: yet the scene they had witnessed, the words and the laughter of the witch, still fearfully dwelt with Ione; and even Glaucus could not thoroughly shake off the impression they bequeathed. The storm had subsided—save, now and then, a low thunder muttered at the distance amidst the darker clouds, or a momentary flash of lightning affronted the sovereignty of the moon. With some difficulty they regained the road, where they found the vehicle already sufficiently repaired for their departure, and the carrucarius calling loudly upon Hercules to tell him where his charge had vanished.

Glaucus vainly endeavoured to cheer the exhausted spirit of Ione; and scarce less vainly to recover the elastic tone of his own natural gaiety. They soon arrived before the gate of the city: as it opened to them, a litter borne by slaves impeded the way.

'It is too late for egress,' cried the sentinel to the inmate of the litter.

'Not so,' said a voice, which the lovers started to hear; it was a voice they well recognised. 'I am bound to the villa of Marcus Polybius. I shall return shortly. I am Arbaces the Egyptian.'

The scruples of him at the gate were removed, and the litter passed close beside the carriage that bore the lovers.

'Arbaces, at this hour!—scarce recovered too, methinks!—Whither and for what can he leave the city?' said Glaucus.

'Alas!' replied Ione, bursting into tears, 'my soul feels still more and more the omen of evil. Preserve us, O ye Gods! or at least,' she murmured inly, 'preserve my Glaucus!'

THE LORD OF THE BURNING BELT AND HIS MINION

Arbaces had tarried only till the cessation of the tempest allowed him, under cover of night, to seek the Saga of Vesuvius. Borne by those of his trustier slaves in whom in all more secret expeditions he was accustomed to confide, he lay extended along his litter, and resigning his sanguine heart to the contemplation of vengeance gratified and love possessed. The slaves in so short a journey moved very little slower than the ordinary pace of mules; and Arbaces soon arrived at the commencement of a narrow path, which the lovers had not been fortunate enough to discover; but which, skirting the thick vines, led at once to the habitation of the witch. Here he rested the litter; and bidding his slaves conceal themselves and the vehicle among the vines from the observation of any chance passenger, he mounted alone, with steps still feeble but supported by a long staff, the drear and sharp ascent.

He paused, as at length he approached the mouth of the cavern, to recover breath; and then, with his wonted collected and stately mien, he crossed the unhallowed threshold.

The fox sprang up at the ingress of this newcomer, and by a long howl announced another visitor to his mistress.

The witch had resumed her seat, and her aspect of grave-like and grim repose. By her feet, upon a bed of dry weeds which half covered it, lay the wounded snake; but the quick eye of the Egyptian caught its scales glittering in the reflected light of the opposite fire, as it writhed,—now contracting, now lengthening, its folds, in pain and unsated anger.

'Down, slave!' said the witch, as before, to the fox; and, as before, the animal dropped to the ground—mute, but vigilant.

'Rise, servant of Nox and Erebus!' said Arbaces, commandingly; 'a superior in thine art salutes thee! rise, and welcome him.'

At these words the hag turned her gaze upon the Egyptian's towering form and dark features. She looked long and fixedly upon him, as he stood before her in his Oriental robe, and folded arms, and steadfast and haughty brow. 'Who art thou,' she said at last, 'that callest thyself greater in art than the Saga of the Burning Fields, and the daughter of the perished Etrurian race?'

'I am he,' answered Arbaces, 'from whom all cultivators of magic, from north to south, from east to west, from the Ganges and the Nile to the vales of Thessaly and the shores of the yellow Tiber, have stooped to learn.'

'There is but one such man in these places,' answered the witch, 'whom the men of the outer world, unknowing his loftier attributes and more secret fame, call Arbaces the Egyptian: to us of a higher nature and deeper knowledge, his rightful appellation is Hermes of the Burning Girdle.'

'Look again,' returned Arbaces: 'I am he.'

As he spoke he drew aside his robe, and revealed a cincture seemingly of fire, that burned around his waist, clasped in the centre by a plate whereon was engraven some sign apparently vague and unintelligible, but which was evidently not unknown to the Saga. She rose hastily, and threw herself at the feet of Arbaces. 'I have seen, then,' said she, in a voice of deep humility, 'the Lord of the Mighty Girdle—vouchsafe my homage.'

'Rise,' said the Egyptian; 'I have need of thee.'

So saying, he placed himself on the same log of wood on which Ione had rested before, and motioned to the witch to resume her seat.

'Thou sayest,' said he, as she obeyed, 'that thou art a daughter of the ancient Etrurian tribes; the mighty walls of whose rock-built cities yet frown above the robber race that hath seized upon their ancient reign. Partly came those tribes from Greece, partly were

they exiles from a more burning and primeval soil. In either case art thou of Egyptian lineage, for the Grecian masters of the aboriginal helot were among the restless sons whom the Nile banished from her bosom. Equally, then, O Saga! thy descent is from ancestors that swore allegiance to mine own. By birth as by knowledge, art thou the subject of Arbaces. Hear me, then, and obey!'

The witch bowed her head.

'Whatever art we possess in sorcery,' continued Arbaces, 'we are sometimes driven to natural means to attain our object. Mark me, then: thou art deeply skilled, methinks, in the secrets of the more deadly herbs; thou knowest those which arrest life, which burn and scorch the soul from out her citadel, or freeze the channels of young blood into that ice which no sun can melt. Do I overrate thy skill? Speak, and truly!'

'Mighty Hermes, such lore is, indeed, mine own. Deign to look at these ghostly and corpse-like features; they have waned from the hues of life merely by watching over the rank herbs which simmer night and day in yon cauldron.'

The Egyptian moved his seat from so unblessed or so unhealthful a vicinity as the witch spoke.

'It is well,' said he; 'thou hast learned that maxim of all the deeper knowledge which saith, "Despise the body to make wise the mind." But to thy task. There cometh to thee by to-morrow's starlight a vain maiden, seeking of thine art a love-charm to fascinate from another the eyes that should utter but soft tales to her own; instead of thy philtres, give the maiden one of thy most powerful poisons. Let the lover breathe his vows to the Shades.'

The witch trembled from head to foot.

'Oh pardon! pardon! dread master,' said she, falteringly, 'but this I dare not. The law in these cities is sharp and vigilant; they will seize, they will slay me.'

'For what purpose, then, thy herbs and thy potions, vain Saga?' said Arbaces, sneeringly.

The witch hid her loathsome face with her hands.

'Oh! years ago,' said she, in a voice unlike her usual tones, so plaintive was it, and so soft, 'I was not the thing that I am now.—I loved, I fancied myself beloved.'

The skeleton frame of the witch shook beneath strong convulsions.

Arbaces gazed upon her with a curious though contemptuous eye.

'And this foul thing has yet human emotions!' thought he; 'still she cowers over the ashes of the same fire that consumes Arbaces!—Such are we all! Mystic is the tie of those mortal passions that unite the greatest and the least.'

He did not reply till she had somewhat recovered herself, and now sat rocking to and fro in her seat, with glassy eyes fixed on the opposite flame, and large tears rolling down her livid cheeks.

'And now, listen to me again! I command thee to obey me! it is for vengeance that I seek thee! This youth whom I would sweep from my path has crossed me, despite my spells:—this thing of purple and broidery, of smiles and glances, soulless and mindless, with no charm but that of beauty—accursed be it!—this insect—this Glaucus—I tell thee, by Orcus and by Nemesis, he must die.'

And working himself up at every word, the Egyptian, forgetful of his debility—of his strange companion—of everything but his own vindictive rage, strode, with large and rapid steps, the gloomy cavern.

'Glaucus! saidst thou, mighty master!' said the witch, abruptly; and her dim eye glared at the name with all that fierce resentment at the memory of small affronts so common amongst the solitary and the shunned.

'Ay, so he is called; but what matters the name? Let it not be heard as that of a living man three days from this date!'

'Hear me!' said the witch, breaking from a short reverie into which she was plunged after this last sentence of the Egyptian. 'Hear me! I am thy thing and thy slave! spare me! If I give to the maiden thou speakest of that which would destroy the life of Glaucus, I shall be surely detected—the dead ever find avengers. Nay, dread man! if thy visit to me be tracked, if thy hatred to Glaucus be known, thou mayest have need of thy archest magic to protect thyself!'

'Ha!' said Arbaces, stopping suddenly short; and as a proof of that blindness with which passion darkens the eyes even of the most acute, this was the first time when the risk that he himself ran by this method of vengeance had occurred to a mind ordinarily wary and circumspect.

'But,' continued the witch, 'if instead of that which shall arrest the heart, I give that which shall sear and blast the brain—which shall make him who quaffs it unfit for the uses and career of life—an abject, raving, benighted thing—smiting sense to drivelling, youth to dotage—will not thy vengeance be equally sated—thy object equally attained?'

'Oh, witch! no longer the servant, but the sister—the equal of Arbaces—how much brighter is woman's wit, even in vengeance, than ours! how much more exquisite than death is such a doom!'

'And,' continued the hag, gloating over her fell scheme, 'in this is but little danger; for by ten thousand methods, which men forbear to seek, can our victim become mad. Mighty Hermes, have I ministered to thee cunningly?'

'Thou shalt have twenty years' longer date for this,' returned Arbaces. 'I will write anew the epoch of thy fate on the face of the pale stars—thou shalt not serve in vain the Master of the Flaming Belt.' So saying, he cast upon the floor a heavy purse, which clinked not unmusically to the ear of the hag, who loved the consciousness of possessing the means to purchase comforts she disdained.

He stayed not to hear the valediction or the thanks of the witch; with a quick step he passed into the moonlit air, and hastened down the mountain.

The witch, who followed his steps to the threshold, stood long at the entrance of the cavern, gazing fixedly on his receding form; and as the sad moonlight streamed over her shadowy form and deathlike face, emerging from the dismal rocks, it seemed as if one gifted, indeed, by supernatural magic had escaped from the dreary Orcus; and, the foremost of its ghostly throng, stood at its black portals—vainly summoning his return, or vainly sighing to rejoin him. The hag, then slowly re-entering the cave, groaningly picked up the heavy purse, took the lamp from its stand, and, passing to the remotest depth of her cell, a black and abrupt passage, which was not visible, save at a near approach, closed round as it was with jutting and sharp crags, yawned before her: she went several yards along this gloomy path, which sloped gradually downwards, as if towards the bowels of the earth, and, lifting a stone, deposited her treasure in a hole beneath, which, as the lamp pierced its secrets, seemed already to contain coins of various value, wrung from the credulity or gratitude of her visitors.

'I love to look at you,' said she, apostrophising the moneys; 'for when I see you I feel that I am indeed of power. And I am to have twenty years' longer life to increase your store! O thou great Hermes!'

She replaced the stone, and continued her path onward for some paces, when she stopped before a deep irregular fissure in the earth. Here, as she bent—strange, rumbling, hoarse, and distant sounds might be heard, while ever and anon, with a loud and grating noise which, to use a homely but faithful simile, seemed to resemble the grinding of steel upon wheels, volumes of streaming and dark smoke issued forth, and rushed spirally along the cavern.

'The Shades are noiser than their wont,' said the hag, shaking her grey locks; and, looking into the cavity, she beheld, far down, glimpses of a long streak of light, intensely but darkly red. 'Strange!' she said, shrinking back; 'it is only within the last two days that dull, deep light hath been visible—what can it portend?'

The fox, who had attended the steps of his fell mistress, uttered a dismal howl, and ran cowering back to the inner cave; a cold shuddering seized the hag herself at the cry of the animal, which, causeless as it seemed, the superstitions of the time considered deeply ominous. She muttered her placatory charm, and tottered back into her cavern, where, amidst her herbs and incantations, she prepared to execute the orders of the Egyptian.

'He called me dotard,' said she, as the smoke curled from the hissing cauldron: 'when the jaws drop, and the grinders fall, and the heart scarce beats, it is a pitiable thing to dote; but when,' she added, with a savage and exulting grin, 'the young, and the beautiful, and the strong, are suddenly smitten into idiocy—ah, *that* is terrible! Burn, flame—simmer herb—swelter toad—I cursed him, and he shall be cursed!'

On that night, and at the same hour which witnessed the dark and unholy interview between Arbaces and the Saga, Apæcides was baptised.

THE PLOT THICKENS

'And you have the courage, then, Julia, to seek the Witch of Vesuvius this evening; in company, too, with that fearful man?'

'Why, Nydia?' replied Julia, timidly; 'dost thou really think there is anything to dread? These old hags, with their enchanted mirrors, their trembling sieves, and their moon-gathered herbs, are, I imagine, but crafty impostors, who have learned, perhaps, nothing but the very charm for which I apply to their skill, and which is drawn but from the knowledge of the field's herbs and simples. Wherefore should I dread?'

'Dost thou not fear thy companion?'

'What, Arbaces? By Dian, I never saw lover more courteous than that same magician! And were he not so dark, he would be even handsome.'

Blind as she was, Nydia had the penetration to perceive that Julia's mind was not one that the gallantries of Arbaces were likely to terrify. She therefore dissuaded her no more: but nursed in her excited heart the wild and increasing desire to know if sorcery had indeed a spell to fascinate love to love.

'Let me go with thee, noble Julia,' said she at length; 'my presence is no protection, but I should like to be beside thee to the last.'

'Thine offer pleases me much,' replied the daughter of Diomed. 'Yet how canst thou contrive it? we may not return until late, they will miss thee.'

'Ione is indulgent,' replied Nydia. 'If thou wilt permit me to sleep beneath thy roof, I will say that thou, an early patroness and friend, hast invited me to pass the day with thee, and sing thee my Thessalian songs; her courtesy will readily grant to thee so light a boon.'

'Nay, ask for thyself!' said the haughty Julia. 'I stoop to request no favour from the Neapolitan!'

'Well, be it so. I will take my leave now; make my request, which I know will be readily granted, and return shortly.'

'Do so; and thy bed shall be prepared in my own chamber.'

With that, Nydia left the fair Pompeian.

On her way back to Ione she was met by the chariot of Glaucus, on whose fiery and curveting steeds was riveted the gaze of the crowded street.

He kindly stopped for a moment to speak to the flower-girl.

'Blooming as thine own roses, my gentle Nydia! and how is thy fair mistress?—recovered, I trust, from the effects of the storm?'

'I have not seen her this morning,' answered Nydia, 'but——'

'But what? draw back—the horses are too near thee.'

'But think you Ione will permit me to pass the day with Julia, the daughter of Diomed?—She wishes it, and was kind to me when I had few friends.'

'The gods bless thy grateful heart! I will answer for Ione's permission.'

'Then I may stay over the night, and return to-morrow?' said Nydia, shrinking from the praise she so little merited.

'As thou and fair Julia please. Commend me to her; and hark ye, Nydia, when thou hearest her speak, note the contrast of her voice with that of the silver-toned Ione.—*Vale!*'

His spirits entirely recovered from the effect of the past night, his locks waving in the wind, his joyous and elastic heart bounding with every spring of his Parthian steeds, a very prototype of his country's god, full of youth and of love—Glaucus was borne rapidly to his mistress.

As the evening darkened, Julia, reclined within her litter, which was capacious enough also to admit her blind companion, took her way to the rural baths indicated by Arbaces. To her natural levity of disposition, her enterprise brought less of terror than of pleasurable excitement; above all, she glowed at the thought of her coming triumph over the hated Neapolitan.

A small but gay group was collected round the door of the villa, as her litter passed by it

to the private entrance of the baths appropriated to the women.

'Methinks, by this dim light,'said one of the bystanders, 'I recognise the slaves of Diomed.'

'True, Clodius,' said Sallust: 'it is probably the litter of his daughter Julia. She is rich, my friend; why dost thou not proffer thy suit to her?'

'Why, I had once hoped that Glaucus would have married her. She does not disguise her attachment; and then, as he gambles freely and with ill-success——'

'The sesterces would have passed to thee, wise Clodius. A wife is a good thing—when it belongs to another man!'

'But,' continued Clodius, 'as Glaucus is, I understand, to wed the Neapolitan, I think I must even try my chance with the dejected maid.'

Dismissing her slaves to that part of the house set apart for their entertainment, Julia and Nydia, avoiding the more public part of the garden, arrived at the place specified by the Egyptian. In a small circular plot of grass the stars gleamed upon the statue of Silenus: —the merry god reclined upon a fragment of rock—the lynx of Bacchus at his feet—and over his mouth he held, with extended arm, a bunch of grapes, which he seemingly laughed to welcome ere he devoured.

'I see not the magician,' said Julia, looking round: when, as she spoke, the Egyptian slowly emerged from the neighbouring foliage, and the light fell palely over his sweeping robes.

'*Salve*, sweet maiden!—But ha! whom hast thou here? we must have no companions!'

'It is but the blind flower-girl, wise magician,' replied Julia: 'herself a Thessalian.'

'Oh! Nydia!' said the Egyptian. 'I know her well.'

Nydia drew back and shuddered.

'Thou hast been at my house, methinks!' said he, approaching his voice to Nydia's ear; 'thou knowest the oath!—Silence and secrecy, now as then, or beware!'

'Yet,' he added, musingly to himself, 'why confide more than is necessary, even in the blind—Julia, canst thou trust thyself alone with me? Believe me, the magician is less formidable than he seems.'

As he spoke, he gently drew Julia aside.

'The witch loves not many visitors at once,' said he: 'leave Nydia here till your return; she can be of no assistance to us: and, for protection—your own beauty suffices—your own beauty and your own rank; yes, Julia, I know thy name and birth. Come, trust thyself with me, fair rival of the youngest of the Naiads!'

The vain Julia was not, as we have seen, easily affrighted; she was moved by the flattery of Arbaces, and she readily consented to suffer Nydia to await her return; nor did Nydia press her presence. At the sound of the Egyptian's voice all her terror of him returned: she felt a sentiment of pleasure at learning she was not to travel in his companionship.

She returned to the Bath-house, and in one of the private chambers waited their return.

Time passed: a light step entered the chamber where Nydia yet indulged her gloomy meditations.

'Oh, thanked be the immortal gods!' said Julia, 'I have returned, I have left that terrible

WATER HEATER

cavern! Come, Nydia! let us away forthwith!'

It was not till they were seated in the litter that Julia again spoke.

'Oh!' said she, tremblingly, 'such a scene! such fearful incantations! and the dead face of the hag!—But, let us talk not of it. I have obtained the potion—she pledges its effect. My rival shall be suddenly indifferent to his eye, and I, I alone, the idol of Glaucus!'

'Glaucus!' exclaimed Nydia.

'Ay! I told thee, girl, at first, that it was *not* the Athenian whom I loved: but I see now that I may trust thee wholly—it *is* the beautiful Greek!'

What then were Nydia's emotions! she had connived, she had assisted, in tearing Glaucus from Ione; but only to transfer, by all the power of magic, his affections yet more hopelessly to another. Her heart swelled almost to suffocation—she gasped for breath—in the darkness of the vehicle, Julia did not perceive the agitation of her companion; she went on rapidly dilating on the promised effect of her acquisition, and on her approaching triumph over Ione, every now and then abruptly digressing to the horror of the scene she had quitted—the unmoved mien of Arbaces, and his authority over the dreadful Saga.

Meanwhile Nydia recovered her self-possession: a thought flashed across her: she slept in the chamber of Julia—she might possess herself of the potion.

They arrived at the house of Diomed, and descended to Julia's apartment, where the night's repast awaited them.

'Drink, Nydia, thou must be cold; the air was chill to-night; as for me, my veins are yet ice.'

And Julia unhesitatingly quaffed deep draughts of the spiced wine.

'Thou hast the potion,' said Nydia; let me hold it in my hands. How small the phial is! of what colour is the draught?'

'Clear as crystal,' replied Julia, as she retook the philtre; 'thou couldst not tell it from this water. The witch assures me it is tasteless. Small though the phial, it suffices for a life's fidelity: it is to be poured into any liquid; and Glaucus will only know what he has quaffed by the effect.'

'Exactly like this water in appearance?'

'Yes, sparkling and colourless as this. How bright it seems! it is as the very essence of moonlit dews. Bright thing! how thou shinest on my hopes through the crystal vase!'

'And how is it sealed?'

'But by one little stopper—I withdraw it now—the draught gives no odour. Strange, that that which speaks to neither sense should thus command all!'

'Is the effect instantaneous?'

'Usually;—but sometimes it remains dormant for a few hours.'

'Oh, how sweet is this perfume!' said Nydia, suddenly, as she took up a small bottle on the table, and bent over its fragrant contents.

'Thinkest thou so? the bottle is set with gems of some value. Thou wouldst not have the bracelet yestermorn;—wilt thou take the bottle?'

'It ought to be such perfumes as these that should remind one who cannot see of the generous Julia. If the bottle be not too costly——'

'Oh! I have a thousand costlier ones: take it, child!'

Nydia bowed her gratitude, and placed the bottle in her vest.

'And the draught would be equally efficacious, whoever administers it?'

'If the most hideous hag beneath the sun bestowed it, such is its asserted virtue that Glaucus would deem her beautiful, and none but her!'

Julia, warmed by wine, and the reaction of her spirits, was now all animation and delight; she laughed loud, and talked on a hundred matters—nor was it till the night had advanced far towards morning that she summoned her slaves and undressed.

When they were dismissed, she said to Nydia, 'I will not suffer this holy draught to quit my presence till the hour comes for its uses. Lie under my pillow, bright spirit, and give me happy dreams!'

So saying, she placed the potion under her pillow. Nydia's heart beat violently.

'Why dost thou drink that unmixed water, Nydia? Take the wine by its side.'

'I am fevered,' replied the blind girl, 'and the water cools me. I will place this bottle by my bedside, it refreshes in these summer nights, when the dews of sleep fall not on our lips. Fair Julia, I must leave thee very early—so Ione bids—perhaps before thou art awake; accept, therefore, now my congratulations.'

'Thanks: when next we meet you may find Glaucus at my feet.'

They had retired to their couches, and Julia, worn out by the excitement of the day, soon slept. But anxious and burning thoughts rolled over the mind of the wakeful Thessalian. She listened to the calm breathing of Julia; and her ear, accustomed to the finest distinctions of sound, speedily assured her of the deep slumber of her companion.

'Now befriend me, Venus!' said she, softly.

She rose gently, and poured the perfume from the gift of Julia upon the marble floor—she rinsed it several times carefully with the water that was beside her, and then easily finding the bed of Julia (for night to her was as day), she pressed her trembling hand under the pillow and seized the potion. Julia stirred not, her breath regularly fanned the burning cheek of the blind girl. Nydia, then, opening the phial, poured its contents into the bottle, which easily contained them; and then refilling the former reservoir of the potion with that limpid water which Julia had assured her it so resembled, she once more placed the phial in its former place. She then stole again to her couch, and waited—with what thoughts!—the dawning day.

The sun had risen—Julia slept still—Nydia noiselessly dressed herself, placed her treasure carefully in her vest, took up her staff, and hastened to quit the house.

The porter, Medon, saluted her kindly as she descended the steps that led to the street:

PERFUME FLASK

she heard him not; her mind was confused and lost in the whirl of tumultuous thoughts, each thought a passion. She felt the pure morning air upon her cheek, but it cooled not her scorching veins.

'Glaucus,' she murmured, 'all the love-charms of the wildest magic could not make thee love me as I love thee. Ione!—ah; away hesitation! away remorse! Glaucus, my fate is in thy smile; and thine! O hope! O joy! O transport, *thy* fate is in these hands!'

BOOK FOUR

A CLASSIC HOST, COOK, AND KITCHEN

It was then the day for Diomed's banquet to the most select of his friends. The graceful Glaucus, the beautiful Ione, the official Pansa, the high-born Clodius, the immortal Fulvius, the exquisite Lepidus, the epicurean Sallust, were not the only honourers of his festival. He expected, also, an invalid senator from Rome (a man of considerable repute and favour at court), and a great warrior from Herculaneum, who had fought with Titus against the Jews, and having enriched himself prodigiously in the wars, was always told by his friends that his country was eternally indebted to his disinterested exertions! The party, however, extended to a yet greater number: for although, critically speaking, it was, at one time, thought inelegant among the Romans to entertain less than three or more than nine at their banquets, yet this rule was easily disregarded by the ostentatious. And we are told, indeed, in history, that one of the most splendid of these entertainers usually feasted a select party of three hundred.

KITCHEN UTENSILS

Diomed, however, more modest, contented himself with doubling the number of the Muses. His party consisted of eighteen, no unfashionable number in the present day.

It was the morning of Diomed's banquet; and Diomed himself, though he greatly affected the gentleman and the scholar, retained enough of his mercantile experience to know that a master's eye makes a ready servant. Accordingly, with his tunic ungirdled on his portly stomach, his easy slippers on his feet, a small wand in his hand, wherewith he now directed the gaze, and now corrected the back, of some duller menial, he went from chamber to chamber of his costly villa.

He did not disdain even a visit to that sacred apartment in which the priests of the festival prepare their offerings. On entering the kitchen, his ears were agreeably stunned by the noise of dishes and pans, of oaths and commands. Small as this indispensable chamber seems to have been in all the houses of Pompeii, it was, nevertheless, usually fitted up with all that amazing variety of stoves and shapes, stewpans and saucepans, cutters and moulds, without which a cook of spirit, no matter whether he be an ancient or a modern, declares it utterly impossible that he can give you anything to eat.

Our story returns to Apæcides. On awaking that day from the broken and feverish sleep which had followed his adoption of a faith so strikingly and sternly at variance with that in which his youth had been nurtured, the young priest could scarcely imagine that he was not yet in a dream; he had crossed the fatal river —the past was henceforth to have no sympathy with the future; the two worlds were distinct and separate,—that which had been, from that which was to be. Slowly he became sensible of the hatred and the horror he should provoke amongst the pious, even if successful; if frustrated in his daring attempt, what penalties might he not incur for an offence hitherto unheard of—for which no specific law, derived from experience, was prepared; and which, for that very reason, precedents, dragged from the sharpest armoury of obsolete and inapplicable legislation, would probably be distorted to meet! His friends,—the sister of his youth,—could he expect justice, though he might receive compassion, from them? This brave and heroic act would by their heathen eyes be regarded, perhaps, as a heinous apostasy,— at the best as a pitiable madness.

The conflict was sharp and keen; but his new feelings triumphed over his old: and a mighty argument in favour of wrestling with the sanctities of old opinions and hereditary forms might be found in the conquest over both, achieved by that humble priest. Had the early Christians been more controlled by 'the solemn plausibilities of custom'—less of democrats in the pure and lofty acceptation of that perverted word,—Christianity would have perished in its cradle!

As each priest in succession slept several nights together in the chambers of the temple, the term imposed on Apæcides was not yet completed; and when he had risen from his couch, attired himself, as usual, in his robes, and left his narrow chamber, he found himself before the altars of the temple.

In the exhaustion of his late emotions he had slept far into the morning, and the vertical sun already poured its fervid beams over the sacred place.

'*Salve*, Apæcides!' said a voice, whose natural asperity was smoothed by long artifice into an almost displeasing softness of tone. 'Thou art late abroad; has the goddess revealed herself to thee in visions?'

'Could she reveal her true self to the people, Calenus, how incenseless would be these altars!'

'That,' replied Calenus, 'may possibly be true; but the deity is wise enough to hold commune with none but priests.'

'A time may come when she will be unveiled without her own acquiescence.'

'It is not likely: she has triumphed for countless ages. And that which has so long stood the test of time rarely succumbs to the lust of novelty. But hark ye, young brother! these sayings are indiscreet.'

'It is not for thee to silence them,' replied Apæcides, haughtily.

'So hot!—yet I will not quarrel with thee. Why, my Apæcides, has not the Egyptian convinced thee of the necessity of our dwelling together in unity? Has he not convinced thee of the wisdom of deluding the people and enjoying ourselves? If not, oh, brother! he is not that great magician he is esteemed.'

'Thou, then, hast shared his lessons?' said Apæcides, with a hollow smile.

'Ay! but I stood less in need of them than thou. Nature had already gifted me with the love of pleasure, and the desire of gain and power. Long is the way that leads the voluptuary to the severities of life; but it is only one step from pleasant sin to sheltering hypocrisy. Beware the vengeance of the goddess, if the shortness of that step be discursed!'

'Beware, thou, the hour when the tomb shall be rent and the rottenness exposed,' returned Apæcides, solemnly. '*Vale!*'

With these words he left the flamen to his meditations. When he got a few paces from the temple, he turned to look back. Calenus had already disappeared in the entry room of the priests, for it now approached the hour of that repast which, called *prandium* by the ancients, answers in point of date to the breakfast of the moderns. The white and graceful fane gleamed brightly in the sun. Upon the altars before it rose the incense and bloomed the garlands. The priest gazed long and wistfully upon the scene—it was the last time that it was ever beheld by him!

He then turned and pursued his way slowly towards the house of Ione; for before possibly the last tie that united them was cut in twain—before the uncertain peril of the next day was incurred, he was anxious to see his last surviving relative, his fondest as his earliest friend.

He arrived at her house, and found her in the garden with Nydia.

'This is kind, Apæcides,' said Ione, joyfully; 'and how eagerly have I wished to see thee!—what thanks do I not owe thee? How churlish hast thou been to answer none of my letters—to abstain from coming hither to receive the expressions of my gratitude! Oh! thou hast assisted to preserve thy sister from dishonour! What, what can she say to thank thee, now thou art come at last?'

'My sweet Ione, thou owest me no gratitude, for thy cause was mine. Let us avoid that subject, let us recur not to that impious man—how hateful to both of us! I may have a speedy opportunity to teach the world the nature of his pretended wisdom and hypocritical severity. But let us sit down, my sister; I am wearied with the heat of the sun; let us sit in yonder shade, and, for a little while longer, be to each other what we have been.'

Beneath a wide plane-tree, with the cistus and the arbutus clustering round them, the living fountain before them, the greensward beneath their feet; the gay cicada, once so dear to Athens, rising merrily ever and anon amidst the grass; the butterfly, beautiful emblem of the soul, dedicated to Psyche, and which has continued to furnish illustrations to the Christian bard, rich in the glowing colours caught from Sicilian skies, hovering about the sunny flowers, itself like a winged flower—in this spot, and this scene, the brother and the sister sat together for the last time on earth.

'Ione, my sister,' said the young convert, 'place your hand upon my brow; let me feel your cool touch. Speak to me, too, for your gentle voice is like a breeze that hath freshness as well as music. Speak to me, but *forbear to bless me!* Utter not one word of those forms of speech which our childhood was taught to consider sacred!'

'Alas! and what then shall I say? Our language of affection is so woven with that of worship, that the words grow chilled and trite if I banish from them allusion to our gods.'

'*Our gods!*' murmured Apæcides, with a shudder: 'thou slightest my request already.'

'Shall I speak then to thee only of Isis?'

'The Evil Spirit! No, rather be dumb for ever, unless at least thou canst—but away, away this talk! Not now will we dispute and cavil; not now will we judge harshly of each other. Thou, regarding me as an apostate! and I all sorrow and shame for thee as an idolater. No, my sister, let us avoid such topics and such thoughts. In thy sweet presence a calm falls over my spirit. For a little while I forget.'

'I will talk to thee then of our early years,' said Ione. 'Shall yon blind girl sing to thee of the days of childhood? Her voice is sweet and musical, and she hath a song on that theme which contains none of those allusions it pains thee to hear.'

'Dost thou remember the words, my sister?' asked Apæcides.

'Methinks yes; for the tune, which is simple, fixed them on my memory.'

'Sing to me then thyself. My ear is not in unison with unfamiliar voices; and thine,

CITY GATES   WALL AND TOWER

DOMESTIC ALTAR

'Ione, full of household associations, has ever been to me more sweet than all the hireling melodies of Lycia or of Crete. Sing to me!'

Ione beckoned to a slave that stood in the portico, and sending for her lute, sang, when it arrived, to a tender and simple air.

Apæcides, yielding to the influence of the silver voice that reminded him of the past, and told but of half the sorrow born to the present, forgot his more immediate and fiery sources of anxious thought. He spent hours in making Ione alternately sing to, and converse with, him; and when he rose to leave her, it was with a calmed and lulled mind.

'Ione,' said he, as he pressed her hand, 'should you hear my name blackened and maligned, will you credit the aspersion?'

'Never, my brother, never!'

'Dost thou not imagine, according to thy belief, that the evil-doer is punished hereafter, and the good rewarded?'

'Can you doubt it?'

'Dost thou think, then, that he who is truly good should sacrifice every selfish interest in his zeal for virtue?'

'He who doth so is the equal of the gods.'

'And thou believest that, according to the purity and courage with which he thus acts, shall be his portion of bliss beyond the grave?'

'So we are taught to hope.'

'Kiss me, my sister. One question more.— Thou art to be wedded to Glaucus: perchance that marriage may separate us more hopelessly—but not of this speak I now;—thou art to be married to Glaucus—dost thou love him? Nay, my sister, answer me by words.'

'Yes!' murmured Ione, blushing.

'Dost thou feel that, for his sake, thou couldst renounce pride, brave dishonour, and incur death? I have heard that when women really love, it is to that excess.'

'My brother, all this could I do for Glaucus, and feel that it were not a sacrifice. There is no sacrifice to those who love, in what is borne for the one we love.'

'Enough! shall woman feel thus for man, and man feel less devotion to his God?'

He spoke no more. His whole countenance seemed instinct and inspired with a divine life: his chest swelled proudly; his eyes glowed: on his forehead was writ the majesty of a man who can dare to be noble! He turned to meet the eyes of Ione—earnest, wistful, fearful;—he kissed her fondly, strained her warmly to his breast, and in a moment more he had left the house.

Long did Ione remain in the same place, mute and thoughtful. The maidens again and again came to warn her of the deepening noon, and her engagement to Diomed's banquet. At length she woke from her reverie, and prepared, not with the pride of beauty, but listless and melancholy, for the festival: one thought alone reconciled her to the promised visit—she should meet Glaucus— she could confide to him her alarm and uneasiness for her brother.

A FASHIONABLE PARTY

Meanwhile Sallust and Glaucus were slowly strolling towards the house of Diomed. Despite the habits of his life, Sallust was not devoid of many estimable qualities. He would have been an active friend, a useful citizen— in short, an excellent man, if he had not taken it into his head to be a philosopher. Brought up in the schools in which Roman plagiarism worshipped the echo of Grecian wisdom, he had imbued himself with those doctrines by which the later Epicureans corrupted the simple maxims of their great master. He gave himself altogether up to pleasure, and imagined there was no sage like a boon companion. Still, however, he had a considerable degree of learning, wit, and good nature; and the hearty frankness of his very vices seemed like virtue itself beside the utter corruption of Clodius and the prostrate effeminacy of Lepidus; and therefore Glaucus liked him the best of his companions; and he, in turn, appreciating the nobler qualities of the Athenian, loved him almost as much as a cold muræna, or a bowl of the best Falernian.

'This is a vulgar old fellow, this Diomed,' said Sallust: 'but he has some good qualities —in his cellar!'

'And some charming ones—in his daughter.'

'True, Glaucus: but you are not much moved by them, methinks. I fancy Clodius is desirous to be your successor.'

'He is welcome.—At the banquet of Julia's beauty, no guest, be sure, is considered a musca.'

'You are severe: but she has, indeed, something of the Corinthian about her—they will be well matched, after all! What good-natured fellows we are to associate with that gambling good-for-nought.'

Diomed's villa is one of the most considerable in point of size at Pompeii.

The merchant affected greatly the man of letters, and, therefore, he also affected a passion for everything Greek; he paid particular attention to Glaucus.

'You will see, my friend,' said he, with a wave of his hand, 'that I am a little classical here. The hall in which we shall sup is borrowed from the Greeks. Noble Sallust, they have not, I am told, this sort of apartment in Rome.'

'Oh!' replied Sallust, with a half smile; 'you Pompeians combine all that is most eligible in Greece and in Rome.'

'You shall see—you shall see, my Sallust,' replied the merchant. 'We have a taste at Pompeii, and we have also money.'

'They are two excellent things,' replied Sallust. 'But, behold, the lady Julia!'

Magnificently robed in white, interwoven with pearls and threads of gold, the handsome Julia entered the apartment.

Scarcely had she received the salutation of the two guests, ere Pansa and his wife, Lepidus, Clodius, and the Roman senator, entered almost simultaneously; then came the widow Fulvia; then the poet Fulvius, like to the widow in name if in nothing else; the warrior from Herculaneum, accompanied by his umbra, next stalked in; afterwards, the less eminent of the guests. Ione yet tarried.

It was the mode among the courteous ancients to flatter whenever it was in their power: accordingly it was a sign of ill-breeding to seat themselves immediately on entering the house of their host. After performing the salutation, which was usually accomplished by the same cordial shake of the right hand which we ourselves retain, and sometimes, by the yet more familiar embrace, they spent several minutes in surveying the apartment, and admiring the bronzes, the pictures, or the furniture, with which it was adorned.

'A beautiful statue this of Bacchus!' said the Roman senator.

'A mere trifle!' replied Diomed.

'What charming paintings!' said Fulvia.

'Mere trifles!' answered the owner.

'Exquisite candelabra!' cried the warrior.

'Exquisite!' echoed his umbra.

'Trifles! trifles!' reiterated the merchant.

Meanwhile, Glaucus found himself by one of the windows of the gallery, which communicated with the terraces, and the fair Julia by his side.

'Is it an Athenian virtue, Glaucus,' said the merchant's daughter, 'to shun those whom we once sought?'

'Fair Julia—no!'

'Yet methinks, it is one of the qualities of Glaucus.'

'Glaucus never shuns a *friend!*' replied the Greek, with some emphasis on the last word.

'May Julia rank among the number of his friends?'

'It would be an honour to the emperor to find a friend in one so lovely.'

'You evade my question,' returned the enamoured Julia. 'But tell me, is it true that you admire the Neapolitan Ione?'

'Does not beauty constrain our admiration?'

'Ah! subtle Greek, still do you fly the meaning of my words. But say, shall Julia be indeed your friend?'

'If she will so favour me, blessed be the gods! The day in which I am thus honoured shall be ever marked in white.'

'Yet, even while you speak, your eye is resting—your colour comes and goes—you move away involuntarily—you are impatient to join Ione!'

For at that moment Ione had entered, and Glaucus had indeed betrayed the emotion noticed by the jealous beauty.

'Can admiration to one woman make me unworthy the friendship of another? Sanction not so, O Julia, the libels of the poets on your sex!'

'Well, you are right—or I will learn to think so. Glaucus, yet one moment! You are to wed Ione; is it not so?'

'If the Fates permit, such is my blessed hope.'

'Accept, then, from me, in token of our new friendship, a present for your bride. Nay, it is the custom of friends, you know, always to present to bride and bridegroom some such little marks of their esteem and favouring wishes.'

'Julia! I cannot refuse any token of friendship from one like you. I will accept the gift as an omen from Fortune herself.'

'Then, after the feast, when the guests retire, you will descend with me to my apartment, and receive it from my hands. Remember!' said Julia, as she joined the wife of Pansa, and left Glaucus to seek Ione.

The widow Fulvia and the spouse of the ædile were engaged in high and grave discussion.

'O Fulvia! I assure you that the last account from Rome declares that the frizzling mode of dressing the hair is growing antiquated; they only now wear it built up in a tower, like Julia's, or arranged as a helmet—the *Galerian* fashion, like mine, you see: it has a fine effect, I think. I assure you, Vespius (Vespius was the name of the Herculaneum hero) admires it greatly.'

'And nobody wears the hair like yon Neapolitan, in the Greek way.'

'What, parted in front, with the knot behind? Oh, no; how ridiculous it is! it reminds one of the statue of Diana! Yet this Ione is handsome, eh?'

'So the men say; but then she is rich: she is to marry the Athenian—I wish her joy. He will not be long faithful, I suspect; those foreigners are very faithless.'

'Oh, Julia!' said Fulvia, as the merchant's daughter joined them; 'have you seen the tiger yet?'

'No!'

'Why, all the ladies have been to see him. He is so handsome!'

'I hope we shall find some criminal or other for him and the lion,' replied Julia. 'Your husband (turning to Pansa's wife) is not so active as he should be in this matter.'

'Why, really, the laws are too mild,' replied the dame of the helmet. 'There are so few offences to which the punishment of the arena can be awarded; and then, too, the gladiators are growing effeminate! The stoutest bestiarii declare they are willing enough to fight a boar or a bull; but as for a lion or a tiger, they think the game too much in earnest.'

'They are worthy of a mitre,' replied Julia, in disdain.

'Oh! have you seen the new house of Fulvius, the dear poet?' said Pansa's wife.

'No: is it handsome?'

'Very!—such good taste. But they say, my dear, that he has such improper pictures! He won't show them to the women: how ill-bred!'

The signal for the feast was given.

Diomed, who was rather ceremonious, had appointed a nomenclator, or appointer of places, to each guest.

The reader understands that the festive board was composed of three tables; one at the centre, and one at each wing. It was only at the outer side of these tables that the guests reclined; the inner space was left untenanted, for the greater convenience of the waiters or ministri. The extreme corner of one of the wings was appropriated to Julia as the lady of the feast; that next her, to Diomed. At one corner of the centre table was placed the ædile; at the opposite corner,

CUPBOARD

the Roman senator—these were the posts of honour. The other guests were arranged, so that the young (gentleman or lady) should sit next each other, and the more advanced in years be similarly matched. An agreeable provision enough, but one which must often have offended those who wished to be thought still young.

The chair of Ione was next to the couch of Glaucus. The seats were veneered with tortoiseshell, and covered with quilts stuffed with feathers, and ornamented with costly embroideries. The sacred salt-cellar and the familiar Lares were not forgotten. Over the table and the seats a rich canopy was suspended from the ceiling. At each corner of the table were lofty candelabra—for though it was early noon, the room was darkened—while from tripods, placed in different parts of the room, distilled the odour of myrrh and frankincense; and upon the abacus, or sideboard, large vases and various ornaments of silver were ranged, much with the same ostentation (but with more than the same taste) that we find displayed at a modern feast.

The custom of grace was invariably supplied by that of libations to the gods; and Vesta, as queen of the household gods, usually received first that graceful homage.

This ceremony being performed, the slaves showered flowers upon the couches and the floor, and crowned each guest with rosy garlands, intricately woven with ribands, tied by the rind of the linden-tree, and each intermingled with the ivy and the amethyst—supposed preventives against the effect of wine; the wreaths of the women only were exempted from these leaves, for it was not the fashion for them to drink wine *in public*. It was then that the president Diomed thought it advisable to institute a *basileus*, or director of the feast—an important office, sometimes chosen by lot; sometimes, as now, by the master of the entertainment.

Diomed was not a little puzzled as to his election. The invalid senator was too grave and too infirm for the proper fulfilment of his duty; the ædile Pansa was adequate enough to the task: but then, to choose the next in official rank to the senator, was an affront to the senator himself. While deliberating between the merits of the others, he caught the mirthful glance of Sallust, and, by a sudden inspiration, named the jovial epicure to the rank of director, or *arbiter bibendi*.

Sallust received the appointment with becoming humility.

'I shall be a merciful king,' said he, 'to those who drink deep; to a recusant, Minos himself shall be less inexorable. Beware!'

The slaves handed round basins of perfumed water, by which lavation the feast commenced: and now the table groaned under the initiatory course.

The conversation, at first desultory and scattered, allowed Ione and Glaucus to carry on those sweet whispers, which are worth all the eloquence in the world. Julia watched them with flashing eyes.

'How soon shall her place be mine!' thought she.

But Clodius, who sat in the centre table, so as to observe well the countenance of Julia, guessed her pique, and resolved to profit by it. He addressed her across the table in set phrases of gallantry; and as he was of high birth and of a showy person, the vain Julia was not so much in love as to be insensible to his attentions.

The slaves, in the interim, were constantly kept upon the alert by the vigilant Sallust, who chased one cup by another with a celerity which seemed as if he were resolved upon exhausting those capacious cellars which the reader may yet see beneath the house of Diomed. The worthy merchant began to repent his choice, as amphora after amphora was pierced and emptied. The slaves, all under the age of manhood (the youngest being about ten years old,—it was they who filled the wine,—the eldest, some five years older, mingled it with water), seemed to share in the zeal of Sallust; and the face of Diomed began to glow as he watched the provoking complacency with which they seconded the exertions of the king of the feast.

The feast proceeded; the guests grew more talkative and noisy; the dessert or last course was already on the table; and the slaves bore round water with myrrh and hyssop for the finishing lavation. At the same time, a small circular table that had been placed in the space opposite the guests suddenly, and as by magic, seemed to open in the centre, and cast up a fragrant shower, sprinkling the table and the guests; while as it ceased the awning above them was drawn aside, and the guests perceived that a rope had been stretched across the ceiling, and that one of those nimble dancers for which Pompeii was so celebrated was now treading his airy measures right over their heads.

One art now yielded to another; and the musicians struck up a soft and mellow air.

The sun begun now to decline, though the revellers, who had worn away several hours, perceived it not in their darkened chamber; and the senator, who was tired, and the warrior, who had to return to Herculaneum, rising to depart, gave the signal for the general dispersion. 'Tarry yet a moment, my friends,' said Diomed; 'if you will go so soon, you must at least take a share in our concluding game.'

So saying, he motioned to one of the ministri, and whispering him, the slave went out, and presently returned with a small bowl containing various tablets carefully sealed,

and, apparently, exactly similar. Each guest was to purchase one of these at the nominal price of the lowest piece of silver: and the sport of this lottery (which was the favourite diversion of Augustus, who introduced it) consisted in the inequality, and sometimes the incongruity, of the prizes, the nature and amount of which were specified within the tablets. For instance, the poet, with a wry face, drew one of his own poems (no physician ever less willingly swallowed his own draught); the warrior drew a case of bodkins, which gave rise to certain novel witticisms relative to Hercules and the distaff; the widow Fulvia obtained a large drinking-cup; Julia, a gentleman's buckle; and Lepidus, a lady's patch-box. The most appropriate lot was drawn by the gambler Clodius, who reddened with anger on being presented to a set of cogged dice. A certain damp was thrown upon the gaiety which these various lots created by an accident that was considered ominous; Glaucus drew the most valuable of all the prizes, a small marble statue of Fortune, of Grecian workmanship: on handing it to him the slave suffered it to drop, and it broke in pieces.

A shiver went round the assembly, and each voice cried spontaneously on the gods to avert the omen.

Glaucus alone, though perhaps as superstitious as the rest, affected to be unmoved.

'Sweet Neapolitan,' whispered he tenderly to Ione, who had turned pale as the broken marble itself, 'I *accept* the omen. It signifies that in obtaining thee, Fortune can give no more,—she breaks *her* image when she blesses me with *thine*.'

In order to divert the impression which this incident had occasioned, Sallust now crowning his cup with flowers, gave the health of their host. This was followed by a similar compliment to the emperor; and then, with a parting cup to Mercury to send them pleasant slumbers, they concluded the entertainment by a last libation, and broke up the party.

Carriages and litters were little used in Pompeii, partly owing to the extreme narrowness of the streets, partly to the convenient smallness of the city. Most of the guests replacing their sandals, which they had put off in the banquet-room, and induing their cloaks, left the house on foot attended by their slaves.

Meanwhile, having seen Ione depart, Glaucus turning to the staircase which led down to the rooms of Julia, was conducted by a slave to an apartment in which he found the merchant's daughter already seated.

'Glaucus!' said she, looking down, 'I see that you really love Ione—she is indeed beautiful.'

'Julia is charming enough to be generous,'

replied the Greek. 'Yes, I love Ione; amidst all the youth who court you, may you have one worshipper as sincere.'

'I pray the gods to grant it! See, Glaucus, these pearls are the present I destine to your bride: may Juno give her health to wear them!'

So saying, she placed a case in his hand, containing a row of pearls of some size and price. It was so much the custom for persons about to be married to receive these gifts, that Glaucus could have little scruple in accepting the necklace, though the gallant and proud Athenian inly resolved to requite the gift by one of thrice its value. Julia then stopping short his thanks, poured forth some wine into a small bowl.

'You have drunk many toasts with my father,' said she, smiling,—'one now with me. Health and fortune to your bride!'

She touched the cup with her lips and then presented it to Glaucus. The customary etiquette required that Glaucus should drain the whole contents; he accordingly did so. Julia, unknowing the deceit which Nydia had practised upon her, watched him with sparkling eyes; although the witch had told her that the effect *might* not be immediate, she yet sanguinely trusted to an expeditious operation in favour of her charms. She was disappointed when she found Glaucus coldly replace the cup, and converse with her in the same unmoved but gentle tone as before. And though she detained him as long as she decorously could do, no change took place in his manner.

'But to-morrow,' thought she, exultingly recovering her disappointment,—'to-morrow, alas for Glaucus!'

Alas for him, indeed!

DRINKING BOWL

THE STORY HALTS FOR A MOMENT

Restless and anxious, Apæcides consumed the day in wandering through the most sequestered walks in the vicinity of the city. The sun was slowly setting as he paused beside a lonely part of the Sarnus, ere yet it wound amidst the evidences of luxury and power. Only through openings in the woods and vines were caught glimpses of the white and gleaming city, in which was heard in the distance no din, no sound, nor 'busiest hum of men.' Amidst the green banks crept the lizard and the grasshopper, and here and there in the brake some solitary bird burst into sudden song, as suddenly stilled. There was deep calm around, but not the calm of night; the air still breathed of the freshness and life of day; the grass still moved to the stir of the insect horde; and on the opposite bank the graceful and white capella passed browsing through the herbage, and paused at the wave to drink.

As Apæcides stood musingly gazing upon the waters, he heard beside him the low bark of a dog.

'Be still, poor friend,' said a voice at hand; 'the stranger's step harms not thy master.' The convert recognised the voice, and, turning, he beheld the old mysterious man whom he had seen in the congregation of the Nazarenes.

The old man was sitting upon a fragment of stone covered with ancient mosses; beside him were his staff and scrip; at his feet lay a small shaggy dog, the companion in how many a pilgrimage perilous and strange.

The face of the old man was as balm to the excited spirit of the neophyte: he approached, and craving his blessing, sat down beside him.

'Thou art provided as for a journey, father,' said he: 'wilt thou leave us yet?'

'My son,' replied the old man, 'the days in store for me on earth are few and scanty; I employ them as becomes me travelling from place to place, comforting those whom God has gathered together in His name, and proclaiming the glory of His Son, as testified to His servant.'

'Thou hast looked, they tell me, on the face of Christ?'

'And the face revived me from the dead. Know, young proselyte to the true faith, that I am he of whom thou readest in the scroll of the Apostle. In the far Judea, and in the city of Nain, there dwelt a widow, humble of spirit and sad of heart; for of all the ties of life one son alone was spared to her. And she loved him with a melancholy love, for he was

the likeness of the lost. And the son died. The reed on which she leaned was broken, the oil was dried up in the widow's cruse. They bore the dead upon his bier; and near the gate of the city, where the crowd were gathered, there came a silence over the sounds of woe, for the Son of God was passing by. The mother, who followed the bier, wept,—not noisily, but all who looked upon her saw that her heart was crushed. And the Lord pitied her, and he touched the bier, and said, 'I SAY UNTO THEE, ARISE.' And the dead man woke and looked upon the face of the Lord. Oh, that calm and solemn brow, that unutterable smile, that careworn and sorrowful face, lighted up with a God's benignity—it chased away the shadows of the grave! I rose, I spoke, I was living, and in my mother's arms —yes, *I* am the dead revived! The people shouted, the funeral horns rung forth merrily: there was a cry, "God has visited His people!" I heard them not—I felt—I saw—nothing— but the face of the Redeemer!'

'From that night I resigned all earthly thought but that of serving HIM. A preacher and a pilgrim, I have traversed the remotest corners of the earth, proclaiming His Divinity, and bringing new converts to His fold. I come as the wind, and as the wind depart; sowing, as the wind sows, the seeds that enrich the world.

'Son, on earth we shall meet no more. Forget not this hour,—what are the pleasures and the pomps of life? As the lamp shines, so life glitters for an hour; but the soul's light is the star that burns for ever, in the heart of illimitable space.'

With these words the old man pressed Apæcides to his breast, and taking up his staff and scrip, the dog bounded cheerily before him, and with slow steps and downcast eyes he went his way.

The convert stood watching his bended form, till the trees shut the last glimpse from his view; and then, as the stars broke forth, he woke from the musings with a start, reminded of his appointment with Olinthus.

THE PHILTRE

When Glaucus arrived at his own home, he found Nydia seated under the portico of his garden. In fact, she had sought his house in the mere chance that he *might* return at an early hour: anxious, fearful, anticipative, she resolved upon seizing the earliest opportunity of availing herself of the love-charm, while at the same time she half hoped the opportunity might be deferred.

It was then, in that fearful burning mood, her heart beating, her cheek flushing, that Nydia awaited the possibility of Glaucus's return before the night. He crossed the portico just as the first stars began to rise, and the heaven above had assumed its most purple robe.

'Ho, my child, wait you for me?'

'Nay, I have been tending the flowers, and did but linger a little while to rest myself.'

'It has been warm,' said Glaucus, placing himself also on one of the seats beneath the colonnade.

'Very.'

'Wilt thou summon Davus? The wine I have drunk heats me, and I long for some cooling drink.'

Here at once, suddenly and unexpectedly, the very opportunity that Nydia awaited presented itself; of himself, at his own free choice, he afforded to her that occasion. She breathed quick—'I will prepare for you myself,' said she, 'the summer draught that Ione loves—of honey and weak wine cooled in snow.'

'Thanks,' said the unconscious Glaucus. 'If Ione love it, enough; it would be grateful were it poison.'

Nydia frowned, and then smiled; she withdrew for a few moments, and returned with the cup containing the beverage. Glaucus took it from her hand. What would not Nydia have given then for one hour's prerogative of sight, to have watched her hopes ripening to effect:—to have seen the first dawn of the imagined love;—to have worshipped with more than Persian adoration the rising of that sun which her credulous soul believed was to break upon her dreary night! Far different, as she stood then and there, were the thoughts, the emotions of the blind girl, from those of the vain Pompeian under a similar suspense. In the last, what poor and frivolous passions had made up the daring whole! What petty pique, what small revenge, what expectation of a paltry triumph, had swelled the attributes of that sentiment

she dignified with the name of love! but in the wild heart of the Thessalian all was pure, uncontrolled, unmodified passion:—erring, unwomanly, frenzied, but debased by no elements of a more sordid feeling. Filled with love as with life itself, how could she resist the occasion of winning love in return!

She leaned for support against the wall, and her face, before so flushed, was now white as snow, and with her delicate hands clasped convulsively together, her lips apart, her eyes on the ground, she waited the next words Glaucus should utter.

Glaucus had raised the cup to his lips, he had already drained about a fourth of its contents, when his eye suddenly glancing upon the face of Nydia, he was so forcibly struck by its alteration, by its intense, and painful, and strange expression, that he paused abruptly, and still holding the cup near his lips, exclaimed,—

'Why, Nydia! Nydia! I say, art thou ill or in pain? Nay, thy face speaks for thee. What ails my poor child?' As he spoke, he put down the cup, and rose from his seat to approach her, when a sudden pang shot coldly to his heart, and was followed by a wild, confused, dizzy sensation at the brain. The floor seemed to glide from under him—his feet seemed to move on air—a mighty and unearthly gladness rushed upon his spirit—he felt too buoyant for the earth—he longed for wings, nay, it seemed in the buoyancy of his new existence, as *if* he possessed them. He burst involuntarily into a loud and thrilling laugh. He clapped his hands—he bounded aloft—he was as a Pythoness inspired; suddenly as it came this preternatural transport passed, though only partially, away. He now felt his blood rushing loudly and rapidly through his veins; it seemed to swell, to exult, to leap along, as a stream that has burst its bounds, and hurries to the ocean. It throbbed in his ear with a mighty sound, he felt it mount to his brow, he felt the veins in the temples stretch and swell as if they could no longer contain the violent and increasing tide —then a kind of darkness fell over his eyes —darkness, but not entire; for through the dim shade he saw the opposite walls glow out, and the figures painted thereon seemed, ghost-like, to creep and glide. What was most strange, he did not feel himself *ill*—he did not sink or quail beneath the dread frenzy that was gathering over him. The novelty of the feelings seemed bright and vivid—he felt as if a younger health had been infused into his frame. He was gliding on to madness— and he knew it not!

Nydia had not answered his first question —she had not been able to reply—his wild and fearful laugh had roused her from her passionate suspense: she could not see his fierce gesture—she could not mark his reeling

and unsteady step as he paced unconsciously to and fro; but she heard the words, broken, incoherent, insane, that gushed from his lips. She became terrified and appalled—she hastened to him, feeling with her arms until she touched his knees, and then falling on the ground she embraced them, weeping with terror and excitement.

'Oh, speak to me! speak! you do not hate me?—speak, speak!'

'By the bright goddess, a beautiful land this Cyprus! Ho! how they fill us with wine instead of blood! now they open the veins of the Faun yonder, to show how the tide within bubbles and sparkles. Come hither, jolly old god! thou ridest on a goat, eh?—what long silky hair he has! He is worth all the coursers of Parthia. But a word with thee—this wine of thine is too strong for us mortals. Oh! beautiful! the boughs are at rest! the green waves of the forest have caught the Zephyr and drowned him! Not a breath stirs the leaves—and I view the Dreams sleeping with folded wings upon the motionless elm; and I look beyond, and I see a blue stream sparkle in the silent noon; a fountain—a fountain springing aloft! Ah! my fount, thou wilt not put out the rays of my Grecian sun, though thou triest ever so hard with thy nimble and silver arms. And now, what form steals yonder through the boughs? she glides like a moonbeam!—she has a garland of oak-leaves on her head. In her hand is a vase upturned, from which she pours pink and tiny shells, and sparkling water. Oh! look on yon face! Man never before saw its like. See! we are alone; only I and she in the wide forest. There is no smile upon her lips—she moves, grave and sweetly sad. Ha! fly, it is a nymph! —it is one of the wild Napææ! Whoever sees her becomes mad—fly! see, she discovers me!'

'Oh! Glaucus! Glaucus! do you not know me? Rave not so wildly, or thou wilt kill me with a word!'

A new change seemed now to operate upon the jarring and disordered mind of the unfortunate Athenian. He put his hand upon Nydia's silken hair; he smoothed the locks— he looked wistfully upon her face, and then, as in the broken chain of thought one or two links were yet unsevered, it seemed that her countenance brought its associations of Ione; and with that remembrance his madness became yet more powerful, and it swayed and tinged by passion, as he burst forth.

'Glaucus! Glaucus!' murmured Nydia, releasing her hold and falling, beneath the excitement of her dismay, remorse, and anguish, insensible on the floor.

'Who calls?' said he in a loud voice. 'Ione, it is she! they have borne her off—we will save her—where is my stilus? Ha, I have it! I come, Ione, to thy rescue! I come! I come!'

So saying, the Athenian with one bound passed the portico, he traversed the house, and rushed with swift but vacillating steps, and muttering audibly to himself, down the starlit streets. The direful potion burnt like fire in his veins, for its effect was made, perhaps, still more sudden from the wine he had drunk previously. Used to the excesses of nocturnal revellers, the citizens, with smiles and winks, gave way to his reeling steps; they naturally imagined him under the influence of the Bromian god, not vainly worshipped at Pompeii; but they who looked twice upon his face started in a nameless fear, and the smile withered from their lips. He passed the more populous streets; and, pursuing mechanically the way to Ione's house, he traversed a more deserted quarter, and entered now the lonely grove of Cybele, in which Apæcides had held his interview with Olinthus.

A REUNION OF DIFFERENT ACTORS

Impatient to learn whether the fell drug had yet been administered by Julia to his hated rival, and with what effect, Arbaces resolved, as the evening came on, to seek her house, and satisfy his suspense. It was customary, as I have before said, for men at that time to carry abroad with them the tablets and the stilus attached to their girdle; and with the girdle they were put off when at home. In fact, under the appearance of a literary instrument, the Romans carried about with them in that same stilus a very sharp and formidable weapon. It was with his stilus that Cassius stabbed Cæsar in the senate-house. Taking, then, his girdle and his cloak, Arbaces left his house, supporting his steps, which were still somewhat feeble (though hope and vengeance had conspired greatly with his own medical science, which was profound, to restore his natural strength), by his long staff: Arbaces took his way to the villa of Diomed.

Brightly and softly bright, fell the moonbeams over the antique grove consecrated to Cybele—the stately trees, whose date went beyond tradition, cast their long shadows over the soil, while through the openings in their boughs the stars shone, still and frequent. The whiteness of the small sacellum in the centre of the grove, amidst the dark foliage, had in it something abrupt and startling; it recalled at once the purpose to which the wood was consecrated,—its holiness and solemnity.

With a swift and stealthy pace, Calenus, gliding under the shade of the trees, reached the chapel, and gently putting back the boughs that completely closed around its rear, settled himself in his concealment; a concealment so complete, what with the fane in front and the trees behind, that no unsuspicious passenger could possibly have detected him. Again, all was apparently solitary in the grove: afar off you heard faintly the voices of some noisy revellers, or the music that played cheerily to the groups that then, as now in those climates, during the nights of summer, lingered in the streets, and enjoyed, in the fresh air and the liquid moonlight, a milder day.

Presently the tall figure of Arbaces, on his way to the house of Diomed, entered the extreme end of the grove; and at the same instant Apæcides, also bound to his appointment with Olinthus, crossed the Egyptian's path.

'Hem! Apæcides,' said Arbaces, recognising the priest at a glance; 'when last we met, you were my foe. I have wished since then to see you, for I would have you still my pupil and my friend.'

Apæcides started at the voice of the Egyptian; and halting abruptly, gazed upon him with a countenance full of contending, bitter, and scornful emotions.

'Villain and impostor!' said he at length; 'thou hast recovered then from the jaws of the grave! But think not again to weave around me thy guilty meshes.—*Retiarius*, I am armed against thee!'

'Hush!' said Arbaces, in a very low voice—but his pride, which in that descendant of kings was great, betrayed the wound it received from the insulting epithets of the priest in the quiver of his lip and the flush of his tawny brow. 'Hush! more low! thou mayest be overhead, and if other ears than mine had drunk those sounds—why——'

'Dost thou threaten?—what if the whole city had heard me?'

'The manes of my ancestors would not have suffered me to forgive thee. But, hold, and hear me. Thou art enraged that I would have offered violence to thy sister.—Nay, peace, peace, but one instant, I pray thee. Thou art right; it was the frenzy of passion and of jealousy—I have repented bitterly of my madness. Forgive me; I, who never implored pardon of living man, beseech thee now to forgive me. Nay, I will atone the insult—I ask thy sister in marriage;—start not, consider,—what is the alliance of yon holiday Greek compared to mine? Wealth unbounded—birth that in its far antiquity leaves your Greek and Roman names the things of yesterday—science—but that thou knowest! Give me thy sister, and my whole life shall atone a moment's error.'

'Egyptian, were even I to consent, my sister loathes the very air thou breathest: but I have my own wrongs to forgive—I may pardon thee that thou hast made me a tool to thy deceits, but never that thou hast seduced me to become the abettor of thy vices—a polluted and a perjured man. Tremble!—even now I prepare the hour in which thou and thy false gods shall be unveiled. Thy lewd and Circean life shall be dragged to day,—thy mumming oracles disclosed—the fane of the idol Isis shall be a byword and a scorn —the name of Arbaces a mark for the hisses of execration! Tremble!'

The flush on the Egyptian's brow was succeeded by a livid paleness. He looked behind, before, around, to feel assured that none were by; and then he fixed his dark and dilating eye on the priest, with such a gaze of wrath and menace, that one, perhaps, less supported than Apæcides by the fervent daring of a divine zeal, could not have faced with unflinching look that lowering aspect. As it was, however, the young convert met it unmoved, and returned it with an eye of proud defiance.

'Apæcides,' said the Egyptian, in a tremulous and inward tone, 'beware! What is it thou wouldst meditate? Speakest thou—reflect, pause before thou repliest—from the hasty influences of wrath, as yet divining no settled purpose, or from some fixed design?'

'I speak from the inspiration of the True God, whose servant I now am,' answered the Christian, boldly; 'and in the knowledge that by His grace human courage has already fixed the date of thy hypocrisy and thy demon's worship; ere thrice the sun has dawned, thou wilt know all! Dark sorcerer, tremble, and farewell!'

All the fierce and lurid passions which he inherited from his nation and his clime, at all times but ill concealed beneath the blandness of craft and the coldness of philosophy, were released in the breast of the Egyptian. Rapidly one thought chased another; he saw before him an obstinate barrier to even a lawful alliance with Ione—the fellow-champion of Glaucus in the struggle which had baffled his designs—the reviler of his name—the threatened desecrator of the goddess he served while he disbelieved—the avowed and approaching revealer of his own impostures and vices.

'Die, then, in thy rashness!' he muttered; 'away, obstacle to my rushing fates!'

And just as the young Christian had turned to depart, Arbaces rasied his hand high over the left shoulder of Apæcides, and plunged his sharp weapon twice into his breast.

Apæcides fell to the ground pierced to the heart,—he fell mute, without even a groan, at the very base of the sacred chapel.

SURGICAL INSTRUMENTS

Arbaces gazed upon him for a moment with the fierce animal joy of conquest over a foe. But presently the full sense of the danger to which he was exposed flashed upon him; he wiped his weapon carefully in the long grass, and with the very garments of his victim; drew his cloak round him, and was about to depart, when he saw, coming up the path, right before him, the figure of a young man, whose steps reeled and vacillated strangely as he advanced: the quiet moonlight streamed full upon his face, which seemed, by the whitening ray, colourless as marble. The Egyptian recognised the face and form of Glaucus. The unfortunate and benighted Greek was chanting a disconnected and mad song, composed from snatches of hymns and sacred odes, all jarringly woven together.

'Ha!' thought the Egyptian, instantaneously divining his state and its terrible cause; 'so, then, the hell-draught works, and destiny hath sent thee hither to crush two of my foes at once!'

Quickly, even ere this thought occurred to him, he had withdrawn on one side of the chapel, and concealed himself amongst the boughs; from that lurking place he watched, as a tiger in his lair, the advance of his second victim. He noted the wandering and restless fire in the bright and beautiful eyes of the Athenian; the convulsions that distorted his statue-like features, and writhed his hueless lip. He saw that the Greek was utterly deprived of reason. Nevertheless, as Glaucus came up to the dead body of Apæcides, from

which the dark red stream flowed slowly over the grass, so strange and ghastly a spectacle could not fail to arrest him, benighted and erring as was his glimmering sense. He paused, placed his hand to his brow, as if to collect himself, and then saying,—

'What ho! Endymion, sleepest thou so soundly? What has the moon said to thee? Thou makest me jealous; it is time to wake,'—he stooped down with the intention of lifting up the body.

Forgetting—feeling not—his own debility, the Egyptian sprung from his hiding-place, and, as the Greek bent, struck him forcibly to the ground, over the very body of the Christian; then, raising his powerful voice to its highest pitch, he shouted,—

'Ho, citizens,—oh! help me!—run hither—hither!—A murder—a murder before your very fane! Help, or the murderer escapes!' As he spoke, he placed his foot on the breast of Glaucus: an idle and superfluous precaution; for the potion operating with the fall, the Greek lay there motionless and insensible, save that now and then his lips gave vent to some vague and raving sounds.

As he there stood awaiting the coming of those his voice still continued to summons, perhaps some remorse, some compunctious visitings—for despite his crimes he was human,—haunted the breast of the Egyptian; the defenceless state of Glaucus—his wandering words—his shattered reason, smote him even more than the death of Apæcides, and he said, half audibly, to himself,—

'Poor clay!—poor human reason; *where is the soul now?* I could spare thee, O my rival—rival never more! But destiny must be obeyed—my safety demands thy sacrifice.' With that, as if to drown compunction, he shouted yet more loudly; and drawing from the girdle of Glaucus the stilus it contained, he steeped it in the blood of the murdered man, and laid it beside the corpse.

And now, fast and breathless, several of the citizens came thronging to the place, some with torches, which the moon rendered unnecessary, but which flared red and tremulously against the darkness of the trees.

'Lift up yon corpse,' said the Egyptian, 'and guard well the murderer.'

They raised the body, and great was their horror and sacred indignation to discover in that lifeless clay a priest of the adored and venerable Isis; but still greater, perhaps, was their surprise, when they found the accused in the brilliant and admired Athenian.

'Glaucus!' cried the bystanders, with one accord; 'is it even credible?'

'I would sooner,' whispered one man to his neighbour, 'believe it to be the Egyptian himself.'

Here a centurion thrust himself into the gathering crowd, with an air of authority.

'How! blood spilt! who the murderer?'

The bystanders pointed to Glaucus.

'He!—by Mars, he has rather the air of being the victim! Who accuses him?'

'I,' said Arbaces, drawing himself up haughtily; and the jewels, which adorned his dress flashing in the eyes of the soldier, instantly convinced that worthy warrior of the witness's respectability.

'Pardon me—your name?' said he.

'Arbaces; it is well known methinks in Pompeii. Passing through the grove, I beheld before me the Greek and the priest in earnest conversation. I was struck by the reeling motions of the first, his violent gestures, and the loudness of his voice; he seemed to me either drunk or mad. Suddenly I saw him raise his stilus—I darted forward—too late to arrest the blow. He had twice stabbed his victim, and was bending over him, when, in my horror and indignation, I struck the murderer to the ground. He fell without a struggle, which makes me yet more suspect that he was not altogether in his senses when the crime was perpetrated; for, recently recovered from a severe illness, my blow was comparatively feeble, and the frame of Glaucus, as you see, is strong and youthful.'

'His eyes are open now—his lips move,' said the soldier. 'Speak, prisoner, what sayest thou to the charge?'

'The charge—ha—ha! Why, it was merrily done; when the old hag set her serpent at me, and Hecate stood by laughing from ear to ear—what could I do? But I am ill—I faint—the serpent's fiery tongue hath bitten me. Bear me to bed, and send for your physician; old Æsculapius himself will attend me if you let him know that I am Greek. Oh, mercy—mercy—I burn!—marrow and brain, I burn!'

And, with a thrilling and fierce groan, the Athenian fell back in the arms of the bystanders.

'He raves,' said the officer, compassionately; 'and in his delirium he has struck the priest. Hath any one present seen him to-day?'

'I,' said one of the spectators, 'beheld him in the morning. He passed my shop and accosted me. He seemed well and sane as the stoutest of us!'

'And I saw him half an hour ago,' said another, 'passing up the streets, muttering to himself with strange gestures, and just as the Egyptian has described.'

'A corroboration of the witness! it must be too true. He must at all events to the prætor; a pity, so young and so rich! But the crime is dreadful: a priest of Isis, in his very robes, too, and at the base itself of our most ancient chapel!'

At these words the crowd were reminded more forcibly, than in their excitement and curiosity they had yet been, of the heinousness of the sacrilege. They shuddered in pious horror.

'No wonder the earth has quaked,' said one, 'when it held such a monster!'

'Away with him to prison—away!' cried they all.

And one solitary voice was heard shrilly and joyously above the rest:—

'The beasts will not want a gladiator now,
 "*Ho, ho, for the merry, merry show!*"'

'True—true—it chances in season for the games!' cried several; and at that thought all pity for the accused seemed vanished. His youth, his beauty, but fitted him better for the purpose of the arena.

'Bring hither some planks—or if at hand, a litter—to bear the dead,' said Arbaces: 'a priest of Isis ought scarcely to be carried to his temple by vulgar hands, like a butchered gladiator.'

At this the bystanders reverently laid the corpse of Apæcides on the ground, with the face upwards; and some of them went in search of some contrivance to bear the body, untouched by the profane.

It was just at that time that the crowd gave way to right and left as a sturdy form forced itself through, and Olinthus the Christian stood immediately confronting the Egyptian. But his eyes, at first, only rested with inexpressible grief and horror on that gory side and upturned face, on which the agony of violent death yet lingered.

'Murdered!' he said. 'Is it thy zeal that has brought thee to this? Have they detected thy noble purpose, and by death prevented their own shame?'

He turned his head abruptly, and his eyes fell full on the solemn features of the Egyptian.

As he looked, you might see in his face, and even the slight shiver of his frame, the repugnance and aversion which the Christian felt for one whom he knew to be so dangerous and so criminal.

'Murder hath been done upon this corpse! Where is the murderer? Stand forth, Egyptian! For, as the Lord liveth, I believe *thou* art the man!'

An anxious and perturbed change might for one moment be detected on the dusky features of Arbaces; but it gave way to the frowning expression of indignation and scorn, as, awed and arrested by the suddenness and vehemence of the charge, the spectators pressed nearer and nearer upon the two more prominent actors.

'I know,' said Arbaces, proudly, 'who is my accuser, and I guess wherefore he thus arraigns me. Men and citizens, know this man for the most bitter of the Nazarenes, if that or Christians be their proper name! What marvel that in his malignity he dares accuse even an Egyptian of the murder of a priest of Egypt!'

'I know him! I know the dog!' shouted several voices. 'It is Olinthus the Christian—or rather the Atheist:—he denies the gods!'

'Peace, brethren,' said Olinthus, with dignity, 'and hear me! This murdered priest of Isis before his death embraced the Christian faith—he revealed to me the dark sins, the sorceries of yon Egyptian—the mummeries and delusions of the fane of Isis. He was about to declare them publicly. *He*, a stranger, unoffending, without enemies! who should shed his blood but one of those who feared his witness? Who might fear that testimony the most?—Arbaces, the Egyptian!'

'You hear him!' said Arbaces; 'you hear him! he blasphemes! Ask him if he believes in Isis!'

'Do I believe in an evil demon?' returned Olinthus, boldly.

A groan and shudder passed through the assembly. Nothing daunted, for prepared at every time for peril, and in the present excitement losing all prudence, the Christian continued,—

'Back, idolaters! this clay is not for your vain and polluting rites—it is to us—to the followers of Christ, that the last offices due to a Christian belong. I claim this dust in the name of the great Creator who has recalled the spirit!'

With so solemn and commanding a voice and aspect the Christian spoke these words, that even the crowd forbore to utter aloud the execration of fear and hatred which in their hearts they conceived.

The centurion pressed forward again.

'In the first place, hast thou, Olinthus, or whatever be thy name, any proof of the charge thou hast made against Arbaces, beyond thy vague suspicions?'

Olinthus remained silent—the Egyptian laughed contemptuously.

'Dost thou claim the body of a priest of Isis as one of the Nazarene or Christian sect?'

'I do.'

THE BAKERS SHOP

The bakery was an important institution and about forty have already been found at Pompeii. They vary in size. the one shown is one of the largest.

A variety of loaves were baked, as were a range of cakes and even dog biscuits.

The flour mills were driven by donkeys or old horses. During Caligula's reign as Emperor, a serious shortage of bread was caused in Rome when he requisitioned all the mill animals for a spectacular in the amphitheatre.

Small mills were worked by freedmen employed by the baker. It was hard, monotonous work.

BAS-RELIEF OF A MILL WITH HORSE

FLOUR MILL
LEFT

GRAIN WAS POURED IN AT TOP OF HOLLOW CYLINDER. IT WAS TURNED AND THE GRAIN CRUSHED BETWEEN IT AND THE INNER CYLINDER FLOUR FELL INTO THE LEAD LINED TROUGH. IT WAS COLLECTED INTO JARS UNTIL REQUIRED.

THE BAKE HOUSE

1 ATRIUM 2 STAIRS TO LIVING ROOMS
3 MILLING ROOM, WITH FOUR DONKEY MILLS 4 OVEN 5 CISTERN & WATER VESSELS 6 KNEADING ROOM
7 BREAD STORAGE 8 DONKEY STABLE
9 MIXING ROOMS 10 SHOPS

KNEADING MACHINE
BELOW

DOUGH WAS PLACED IN HOLLOW LAVA BASIN (ABOUT TWO FOOT IN DIAMETER). THE ARM WITH BLADES WAS THEN TURNED AND THE DOUGH MIXED AGAINST THE ARMS SET IN THE BASIN.

THESE LOAVES WERE FOUND IN AN OVEN IN POMPEII. THEY WERE STAMPED TO SHOW THE BAKER & TYPE OF FLOUR.

THE OVEN

OVEN WAS ENCLOSED IN A SMOKE CHAMBER WITH AN OPENING ABOVE FOR DRAUGHT A FIRE WAS LIT IN THE OVEN AND WHEN 'BAKING' HEAT WAS REACHED THE ASHES WERE RAKED INTO ASH PIT. LOAVES WERE INSERTED & OVEN FRONT CLOSED. WATER JAR TO MOISTEN BREAD IN BAKING.

TWO METHODS OF HARNESSING A TEAM OF FOUR

CARRUS

THE CARRUS WAS PULLED BY TWO OR FOUR HORSES. THE AWNINGS WERE USED FOR VENTILATION. USED FOR LONG JOURNEYS. THE TRAVELLERS WOULD PLAN THEIR JOURNEYS TO STAY WITH FRIENDS IF POSSIBLE SINCE THE WAYSIDE INNS WERE OFTEN DIRTY AND DISORDERLY.

CONSTRUCTION OF A ROMAN ROAD

1. PARALLEL DITCHES CUT TO SUITABLE DEPTH.

2. EARTH BETWEEN DITCHES REMOVED AND STONES SET ON EITHER SIDE.

3. LAYERS OF SAND (& SOMETIMES CHALK), LARGE STONES FIXED WITH CEMENT AND COMPRESSED GRAVEL SAND, EARTH & BRICK MIXED TOGETHER. FINAL SURFACE OF STONES OR PEBBLES WELL RAMMED DOWN.

IF THE LAYERS HAD TO BE REDUCED (THROUGH LACK OF TIME, MONEY OR MATERIALS) A FOUNDATION OF LARGE STONES WAS LAID.

IF THE GROUND WAS MARSHY, WOODEN PILES WOULD BE SUNK AND A TIMBER FRAME WORK USED AS A FOUNDATION

TOWN ROADS HAD STEPPING STONES, AND SOMETIMES CULVERTS WHICH LED OFF WATER TO DRAINS.

TRAVELLING CLOAK

ROAD SYSTEM AT THE HEIGHT OF THE EMPIRE

FARM CART WITH SOLID WHEELS, WITH WICKER BASKET. USUALLY PULLED BY OXEN

TWO MAN LITTER, FROM A ROMAN RELIEF

CHARIOT THIS ONE FOR SPECIAL OCCASIONS, EVERYDAY ONES WOULD BE MORE PLAIN.

WINE CART: WINE HELD IN A SEWN ANIMAL SKIN..AMPHOREA FILLED FROM LEG

TWO WHEELED OPEN CART, WITH WICKER BODY.

HORSE TRAPPINGS FOUND IN POMPEII

MILESTONE: THESE WERE SET UP ALONG ALL THE ROADS IN THE EMPIRE

CCXVI
IMP.C AESARDIV
TRAIANI·PARHIC
DIVI·NERVAE·NT
NVS·HADRIANVS
PONT·MAX·TRIB·
COS·III·VI·AM·IVLI
AVG·A·FLVM·IN·ETIA
BIA·QVAE·VETVSTA
INTERCIDERAT·SL
PECVNIA·RESTID
DCV

GROMA: USED TO LAY-OUT ROADS AND BOUND-ARIES. FOUND IN POMPEII

DURING THE HEIGHT OF THE EMPIRE THERE WERE MORE THAN 87,500 MILES OF WELL MAINTAINED ROADS. TRAVEL WAS COMPARATIVELY SWIFT, BUT AS VEHICLES HAD NO SPRINGS IT WAS RATHER UNCOMFORTABLE.

POLITICAL AND SOCIAL ORGANISATION

The Pompeian administrative system was a miniature of the State one. The Emperor and Senate took little interest in local provincial affairs unless the circumstances were exceptional.

The official qualifications for election to office were being born a free man, no criminal record, and money. If lack of money made it necessary to work, then the work had to be in one of the professions. Freedmen (see Glossary) who had enough money could also stand for office. Tradesmen were considered only if no other candidates were available.

STATUE OF M. HOLCONIUS RUFUS. A LEADING POMPEIAN HE HAD A DISTINGUISHED CAREER BEING: CHIEF MAGISTRATE THREE TIMES, CENSUS MAGISTRATE TWICE, MILITARY TRIBUNE, PRIEST OF AUGUSTUS TWICE, AND PATRON OF THE COLONY

CHIEF MAGISTRATES (DUOVIRI) 2

CONTROLLED PUBLIC FUNDS.
ONE APPOINTED AS CHAIRMAN
WHO HAD AS ASSISTANTS:
2 GUARDS, 2 MESSENGERS, 1 ATTENDANT, 1 LETTER COPIER, 1 SOOTHSAYER, 1 HERALD, 1 PIPE PLAYER, 2 SECRETARIES
EVERY FIVE YEARS TWO SPECIAL MAGISTRATES WERE APPOINTED TO TAKE THE STATE CENSUS

MAGISTRATES (DECURIONS) 80-100

SAT & VOTED AT COUNCIL MEETINGS

AEDILES 2

ELECTED EVERY YEAR. YOUNG MEN AT START OF POLITICAL LIFE HAD GENERAL ADMINISTRATION DUTIES
ASSISTED BY 1 SECRETARY 1 SOOTHSAYER, 4 PUBLIC SLAVES, 1 HERALD 1 PIPE PLAYER

LOWER OFFICIALS: (PART ADMINISTRATIVE, PART RELIGIOUS)

AUGUSTALES
IN CHARGE OF RAISING MONEY FOR THE IMPERIAL CULT
USUALLY FREEDMEN PROBABLY APPOINTED BY THE EMPEROR

PRIESTS, (FOR PUBLIC CEREMONIES)
NUMBER VARIED, ELECTED ANNUALY FROM THE MAGISTRATES
PRIESTESS'
HIGH PRIESTESS OF VENUS & CERES

COMITA
POPULAR ASSEMBLY (ELECTED BY MAGISTRATES)
MADE UP OF CITIZENS ELIGIBLE TO VOTE
VOTED ON RESOLUTIONS MADE BY MAGISTRATES

A SIMPLIFIED VERSION OF THE CITY COUNCIL OF POMPEII

'Swear then by yon fane, yon statue of Cybele, by yon most ancient sacellum in Pompeii, that the dead man embraced your faith!'

'Vain man! I disown your idols! I abhor your temples! How can I swear by Cybele then?'

And as he spoke he strode across to the fane, and ere any of the bystanders were aware of his purpose, he, in his compassion or his zeal, struck the statue of wood from its pedestal.

'See!' cried he, 'your goddess cannot avenge herself. Is this a thing to worship?'

Further words were denied to him: so gross and daring a sacrilege—of one, too, of the most sacred of their places of worship—filled even the most lukewarm with rage and horror. With one accord the crowd rushed upon him, seized, and but for the interference of the centurion, they would have torn him to pieces.

'Peace!' said the soldier, authoritatively,— 'refer we this insolent blasphemer to the proper tribunal—time has been already wasted. Bear we both the culprits to the magistrates; place the body of the priest on the litter—carry it to his own home.'

At this moment a priest of Isis stepped forward. 'I claim these remains, according to the custom of the priesthood.'

'The flamen be obeyed,' said the centurion. 'How is the murderer?'

'Insensible or asleep.'

'Were his crimes less, I could pity him. On!'

Arbaces, as he turned, met the eye of that priest of Isis—it was Calenus; and something there was in that glance, so significant and sinister, that the Egyptian muttered to himself,—

'Could he have witnessed the deed?'

A girl darted from the crowd, and gazed hard on the face of Olinthus. '*By Jupiter, a stout knave! I say, we shall have a man for the tiger now; one for each beast!*'

'Ho!' shouted the mob; 'a man for the lion, and another for the tiger! What luck! Io Pæan!'

LEG IRONS
FOR PUNISHING
GLADIATORS

FRIENDSHIP TESTED – ENMITY SOFTENED

The night was somewhat advanced, and the gay lounging-places of the Pompeians were still crowded. You might observe in the countenances of the various idlers a more earnest expression than usual. They talked in large knots and groups, as if they sought by numbers to divide the half-painful, half-pleasurable anxiety which belonged to the subject on which they conversed: it was a subject of life and death.

A young man passed briskly by the graceful portico of the Temple of Fortune—so briskly, indeed, that he came with no slight force full against the rotund and comely form of that respectable citizen Diomed, who was retiring homeward to his suburban villa.

'Holloa!' groaned the merchant, recovering with some difficulty his equilibrium; 'have you no eyes? or do you think I have no feeling? By Jupiter! you have well nigh driven out the divine particle; such another shock, and my soul will be in Hades!'

'Ah, Diomed! is it you? forgive my inadvertence. I was absorbed in thinking of the reverses of life. Our poor friend, Glaucus, eh! who could have guessed it?'

'Well, but tell me, Clodius, is he really to be tried by the senate?'

'Yes; they say the crime is of so extraordinary a nature that the senate itself must adjudge it; and so the lictors are to induct him formally.'

'He has been accused publicly, then?'

'To be sure; where have you been not to hear that?'

'Why, I have only just returned from Neapolis, whither I went on business the very morning after his crime;—so shocking, and at my house the same night that it happened!'

'There is no doubt of his guilt,' said Clodius, shrugging his shoulders; 'and as these crimes take precedence of all little undignified peccadilloes, they will hasten to finish the sentence previous to the games.'

'The games! Good gods!' replied Diomed, with a slight shudder: 'can they adjudge him to the beasts?—so young, so rich!'

'True; but then he is a Greek. Had he been a Roman, it would have been a thousand pities. These foreigners can be borne with in their prosperity; but in adversity we must not forget that they are in reality slaves. However, we of the upper classes are always tender-hearted; and he would certainly get off tolerably well if he were left to us: for, between ourselves, what is a paltry priest of Isis!—what Isis herself? But the common

people are superstitious; they clamour for the blood of the sacrilegious one. It is dangerous not to give way to public opinion.'

'And the blasphemer—the Christian, or Nazarene, or whatever else he be called?'

'Oh, poor dog! if he will sacrifice to Cybele or Isis, he will be pardoned—if not, the tiger has him. At least, so I suppose; but the trial will decide. We talk while the urn's still empty. And the Greek may yet escape the deadly θ of his own alphabet. But enough of this gloomy subject. How is the fair Julia?'

'Well, I fancy.'

'Commend me to her. But hark! the door yonder creaks on its hinges; it is the house of the prætor. Who comes forth? By Pollux! it is the Egyptian! What can he want with our official friend!'

'Some conference touching the murder, doubtless,' replied Diomed; 'but what was supposed to be the inducement to the crime? Glaucus was to have married the priest's sister.'

'Yes: some say Apæcides refused the alliance. It might have been a sudden quarrel. Glaucus was evidently drunk;—nay, so much so as to have been quite insensible when taken up, and I hear is still delirious—whether with wine, terror, remorse, the Furies, or the Bacchanals, I cannot say.'

'Poor fellow!—he has good counsel?'

'The best—Caius Pollio, an eloquent fellow enough.'

Leaving the less active Diomed to regain his villa, Clodius strode on, humming a Greek air, and perfuming the night with the odours that steamed from his snowy garments and flowing locks.

'If,' thought he, 'Glaucus feed the lion, Julia will no longer have a person to love better than me; she will certainly doat on me;—and so, I suppose, I must marry. By the gods! the twelve lines begin to fail—men look suspiciously at my hand when it rattles the dice. That infernal Sallust insinuates cheating; and if it be discovered that the ivory is clogged, why farewell to the merry supper and the perfumed billet;—Clodius is undone! Better marry, then, while I may, renounce gaming, and push my fortune (or rather the gentle Julia's) at the imperial court.'

Thus muttering the schemes of his ambition, if by that high name the projects of Clodius may be called, the gamester found himself suddenly accosted; he turned and beheld the dark brow of Arbaces.

'Hail, noble Clodius! pardon my interruption; and inform me, I pray you, which is the house of Sallust?'

'It is but a few yards hence, wise Arbaces. But does Sallust entertain to-night?'

'I know not,' answered the Egyptian; 'nor am I, perhaps, one of those whom he would seek as a boon companion. But thou knowest that his house holds the person of Glaucus, the murderer.'

'Ay! he, good-hearted epicure, believes in the Greek's innocence! You remind me that he has become his surety; and, therefore, till the trial, is responsible for his appearance. Well, Sallust's house is better than a prison, especially that wretched hole in the forum. But for what can *you* seek Glaucus?'

'Why, noble Clodius, if we could save him from execution it would be well. The condemnation of the rich is a blow upon society itself. I should like to confer with him—for I hear he has recovered his senses—and ascertain the motives of his crime; they may be so extenuating as to plead in his defence.'

'You are benevolent, Arbaces.'

'Benevolence is the duty of one who aspires to wisdom,' replied the Egyptian, modestly. 'Which way lies Sallust's mansion?'

'I will show you,' said Clodius, 'if you will suffer me to accompany you a few steps. But, pray what has become of the poor girl who was to have been wed the Athenian—the sister of the murdered priest?'

'Alas! well-nigh insane! Sometimes she utters imprecations on the murderer—then suddenly stops short—then cries, "But *why* curse? Oh, my brother! Glaucus was *not* thy murderer—never will I believe it!" Then she begins again, and again stops short, and mutters awfully to herself, "Yet if it were indeed he?"'

'Unfortunate Ione!'

'But it is well for her that those solemn cares to the dead which religion enjoins have hitherto greatly absorbed her attention from Glaucus and herself: and, in the dimness of her senses, she scarcely seems aware that Glaucus is apprehended and on the eve of trial. When the funeral rites due to Apæcides are performed, her apprehension will return; and then I fear me much that her friends will be revolted by seeing her run to succour and aid the murderer of her brother!'

'Such scandal should be prevented.'

'I trust I *have* taken precautions to that effect. I am her lawful guardian, and have just succeeded in obtaining permission to escort her, after the funeral of Apæcides, to my own house; there, please the gods! she will be secure.'

'You have done well, sage Arbaces. And, now, yonder is the house of Sallust. The gods keep you! Yet, hark you, Arbaces—why so gloomy and unsocial? Men say you *can* be gay—why not let me initiate you into the pleasures of Pompeii?—I flatter myself no one knows them better.'

'I thank you, noble Clodius: under your auspices I might venture, I think, to wear the philyra: but, at my age, I should be an awkward pupil.'

'Oh, never fear; I have made converts of

fellows of seventy. The rich, too, are never old.'

'You flatter me. At some future time I will remind you of your promise.'

'You may command Marcus Clodius at all times:—and so, *vale!*'

'Now,' said the Egyptian, soliloquising, 'I am not wantonly a man of blood; I would willingly save this Greek, if, by confessing the crime, he will lose himself for ever to Ione, and for ever free me from the chance of discovery; and I *can* save him by persuading Julia to own the philtre, which will be held

DOOR HINGE

his excuse. But if he do not confess the crime' why Julia must be shamed from the confession, and he must die!—die, lest he prove my rival with the living—die, that he may be my proxy with the dead! Will he confess?—can he not be persuaded that in his delirium he struck the blow? To me it would give far greater safety than even his death. Hem! we must hazard the experiment.'

Sweeping along the narrow street, Arbaces now approached the house of Sallust, when he beheld a dark form wrapped in a cloak, and stretched at length across the threshold of the door.

So still lay the figure, and so dim was its outline, that any other than Arbaces might have felt a superstitious fear, lest he beheld one of those grim *lemures*, who, above all other spots, haunted the threshold of the homes they formerly possessed. But not for Arbaces were such dreams.

'Rise!' said he, touching the figure with his foot; 'thou obstructest the way!'

'Ha! who art thou?' cried the form, in a sharp tone; and as she raised herself from the ground, the starlight fell full on the pale face and fixed but sightless eyes of Nydia the Thessalian. 'Who art thou? I know the burden of thy voice.'

'Blind girl! what dost thou here at this late hour? Fie!—is this seeming thy sex or years? Home, girl!'

'I know thee,' said Nydia, in a low voice, 'thou art Arbaces the Egyptian:' then, as if inspired by some sudden impulse, she flung herself at his feet, and clasping his knees, exclaimed, in a wild and passionate tone, 'Oh dread and potent man! save him—save him! He is not guilty—it is I! He lies within, ill—dying, and I—I am the hateful cause! And they will not admit me to him—they spurn the blind girl from the hall. Oh, heal him! thou knowest some herb—some spell—some counter-charm, for it is a potion that hath wrought this frenzy!'

'Hush, child! I know all—thou forgettest that I accompanied Julia to the saga's home. Doubtless her hand administered the draught; but her reputation demands thy silence. Reproach not thyself—what must be, must: meanwhile, I seek the criminal—he may yet be saved. Away!'

Thus saying, Arbaces extricated himself from the clasp of the despairing Thessalian, and knocked loudly at the door.

In a few moments the heavy bars were heard suddenly to yield, and the porter, half opening the door, demanded who was there.

'Arbaces—important business to Sallust relative to Glaucus. I come from the prætor.'

The porter, half yawning, half groaning, admitted the tall form of the Egyptian. Nydia sprang forward. 'How is he?' she cried; 'tell me—tell me!'

'Ho, mad girl! is it thou still?—for shame! Why, they say he is sensible.'

'The gods be praised!—and you will not admit me? Ah! I beseech thee——'

'Admit thee!—no. A pretty salute I should prepare for these shoulders were I to admit such things as thou! Go home!'

The door closed, and Nydia, with a deep sigh, laid herself down once more on the cold stones; and, wrapping her cloak round her face, resumed her weary vigil.

Meanwhile Arbaces had already gained the triclinium, where Sallust, with his favourite freedman, sat late at supper.

GLASS CUP

'What! Arbaces! and at this hour!—Accept this cup.'

'Nay, gentle Sallust; it is on business, not pleasure, that I venture to disturb thee. How doth thy charge?—they say in the town that he has recovered sense.'

'Alas! and truly,' replied the good-natured but thoughtless Sallust, wiping the tear from his eyes; 'but so shattered are his nerves and frame that I scarcely recognise the brilliant and gay carouser I was wont to know. Yet, strange to say, he cannot account for the cause of the sudden frenzy that seized him—he retains but a dim consciousness of what hath passed; and, despite thy witness, wise Egyptian, solemnly upholds his innocence of the death of Apæcides.'

'Night wanes,' said the Egyptian; 'suffer me to see thy ward now.'

Sallust nodded assent, and led the way to a small chamber, guarded without by two dozing slaves. The door opened; at the request of Arbaces, Sallust withdrew—the Egyptian was alone with Glaucus.

The Egyptian seated himself quietly beside the bed; Glaucus still lay mute and unconscious of his presence. At length, after a considerable pause, Arbaces thus spoke:—

'Glaucus, we have been enemies. I come to thee alone and in the dead of night—thy friend, perhaps thy saviour.'

As the steed starts from the path of the tiger, Glaucus sprang up breathless—alarmed, panting at the abrupt voice, the sudden apparition of his foe. Their eyes met, and neither, for some moments, had power to withdraw his gaze. The flush went and came over the face of the Athenian, and the bronzed cheek of the Egyptian grew a shade more pale. At length, with an inward groan, Glaucus turned away, drew his hand across his brow, sunk back, and muttered,—

'Am I still dreaming?'

'No, Glaucus, thou art awake. By this right hand and my father's head, thou seest one who may save thy life. Hark! I know what thou hast done, but I know also its excuse, of which thou thyself art ignorant. Thou hast committed murder, it is true—a sacrilegious murder: frown not—start not—these eyes saw it. But I can save thee—I can prove how thou wert bereaved of sense, and made not a free thinking and free-acting man. But in order to save thee, thou must confess thy crime. Sign but this paper, acknowledging thy hand in the death of Apæcides, and thou shalt avoid the fatal urn.'

'What words are these?—Murder and Apæcides!—Did I not see him stretched on the ground bleeding and a corpse? and wouldst thou persuade me that *I* did the deed? Man, thou liest! Away!'

'Be not rash—Glaucus, be not hasty; the deed is proved. Come, come, thou mayst well be excused for not recalling the act of thy delirium, and which thy sober senses would have shunned even to contemplate. But let me try to refresh thy exhausted and weary memory. Thou knowest thou wert walking with the priest, disputing about his sister; thou knowest he was intolerant, and half a Nazarene, and he sought to convert thee, and ye had hot words; and he calumniated thy mode of life, and swore he would not marry Ione to thee—and then, in thy wrath and thy frenzy, thou didst strike the sudden blow. Come, come; you can recollect this!—read this papyrus, it runs to that effect—sign it, and thou art saved.'

'Barbarian, give me the written lie, that I may tear it! *I* the murderer of Ione's brother: *I* confess to have injured one hair of the head of him she loved! Let me rather perish a thousand times!'

'Beware!' said Arbaces, in a low and hissing tone: 'there is but one choice—thy confession and thy signature, or the amphitheatre and the lion's maw!'

As the Egyptian fixed his eyes upon the sufferer, he hailed with joy the signs of evident emotion that seized the latter at these words. A slight shudder passed over the Athenian's frame—his lip fell—an expression of sudden fear and wonder betrayed itself in his brow and eye.

'Great gods!' he said, in a low voice, 'what reverse is this? It seems but a little day since life laughed out from amidst roses—Ione mine—youth, health, love lavishing on me their treasures; and now—pain, madness, shame, death! And for what? What have I done? Oh, I am mad still?'

'Sign, and be saved!' said the soft, sweet voice of the Egyptian.

'Tempter, never!' cried Glaucus, in the reaction of rage. 'Thou knowest me not: thou knowest not the haughty soul of an Athenian! Go! leave me to live without self-reproach—or to perish without fear!'

'Bethink thee well! the lion's fangs: the hoots of the brutal mob: the vulgar gaze on thy dying agony and mutilated limbs: thy name degraded; thy corpse unburied; the shame thou wouldst avoid clinging to thee for aye and ever!'

'Thou ravest! *thou* art the madman! shame is not in the loss of other men's esteem,—it is in the loss of our own. Wilt thou go?—my eyes loathe the sight of thee! hating ever, I despise thee now!'

'I go,' said Arbaces, stung and exasperated, but not without some pitying admiration of his victim,—'I go; we meet twice again—once at the Trial, once at the Death! Farewell!'

The Egyptian rose slowly, gathered his robes about him, and left the chamber. He sought Sallust for a moment, whose eyes began to reel with the vigils of the cup: 'He is still, unconscious, or still obstinate; there is no hope for him.'

'Say not so,' replied Sallust, who felt but little resentment against the Athenian's accuser, for he possessed no great austerity of virtue, and was rather moved by his friend's reverses than persuaded of his innocence.

'We shall see,' said the Egyptian.

Suddenly the bolts were again withdrawn—the door unclosed; Arbaces was in the open street; and poor Nydia once more started from her long watch.

'Wilt thou save him?' she cried, clasping her hands.

'Child, follow me home; I would speak to thee—it is for his sake I ask it.'

'And thou wilt save him?'

No answer came forth to the thirsting ear of the blind girl: Arbaces had already proceeded far up the street; she hesitated a moment, and then followed his steps in silence.

'I must secure this girl,' said he, musingly, 'lest she give evidence of the philtre; as to the vain Julia, she will not betray herself.'

A CLASSIC FUNERAL

While Arbaces had been thus employed, Sorrow and Death were in the house of Ione. It was the night preceding the morn in which the solemn funeral rites were to be decreed to the remains of the murdered Apæcides. The corpse had been removed from the temple of Isis to the house of the nearest surviving relative, and Ione had heard, in the same breath, the death of her brother and the accusation against her betrothed. That first violent anguish which blunts the sense to all but itself, and the forbearing silence of her slaves, had prevented her learning minutely the circumstances attendant on the fate of her lover. His illness, his frenzy, and his approaching trial, were unknown to her. She learned only the accusation against him, and at once indignantly rejected it; nay, on hearing that Arbaces was the accuser, she required no more to induce her firmly and solemnly to believe that the Egyptian himself was the criminal.

The stars were fading one by one from the grey heavens, and night slowly receding before the approach of morn, when a dark group stood motionless before Ione's door. High and slender torches, made paler by the unmellowed dawn, cast their light over various countenances, hushed for the moment in one solemn and intent expression. And now there arose a slow and dismal music, which accorded sadly with the rite, and floated far along the desolate and breathless streets.

As the hymn died away, the group parted in twain; and placed upon a couch, spread with a purple pall, the corpse of Apæcides was carried forth, with the feet foremost. The designator, or marshal of the sombre ceremonial, accompanied by his torch-bearers, clad in black, gave the signal, and the procession moved dreadly on.

First went the musicians, playing a slow march—the solemnity of the lower instruments broken by many a louder and wilder burst of the funeral trumpet: next followed the hired mourners, chanting their dirges to the dead; and the female voices were mingled with those of boys, whose tender years made still more striking the contrast of life and death—the fresh leaf and the withered one. But the players, the buffoons, the archimimus (whose duty it was to personate the dead)—these, the customary attendants at ordinary funerals, were banished from a funeral attended with so many terrible associations.

The priests of Isis came next in their snowy garments, barefooted, and supporting sheaves of corn; while before the corpse were carried the images of the deceased and his many Athenian forefathers. And behind the bier followed, amidst her women, the sole surviving relative of the dead—her head bare, her locks dishevelled, her face paler than marble, but composed and still, save ever and anon, as some tender thought—awakened by the music, flashed upon the dark lethargy of woe, she covered that countenance with her hands, and sobbed unseen; for hers were not the noisy sorrow, the shrill lament, the ungoverned gesture, which characterised those who honoured less faithfully. In that age, as in all, the channel of deep grief flowed hushed and still.

And so the procession swept on, till it had traversed the streets, passed the city gate, and gained the Place of Tombs without the wall, which the traveller yet beholds.

Raised in the form of an altar—of unpolished pine, amidst whose interstices were placed preparations of combustible matter—stood the funeral pyre; and around it drooped the dark and gloomy cypresses so consecrated by song to the tomb.

As soon as the bier was placed upon the pile, the attendants parting on either side, Ione passed up to the couch, and stood before the unconscious clay for some moments motionless and silent. The features of the dead had been composed from the first agonised expression of violent death. The sister gazed, and not a sound was heard

CROSS SECTION OF URN

CROSS SECTION OF TOMB WITH URNS IN NICHES

amidst the crowd; there was something terrible, yet softening, also, in the silence; and when it broke, it broke sudden and abrupt—it broke, with a loud and passionate cry—the vent of long-smothered despair.

'My brother! my brother!' cried the poor orphan, falling upon the couch; 'thou whom the worm on thy path feared not—what enemy couldst thou provoke? Oh, is it in truth come to this? Awake! awake! We grew together! Are we thus torn asunder? Thou art not dead—thou sleepest. Awake! awake!'

The sound of her piercing voice aroused the sympathy of the mourners, and they broke into loud and rude lament. This

CYMBALS

PIPE

FLUTES

startled, this recalled Ione; she looked up hastily and confusedly, as if for the first time sensible of the presence of those around.

'*Ah!*' she murmured with a shiver, '*we are not then alone!*'

With that, after a brief pause, she rose; and her pale and beautiful countenance was again composed and rigid. With fond and trembling hands, she unclosed the lids of the deceased; but when the dull glazed eye, no longer beaming with love and life, met hers, she shrieked aloud, as if she had seen a spectre. Once more recovering herself she kissed again and again the lids, the lips, the brow; and with mechanic and unconscious hand, received from the high priest of her brother's temple the funeral torch.

The sudden burst of music, the sudden song of the mourners announced the birth of the sanctifying flame.

And now high and far into the dawning skies broke the fragrant fire, it flushed luminously across the gloomy cypresses—it shot above the massive walls of the neighbouring city; and the early fisherman started to behold the blaze reddening on the waves of the creeping sea.

But Ione sat down apart and alone, and, leaning her face upon her hands, saw not the flame, nor heard the lamentation of the music: she felt only one sense of loneliness,—she had not yet arrived to that hallowing sense of comfort, when we know that we are *not* alone —that the dead are with us!

The breeze rapidly aided the effect of the combustibles placed within the pile. By degrees the flame wavered, lowered, dimmed, and slowly, by fits and unequal starts, died away—emblem of life itself; where, just before, all was restlessness and flame, now lay the dull and smouldering ashes.

The last sparks were extinguished by the attendants—the embers were collected.

Steeped in the rarest wine and the costliest odours, the remains were placed in a silver urn, which was solemnly stored in one of the neighbouring sepulchres beside the road; and they placed within it the vial full of tears, and the small coin which poetry still consecrated to the grim boatman. And the sepulchre was covered with flowers and chaplets, and incense kindled on the altar, and the tomb hung round with many lamps.

But the next day, when the priest returned with fresh offerings to the tomb, he found that to the relics of heathen superstition some unknown hands had added a green palm-branch. He suffered it to remain, unknowing that it was the sepulchral emblem of Christianity.

TOMBSTONE

IVNONI
TICHES·IVLIAE
AVGVSTAE·VENER

FRONT   BACK

AN ADVENTURE HAPPENS TO IONE

While some stayed behind to share with the priests the funeral banquet, Ione and her handmaids took homeward their melancholy way. And now (the last duties to her brother performed) her mind awoke from its absorption, and she thought of her affianced, and the dread charge against him. Not—as we have before said—attaching even a momentary belief to the unnatural accusation, but nursing the darkest suspicion against Arbaces, she felt that justice to her lover and to her murdered relative demanded her to seek the prætor, and communicate her impression, unsupported as it might be. Questioning her maidens, who had hitherto—kindly anxious, as I have said, to save her the additional agony—refrained from informing her of the state of Glaucus, she learned that he had been dangerously ill: that he was in custody, under the roof of Sallust; that the day of his trial was appointed.

'Averting gods,' she exclaimed; 'and have I been so long forgetful of him? Have I seemed to shun him? O! let me hasten to do him justice—to show that I, the nearest relative of the dead, believe him innocent of the charge. Quick! quick! let us fly. Let me soothe—tend—cheer him! and if they will not believe me; if they will not lead to my conviction; if they sentence him to exile or to death, let me share the sentence with him!'

Instinctively she hastened her pace, confused and bewildered, scarce knowing whither she went; now designing first to seek the prætor, and now to rush to the chamber of Glaucus. She hurried on—she passed the gate of the city—she was in the long street leading up the town. The houses were opened, but none were yet astir in the streets; the life of the city was scarce awake—when lo! she came suddenly upon a small knot of men standing beside a covered litter. A tall figure stepped from the midst of them, and Ione shrieked aloud to behold Arbaces.

'Fair Ione!' said he, gently, and appearing not to heed her alarm: 'my ward, my pupil! forgive me if I disturb thy pious sorrows; but the prætor, solicitous of thy honour, and anxious that thou mayest not rashly be implicated in the coming trial; knowing the strange embarrassment of thy state (seeking justice for thy brother, but dreading punishment to thy betrothed)—sympathising, too, with thy unprotected and friendless condition, and deeming it harsh that thou shouldst be suffered to act unguided and mourn alone—hath wisely and paternally confided thee to the care of thy lawful guardian. Behold the writing which intrusts thee to my charge!'

'Dark Egyptian!' cried Ione, drawing herself proudly aside; 'begone! It is thou that hast slain my brother! Is it to thy care, thy hands, yet reeking with his blood, that they will give the sister? Ha! thou turnest pale! thy conscience smites thee! thou tremblest at the thunderbolt of the avenging god! Pass on, and leave me to my woe!'

'Thy sorrows unstring thy reason, Ione,' said Arbaces, attempting in vain his usual calmness of tone. 'I forgive thee. Thou wilt find me now, as ever, thy surest friend. But the public streets are not the fitting place for us to confer—for me to console thee. Approach, slaves! Come, my sweet charge, the litter awaits thee.'

The amazed and terrified attendants gathered round Ione, and clung to her knees.

'Arbaces,' said the eldest of the maidens, 'this is surely not the law! For nine days after the funeral, is it not written that the relatives of the deceased shall not be molested in their homes, or interrupted in their solitary grief?'

'Woman!' returned Arbaces, imperiously waving his hand, 'to place a ward under the roof of her guardian is not against the funeral laws. I tell thee I have the fiat of the prætor. This delay is indecorous. Place her in the litter.'

So saying, he threw his arm firmly round the shrinking form of Ione. She drew back, gazed earnestly in his face, and then burst into hysterical laughter:—

'Ha, ha! this is well—well! Excellent guardian—paternal law! Ha, ha!' And, startled herself at the dread echo of that shrill and maddened laughter, she sunk, as it died away, lifeless upon the ground. . . . A minute more, and Arbaces had lifted her into the litter. The bearers moved swiftly on, and the unfortunate Ione was soon borne from the sight of her weeping handmaids.

WHAT BECOMES OF NYDIA IN THE HOUSE OF ARBACES

It will be remembered that, at the command of Arbaces, Nydia followed the Egyptian to his home, and conversing there with her, he learned from the confession of her despair and remorse, that her hand, and not Julia's, had administered to Glaucus the fatal potion. At another time the Egyptian might have conceived a philosophical interest in sounding the depths and origin of the strange and absorbing passion which, in blindness and in slavery, this singular girl had dared to cherish; but at present he spared no thought from himself. As, after her confession, the poor Nydia threw herself on her knees before him, and besought him to restore the health and save the life of Glaucus—for in her youth and ignorance she imagined the dark magician all-powerful to effect both—Arbaces, with unheeding ears, was noting only the new expediency of detaining Nydia a prisoner until the trial and fate of Glaucus were decided.

'Daughter,' said Arbaces, waking from his reverie, 'thou must rest here; it is not meet for thee to wander along the streets, and be spurned from the threshold by the rude feet of slaves. I have compassion on thy soft crime—I will do all to remedy it. Wait here patiently for some days, and Glaucus shall be restored.' So saying, and without waiting for her reply, he hastened from the room, drew the bolt across the door, and consigned the care and wants of his prisoner to the slave who had the charge of that part of the mansion.

Alone, then, and musingly, he waited the morning light, and with it repaired, as we have seen, to possess himself of the person of Ione.

His primary object, with respect to the unfortunate Neapolitan, was that which he had really stated to Clodius, viz., to prevent her interesting herself actively in the trial of Glaucus, and also to guard against her accusing him (which she would, doubtless, have done) of his former act of perfidy and violence towards her, his ward—denouncing his causes for vengeance against Glaucus—unveiling the hypocrisy of his character—and casting any doubt upon his veracity in the charge which he had made against the Athenian. Not till he had encountered her that morning—not till he had heard her loud denunciations—was he aware that he had also another danger to apprehend in her suspicion of his crime. He hugged himself now at the thought that these ends were effected: that one, at once the object of his passion and

his fear, was in his power. He believed more than ever the flattering promises of the stars; and when he sought Ione in that chamber in the inmost recesses of his mysterious mansion to which he had consigned her—when he found her overpowered by blow upon blow, and passing from fit to fit, from violence to torpor, in all the alternations of hysterical disease—he thought more of the loveliness which no frenzy could distort than of the woe which he had brought upon her; and, having Ione now in his possession, he secretly resolved, as soon as he had witnessed the last agony of his rival, to transport his wealth—and her, the costliest treasure of all, to some distant shore.

ROMAN LOCK

1. KEY IS INSERTED INTO LOCK 2. AND FITS OVER PEGS 3. WITH SPRINGS ATTACHED WHEN KEY IS FULLY PUSHED DOWN THE BOLT

4. CAN BE WITHDRAWN

NYDIA AFFECTS THE SORCERESS

When the Thessalian found that Arbaces returned to her no more—when she was left, hour after hour, to all the torture of that miserable suspense which was rendered by blindness doubly intolerable, she began, with outstretched arms, to feel around her prison for some channel of escape; and finding the only entrance secure, she called aloud, and with the vehemence of a temper naturally violent, and now sharpened by impatient agony.

'Ho, girl!' said the slave in attendance, opening the door; 'art thou bit by a scorpion? or thinkest thou that we are dying of silence here, and only to be preserved, like the infant Jupiter, by a hullabaloo?'

'Where is thy master? and wherefore am I caged here? I want air and liberty: let me go forth!'

'Alas! little one, hast thou not seen enough of Arbaces to know that his will is imperial! He hath ordered thee to be caged; and caged thou art, and I am thy keeper. Thou canst not have air and liberty; but thou mayst have what are much better things—food and wine.'

'Proh Jupiter!' cried the girl, wringing her hands; 'and why am I thus imprisoned? What can the great Arbaces want with so poor a thing as I am?'

'That I know not, unless it be to attend on thy new mistress, who has been brought hither this day.'

'What! Ione here?'

'Yes, poor lady; she liked it little, I fear. Yet, by the Temple of Castor! Arbaces is a gallant man to the women. Thy lady is his ward, thou knowest.'

'Wilt thou take me to her?'

'She is ill—frantic with rage and spite. Besides, I have no orders to do so; and I never think for myself. When Arbaces made

me slave of these chambers, he said, "I have but one lesson to give thee;—while thou servest me, thou must have neither ears, eyes, nor thought; thou must be but one quality—obedience." '

'But what harm is there in seeing Ione?'

'That I know not; but if thou wantest a companion, I am willing to talk to thee, little one, for I am solitary enough in my dull cubiculum. And, by the way, thou art Thessalian—knowest thou not some cunning amusement of knife and shears, some pretty trick of telling fortunes, as most of thy race do, in order to pass the time?'

'Tush, slave, hold thy peace! or, if thou wilt speak, what hast thou heard of the state of Glaucus?'

'Why, my master has gone to the Athenian's trial; Glaucus will smart for it!'

'For what?'

'The murder of the priest Apæcides.'

'Ha!' said Nydia, pressing her hands to her forehead; 'something of this I have indeed heard, but understand not. Yet, who will dare to touch a hair of his head?'

'That will the lion, I fear.'

'Averting gods! what wickedness dost thou utter?'

'Why, only that, if he be found guilty, the lion, or may be the tiger, will be his executioner.'

Nydia leaped up, as if an arrow had entered her heart; she uttered a piercing scream; then, falling before the feet of the slave, she cried, in a tone that melted even his rude heart,—

'Ah! tell me thou jestest—thou utterest not the truth—speak, speak!'

'Why, by my faith, blind girl, I know nothing of the law; it may not be so bad as I say. But Arbaces is his accuser, and the people desire a victim for the arena. Cheer thee! But what hath the fate of the Athenian to do with thine?'

'No matter, no matter—he has been kind to me: thou knowest not, then, what they will do? Arbaces his accuser! O fate! The people

—the people! Ah! *they* can look upon his face —who will be cruel to the Athenian!—Yet was not Love itself cruel to him?'

So saying, her head drooped upon her bosom: she sunk into silence; scalding tears flowed down her cheeks; and all the kindly efforts of the slave were unable either to console her or distract the absorption of her reverie.

When his household cares obliged the ministrant to leave her room, Nydia began to re-collect her thoughts. Arbaces was the accuser of Glaucus; Arbaces had imprisoned her here; was not that a proof that her liberty might be serviceable to Glaucus? She possessed much of the craft of her sex, and it had been increased in her breast by her early servitude. What slave was ever destitute of cunning? She resolved to practise upon her keeper; and calling suddenly to mind his superstitious query as to her Thessalian art, she hoped by that handle to work out some method of release. These doubts occupied her mind during the rest of the day and the long hours of night; and, accordingly, when Sosia visited her the following morning, she hastened to divert his garrulity into that channel in which it had before evinced a natural disposition to flow.

She was aware, however, that her only chance of escape was at night; and accordingly she was obliged, with a bitter pang at the delay, to defer till then her purposed attempt.

'The night,' said she, 'is the sole time in which we can well decipher the decrees of Fate—then it is thou must seek me. But what desirest thou to learn?'

'By Pollux! I should like to know as much as my master; but that is not to be expected. Let me know, at least, whether I shall save enough to purchase my freedom, or whether this Egyptian will give it me for nothing. He does such generous things sometimes. Next, supposing that be true, shall I possess myself of that snug taberna among the Myropolia, which I have long had in my eye? 'Tis a genteel trade that of a perfumer, and suits a retired slave who has something of a gentleman about him!'

'Ay! so you would have precise answers to those questions?—there are various ways of satisfying you. There is the Lithomanteia, or Speaking-stone, which answers your prayer with an infant's voice; but, then, we have not that precious stone with us—costly is it and rare. Then there is the Gastromanteia, whereby the demon casts pale and deadly images upon the water, prophetic of the future. But this art requires also glasses of a peculiar fashion, to contain the consecrated liquid, which we have not. I think, therefore, that the simplest method of satisfying your desire would be by the Magic of Air.'

LOCK AND KEY

'I trust,' said Sosia, tremulously, 'that there is nothing very frightful in the operation? I have no love for apparitions.'

'Fear not; thou wilt see nothing; thou wilt only hear by the bubbling of water whether or not thy suit prospers. First, then, be sure, from the rising of the evening star, that thou leavest the garden-gate somewhat open, so that the demon may feel himself invited to enter therein; and place fruits and water near the gate as a sign of hospitality; then, three hours after twilight, come here with a bowl of the coldest and purest water, and thou shalt learn all, according to the Thessalian lore my mother taught me. But forget not the garden-gate—all rests upon that: it must be open when you come, and for three hours previously.'

'Trust me,' replied the unsuspecting Sosia; 'I know what a gentleman's feelings are when a door is shut in his face, as the cookshop's hath been in mine many a day; and I know, also, that a person of respectability, as a demon of course is, cannot but be pleased, on the other hand, with any little mark of courteous hospitality. Meanwhile, pretty one, here is thy morning's meal.'

'But what of the trial?'

'Oh, the lawyers are still at it—talk, talk—it will last over till to-morrow.'

'To-morrow? You are sure of that?'

'So I hear.'

'And Ione?'

'By Bacchus! she must be tolerably well, for she was strong enough to make my master stamp and bite his lip this morning. I saw him quit her apartment with a brow like a thunder-storm.'

'Lodges she near this?'

'No—in the upper apartments. But I must not stay prating here longer.—*Vale!*'

MONEY CHANGERS BOOTH

A WASP VENTURES INTO THE SPIDER'S WEB

The second night of the trial had set in; and it was nearly the time in which Sosia was to brave the dread Unknown, when there entered, at that very garden-gate which the slave had left ajar—not, indeed, one of the mysterious spirits of earth or air, but the heavy and most human form of Calenus, the priest of Isis. He scarcely noted the humble offerings of indifferent fruit, and still more indifferent wine, which the pious Sosia had deemed good enough for the invisible stranger they were intended to allure. 'Some tribute,' thought he, 'to the garden god. By my father's head! if his deityship were never better served, he would do well to give up the godly profession. Ah! were it not for us priests, the gods would have a sad time of it. And now for Arbaces—I am treading a quicksand, but it ought to cover a mine. I have the Egyptian's life in my power—what will he value it at?'

As he thus soliloquised, he crossed through the open court into the peristyle, where a few lamps here and there broke upon the empire of the starlit night; and issuing from one of the chambers that bordered the colonnade, suddenly encountered Arbaces.

'Ho! Calenus—seekest thou me?' said the Egyptian; and there was a little embarrassment in his voice.

'Shall we within to your chamber, Arbaces?'

'As you will; but the night is clear and balmy—I have some remains of languor yet lingering on me from my recent illness—the air refreshes me—let us walk in the garden—we are equally alone there.'

'With all my heart,' answered the priest; and the two *friends* passed slowly to one of the many terraces which, bordered by marble vases and sleeping flowers, intersected the garden.

'It is a lovely night,' said Arbaces—'blue and beautiful as that on which, twenty years ago, the shores of Italy first broke upon my view. My Calenus, age creeps upon us—let us, at least, feel that we have lived.'

'Thou, at least, mayst arrogate that boast,' said Calenus, beating about, as it were, for an opportunity to communicate the secret which weighed upon him, and feeling his usual awe of Arbaces still more impressively that night, from the quiet and friendly tone of dignified condescension which the Egyptian assumed—'Thou, at least, mayst arrogate that boast. Thou hast had countless wealth—a frame on whose close-woven fibres disease can find no space to enter—prosperous love—inexhaustible pleasure—and, even at this hour, triumphant revenge.'

'Thou alludest to the Athenian. Ay, to-morrow's sun the fiat of his death will go forth. The senate does not relent. But thou mistakest: his death gives me no other gratification than that it releases me from a rival in the affections of Ione. I entertain no other sentiment of animosity against that unfortunate homicide.'

'Homicide!' repeated Calenus, slowly and meaningly; and, halting as he spoke, he fixed his eyes upon Arbaces. The stars shone pale and steadily on the proud face of their prophet, but they betrayed there no change: the eyes of Calenus fell disappointed and abashed. He continued rapidly—'Homicide! it is well to charge him with that crime; but thou, of all men, knowest that he is innocent.'

'Explain thyself,' said Arbaces, coldly; for he had prepared himself for the hint his secret fears had foretold.

'Arbaces,' answered Calenus, sinking his voice into a whisper, 'I was in the sacred grove, sheltered by the chapel and the surrounding foliage. I overheard—I marked the whole. I saw thy weapon pierce the heart of Apæcides. I blame not the deed—it destroyed a foe and an apostate.'

'Thou sawest the whole!' said Arbaces, drily; 'so I imagined—thou wert alone?'

'Alone!' returned Calenus, surprised at the Egyptian's calmness.

'And wherefore wert thou hid behind the chapel at that hour?'

'Because I had learned the conversion of Apæcides to the Christian faith—because I knew that on that spot he was to meet the fierce Olinthus—because they were to meet there to discuss plans for unveiling the sacred mysteries of our goddess to the people—and I was there to detect, in order to defeat them.'

'Hast thou told living ear what thou didst witness?'

'No, my master: the secret is locked in thy servant's breast.'

'What! even thy kinsman Burbo guesses it not! Come the truth!'

'By the gods——'

'Well, then, Calenus, what wouldst thou have me pay thee?'

'Thy life is very precious, and thy wealth is very great,' returned the priest, grinning.

'Wittier and more witty. But speak out—what shall be the sum?'

'Arbaces, I have heard that in thy secret treasury below, beneath those rude Oscan arches which prop thy stately halls, thou hast piles of gold, of vases, and of jewels, which might rival the receptacles of the wealth of the deified Nero. Thou mayst easily spare out of those piles enough to make Calenus among the richest priests of Pompeii, and yet not miss the loss.'

'Come, Calenus,' said Arbaces, winningly, and with a frank and generous air, 'thou art an old friend, and hast been a faithful servant. Thou canst have no wish to take away my life, nor I a desire to stint thy reward: thou shalt descend with me to that treasury thou referrest to, thou shalt feast thine eyes with the blaze of uncounted gold and the sparkle of priceless gems; and thou shalt for thy own reward, bear away with thee this night as much as thou canst conceal beneath thy robes. Nay, when thou hast once seen what thy friend possesses, thou wilt learn how foolish it would be to injure one who has so much to bestow. When Glaucus is no more, thou shalt pay the treasury another visit. Speak I frankly and as a friend?'

'Oh, greatest, best of men!' cried Calenus, almost weeping with joy, 'canst thou thus forgive my injurious doubts of thy justice, thy generosity?'

'Hush! one other turn and we will descend to the Oscan arches.'

THE SLAVE CONSULTS THE ORACLE

Impatiently Nydia awaited the arrival of the no less anxious Sosia. Fortifying his courage by plentiful potations of a better liquor than that provided for the demon, the credulous ministrant stole into the blind girl's chamber.

'Well, Sosia, and art thou prepared? Hast thou the bowl of pure water?'

'Verily, yes: but I tremble a little. You are sure I shall not see the demon? I have heard that those gentlemen are by no means of a handsome person or a civil demeanour.'

'Be assured! And hast thou left the garden-gate gently open?'

'Yes; and placed some beautiful nuts and apples on a little table close by?'

'That's well. And the gate is open now, so that the demon may pass through it?'

'Surely it is.'

'Well, then, open this door; there—leave it just ajar. And now, Sosia, give me the lamp.'

'What, you will not extinguish it?'

'No; but I must breathe my spell over its ray. There is a spirit in fire. Seat thyself.'

The slave obeyed; and Nydia, after bending for some moments silently over the lamp, rose, and chanted in a low voice.

'The spectre *is* certainly coming,' said Sosia. 'I feel him running along my hair!'

'Place thy bowl of water on the ground. Now, then, give me thy napkin, and let me fold up thy face and eyes.'

'Ay! that's always the custom with these charms. Not so tight, though: gently—gently!'

'There—thou canst not see?'

'See, by Jupiter! No! nothing but darkness.'

'Address, then, to the spectre whatever question thou wouldst ask him, in a low-whispered voice, three times. If thy question is answered in the affirmative, thou wilt hear the water ferment and bubble before the demon breathes upon it; if in the negative, the water will be quite silent.'

'But you will not play any trick with the water, eh?'

'Let me place the bowl under thy feet—so. Now thou wilt perceive that I cannot touch it without thy knowledge.'

'Very fair. Now, then, O Bacchus! befriend me. Thou knowest that I have always loved thee better than all the other gods, and I will dedicate to thee that silver cup I stole last year from the burly carptor (butler), if thou wilt but befriend me with this water-loving demon. And thou, O Spirit! listen and hear me. Shall I be enabled to purchase my freedom next year? Thou knowest; for, as thou livest in the air, the birds have doubtless acquainted thee with every secret of this house,—thou knowest that I have filched and pilfered all that I honestly—that is, safely—

OIL LAMP AND STAND

WATER BOWL

MONEY BOXES

could lay finger upon for the last three years, and I yet want two thousand sesterces of the full sum. Shall I be able, O good Spirit! to make up the deficiency in the course of this year? Speak—Ha! does the water bubble? No; all is as still as a tomb.—Well, then, if not this year, in two years?—Ah! I hear something; the demon is scratching at the door; he'll be here presently.—In two years, my good fellow: come now, two; that's a very reasonable time. What! dumb still! Two years and a half—three—four? Ill fortune to you, friend demon! You are not a lady, that's clear, or you would not keep silence so long. Five—six—sixty years? and may Pluto seize you! I'll ask no more.' And Sosia, in a rage, kicked down the water over his legs. He then, after much fumbling and more cursing, managed to extricate his head from the napkin in which it was completely folded—stared round—and discovered that he was in the dark.

'What, ho! Nydia; the lamp is gone. Ah, traitress; and thou art gone too; but I'll catch thee—thou shalt smart for this!'

The slave groped his way to the door; it was bolted from without: he was a prisoner instead of Nydia. What could he do? He did not dare to knock loud—to call out—lest Arbaces should overhear him, and discover how he had been duped; and Nydia, meanwhile, had probably already gained the garden-gate, and was fast on her escape.

'But,' thought he, 'she will go home, or, at least, be somewhere in the city. To-morrow, at dawn, when the slaves are at work in the peristyle, I can make myself heard; then I can go forth and seek her. I shall be sure to find and bring her back, before Arbaces knows a word of the matter. Ah! that's the best plan. Little traitress, my fingers itch at thee: and to leave only a bowl of water, too!

Had it been wine, it would have been some comfort.'

While Sosia, thus entrapped, was lamenting his fate, and revolving his schemes to repossess himself of Nydia, the blind girl, with that singular precision and dexterious rapidity of motion, which, we have before observed, was peculiar to her, had passed lightly along the peristyle, threaded the opposite passage that led into the garden, and, with a beating heart, was about to proceed towards the gate, when she suddenly heard the sound of approaching steps, and distinguished the dreaded voice of Arbaces himself. She paused for a moment in doubt and terror; then suddenly it flashed across her recollection that there was another passage which was little used except for the admission of the fair partakers of the Egyptian's secret revels, and which wound along the basement of that massive fabric towards a door which also communicated with the garden. By good fortune it might be open. At that thought, she hastily retraced her steps, descended the narrow stairs at the right, and was soon at the entrance of the passage. Alas! the door at the entrance was closed and secured. While she was yet assuring herself that it was indeed locked, she heard behind her the voice of Calenus, and, a moment after, that of Arbaces in low reply. She could not stay there; they were probably passing to that very door. She sprang onward, and felt herself in unknown ground. The air grew damp and chill; this reassured her. She thought she might be among the cellars of the luxurious mansion, or, at least, in some rude spot not likely to be visited by its haughty lord, when again, her quick ear caught steps and the sound of voices. On, on, she hurried, extending her arms, which now frequently encountered pillars of thick and massive form. With a tact, doubled in acuteness by her fear, she escaped these perils, and continued her way, the air growing more and more damp as she proceeded; yet, still, as she ever and anon paused for breath, she heard the advancing steps and the indistinct murmur of voices. At length she was abruptly stopped by a wall that seemed the limit of her path. Was there no spot in which she could hide? No aperture? no cavity? There was none! She stopped, and wrung her hands in despair; then again, nerved as the voices neared upon her, she hurried on by the side of the wall; and coming suddenly against one of the sharp buttresses that here and there jutted boldly forth, she fell to the ground. Though much bruised, her senses did not leave her; she uttered no cry; nay, she hailed the accident that had led her to something like a screen; and creeping close up to the angle formed by the buttress, so that on one side at least she was sheltered from view, she gathered her slight and small form into its smallest compass, and breathlessly awaited her fate.

Meanwhile Arbaces and the priest were taking their way to that secret chamber whose stores were so vaunted by the Egyptian. They were in a vast subterranean atrium, or hall; the low roof was supported by short, thick pillars of an architecture far remote from the Grecian graces of that luxuriant period. The single and pale lamp, which Arbaces bore, shed but an imperfect ray over the bare and rugged walls, in which the huge stones, without cement, were fitted curiously and uncouthly into each other. The disturbed reptiles glared dully on the intruders, and then crept into the shadow of the walls.

Calenus shivered as he looked around and breathed the damp, unwholesome air.

'Yet,' said Arbaces, with a smile, perceiving his shudder, 'it is these rude abodes that furnish the luxuries of the halls above. They are like the labourers of the world,—we despise their ruggedness, yet they feed the very pride that disdains them.'

'And whither goes yon dim gallery to the left?' asked Calenus; 'in this depth of gloom it seems without limit, as if winding into Hades.'

'On the contrary, it does but conduct to the upper rooms,' answered Arbaces, carelessly: 'it is to the right that we steer to our bourn.'

The hall, like many in the more habitable regions of Pompeii, branched off at the extremity into two wings or passages; the length of which, not really great, was to the eye considerably exaggerated by the sudden gloom against which the lamp so faintly struggled. To the right of these *alæ* the two comrades now directed their steps.

'The gay Glaucus will be lodged to-morrow in apartments not much drier, and far less spacious than this,' said Calenus, as they passed by the very spot where, completely wrapped in the shadow of the broad, projecting buttress, cowered the Thessalian.

'Ay, but then he will have dry room, and ample enough, in the arena on the following day. And to think' continued Arbaces, slowly, and very deliberately—'to think that a word of thine could save him, and consign Arbaces to his doom!'

'That word shall never be spoken,' said Calenus.

'Right, my Calenus! it never shall,' returned Arbaces, familiarly leaning his arm on the priest's shoulder: 'and now, halt—we are at the door.'

The light trembled against a small door deep set in the wall, and guarded strongly by many plates and bindings of iron, that intersected the rough and dark wood. From his girdle Arbaces now drew a small ring, holding three or four short but strong keys. Oh, how beat the griping heart of Calenus, as he heard the rusty wards growl, as if resenting the admission to the treasures they guarded!

'Enter, my friend,' said Arbaces, 'while I hold the lamp on high, that thou mayst glut thine eyes on the yellow heaps.'

The impatient Calenus did not wait to be twice invited; he hastened towards the aperture.

Scarce had he crossed the threshold, when the strong hand of Arbaces plunged him forwards.

'*The word shall never be spoken!*' said the Egyptian, with a loud exultant laugh, and closed the door upon the priest.

Calenus had been precipitated down several steps, but not feeling at the moment the pain of his fall, he sprung up again to the door, and beating at it fiercely with his clenched fist, he cried aloud in what seemed more a beast's howl than a human voice, so keen was his agony and despair: 'Oh, release me, release me, and I will ask no gold!'

The words but imperfectly penetrated the massive door, and Arbaces again laughed. Then, stamping his foot violently, rejoined, perhaps to give vent to his long-stifled passions,—

'All the gold of Dalmatia,' cried he, 'will not buy thee a crust of bread. Starve, wretch! thy dying groans will never wake even the echo of these vast halls; nor will the air ever reveal, as thou gnawest, in thy desperate famine, thy flesh from thy bones, that so perishes the man who threatened, and could have undone, Arbaces! Farewell!'

'Oh, pity—mercy! Inhuman villain; was it for this——'

NYDIA ACCOSTS CALENUS

What words of terror, yet of hope, had Nydia overheard! The next day Glaucus was to be condemned; yet there lived one who could save him, and adjudge Arbaces to his doom, and that one breathed within a few steps of her hiding-place! She caught his cries and shrieks—his imprecations—his prayers, though they fell choked and muffled on her ear. He was imprisoned, but she knew the secret of his cell: could she but escape—could she but seek the prætor, he might yet in time be given to light, and preserve the Athenian. Her emotions almost stifled her; her brain reeled—she felt her sense give way—but by a violent effort she mastered herself; and, after listening intently for several minutes, till she was convinced that Arbaces had left the space to solitude and herself, she crept on as her ear guided her to the very door that had closed upon Calenus. Here she more distinctly caught his accents of terror and despair. Thrice she attempted to speak, and thrice her voice failed to penetrate the folds of the heavy door. At length finding the lock, she applied her lips to its small aperture, and the prisoner distinctly heard a soft tone breathe his name.

His blood curdled—his hair stood on end. That awful solitude, what mysterious and preternatural being could penetrate! 'Who's there?' he cried, in new alarm; 'what spectre —what dread *larva*, calls upon the lost Calenus?'

'Priest,' replied the Thessalian, 'unknown to Arbaces, I have been, by the permission of the gods, a witness to his perfidy. If I myself can escape from these walls, I may save thee. But let thy voice reach my ear through this narrow passage, and answer what I ask.'

'Ah, blessed spirit,' said the priest, exultingly, and obeying the suggestion of Nydia, 'save me, and I will sell the very cups on the altar to pay thy kindness.'

'I want not thy gold—I want thy secret. Did I hear aright?—Canst thou save the Athenian Glaucus from the charge against his life?'

'I can—I can!—therefore (may the Furies blast the foul Egyptian!) hath Arbaces snared me thus, and left me to starve and rot!'

'They accuse the Athenian of murder: canst thou disprove the accusation?'

'Only free me, and the proudest head of Pompeii is not more safe than his. I saw the deed done—I saw Arbaces strike the blow; I can convict the true murderer and acquit the innocent man. But if I perish, he dies also. Dost thou interest thyself for him? Oh, blessed stranger, in my heart is the urn which condemns or frees him!'

'And thou wilt give full evidence of what thou knowest?'

'Will!—Oh! were hell at my feet—yes! Revenge on the false Egyptian!—revenge!— revenge! revenge!'

As through his ground teeth Calenus shrieked forth those last words, Nydia felt that in his worst passions was her certainty of his justice to the Athenian. Her heart beat: was it to be her proud destiny to preserve her idolised—her adored? 'Enough,' said she, 'the powers that conducted me hither will carry me through all. Yes, I feel that I shall deliver thee. Wait in patience and hope.'

So, saying, she glided away, and felt with extended arms along the pillared space until she had gained the farther end of the hall and the mouth of the passage that led to the upper air. But there she paused; she felt that it would be more safe to wait awhile, until the night was so far blended with the morning that the whole house would be buried in sleep, and so that she might quit it unobserved. She, therefore, once more laid herself down, and counted the weary moments. In her sanguine heart, joy was the predominant emotion. Glaucus was in deadly peril—but *she* should save him!

KEY

ARBACES AND IONE

When Arbaces had warmed his veins by large draughts of that spiced and perfumed wine so valued by the luxurious, he felt more than usually elated and exultant of heart. There is a pride in triumphant ingenuity, not less felt, perhaps, though its object be guilty. Our vain human nature hugs itself in the consciousness of superior craft and self-obtained success—afterwards comes the horrible reaction of remorse.

But remorse was not a feeling which Arbaces was likely ever to experience for the fate of the base Calenus. He swept from his remembrance the thought of the priest's agonies and lingering death: he felt only that a great danger was passed, and a possible foe silenced; all left to him now would be to account to the priesthood for the disappearance of Calenus; and this he imagined it would not be difficult to do.

Accosting the slave in attendance without, he inquired if Ione had yet retired to rest; and learning that she was still up, and unusually quiet and composed, he ventured into her presence. He found his beautiful ward sitting before a small table, and leaning her face upon both her hands in the attitude of thought. Yet the expression of the face itself possessed not its wonted bright and Psyche-like expression of sweet intelligence; the lips were apart—the eye vacant and unheeding—and the long dark hair, falling neglected and dishevelled upon her neck, gave by the contrast additional paleness to a cheek which had already lost the roundness of its contour.

Arbaces gazed upon her a moment ere he advanced. She, too, lifted up her eyes; and when she saw who was the intruder, shut them with an expression of pain, but did not stir.

'Give me back my brother and my betrothed,' said Ione, in a calm and imploring tone, and a few large tears rolled unheeded down her cheeks.

'Would that I could restore the one and save the other!' returned Arbaces, with apparent emotion. 'Yes; to make thee happy I would renounce my ill-fated love, and gladly join thy hand to the Athenian's. And think not, O Ione, that I would follow thee longer with a prayer of love. I know it is in vain.. Suffer me only to weep—to mourn with thee Forgive a violence deeply repented, and that shall offend no more. Let me be to thee only what I once was—a friend, a father, a protector. Ah, Ione! spare me and forgive.'

'I forgive thee. Save but Glaucus, and I will renounce him. Oh! if thou really lovest me—if thou art human—remember my father's ashes, remember my childhood, think of all the hours we passed happily together, and save my Glaucus!'

Strange convulsions shook the frame of the Egyptian; his features worked fearfully—he turned his face aside, and said, in a hollow voice, 'If I could save him, even now, I would; but the Roman law is stern and sharp. Yet if I *could* succeed—if I *could* rescue and set him free—wouldst thou be mine—my bride?'

'Thine?' repeated Ione, rising: 'thine!—thy bride? My brother's blood is unavenged: *who* slew him? O Nemesis, can I even sell, for the life of Glaucus, thy solemn trust? Arbaces—*thine?* Never.'

'Ione, Ione!' cried Arbaces, passionately; 'why these mysterious words?—why dost thou couple my name with the thought of thy brother's death?'

'My dreams couple it—and dreams are from the gods.'

'Enough, Ione. All that I can do for Glaucus shall be done; but blame me not if I fail. Inquire of my foes, even, if I have not sought, if I do not seek, to turn aside the sentence from his head; and judge me accordingly. Sleep then, Ione. Night wanes; I leave thee to rest,—and mayst thou have kinder dreams of one who has no existence but in thine.'

Without waiting a reply, Arbaces hastily withdrew; afraid, perhaps, to trust himself further to the passionate prayer of Ione, which racked him with jealousy, even while it touched him to compassion. But compassion itself came too late. Had Ione even pledged him her hand as his reward, he could not now—his evidence given—the populace excited—have saved the Athenian. Still, made sanguine by his very energy of mind, he threw himself on the chances of the future, and believed he should yet triumph over the woman that had so entangled his passions.

As his attendants assisted to unrobe him for the night, the thought of Nydia flashed across him. He felt it was necessary that Ione should never learn of her lover's frenzy, lest it might excuse his imputed crime; and it was possible that her attendants might inform her that Nydia was under his roof, and she might desire to see her. As this idea crossed him, he turned to one of his freedmen,—

'Go, Callias,' said he, 'forthwith to Sosia, and tell him, that on no pretence is he to suffer the blind slave Nydia out of her chamber. But, stay—first seek those in attendance upon my ward, and caution them not to inform her that the blind girl is under my roof. Go—quick!'

The freedman hastened to obey. After having discharged his commission with respect to Ione's attendants, he sought the worthy Sosia. He found him not in the little cell which was apportioned for his cubiculum; he called his name aloud, and from Nydia's chamber, close at hand, he heard the voice of Sosia reply,—

'Oh, Callias, is it you that I hear?—the gods be praised! Open the door, I pray you!'

Callias withdrew the bolt, and the rueful face of Sosia hastily protruded itself.

'What!—in the chamber with that young girl, Sosia! *Proh pudor!* Are there not fruits ripe enough on the wall, but that thou must tamper with such green——'

'Name not the little witch!' interrupted Sosia, impatiently; 'she will be my ruin!' And he forthwith imparted to Callias the history of the Air Demon, and the escape of the Thessalian.

'Hang thyself, then, unhappy Sosia! I am just charged from Arbaces with a message to thee; on no account art thou to suffer her, even for a moment, from that chamber!'

'*Me miserum!*' exclaimed the slave. 'What can I do!—by this time she may have visited half Pompeii. But to-morrow I will undertake

BRONZE TABLE

78

to catch her in her old haunts. Keep but my counsel, my dear Callias.'

The good-natured Callias consented to assist the slave; and after vainly searching the chambers at hand, and the recesses of the peristyle, they entered the garden.

It was about this time that Nydia had resolved to quit her hiding-place, and venture forth on her way. Lightly, tremulously holding her breath, which ever and anon broke forth in quick convulsive gasps,—now gliding by the flower-wreathed columns that bordered the peristyle—now darkening the still moonshine that fell over its tesselated centre—now ascending the terrace of the garden—now gliding amidst the gloomy and breathless trees, she gained the fatal door—to find it locked!

'Hush, Callias!—let her go on. Let us see what she will do when she has convinced herself that the door is honest.'

'Look! she raises her face to the heavens—she mutters—she sinks down despondent! No! by Pollux, she has some new scheme! She will not resign herself! By Jupiter, a tough spirit! See, she springs up—she retraces her steps—she thinks of some other chance! —I advise thee, Sosia, to delay no longer: seize her ere she quit the garden,—now!'

'Ah! runaway! I have thee—eh?' said Sosia, seizing upon the unhappy Nydia.

And, catching the light weight in his arms, Sosia soon gained the house, and reached the chamber from which Nydia had escaped. There, removing the gag, he left her to a solitude so racked and terrible, that out of Hades its anguish could scarcely be exceeded.

KEYS

THE DUNGEON AND ITS VICTIMS

It was now late on the third and last day of the trial of Glaucus and Olinthus. A few hours after the court had broke up and judgment been given, a small party of the fashionable youth at Pompeii were assembled round the fastidious board of Lepidus.

'So Glaucus denies his crime to the last?' said Clodius.

'Yes; but the testimony of Arbaces was convincing; he saw the blow given,' answered Lepidus.

'What could have been the cause?'

'Why, the priest was a gloomy and sullen fellow. He probably rated Glaucus soundly about his gay life and gaming habits, and ultimately swore he would not consent to his marriage with Ione. High words arose; Glaucus seems to have been full of the passionate god, and struck in sudden exasperation. Such, at least, is the shrewd conjecture of Arbaces, who seems to have been most kind and forbearing in his testimony.'

'Yes; he has made himself generally popular by it. But, in consideration of these extenuating circumstances, the senate should have relaxed the sentence.'

'And they *would* have done so, but for the people; but *they* were outrageous. The priest had spared no pains to excite them; and they imagined—the ferocious brutes!—because Glaucus was a rich man and a gentleman, that he was likely to escape; and therefore they were inveterate against him, and doubly resolved upon his sentence.'

'He looks sadly altered; but how composed and fearless!'

'Ay, we shall see if his firmness will last over to-morrow. But what merit in courage, when that atheistical hound, Olinthus, manifested the same?'

'The blasphemer! Yes,' said Lepidus, with pious wrath, 'no wonder that one of the decurions was, but two days ago, struck dead by lightning in a serene sky. The gods feel vengeance against Pompeii while the vile desecrator is alive within its walls.'

'Yet so lenient was the senate, that had he but expressed his penitence, and scattered a few grains of incense on the altar of Cybele, he would have been let off. I doubt whether these Nazarenes, had they the state religion, would be as tolerant to us, supposing we had kicked down the image of their Deity, blasphemed their rites, and denied their faith.'

'They give Glaucus one chance, in consideration of the circumstances; they allow

him, against the lion, the use of the same stilus wherewith he smote the priest.'

'Hast thou seen the lion? hast thou looked at his teeth and fangs, and wilt thou call *that* a chance? Why, sword and buckler would be mere reed and papyrus against the rush of the mighty beast! No, I think the true mercy has been, not to leave him long in suspense; and it was therefore fortunate for him that our benign laws are slow to pronounce, but swift to execute; and that the games of the amphitheatre had been, by a sort of providence, so long since fixed for to-morrow. He who awaits death, dies twice.'

'As for the Atheist,' said Clodius, 'he is to cope the grim tiger naked-handed. Well, these combats are past betting on. We will take the odds?'

A peal of laughter announced the ridicule of the question.

'Poor Clodius!' said the host; 'to lose a friend is something; but to find no one to bet on the chance of his escape is a worse misfortune to thee.'

After his condemnation, Glaucus was admitted no more to the gentle guardianship of Sallust, the only friend of his distress. He was led along the forum till the guards stopped at a small door by the side of the temple of Jupiter. The door opened in the centre in a somewhat singular fashion, revolving round on its hinges, as it were, like a modern turnstile, so as only to leave half the threshold open at the same time. Through this narrow aperture they thrust the prisoner, placed before him a loaf and a pitcher of water, and left him to darkness, and, as he thought, to solitude. So sudden had been that revolution of fortune which had prostrated him from the palmy height of youthful pleasure and successful love to the lowest abyss of ignominy, and the horror of a most bloody death, that he could scarcely convince himself that he was not held in the meshes of some fearful dream. .

A voice from the recess of the darkness asked, 'Who is my companion in this awful hour? Athenian Glaucus, it is thou?'

'So, indeed, they called me in mine hour of fortune: they may have other names for me now. And *thy* name, stranger?'

'Is Olinthus, thy co-mate in the prison as the trial.'

'What! he whom they call the Atheist? Is it the injustice of men that hath taught thee to deny the providence of the gods?'

'Alas!' answered Olinthus: 'thou, not I, art the true Atheist, for thou deniest the sole true God—the Unknown One—to whom thy Athenian fathers erected an altar. It is in this hour that I know my God. He is with me in the dungeon; His smile penetrates the darkness; on the eve of death my heart whispers immortality, and earth recedes from me but to bring the weary soul nearer unto heaven.'

'Tell me,' said Glaucus, abruptly, 'did I not hear thy name coupled with that of Apæcides in my trial? Dost thou believe me guilty?'

'God alone reads the heart! but my suspicion rested not upon thee.'

'On whom then?'

'Thy accuser, Arbaces.'

'Ha! thou cheerest me: and wherefore?'

'Because I know the man's evil breast, and he had cause to fear him who is now dead.'

With that, Olinthus proceeded to inform Glaucus of those details which the reader already knows, the conversion of Apæcides, the plan they had proposed for the detection of the impostures of the Egyptian priestcraft, and of the seductions practised by Arbaces upon the youthful weakness of the proselyte. 'Therefore,' concluded Olinthus, 'had the deceased encountered Arbaces, reviled his treasons, and threatened detection, the place, the hour, might have favoured the wrath of the Egyptian, and passion and craft alike dictated the fatal blow.'

'It must have been so!' cried Glaucus, joyfully. 'I am happy.'

'Yet what, O unfortunate! avails to thee now the discovery? Thou art condemned and fated; and in thine innocence thou wilt perish.'

'But I shall *know myself* guiltless; and in my mysterious madness I had fearful, though momentary, doubts. Yet tell me, man of a strange creed, thinkest thou that for small errors, or for ancestral faults, we are for ever abandoned and accursed by the powers above, whatever name thou allottest to them?'

'God is just, and abandons not His creatures for their mere human frailty. God is merciful, and curses none but the wicked who repent not.'

'Yet it seemeth to me as if, in the divine anger, I had been smitten by a sudden madness, a supernatural and solemn frenzy, wrought not by human means.'

'There are demons on earth,' answered the Nazarene, fearfully, 'as well as there are God and His Son in heaven; and since thou acknowledgest not the last, the first may have had power over thee.'

Glaucus did not reply, and there was a silence for some minutes. At length the Athenian said, in a changed, and soft, and half-hesitating voice, 'Christian, believest thou, among the doctrines of thy creed, that the dead live again—that they who have loved here are united hereafter—that beyond the grave our good name shines pure from the mortal mists that unjustly dim it in the gross-eyed world—and that the streams which are divided by the desert and the rock meet in the solemn Hades, and flow once more into one?'

'Believe I that, O Athenian? No, I do not believe—I *know*! and it is that beautiful and blessed assurance which supports me now. O Cyllene!' continued Olinthus, passionately, 'bride of my heart! torn from me in the first month of our nuptials, shall I not see thee yet, and ere many days be past? Welcome, welcome death, that will bring me to heaven and thee!'

'Tell me, then, thy doctrines, and expound to me thy hopes,' said Glaucus, earnestly.

Olinthus was not slow to obey that prayer; and there—as oftentimes in the early ages of the Christian creed—it was in the darkness of the dungeon, and over the approach of dea‍ that the dawning Gospel shed its soft a‍ ‍secrating rays.

1 ENTRANCE
2 DOOR KEEPER
3 ATHLETES WAITING ROOM
4 ARMS FOUND HERE
5 GUARD ROOM
6 STAIRS TO OVERSEERS ROOMS
7 KITCHEN
8 MESS ROOM

GLADIATORS BARRACKS

A CHANCE FOR GLAUCUS

The hours passed in lingering torture over the head of Nydia from the time in which she had been replaced in her cell.

Sosia, as if afraid he should be again outwitted, had refrained from visiting her until late in the morning of the following day, and then he but thrust in the periodical basket of food and wine, and hastily reclosed the door. That day rolled on, and Nydia felt herself pent—barred—inexorably confined, when that day was the judgment-day of Glaucus, and when her release would have saved him! Yet knowing, almost impossible as seemed her escape, that the sole chance for the life of Glaucus rested on her, this young girl, frail, passionate, and acutely susceptible as she was—resolved not to give way to a despair that would disable her from seizing whatever opportunity *might* occur. She kept her senses whenever, beneath the whirl of intolerable thought, they reeled and tottered; nay, she took food and wine that she might sustain her strength—that she might be prepared!

She revolved scheme after scheme of escape, and was forced to dismiss all. Yet Sosia was her only hope, the only instrument with which she could tamper. She waited burningly till Sosia should again appear: but as hour after hour passed, and he came not, she grew impatient. Every never beat with fever; she could endure the solitude no longer—she groaned, she shrieked aloud—she beat herself against the door. Her cries echoed along the hall, and Sosia, in peevish anger, hastened to see what was the matter, and silence his prisoner if possible.

'Ho! ho! what is this?' said he, surlily. 'Young slave, if thou screamest out thus, we must gag thee again. My shoulders will smart for it, if thou art heard by my master.'

'Kind Sosia, chide me not—I cannot endure to be so long alone,' answered Nydia; 'the solitude appals me. Sit with me, I pray, a little while. Nay, fear not that I should attempt to escape; place thy seat before the door. Keep thine eye on me—I will not stir from this spot.'

'I am sure I do not wish to be churlish; and so far as a little innocent chat goes, I have no objection to indulge you. But mind, no tricks—no more conjuring!'

'No, no; tell me, dear Sosia, what is the hour?'

'It is already evening—the goats are going home.'

'O gods! how went the trial?'

'Both condemned!'

Nydia repressed the shriek. 'Well—well, I thought it would be so. When do they suffer?'

'To-morrow, in the amphitheatre. If it were not for thee, little wretch, I should be allowed to go with the rest and see it.'

Nydia leant back for some moments. Nature could endure no more—she had fainted away. But Sosia did not perceive it, for it was the dusk of eve, and he was full of his own privations. He went on lamenting the loss of so delightful a show, and accusing the injustice of Arbaces for singling him out from all his fellows to be converted into a gaoler; and ere he had half finished, Nydia, with a deep sigh, recovered the sense of life.

'Thou sighest, blind one, at my loss! Well, that is some comfort. So long as you acknowledge how much you cost me, I will endeavour not to grumble. It is hard to be ill-treated, and yet not pitied.'

'Sosia, how much dost thou require to make up the purchase of thy freedom?'

'How much? Why, about two thousand sesterces.'

'The gods be praised! not more? Seest thou these bracelets and this chain? They are well worth double that sum. I will give them thee if——'

'Tempt me not: I cannot release thee. Arbaces is a severe and awful master. Who knows but I might feed the fishes of the Sarnus? Alas! all the sesterces in the world would not buy me back into life. Better a live dog than a dead lion.'

'Sosia, thy freedom! Think well! If thou wilt let me out only for one little hour!—let me out at midnight—I will return ere to-morrow's dawn; nay, thou canst go with me.'

'No,' said Sosia, sturdily, 'a slave once disobeyed Arbaces, and he was never more heard of.'

'But the law gives a master no power over the life of a slave.'

'The law is very obliging, but more polite than efficient. I know that Arbaces always gets the law on his side. Besides, if I am once dead, what law can bring me to life again!'

Nydia wrung her hands. 'Is there no hope, then?' said she, convulsively.

'None of escape till Arbaces gives the word.'

'Well, then,' said Nydia, quickly, 'thou wilt not, at least, refuse to take a letter for me: thy master cannot kill thee for that.'

'To whom?'

'The prætor.'

'To a magistrate? No—not I. I should be made a witness in court, for what I know; and the way they cross-examine the slaves is by the torture.'

'Pardon: I meant not the prætor—it was a word that escaped me unawares: I meant quite another person—the gay Sallust.'

'Oh! and what want you with him?'

'Glaucus was my master; he purchased me from a cruel lord. He alone has been kind to me. He is to die. I shall never live happily if I cannot, in his hour of trial and doom, let him know that one heart is grateful to him. Sallust is his friend; he will convey my message.'

'Give me the trinkets, and I will take the letter. Yet stay—thou art a slave—thou hast no right to these ornaments—they are thy master's.'

'They were the gifts of Glaucus; he is my master. What chance hath he to claim them? Who else will know they are in my possession?'

'Enough—I will bring thee the papyrus.'

'No, not papyrus—a tablet of wax and a stilus.'

STILUS

When the tablet was brought to her, she thus painfully traced some words in Greek, the language of her childhood, and which almost every Italian of the higher ranks was then supposed to know. She carefully wound round the epistle the protecting thread, and covered its knot with wax; and ere she placed it in the hands of Sosia, she thus addressed him:—

'Sosia, I am blind and in prison. Thou mayst think to deceive me—thou mayst pretend only to take the letter to Sallust—thou mayst not fulfil thy charge: but here I solemnly dedicate thy head to vengeance, thy soul to the infernal powers, if thou wrongest thy trust; and I call upon thee to place thy right hand of faith in mine, and repeat after me these words:—"By the ground on which we stand—by the elements which contain life and can curse life—by Orcus, the all-avenging—by the Olympian Jupiter, the all-seeing—I swear that I will honestly discharge my trust, and faithfully deliver into the hands of Sallust this letter! And if I perjure myself in this oath, may the full curses of heaven and hell be wreaked upon me!" Enough!—I trust thee—take thy reward. It is already dark—depart at once.'

'Thou art a strange girl, and thou hast frightened me terribly; but it is all very natural: and if Sallust is to be found, I give him this letter as I have sworn. By my faith, I may have my little peccadilloes! but perjury—no! I leave *that* to my betters.'

With this Sosia withdrew, carefully passing the heavy bolt athwart Nydia's door—carefully locking its wards: and, hanging the key to his girdle, he retired to his own den, enveloped himself from head to foot in a huge disguising cloak, and slipped out by the back way undisturbed and unseen.

The streets were thin and empty. He soon gained the house of Sallust. The porter bade him leave his letter, and be gone; for Sallust was so grieved at the condemnation of Glaucus, that he could not on any account be disturbed.

'Nevertheless, I have sworn to give this letter into his own hands—do so I must!' And Sosia, well knowing by experience that Cerberus loves a sop, thrust some half a dozen sesterces into the hand of the porter.

'Well, well,' said the latter, relenting, 'you may enter if you will; but, to tell you the truth, Sallust is drinking himself out of his grief. It is his way when anything disturbs him. He orders a capital supper, the best wine, and does not give over till everything is out of head—but the liquor.'

'An excellent plan—excellent! Ah, what it is to be rich! If I were Sallust, I would have some grief or another every day. But just say a kind word for me with the atriensis—I see him coming.'

Sallust was too sad to receive company; he was too sad, also, to drink alone; so, as was his wont, he admitted his favourite freedman to his entertainment, and a stranger banquet never was held. For ever and anon, the kind-hearted epicure sighed, whimpered, wept outright, and then turned with double zest to some new dish or his refilled goblet.

It was at this moment that Sosia was admitted to the presence of the disconsolate carouser.

'Ho—what art thou?'

'Merely a messenger to Sallust. I give him this billet from a young female. There is no answer that I know of. May I withdraw?'

Thus said the discreet Sosia, keeping his face muffled in his cloak, and speaking with a feigned voice, so that he might not hereafter be recognised.

GONG

'By the gods—a pimp! Unfeeling wretch! —do you not see my sorrows? Go!—and the curses of Pandarus with you!'

Sosia lost not a moment in retiring.

Sosia's path lay along a narrow lane that led towards the amphitheatre and its adjacent palaces. Suddenly, as he turned a sharp corner he found himself in the midst of a considerable crowd. Men, women, and children, all were hurrying or laughing, talking, gesticulating; and, ere he was aware of it, the worthy Sosia was borne away with the noisy stream.

'What now?' he asked of his nearest neighbour, a young artificer; 'what now? Where are all these good folks thronging? Does any rich patron give away alms or viands to-night?'

'Not so, man—better still,' replied the artificer; 'the noble Pansa—the people's friend—has granted the public leave to see the beasts in their *vivaria*. By Hercules! they will not be seen so safely by some persons to-morrow.'

' 'Tis a pretty sight,' said the slave, yielding to the throng that impelled him onward; 'and since I may not go to the sports to-morrow, I may as well take a peep at the beasts to-night.'

'You will do well,' returned his new acquaintance, 'a lion and a tiger are not to be seen at Pompeii every day.'

The crowd had now arrived at the place of destination; but as the cell in which the wild beasts were confined was extremely small and narrow, tenfold more vehement than it hitherto had been was the rush of the aspirants to obtain admittance. Two of the officers of the amphitheatre, placed at the entrance, very wisely mitigated the evil by dispensing to the foremost only a limited number of tickets at a time, and admitting no new visitors till their predecessors had sated their curiosity. Sosia, who was a tolerably stout fellow, and not troubled with any remarkable scruples of diffidence or good breeding, contrived to be among the first of the initiated.

Separated from his companion the artificer, Sosia found himself in a narrow cell of oppressive heat and atmosphere, and lighted by several rank and flaring torches.

The animals, usually kept in different vivaria, or dens, were now, for the greater entertainment of the visitors, placed in one, but equally indeed divided from each other by strong cages protected by iron bars.

There they were, the fell and grim wanderers of the desert, who have now become almost the principal agents of this story. The lion, who, as being the more gentle by nature than his fellow-beast, had been more incited to ferocity by hunger, stalked restlessly and fiercely to and fro his narrow confines: his eyes were lurid with rage and famine: and as, every now and then, he paused and glared around, the spectators fearfully pressed backward, and drew their breath more quickly. But the tiger lay quiet and extended at full length in his cage, and only by an occasional play of his tail, or a long impatient yawn, testified any emotion at his confinement, or at the crowd which honoured him with his presence.

'I have seen no fiercer beast than yon lion even in the amphitheatre of Rome,' said a gigantic and sinewy fellow who stood at the right hand of Sosia.

'I feel humbled when I look at his limbs,' replied, at the left of Sosia, a slighter and younger figure, with his arms folded on his breast.

The slave looked first at one, and then at the other. '*Virtus in medio!*—virtue is ever in the middle!' muttered he to himself; 'a goodly neighbourhood for thee, Sosia—a gladiator on each side!'

'That is well said, Lydon,' returned the huger gladiator, 'I feel the same.'

'And to think,' observed Lydon, in a tone of deep feeling, 'to think that the noble Greek, he whom we saw but a day or two since before us, so full of youth, and health, and joyousness, is to feast yon monster!'

'Why not?' growled Niger, savagely: 'many an honest gladiator has been compelled to a like combat by the emperor—why not a wealthy murderer by the law?'

Lydon sighed, shrugged his shoulders, and remained silent. Meanwhile the common gazers listened with staring eyes and lips apart: the gladiators were objects of interest as well as the beasts—they were animals of the same species; so the crowd glanced from one to the other—the men and the brutes;— whispering their comments and anticipating the morrow.

'Well!' said Lydon, turning away, 'I thank the gods that it is not the lion or the tiger *I* am to contend with; even you, Niger, are a gentler combatant than they.'

'But equally dangerous,' said the gladiator, with a fierce laugh; and the bystanders, admiring his vast limbs and ferocious countenance, laughed too.

'That as it may be,' answered Lydon, carelessly, as he pressed through the throng and quitted the den.

'I may as well take advantage of his shoulders,' thought the prudent Sosia, hastening to follow him: 'the crowd always give way to a gladiator, so I will keep close behind, and come in for a share of his consequence.'

The son of Medon strode quickly through the mob, many of whom recognised his features and profession.

'That is young Lydon, a brave fellow: he fights to-morrow,' said one.

'Ah! I have a bet on him,' said another, 'see how firmly he walks!'

GLADIATOR'S OUTFIT

SHIELD

GLADIATOR'S HELMET

LEG-GUARD

'Good luck to thee, Lydon!' said a third.

'Lydon, you have my wishes,' half whispered a fourth, smiling (a comely woman of the middle class)—'and if you win, why, you may hear more of me.'

'A handsome man, by Venus!' cried a fifth, who was a girl scarce in her teens. 'Thank you,' returned Sosia, gravely taking the compliment to himself.

However strong the purer motives of Lydon, and certain though it be that he would never have entered so bloody a calling but from the hope of obtaining his father's freedom, he was not altogether unmoved by the notice he excited. He forgot that the voices now raised in commendation might, on the morrow, shout over his death-pangs.

By nature fierce and reckless, as well as generous and warm-hearted, he was already imbued with the pride of a profession that he fancied he disdained, and affected by the influence of a companionship that in reality he loathed. He saw himself now a man of importance; his step grew yet lighter, and his mien more elate.

'Niger,' said he, turning suddenly, as he had now threaded the crowd; 'we have often quarrelled; we are not matched against each other, but one of us, at least, may reasonably expect to fall—give us thy hand.'

'Most readily,' said Sosia, extending his palm.

'Ha! what fool is this? Why, I thought Niger was at my heels!'

'I forgive the mistake,' replied Sosia, condescendingly: 'don't mention it; the error was easy—I and Niger are somewhat of the same build.'

'Ha! ha! that is excellent! Niger would have slit thy throat had he heard thee!'

'You gentlemen of the arena have a most disagreeable mode of talking,' said Sosia; 'let us change the conversation.'

'*Vah! vah!*' said Lydon, impatiently; 'I am in no humour to converse with thee!'

'Why, truly,' returned the slave, 'you must have serious thoughts enough to occupy your mind: to-morrow is, I think, your first essay in the arena. Well, I am sure you will die bravely!'

'May thy words fall on thine own head!' said Lydon, superstitiously, for he by no means liked the blessing of Sosia. '*Die!* No— I trust *my* hour is not yet come.'

'He who plays at dice with death must expect the dog's throw,' replied Sosia, maliciously. 'But you are a strong fellow, and I wish you all imaginable luck; and so, *vale!*'

With that the slave turned on his heel, and took his way homeward.

'I trust the rogue's words are not ominous,' said Lydon, musingly. 'In my zeal for my father's liberty, and my confidence in my own thews and sinews, I have not contemplated the possibility of death. My poor father! I am thy only son!—if I were to fall——'

BOOK FIVE

THE DREAM OF ARBACES

The awful night preceding the fierce joy of the amphitheatre rolled drearily away, and greyly broke forth the dawn of THE LAST DAY OF POMPEII! The air was uncommonly calm and sultry—a thin and dull mist gathered over the valleys and hollows of the broad Campanian fields. But yet it was remarked in surprise by the early fishermen, that, despite the exceeding stillness of the atmosphere, the waves of the sea were agitated, and seemed, as it were, to run disturbedly back from the shore; while along the blue and stately Sarnus there crept a hoarse and sullen murmur, as it glided by the laughing plains and the gaudy villas of the wealthy citizens. Clear above the low mist rose the time-worn towers of the immemorial town, the red-tiled roofs of the bright streets, the solemn columns of many temples, and the statue-crowned portals of the Forum and the Arch of Triumph. Far in the distance, the outline of the circling hills soared above the vapours, and mingled with the changeful hues of the morning sky. The cloud that had so long rested over the crest of Vesuvius had suddenly vanished, and its rugged and haughty brow looked without a frown over the beautiful scenes below.

Despite the earliness of the hour, the gates of the city were already opened. Horsemen upon horsemen, vehicle after vehicle, poured rapidly in; and the voices of numerous pedestrian groups, clad in holiday attire, rose high in joyous and excited merriment; the streets were crowded with citizens and strangers from the populous neighbourhood of Pompeii; and noisily—fast—confusedly swept the many streams of life towards the fatal show.

Despite the vast size of the amphitheatre, seemingly so disproportioned to the extent of the city, and formed to include nearly the whole population of Pompeii itself, so great, on extraordinary occasions, was the concourse of strangers from all parts of Campania, that the space before it was usually crowded for several hours previous to the commencement of the sports, by such persons as were not entitled by their rank to appointed and special seats. And the intense curiosity which the trial and sentence of two criminals so remarkable had occasioned, increased the crowd on this day to an extent wholly unprecedented.

While the common people, with the lively vehemence of their Campanian blood, were thus pushing, scrambling, hurrying on,—yet, amidst all their eagerness, preserving, as is now the wont with Italians in such meetings, a wonderful order and unquarrelsome good

humour, a strange visitor to Arbaces was threading her way to his sequestered mansion. At the sight of her quaint and primæval garb —of her wild gait and gestures—the passengers she encountered touched each other and smiled; but as they caught a glimpse of her countenance, the mirth was hushed at once, for the face was as the face of the dead; and, what with the ghastly features and obsolete robes of the stranger, it seemed as if one long entombed had risen once more amongst the living. In silence and awe each group gave way as she passed along, and she soon gained the broad porch of the Egyptian's palace.

The black porter, like the rest of the world, astir at an unusual hour, started as he opened the door to her summons.

The sleep of the Egyptian had been unusually profound during the night; but, as the dawn approached, it was disturbed by strange and unquiet dreams, which impressed him the more as they were coloured by the peculiar philosophy he embraced.

He thought that he was transported to the bowels of the earth, and that he stood alone in a mighty cavern supported by enormous columns of rough and primæval rock, lost, as they ascended, in the vastness of a shadow athwart whose eternal darkness no beam of day had ever glanced. And in the space between these columns were huge wheels, that whirled round and round unceasingly, and with a rushing and roaring noise. Only to the right and left extremities of the cavern, the space between the pillars was left bare, and the apertures stretched away into galleries —not wholly dark, but dimly lighted by wandering and erratic fires, that, meteor-like, now crept (as the snake creeps) along the rugged and dank soil; and now leaped fiercely to and fro, darting across the vast gloom in wild gambols—suddenly disappearing, and as suddenly bursting into tenfold brilliancy and power. And while he gazed wonderingly upon the gallery to the left, thin, mist-like, aerial shapes passed slowly up; and when they had gained the hall they seemed to rise aloft, and to vanish, as the smoke vanishes, in the measureless ascent.

He turned in fear towards the opposite extremity—and behold! there came swiftly, from the gloom above, similar shadows, which swept hurriedly along the gallery to the right, as if borne involuntarily adown the sides of some invisible stream; and the faces of these spectres were more distinct than those that emerged from the opposite passage; and on some was joy, and on others sorrow— some were vivid with expectation and hope, some unutterably dejected by awe and horror. And so they passed, swift and constantly on, till the eyes of the gazer grew dizzy and blinded with the whirl of an ever-varying

FISH HOOKS

succession of things impelled by a power apparently not their own.

The scene suddenly changed. Arbaces was in a place of human bones; and lo! in the midst of them was a skull, and the skull, still retaining its fleshless hollows, assumed slowly, and in the mysterious confusion of a dream, the face of Apæcides; and forth from the grinning jaws there crept a small worm, and it crawled to the feet of Arbaces. He attempted to stamp on it and crush it; but it became longer and larger with that attempt. It swelled and bloated till it grew into a vast serpent: it coiled itself round the limbs of Arbaces; it crunched his bones; it raised its glaring eyes and poisonous jaws to his face. He writhed in vain; he withered—he gasped—beneath the influence of the blighting breath—he felt himself blasted into death. And then a voice came from the reptile, which still bore the face of Apæcides and rang in his reeling ear,—

'THY VICTIM IS THY JUDGE! THE WORM THOU WOULDST CRUSH BECOMES THE SERPENT THAT DEVOURS THEE!'

With a shriek of wrath, and woe, and despairing resistance, Arbaces awoke—his hair on end—his brow bathed in dew—his eyes glazed and staring—his mighty frame quivering as an infant's, beneath the agony of that dream. He awoke—he collected himself—he blessed the gods whom he disbelieved, that he *was* in a dream;—he turned his eyes from side to side—he saw the dawning light break through his small but lofty window—he was in the Precincts of Day—he rejoiced—he smiled, his eyes fell, and opposite to him he beheld the ghastly features, the lifeless eye, the livid lip—of the hag of Vesuvius!

'Ha!' he cried, placing his hands before his eyes, as to shut out the grisly vision, 'do I dream still?—Am I with the dead?'

'Mighty Hermes—no! Thou art with one death-like, but not dead. Recognise thy friend and slave.'

There was a long silence. Slowly the shudders that passed over the limbs of the Egyptian chased each other away, faintlier and faintlier dying till he was himself again.

'It was a dream, then,' said he. 'Well—let me dream no more, or the day cannot compensate for the pangs of night. Woman, how camest thou here, and wherefore?'

'I came to warn thee,' answered the sepulchral voice of the saga.

'Warn me! The dream lied not, then? Of what peril?'

'Listen to me. Some evil hangs over this fated city. Fly while it be time. Thou knowest that I hold my home on that mountain beneath which old tradition saith there yet burn the fires of the river of Phlegethon; and in my cavern is a vast abyss, and in that

abyss I have of late marked a red and dull stream creep slowly, slowly on; and heard many and mighty sounds hissing and roaring through the gloom. But last night, as I looked thereon, behold the stream was no longer dull, but intensely and fiercely luminous; and while I gazed, the beast that liveth with me, and was cowering by my side, uttered a shrill howl, and fell down and died, and the slaver and froth were round his lips. I crept back to my lair; but I distinctly heard, all the night, the rock shake and tremble; and, though the air was heavy and still, there were the hissing of pent winds, and the grinding as of wheels, beneath the ground. So, when I rose this morning at the very birth of dawn, I looked again down the abyss, and I saw vast fragments of stone borne black and floatingly over the lurid stream; and the stream itself was broader, fiercer, redder than the night before. Then I went forth, and ascended to the summit of the rock: and in that summit there appeared a sudden and vast hollow, which I had never perceived before, from which curled a dim, faint smoke; and the vapour was deathly, and I gasped, and sickened, and nearly died. I returned home. I took my gold and my drugs, and left the habitation of many years; for I remembered the dark Etruscan prophecy which saith, "When the mountain opens, the city shall fall—when the smoke crowns the Hill of the Parched Fields, there shall be woe and weeping in the hearths of the Children of the Sea." Dread master, ere I leave these walls for some more distant dwelling, I come to thee. As thou livest, know I in my heart that the earthquake that sixteen years ago shook this city to its solid base, was but the forerunner of more deadly doom. The walls of Pompeii are built above the fields of the Dead, and the rivers of the sleepless Hell. Be warned and fly!'

'Witch, I thank thee for thy care of one not ungrateful. On yon table stands a cup of gold; take it, it is thine. I dreamt not that there lived one, out of the priesthood of Isis, who would have saved Arbaces from destruction. The signs thou hast seen in the bed of the extinct volcano,' continued the Egyptian, musingly, 'surely tell of some coming danger to the city; perhaps another earthquake fiercer than the last. Be that as it may, there is a new reason for my hastening from these walls.'

The hag, who had placed the costly gift of Arbaces in the loose folds of her vest, now rose to depart. When she had gained the door she paused, turned back, and said, 'This may be the last time we meet on earth; but whither flieth the flame when it leaves the ashes?—Wandering to and fro, up and down as an exhalation on the morass, the flame may be seen in the marshes of the lake below; and the witch and the Magian, the pupil and the master, the great one and the accursed one, may meet again. Farewell!'

'Out, croker!' muttered Arbaces, as the door closed on the hag's tattered robes; and, impatient of his own thoughts, not yet recovered from the past dream, he hastily summoned his slaves.

THE AMPHITHEATRE

Nydia, assured by the account of Sosia, on his return home, and satisfied that her letter was in the hands of Sallust, gave herself up once more to hope. Sallust would surely lose no time in seeking the prætor—in coming to the house of the Egyptian—in releasing her—

in breaking the prison of Calenus. That very night Glaucus would be free. Alas! the night passed—the dawn broke; she heard nothing but the hurried footsteps of the slaves along the hall and peristyle, and their voices in preparation for the show. By-and-by, the commanding voice of Arbaces broke on her ear—a flourish of music rung out cheerily: the long procession were sweeping to the amphitheatre to glut their eyes on the death-pangs of the Athenian!

The procession of Arbaces moved along slowly, and with much solemnity, till now, arriving at the place where it was necessary for such as came in litters or chariots to alight, Arbaces descended from his vehicle, and proceeded to the entrance by which the more distinguished spectators were admitted. His slaves, mingling with the humbler crowd, were stationed by officers who received their tickets in places in the *popularia* (the seats apportioned to the vulgar). And now, from the spot where Arbaces sat, his eyes scanned the mighty and impatient crowd that filled the stupendous theatre.

On the upper tier (but apart from the male spectators) sat the women, their gay dresses resembling some gaudy flower-bed; it is needless to add that they were the most talkative part of the assembly; and many were the looks directed up to them, especially from the benches appropriated to the young and the unmarried men. On the lower seats round the arena sat the more high-born and wealthy visitors—the magistrates and those of senatorial or equestrian dignity; the passages which, by corridors at the right and left, gave access to these seats, at either end of the oval arena, were also the entrances for the combatants. Strong palings at these passages prevented any unwelcome eccentricity in the movements of the beasts, and confined them to their appointed prey. Around the parapet which was raised above the arena, and from which the seats gradually rose, were gladiatorial inscriptions, and paintings wrought in fresco, typical of the entertainments for which the place was designed. Throughout the whole building wound invisible pipes, from which, as the day advanced, cooling and fragrant showers were to be sprinkled over the spectators. The officers of the amphitheatre were still employed in the task of fixing the vast awning (or *velaria*) which covered the whole, and which luxurious invention the Campanians arrogated to themselves: it was woven of the whitest Apulian wool, and variegated with broad stripes of crimson. Owing either to some inexperience on the part of the workmen, or to some defect in the machinery, the awning, however, was not arranged that day so happily as usual; indeed, from the immense space of the circumference, the task was always one of great

difficulty and art—so much so, that it could seldom be adventured in rough or windy weather. But the present day was so remarkably still that there seemed to the spectators no excuse for the awkwardness of the artificers; and when a large gap in the back of the awning was still visible, from the obstinate refusal of one part of the *velaria* to ally itself with the rest, the murmurs of discontent were loud and general.

The ædile Pansa, at whose expense the exhibition was given, looked particularly annoyed at the defect, and vowed bitter vengeance on the head of the chief officer of the show, who, fretting, puffing, perspiring, busied himself in idle orders and unavailing threats.

The hubbub ceased suddenly—the operators desisted—the crowd were stilled—the gap was forgotten—for now, with a loud and warlike flourish of trumpets, the gladiators, marshalled in ceremonious procession, entered the arena. They swept round the oval space very slowly and deliberately, in order to give the spectators full leisure to admire their stern serenity of feature—their brawny limbs and various arms, as well as to form such wagers as the excitement of the moment might suggest.

'Oh!' cried the widow Fulvia, to the wife of Pansa, as they leaned down from their lofty bench, 'do you see that gigantic gladiator? how drolly he is dressed!'

'Yes,' said the ædile's wife, with complacent importance, for she knew all the names and qualities of each combatant; 'he is a *retiarius* or netter; he is armed only, you see, with a three-pronged spear like a trident, and a net; he wears no armour, only the fillet and the tunic. He is a mighty man, and is to fight with Sporus, yon thick-set gladiator, with the round shield and drawn sword, but without body armour; he has not his helmet on now, in order that you may see his face—how fearless it is!—by-and-by he will fight with his vizor down.'

'But surely a net and a spear are poor arms against a shield and sword?'

'That shows how innocent you are, my dear Fulvia; the retiarius has generally the best of it.'

'But who is yon handsome gladiator, nearly naked—is it not quite improper? By Venus! but his limbs are beautifully shaped!'

'It is Lydon, a young untried man! he has the rashness to fight yon other gladiator similarly dressed, or rather undressed—Tetraides. They fight first in the Greek fashion, with the cestus; afterwards they put on armour, and try sword and shield.'

'He is a proper man, this Lydon; and the women, I am sure, are on his side.'

'So are not the experienced betters; Clodius offers three to one against him!'

'Oh, Jove! how beautiful!' exclaimed the widow, as two gladiators, armed *cap-à-pie*, rode round the arena on light and prancing steeds. Resembling much the combatants in the tilts of the middle age, they bore lances and round shields beautifully inlaid: their armour was woven intricately with bands of iron, but it covered only the thighs and the right arms; short cloaks, extending to the seat, gave a picturesque and graceful air to

THE AMPHITHEATRE

their costume; their legs were naked, with the exception of sandals, which were fastened a little above the ankle. 'Oh, beautiful! Who are these?' asked the widow.

'The one is named Berbix—he has conquered twelve times; the other assumes the arrogant name of Nobilior. They are both Gauls.'

While thus conversing, the first formalities of the show were over. To these succeeded a feigned combat with wooden swords between the various gladiators matched against each other. Amongst these, the skill of two Roman gladiators, hired for the occasion, was the most admired; and next to them the most graceful combatant was Lydon. This sham contest did not last above an hour, nor did it attract any very lively interest, except among those connoisseurs of the arena to whom art was preferable to more coarse excitement; the body of the spectators were rejoiced when it was over, and when the sympathy rose to terror. The combatants were now arranged in pairs, as agreed beforehand; their weapons examined; and the grave sports of the day commenced amidst the deepest silence—broken only by an exciting and preliminary blast of warlike music.

It was often customary to begin the sports by the most cruel of all, and some bestiarius, or gladiator appointed to the beasts, was slain first, as an initiatory sacrifice. But in the present instance, the experienced Pansa thought it better that the sanguinary drama should advance, not decrease, in interest; and, accordingly, the execution of Olinthus and Glaucus was reserved for the last. It was arranged that the two horsemen should first occupy the arena; that the foot gladiators, paired off, should then be loosed indiscriminately on the stage; that Glaucus and the lion should next perform their part in the bloody spectacle; and the tiger and the Nazarene be the grand finale. And, in the spectacles of Pompeii, the reader of Roman history must limit his imagination, nor expect to find those vast and wholesale exhibitions of magnificent slaughter with which a Nero or a Caligula regaled the inhabitants of the Imperial City The Roman shows, which absorbed the more celebrated gladiators, and the chief proportion of foreign beasts, were indeed the very reason why, in the lesser towns of the empire, the sports of the amphitheatre were comparatively humane and rare; and in this, as in other respects, Pompeii was but the miniature, the microcosm of Rome. Still, it was an awful and imposing spectacle, with which modern times have, happily, nothing to compare:—a vast theatre, rising row upon row, and swarming with human beings, from fifteen to eighteen thousand in number, intent upon no fictitious representation—no tragedy of the stage—but the actual victory or

defeat, the exultant life or the bloody death, of each and all who entered the arena!

The two horsemen were now at either extremity of the lists (if so they might be called); and, at a given signal from Pansa, the combatants started simultaneously as in full collision, each advancing his round buckler, each poising on high his light yet sturdy javelin; but just when within three paces of his opponent, the steed of Berbix suddenly halted, wheeled round, and, as Nobilior was borne rapidly by, his antagonist spurred upon him. The buckler of Nobilior, quickly and skilfully extended, received a blow which otherwise would have been fatal.

'Well done, Nobilior!' cried the prætor, giving the first vent to the popular excitement.

'Bravely struck, my Berbix!' answered Clodius from his seat.

And the wild murmur, swelled by many a shout, echoed from side to side.

The vizors of both the horsemen were completely closed (like those of the knights in after times), but the head was, nevertheless, the great point of assault; and Nobilior, now wheeling his charger with no less adroitness than his opponent, directed his spear full on the helmet of his foe. Berbix raised his buckler to shield himself, and his quick-eyed antagonist, suddenly lowering his weapon, pierced him through the breast. Berbix reeled and fell.

'Nobilior! Nobilior!' shouted the populace.

'I have lost ten sestertia,' said Clodius, between his teeth.

'Habet!—he has it,' said Pansa, deliberately.

The populace, not yet hardened into cruelty, made the signal of mercy; but as the attendants of the arena approached, they found the kindness came too late;—the heart of the Gaul had been pierced, and his eyes were set in death. It was his life's blood that flowed so darkly over the sand and sawdust of the arena.

'It is a pity it was so soon over—there was little enough for one's trouble,' said the widow Fulvia.

'Yes—I have no compassion for Berbix. Any one might have seen that Nobilior did but feint. Mark, they fix the fatal hook to the body—they drag him away to the spoliarium—they scatter new sand over the stage! Pansa regrets nothing more than that he is not rich enough to strew the arena with borax and cinnabar, as Nero used to do.'

'Well, if it has been a brief battle, it is quickly succeeded. See my handsome Lydon on the arena—ay—and the net-bearer too, and the swordsmen! Oh, charming!'

There were now on the arena six combatants: Niger and his net, matched against Sporus with his shield and his short broadsword; Lydon and Tetraides, naked save by a cincture round the waist, each armed only

with a heavy Greek cestus—and two gladiators from Rome, clad in complete steel, and evenly matched with immense bucklers and pointed swords.

The initiatory contest between Lydon and Tetraides being less deadly than that between the other combatants, no sooner had they advanced to the middle of the arena than, as by common consent, the rest held back, to see how that contest should be decided, and wait till fiercer weapons might replace the cestus, ere they themselves commenced hostilities. They stood leaning on their arms and apart from each other, gazing on the show, which, if not bloody enough, thoroughly to please the populace, they were still inclined to admire, because its origin was of their ancestral Greece.

No person could, at first glance, have seemed less evenly matched than the two antagonists. Tetraides, though not taller than Lydon, weighed considerably more; the natural size of his muscles was increased, to the eyes of the vulgar, by masses of solid flesh; for, as it was a notion that the contest of the cestus fared easiest with him who was plumpest, Tetraides had encouraged to the utmost his hereditary predisposition to the portly. His shoulders were vast, and his lower limbs thick-set, double-jointed, and slightly curved outward, in that formation which takes so much from beauty to give so largely to strength. But Lydon, except that he was slender, even almost to meagreness, was beautifully and delicately proportioned; and the skilful might have perceived that, with much less compass of muscle than his foe, that which he had was more seasoned—iron and compact. In proportion, too, as he wanted flesh, he was likely to possess activity; and a haughty smile on his resolute face which strongly contrasted the solid heaviness of his enemy's gave assurance to those who beheld it, and united their hope to their pity: so that, despite the disparity of their seeming strength, the cry of the multitude was nearly as loud for Lydon as for Tetraides.

Whoever is acquainted with the modern prize-ring—whoever has witnessed the heavy and disabling strokes which the human fist, skilfully directed, hath the power to bestow—may easily understand how much that happy facility would be increased by a band carried by thongs of leather round the arm as high as the elbow, and terribly strengthened about the knuckles by a plate of iron, and sometimes a plummet of lead. Yet this, which was meant to increase, perhaps rather diminished, the interest of the fray: for it necessarily shortened its duration.

'Guard thyself!' growled Tetraides, moving nearer and nearer to his foe, who rather shifted round him than receded.

Lydon did not answer, save by a scornful

glance of his quick, vigilant eye. Tetraides struck—it was as the blow of a smith on a vice; Lydon sank suddenly on one knee—the blow passed over his head. Not so harmless was Lydon's retaliation: he quickly sprung to his feet, and aimed his cestus full on the broad breast of his antagonist. Tetraides reeled—the populace shouted.

'You are unlucky to-day,' said Lepidus to Clodius: 'you have lost one bet—you will lose another.'

'By the gods! my bronzes go to the auctioneer if that is the case. I have no less than a hundred sestertia upon Tetraides. Ha, ha! see how he rallies! That was a home stroke: he has cut open Lydon's shoulder.—A Tetraides!—a Tetraides!'

'But Lydon is not disheartened. By Pollux! how well he keeps his temper. See how dexterously he avoids those hammer-like hands!—dodging now here, now there—circling round and round. Ah, poor Lydon! he has it again.'

'Three to one still on Tetraides! What say you, Lepidus?'

'Well, nine sestertia to three—be it so! What! again, Lydon? He stops—he gasps for breath. By the gods, he is down; No—he is again on his legs. Brave Lydon! Tetraides is encouraged—he laughs loud—he rushes on him.'

'Fool—success blinds him—he should be cautious. Lydon's eye is like the lynx's,' said Clodius, between his teeth.

'Ha, Clodius! saw you that? Your man totters! Another blow—he falls—he falls!'

'Earth revives him, then. He is once more up; but the blood rolls down his face.'

'By the thunderer! Lydon wins it. See how he presses on him! That blow on the temple would have crushed an ox! it *has* crushed Tetraides. He falls again—he cannot move—*habet!*—*habet!*'

'*Habet!*' repeated Pansa. 'Take them out and give them the armour and swords.'

'Noble editor,' said the officers, 'we fear that Tetraides will not recover in time; howbeit, we will try.'

'Do so.'

In a few minutes the officers, who had dragged off the stunned and insensible gladiator, returned with rueful countenances. They feared for his life; he was utterly incapacitated from re-entering the arena.

'In that case,' said Pansa, 'hold Lydon a *subdititius*, and the first gladiator that is vanquished, let Lydon supply his place with the victor.'

The people shouted their applause at this sentence: then they again sunk into deep silence. The trumpet sounded loudly. The four combatants stood each against each in prepared and stern array.

'Dost thou recognise the Romans, my

Clodius; are they among the celebrated, or are they merely *ordinarii?*'

'Eumolpus is a good second-rate swordsman, my Lepidus. Nepimus, the lesser man, I have never seen before: but he is the son of one of the imperial *fiscales*, and brought up in a proper school; doubtless they will show sport, but I have no heart for the game; I cannot win back my money—I am undone. Curses on that Lydon! who could have supposed he was so dexterous or so lucky?'

'Well, Clodius, shall I take compassion on you, and accept your own terms with these Romans?'

'An even ten sestertia on Eumolpus, then?'

'What! when Nepimus is untried? Nay, nay; that is too bad.'

'Well—ten to eight?'

'Agreed.'

While the contest in the amphitheatre had thus commenced, there was one in the loftier benches for whom it had assumed, indeed, a poignant—a stifling interest. The aged father of Lydon, despite his Christian horror of the spectacle, in his agonised anxiety for his son, had not been able to resist being the spectator of his fate. One amidst a fierce crowd of strangers—the lowest rabble of the populace—the old man saw, felt nothing, but the form—the presence of his brave son! Not a sound had escaped his lips when twice he had seen him fall to the earth;—only he had turned paler, and his limbs trembled. But he had uttered one low cry when he saw him victorious; unconscious, alas! of the more fearful battle to which that victory was but a prelude.

'My gallant boy!' said he, and wiped his eyes.

'Is he thy son?' said a brawny fellow to the right of the Nazarene; 'he has fought well: let us see how he does by-and-by. Hark! he is to fight the first victor. Now, old boy, pray the gods that that victor be neither of the Romans! nor, next to them, the giant Niger.'

The old man sat down again and covered his face. The fray for the moment was indifferent to him—Lydon was not one of the combatants. Yet—yet—the thought flashed across him—the fray was indeed of deadly interest—the first who fell was to make way for Lydon! He started, and bent down, with straining eyes and clasped hands to view the encounter.

The first interest was attracted towards the combat of Niger with Sporus; for this species of contest, from the fatal result which usually attended it, and from the great science it required in either antagonist, was always peculiarly inviting to the spectators.

They stood at a considerable distance from each other. The singular helmet which Sporus wore (the vizor of which was down) concealed his face; but the features of Niger

GLADIATOR'S HELMET

attracted a fearful and universal interest from their compressed and vigilant ferocity. Thus they stood for some moments, each eyeing each, until Sporus began slowly, and with great caution, to advance, holding his sword pointed, like a modern fencer's, at the breast of his foe. Niger retreated as his antagonist advanced, gathering up his net with his right hand, and never taking his small glittering eye from the movements of the swordsman. Suddenly when Sporus had approached nearly at arm's length, the retiarius threw himself forward, and cast his net. A quick inflection of body saved the gladiator from the deadly snare! he uttered a sharp cry of joy and rage, and rushed upon Niger: but Niger had already drawn in his net, thrown it across his shoulders, and now fled round the lists with a swiftness which the *secutor* in vain endeavoured to equal. The people laughed and shouted aloud, to see the ineffectual efforts of the broad-shouldered gladiator to overtake the flying giant: when, at that moment, their attention was turned from these to the two Roman combatants.

They had placed themselves at the onset face to face, at the distance of modern fencers from each other: but the extreme caution which both evinced at first had prevented any warmth of engagement, and allowed the spectators full leisure to interest themselves in the battle between Sporus and his foe. But the Romans were now heated into full and fierce encounter: they pushed—returned—advanced on—retreated from—each other with all that careful yet scarcely perceptible caution which characterises men well experienced and equally matched. But at this moment, Eumolpus, the elder gladiator, by that dexterous back-stroke which was considered in the arena so difficult to avoid, had wounded Nepimus in the side. The people shouted; Lepidus turned pale.

'Ho!' said Clodius, 'the game is nearly over. If Eumolpus fights now the quiet fight, the other will gradually bleed himself away.'

'But, thank the gods! he does *not* fight the backward fight. See!—he presses hard upon Nepimus. By Mars! but Nepimus had him there! the helmet rang again!—Clodius, I shall win!'

'Why do I ever bet but at the dice?' groaned Clodius to himself;—'or why cannot one cog a gladiator?'

'A Sporus!—a Sporus!' shouted the populace, as Niger having now suddenly paused, had again cast his net, and again unsuccessfully. He had not retreated this time with sufficient agility—the sword of Sporus had inflicted a severe wound upon his right leg; and, incapacitated to fly, he was pressed hard by the fierce swordsman. His great height and length of arm still continued, however, to give him no despicable advantages; and steadily keeping his trident at the front of his foe, he repelled him successfully for several minutes. Sporus now tried, by great rapidity of evolution, to get round his antagonist, who necessarily moved with pain and slowness. In so doing, he lost his caution —he advanced too near to the giant—raised his arm to strike, and received the three points of the fatal spear full in his breast! He sank on his knee. In a moment more, the deadly net was cast over him, he struggled against its meshes in vain; again—again— again he writhed mutely beneath the fresh strokes of the trident—his blood flowed fast through the net and redly over the sand. He lowered his arms in acknowledgment of defeat.

The conquering retiarius withdrew his net, and leaning on his spear, looked to the audience for their judgment. Slowly, too, at the same moment, the vanquished gladiator rolled his dim and despairing eyes around the theatre. From row to row, from bench to bench, there glared upon him but merciless and unpitying eyes.

Hushed was the roar—the murmur! The silence was dread, for in it was no sympathy; not a hand—no, not even a woman's hand— gave the signal of charity and life! Sporus had never been popular in the arena; and, lately, the interest of the combat had been excited on behalf of the wounded Niger. The people were warmed into blood—the *mimic* fight had ceased to charm; the interest had mounted up to the desire of sacrifice and the thirst of death!

The gladiator felt that his doom was sealed: uttered no prayer—no groan. The people

gave the signal of death! In dogged but agonised submission, he bent his neck to receive the fatal stroke. And now, as the spear of the retiarius was not a weapon to inflict instant and certain death, there stalked into the arena a grim and fatal form, brandishing a short, sharp sword, and with features utterly concealed beneath its vizor. With slow and measured steps, this dismal headsman approached the gladiator, still kneeling—laid the left hand on his humbled crest—drew the edge of the blade across his neck—turned round to the assembly, lest, in the last moment, remorse should come upon them; the dread signal continued the same: the blade glittered brightly in the air—fell—and the gladiator rolled upon the sand; his limbs quivered—were still,—he was a corpse.

His body was dragged at once from the arena through the gate of death, and thrown into the gloomy den termed technically the spoliarium. And ere it had well reached that destination, the strife between the remaining combatants was decided. The sword of Eumolpus had inflicted the death wound upon the less experienced combatant. A new victim was added to the receptacle of the slain.

Throughout that mighty assembly there now ran a universal movement; the people breathed more freely, and resettled themselves in their seats. A grateful shower was cast over every row from the concealed conduits. In cool and luxurious pleasure they talked over the late spectacle of blood. Eumolpus removed his helmet, and wiped his brows; his close-curled hair and short beard, his noble Roman features and bright dark eye attracted the general admiration. He was fresh, unwounded, unfatigued.

The editor paused, and proclaimed aloud that, as Niger's wound disabled him from again entering the arena, Lydon was to be the successor to the slaughtered Nepimus, and the new combatant of Eumolpus.

'Yet, Lydon,' added he, 'if thou wouldst decline the combat with one so brave and tried, thou mayst have full liberty to do so. Eumolpus is not the antagonist that was originally decreed for thee. Thou knowest best how far thou canst cope with him. If thou failest, thy doom is honourable death; if thou conquerest, out of my own purse I will double the stipulated prize.'

The people shouted applause. Lydon stood in the lists, he gazed around; high above he beheld the pale face, the straining eyes, of his father. He turned away irresolute for a moment. No! the conquest of the cestus was not sufficient—he had not yet won the prize of victory—his father was still a slave!

'Noble ædile!' he replied, in a firm and deep tone, 'I shrink not from this combat. For the honour of Pompeii, I demand that

one trained by its long-celebrated lanista shall do battle with this Roman.'

The people shouted louder than before.

'Four to one against Lydon!' said Clodius to Lepidus.

'I would not take twenty to one! Why, Eumolpus is a very Achilles, and this poor fellow is but a *tyro!*'

Eumolpus gazed hard on the face of Lydon; he smiled; yet the smile was followed by a slight and scarce audible sigh—a touch of compassionate emotion, which custom conquered the moment the heart acknowledged it.

And now both, clad in complete armour, the sword drawn, the vizor closed, the two last combatants of the arena (ere man, at least, was matched with beast), stood opposed to each other.

It was just at this time that a letter was delivered to the prætor by one of the attendants of the arena; he removed the cincture— glanced over it for a moment—his countenance betrayed surprise and embarrassment. He re-read the letter, and then muttering,— 'Tush! it is impossible!—the man must be drunk, even in the morning, to dream of such follies!'—threw it carelessly aside, and gravely settled himself once more in the attitude of attention to the sports.

The interest of the public was wound up very high. Eumolpus had at first won their favour; but the gallantry of Lydon, and his well-timed allusion to the honour of the Pompeian lanista had afterwards given the latter the preference in their eyes.

'Holla, old fellow!' said Medon's neighbour to him. 'Your son is hardly matched; but never fear, the editor will not permit him to be slain—no, nor the people neither; he has behaved too bravely for that. Ha! that was a home thrust!—well averted, by Pollux! At him again, Lydon!—they stop to breathe! What art thou muttering, old boy?'

'Prayers!' answered Medon, with a more calm and hopeful mien than he had yet maintained.

'Prayers!—trifles! The time for gods to carry a man away in a cloud is gone now. Ha! Jupiter! what a blow! Thy side—thy side!— take care of thy side, Lydon!'

There was a convulsive tremor throughout the assembly. A fierce blow from Eumolpus, full on the crest had brought Lydon to his knee.

'*Habet!*—he has it!' cried a shrill female voice; 'he has it!'

Meanwhile Lydon, who had hitherto defended himself with great skill and valour, began to give way before the vigorous assaults of the practised Roman; his arm grew tired, his eye dizzy, he breathed hard and painfully. The combatants paused again for breath.

'Young man,' said Eumolpus, in a low voice,

'desist; I will wound thee slightly—then lower thy arms; thou hast propitiated the editor and the mob—thou wilt be honourably saved!'

'And my father still enslaved!' groaned Lydon to himself. 'No! death or his freedom.'

At that thought, and seeing that, his strength not being equal to the endurance of the Roman, everything depended on a sudden and desperate effort, he threw himself fiercely on Eumolpus; the Roman warily retreated—Lydon thrust again—Eumolpus drew himself aside—the sword grazed his cuirass—Lydon's breast was exposed—the Roman plunged his sword through the joints of the armour, not meaning, however, to inflict a deep wound; Lydon, weak and exhausted, fell forward, fell on the point: it passed through and through, even to the back. Eumolpus drew forth his blade; Lydon still made an effort to regain his balance—his sword left his grasp—he struck mechanically at the gladiator with his naked hand, and fell prostrate on the arena. With one accord, editor and assembly made the signal of mercy—the officers of the arena approached—they took off the helmet of the vanquished. He still breathed; his eyes rolled fiercely on his foe; the savageness he had acquired in his calling glared from his gaze, and lowered upon the brow darkened already with the shades of death; then, with a convulsive groan, with a half start, he lifted his eyes above. They rested not on the face of the editor nor on the pitying brows of his relenting judges. He saw them not; they were as if the vast space was desolate and bare; one pale agonising face alone was all he recognised —one cry of a broken heart was all that, amidst the murmurs and the shouts of the populace, reached his ear. The ferocity vanished from his brow; a soft, a tender expression of sanctifying but despairing filial love played over his features—played—waned—darkened! His face suddenly became locked and rigid, resuming its former fierceness. He fell upon the earth.

'Look to him,' said the ædile; 'he has **done** his duty!'

The officers dragged him off to the spoliarium.

'A true type of glory, and of its fate!' murmured Arbaces to himself; and his eye, glancing round the amphitheatre, betrayed so much of disdain and scorn, that whoever encountered it felt his breath suddenly arrested, and his emotions frozen into one sensation of abasement and of awe.

Again rich perfumes were wafted around the theatre; the attendants sprinkled fresh sand over the arena.

'Bring forth the lion and Glaucus the Athenian,' said the editor.

And a deep and breathless hush of over-wrought interest, and intense (yet, strange to say, not unpleasing) terror lay, like a mighty and awful dream, over the assembly.

SALLUST READS NYDIA'S LETTER

THRICE had Sallust awakened from his morning sleep, and thrice, recollecting that his friend was that day to perish, had he turned himself with a deep sigh once more to court oblivion. His sole object in life was to avoid pain; and where he could not avoid, at least to forget it.

At length, unable any longer to steep his consciousness in slumber, he raised himself from his incumbent posture, and discovered his favourite freedman sitting by his bedside as usual; for Sallust, who, as I have said, had a gentlemanlike taste for the polite letters, was accustomed to be read to for an hour or so previous to his rising in the morning.

'No books to-day! no more Tibullus! no more Pindar for me! Pindar! alas, alas! the very name recalls those games to which our arena is the savage successor. Has it begun—the amphitheatre? are its rites commenced?'

'Long since, O Sallust! Did you not hear the trumpets and the trampling feet?'

'Ay, ay; but the gods be thanked, I was drowsy, and had only to turn round to fall asleep again.'

'The gladiators must have been long in the ring?'

'The wretches! None of my people have gone to the spectacle?'

'Assuredly not; your orders were too strict.'

'That is well—would the day were over! What is that letter yonder on the table?'

'That! Oh, the letter brought to you last night, when you were—too—too——'

'Drunk to read it, I suppose. No matter, it cannot be of much importance.'

'Shall I open it for you, Sallust?'

'Do: anything to divert my thoughts. Poor Glaucus!'

The freedman opened the letter. 'What! Greek?' said he: 'some learned lady, I suppose.' He glanced over the letter, and for

BED ALSO USED AS COUCH FOR RECLINING

some moments the irregular lines traced by the blind girl's hand puzzled him. Suddenly, however, his countenance exhibited emotion and surprise. 'Good gods! noble Sallust! what have we done not to attend to this before? Hear me read!

' "Nydia, the slave, to Sallust, the friend of Glaucus! I am a prisoner in the house of Arbaces. Hasten to the prætor! procure my release, and we shall yet save Glaucus from the lion. There is another prisoner within these walls, whose witness can exonerate the Athenian from the charge against him;—one who saw the crime—who can prove the criminal in a villain hitherto unsuspected. Fly! hasten! quick! quick! Bring with you armed men, lest resistance be made, and a cunning and dexterous smith; for the dungeon of my fellow-prisoner is thick and strong. Oh! by thy right hand and thy father's ashes, lose not a moment!" '

'Great Jove!' exclaimed Sallust, starting, 'and this day—nay, within this hour, perhaps, he dies. What is to be done? I will instantly to the prætor.'

'Nay; not so. The prætor (as well as Pansa, the editor himself) is the creature of the mob; and the mob will not hear of delay; they will not be balked in the very moment of expectation. Besides, the publicity of the appeal would forewarn the cunning Egyptian. It is evident that he has some interest in these concealments. No; fortunately thy slaves are in thy house.'

'I seize thy meaning,' interrupted Sallust: 'arm the slaves instantly. The streets are empty. We will ourselves hasten to the house of Arbaces , and release the prisoners. Quick! quick! What ho! Davus there! My gown and sandals, the papyrus and a reed. I will write to the prætor, to beseech him to delay the sentence of Glaucus, for that, within an hour, we may yet prove him innocent. So, so, that is well. Hasten with this, Davus, to the prætor, at the amphitheatre. See it given to his own hand. Now then, O ye gods! whose providence Epicurus denied, befriend me, and I will call Epicurus a liar!'

DECORATION FROM BEDSTEAD

THE AMPHITHEATRE ONCE MORE

Glaucus and Olinthus had been placed together in that gloomy and narrow cell in which the criminals of the arena awaited their last and fearful struggle. Their eyes, of late accustomed to the darkness, scanned the faces of each other in this awful hour, and by that dim light, the paleness, which chased away the natural hues from either cheek, assumed a yet more ashy and ghastly whiteness. Yet their brows were erect and dauntless—their limbs did not tremble—their lips were compressed and rigid. The religion of the one, the pride of the other, the conscious innocence of both, and, it may be, the support derived from their mutual companionship, elevated the victim into the hero.

'Hark! hearest thou that shout? They are growling over their human blood,' said Olinthus.

'I hear; my heart grows sick; but the gods support me.'

'The gods! O rash young man! in this hour recognise only the One God. Have I not taught thee in the dungeon, wept for thee, prayed for thee?—in my zeal and in my agony, have I not thought more of thy salvation than my own?'

'Brave friend!' answered Glaucus, solemnly, 'I have listened to thee with awe, with wonder, and with a secret tendency towards conviction. Had our lives been spared, I might gradually have weaned myself from the tenets of my own faith, and inclined to thine; but, in this last hour it were a craven thing, and a base, to yield to hasty terror what should only be the result of lengthened meditation. Speak we no more of this. Hush! Dost thou hear them drag yon heavy body through the passage? Such as that clay will be ours soon.'

'O Heaven! O Christ! already I behold ye!' cried the fervent Olinthus, lifting up his hands; 'I tremble not—I rejoice that the prison-house shall be soon broken.'

Glaucus bowed his head in silence. He felt the distinction between his fortitude and that of his fellow-sufferer. The heathen did not tremble; but the Christian exulted.

The door swung gratingly back—the gleam of spears shot along the walls.

'Glaucus the Athenian, thy time has come,' said a loud and clear voice; 'the lion awaits thee.'

'I am ready,' said the Athenian. 'Brother and co-mate, one last embrace! Bless me—and farewell!'

The Christian opened his arms—he clasped the young heathen to his breast—he kissed his forehead and cheek—he sobbed aloud—his tears flowed fast and hot over the features of his new friend.

'Oh! could I have converted thee, I had not wept. Oh! that I might say to thee, "We two shall sup this night in Paradise!" '

'It may be so yet,' answered the Greek, with a tremulous voice. 'They whom death part not, may meet yet beyond the grave: on the earth—on the beautiful, the beloved earth, farewell for ever!—Worthy officer, I attend you.'

Glaucus tore himself away; and when he came forth into the air, its breath, which, though sunless, was hot and arid, smote witheringly upon him. His frame, not yet restored from the effects of the deadly draught, shrank and trembled. The officers supported him.

'Courage!' said one; 'thou art young, active, well knit. They give thee a weapon! despair not, and thou mayst yet conquer.'

Glaucus did not reply; but, ashamed of his infirmity, he made a desperate and convulsive effort, and regained the firmness of his nerves. They anointed his body, completely naked, save by a cincture round the loins, placed the stilus (vain weapon!) in his hand, and led him into the arena.

And now when the Greek saw the eyes of thousands and tens of thousands upon him, he no longer felt that he was mortal. All evidence of fear—all fear itself—was gone. A red and haughty flush spread over the paleness of his features—he towered aloft to the full of his glorious stature. In the elastic beauty of his limbs and form, in his intent but unfrowning brow, in the high disdain, and in the indomitable soul, which breathed visibly, which spoke audibly, from his attitude, his lip, his eye,—he seemed the very incarnation, vivid and corporeal, of the valour of his land —of the divinity of its worship—at once a hero and a god!

The murmur of hatred and horror at his crime, which had greeted his entrance, died into the silence of involuntary admiration and half-compassionate respect; and with a quick and convulsive sigh, that seemed to move the whole mass of life as if it were one body, the gaze of the spectators turned from the Athenian to a dark uncouth object in the centre of the arena. It was the grated den of the lion!

'By Venus, how warm it is!' said Fulvia; 'yet there is no sun. Would that those stupid sailors could have fastened up that gap in the awning!'

'Oh! it is warm, indeed. I turn sick—I faint!' said the wife of Pansa; even her experienced stoicism giving way at the struggle about to take place.

The lion had been kept without food for twenty-four hours, and the animal had, during the whole morning, testified a singular and restless uneasiness, which the keeper had attributed to the pangs of hunger. Yet its bearing seemed rather that of fear than of rage; its roar was painful and distressed; it hung its head—snuffed the air through the bars—then lay down—started again—and again uttered its wild and far-resounding cries. And now, in its den, it lay utterly dumb and mute, with distended nostrils forced hard against the grating, and disturbing with a heaving breath, the sand below on the arena.

The editor's lip quivered, and his cheek grew pale; he looked anxiously around—hesitated—delayed; the crowd became impatient. Slowly he gave the sign; the keeper, who was behind the den, cautiously removed the grating, and the lion leaped forth with a mighty and glad roar of release. The keeper hastily retreated through the grated passage leading from the arena, and left the lord of the forest—and his prey.

Glaucus had bent his limbs so as to give himself the firmest posture at the expected rush of the lion, with his small and shining weapon raised on high, in the faint hope that *one* well-directed thrust (for he knew that he should have time but for *one*) might penetrate through the eye to the brain of his grim foe.

But, to the unutterable astonishment of all, the beast seemed not even aware of the presence of the criminal.

At the first moment of its release it halted abruptly in the arena, raised itself half on end, snuffing the upward air with impatient sighs; then suddenly it sprang forward, but not on the Athenian. At half-speed it circled round and round the space, turning its vast head from side to side with an anxious and perturbed gaze, as if seeking only some avenue of escape; once or twice it endeavoured to leap up the parapet that divided it from the audience, and, on failing, uttered rather a baffled howl than its deep-toned and kingly roar. It evinced no sign, either of wrath or hunger; its tail dropped along the sand, instead of lashing its gaunt sides; and its eye, though it wandered at times to Glaucus, rolled again listlessly from him. At length, as if tired of attempting to escape, it crept with a moan into its cage, and once more laid itself down to rest.

The first surprise of the assembly at the apathy of the lion soon grew converted into resentment at its cowardice; and the populace already merged their pity for the fate of Glaucus into angry compassion for their own disappointment.

The editor called to the keeper.

'How is this? Take the goad, prick him forth, and then close the door of the den.'

As the keeper, with some fear, but more astonishment, was preparing to obey, a loud cry was heard at one of the entrances of the arena; there was a confusion, a bustle—voices of remonstrance suddenly breaking forth, and suddenly silenced at the reply. All eyes turned in wonder at the interruption, towards the quarter of the disturbance; the crowd gave way, and suddenly Sallust appeared on the senatorial benches, his hair dishevelled—breathless—heated—half-exhausted. He cast his eyes hastily round the ring. 'Remove the Athenian,' he cried; 'haste—he is innocent! Arrest Arbaces the Egyptian—HE is the murder of Apæcides!'

'Art thou mad, O Sallust!' said the prætor, rising from his seat. 'What means this raving?'

'Remove the Athenian!—Quick! or his blood be on your head. Prætor, delay, and you answer with your own life to the emperor! I bring with me the eye-witness to the death of the priest Apæcides. Room there!—stand back!—give way! People of Pompeii, fix every eye upon Arbaces—there he sits! Room there for the priest Calenus!'

Pale, haggard, fresh from the jaws of famine and of death, his face fallen, his eyes dull as a vulture's, his broad frame gaunt as a skeleton,—Calenus was supported into the very row in which Arbaces sat. His releasers had given him sparingly of food; but the chief sustenance that nerved his feeble limbs was revenge!

'The priest Calenus!—Calenus!' cried the mob. '*Is* it he? No—it is a dead man?'

'It *is* the priest Calenus,' said the prætor, gravely. 'What hast thou to say?'

'Arbaces of Egypt is the murderer of Apæcides, the priest of Isis; these eyes saw him deal the blow. It is from the dungeon into which he plunged me—it is from the darkness and horror of a death by famine—that the gods have raised me to proclaim his crime! Release the Athenian—he is innocent!'

'It is for this, then, that the lion spared him.—A miracle! a miracle!' cried Pansa.

'A miracle! a miracle!' shouted the people; 'remove the Athenian—*Arbaces to the lion!*'

And that shout echoed from hill to vale—from coast to sea—'*Arbaces to the lion!*'

'Officers, remove the accused Glaucus—remove, but guard him yet,' said the prætor. 'The gods lavish their wonders upon this day.'

As the prætor gave the word of release, there was a cry of joy—a female voice—a child's voice—and it was of joy! It rang through the heart of the assembly with electric force—it was touching, it was holy, that child's voice! And the populace echoed it back with sympathising congratulation!

'Silence!' said the grave prætor—'who is there?'

'The blind girl—Nydia,' answered Sallust; 'it is her hand that has raised Calenus from the grave, and delivered Glaucus from the lion.'

'Of this hereafter,' said the prætor. 'Calenus, priest of Isis, thou accusest Arbaces of the murder of Apæcides?'

'I do.'

'Thou didst behold the deed?'

'Prætor—with these eyes——'

'Enough at present—the details must be reserved for more suiting time and place. Arbaces of Egypt, thou hearest the charge against thee—thou has not yet spoken—what hast thou to say?'

The gaze of the crowd had been long riveted on Arbaces: but not until the confusion which he had betrayed at the first charge of Sallust and the entrance of Calenus had subsided. At the shout, 'Arbaces to the lion!' he had indeed trembled, and the dark bronze of his cheek had taken a paler hue. But he had soon recovered his haughtiness and self-control. Proudly he returned the angry glare of the countless eyes around him; and replying now to the question of the prætor, he said, in that accent so peculiarly tranquil and commanding, which characterised his tones,—

'Prætor, this charge is so mad that it scarcely deserves reply. My first accuser is the noble Sallust—the most intimate friend of Glaucus! my second is a priest; I revere his garb and calling—but, people of Pompeii! ye know somewhat of the character of Calenus—he is griping and gold-thirsty to a proverb; the witness of such men is to be bought! Prætor, I am innocent!'

'Sallust,' said the magistrate, 'where found you Calenus?'

'In the dungeons of Arbaces.'

'Egyptian,' said the prætor, frowning, 'thou didst, then, dare to imprison a priest of the gods—and wherefore?'

'Hear me,' answered Arbaces, rising calmly, but with agitation visible in his face. 'This man came to threaten that he would make against me the charge he has now made, unless I would purchase his silence with half my fortune: I remonstrated—in vain. Peace there—let not the priest interrupt me! Noble prætor—and ye, O people! I was a stranger in the land—I knew myself innocent of crime—but the witness of a priest against me might yet destroy me. In my perplexity I decoyed him to the cell whence he has been released, on pretence that it was the coffer-house of my gold. I resolved to detain him there until the fate of the true criminal was sealed, and his threats could avail no longer; but I meant no worse. I may have erred—but who amongst ye will not acknowledge the equity of self-preservation? Were I guilty, why was the witness of this priest silent at the trial?—*then* I had not detained or concealed him. Why did he not proclaim my guilt when I proclaimed that of Glaucus? Prætor, this needs an answer. For the rest, I throw myself on your laws. I demand their protection. Remove hence the accused and the accuser. I will willingly meet, and cheerfully abide by, the decision of the legitimate tribunal. This is no place for further parley.'

'He says right,' said the prætor. 'Ho! guards—remove Arbaces—guard Calenus! Sallust, we hold you responsible for your accusation. Let the sports be resumed.'

'What!' cried Calenus, turning round to the people, 'shall Isis be thus contemned? Shall the blood of Apæcides yet cry for vengeance? Shall justice be delayed now, that it may be frustrated hereafter? Shall the lion be cheated of his lawful prey? A god! a god! —I feel the god rush to my lips! *To the lion —to the lion with Arbaces!*'

His exhausted frame could support no longer the ferocious malice of the priest; he sank on the ground in strong convulsions— the foam gathered to his mouth—he was as a man, indeed, whom a supernatural power had entered! The people saw and shuddered.

'It is a god that inspires the holy man! *To the lion with the Egyptian!*'

With that cry up sprang—on moved— thousands upon thousands! They rushed from the heights—they poured down in the direction of the Egyptian. In vain did the

ædile command—in vain did the prætor lift his voice and proclaim the law. The people had been already rendered savage by the exhibition of blood—they thirsted for more— their superstition was aided by their ferocity. Aroused—inflamed by the spectacle of their victims, they forgot the authority of their rulers. It was one of those dread popular convulsions common to crowds wholly ignorant, half free and half servile; and which the peculiar constitution of the Roman provinces so frequently exhibited. The power of the prætor was as a reed beneath the whirl-wind; still, at his word the guards had drawn themselves along the lower benches, on which the upper classes sat separate from the vulgar. They made but a feeble barrier—the waves of the human sea halted for a moment, to enable Arbaces to count the exact moment of his doom! In despair, and in a terror which beat down even pride, he glanced his eyes over the rolling and rushing crowd—when, right above them, through the wide chasm which had been left in the velaria, he beheld a strange and awful apparition—he beheld— and his craft restored his courage!

He stretched his hand on high; over his lofty brow and royal features there came an expression of unutterable solemnity and command.

'Behold!' he shouted with a voice of thunder, which stilled the roar of the crowd; 'behold how the gods protect the guiltless! The fires of the avenging Orcus burst forth against the false witness of my accusers!'

The eyes of the crowd followed the gesture of the Egyptian, and beheld, with ineffable dismay, a vast vapour shooting from the summit of Vesuvius, in the form of a gigantic pine-tree; the trunk, blackness,—the bran-ches, fire!—a fire that shifted and wavered in its hues with every moment, now fiercely luminous, now of a dull and dying red, that again blazed terrifically forth with intolerable glare!

There was a dead, heart-sunken silence— through which there suddenly broke the roar of the lion, which was echoed back from within the building by the sharper and fiercer yells of its fellow-beast. Dread seers were they of the Burden of the Atmosphere, and wild prophets of the wrath to come!

Then there arose on high the universal shrieks of women; the men stared at each other, but were dumb. At that moment they felt the earth shake beneath their feet; the walls of the theatre trembled: and, beyond in the distance, they heard the crash of falling roofs; an instant more and the mountain-cloud seemed to roll towards them, dark and rapid, like a torrent; at the same time, it cast forth from its bosom a shower of ashes mixed with vast fragments of burning stone! Over the crushing vines,—over the desolate streets, —over the amphitheatre itself,—far and wide, —with many a mighty splash in the agitated sea,—fell that awful shower!

No longer thought the crowd of justice or of Arbaces; safety for themselves was their sole thought. Each turned to fly—each dash-ing, pressing, crushing, against the other. Trampling recklessly over the fallen—amidst groans, and oaths, and prayers, and sudden shrieks, the enormous crowd vomited itself forth through the numerous passages.

MONEY CHEST

THE CELL OF THE PRISONER AND THE DEN OF THE DEAD

PORTABLE LAMP

Stunned by his reprieve, doubting that he was awake, Glaucus had been led by the officers of the arena into a small cell within the walls of the theatre. They threw a loose robe over his form, and crowded round in congratulation and wonder. There was an impatient and fretful cry without the cell; the throng gave way, and the blind girl, led by some gentler hand, flung herself at the feet of Glaucus.

'It is *I* who have saved thee,' she sobbed; 'now let me die!'

'Nydia, my child!—my preserver!'

'Oh, let me feel thy touch—thy breath! Yes, yes, thou livest! We are not too late! That dread door, methought it would never yield! and Calenus—oh! his voice was as the dying wind among tombs:—we had to wait,—gods! it seemed hours ere food and wine restored to him something of strength. But thou livest! thou livest yet! And I—I have saved thee!'

This affecting scene was soon interrupted by the event just described.

'The mountain! the earthquake!' resounded from side to side. The officers fled with the rest; they left Glaucus and Nydia to save themselves as they might.

As the sense of the dangers around them flashed on the Athenian, his generous heart recurred to Olinthus. He, too, was reprieved from the tiger by the hand of gods; should he be left to a no less fatal death in the neighbouring cell? Taking Nydia by the hand, Glaucus hurried across the passages; he gained the den of the Christian! He found Olinthus kneeling in prayer.

'Arise! arise! my friend,' he cried. 'Save thyself, and fly! See! Nature is thy dread deliverer!' He led forth the bewildered Christian, and pointed to a cloud which advanced darker and darker, disgorging forth showers of ashes and pumice stones;—and bade him hearken to the cries and trampling rush of the scattered crowd.

'This is the hand of God—God be praised!' said Olinthus, devoutly.

'Fly! seek thy brethren! Concert with them thy escape. Farewell!'

Olinthus did not answer, neither did he mark the retreating form of his friend.

At length he roused himself, and hurried on, he scarce knew whither.

The open doors of a dark, desolate cell suddenly appeared on his path; through the gloom within there flared and flickered a single lamp; and by its light he saw three grim and naked forms stretched on the earth in death. His feet were suddenly arrested; for, amidst the terrors of that drear recess—the spoliarium of the arena—he heard a low voice calling on the name of Christ!

He could not resist lingering at that appeal: he entered the den, and his feet were dabbled in the slow streams of blood that gushed from the corpses over the sand.

'Who,' said the Nazarene, 'calls upon the son of God?'

No answer came forth; and turning round, Olinthus beheld, by the light of the lamp, an old grey-headed man sitting on the floor, and supporting in his lap the head of one of the dead.

'Medon!' said Olinthus, pityingly, 'arise, and fly! God is forth upon the wings of the elements! The New Gomorrah is doomed!—Fly, ere the fires consume thee!'

'He was ever so full of life!—he *cannot* be dead! Come hither!—place your hand on his heart!—sure it beats yet?'

'Brother, the soul has fled! We will remember it in our prayers! Thou canst not reanimate the dumb clay! Come, come—hark! while I speak, yon crashing walls!—hark! yon agonising cries! Not a moment is to be lost!—Come!'

'I hear nothing!' said Medon, shaking his grey hair. 'The poor boy, his love murdered him!'

'Come! come! forgive this friendly force.'

'What! Who could sever the father from the son?' And Medon clasped the body tightly in his embrace, and covered it with passionate kisses. 'Go!' said he, lifting up his face for one moment. 'Go!—we must be alone!'

'Alas!' said the compassionate Nazarene, 'Death hath severed ye already!'

The old man smiled very calmly. 'No, no, no!' he muttered, his voice growing lower with each word,—'Death has been more kind!'

With that his head drooped on his son's breast—his arms relaxed their grasp. Olinthus caught him by the hand—the pulse had ceased to beat! The last words of the father were the words of truth,—*Death had been more kind!*

Meanwhile Glaucus and Nydia were pacing swiftly up the perilous and fearful streets. The Athenian had learned from his preserver that Ione was yet in the house of Arbaces. Thither he fled, to release—to save her! The few slaves whom the Egyptian had left at his mansion when he had repaired in long procession to the amphitheatre, had been able to offer no resistance to the armed band of Sallust; and when afterwards the volcano broke forth, they had huddled together, stunned and frightened, in the inmost recesses of the house. Even the tall Ethiopian had forsaken his post at the door; and Glaucus (who left Nydia without—the poor Nydia, jealous once more, even in such an hour!) passed on through the vast hall without meeting one from whom to learn the chamber of Ione. Even as he passed, however, the darkness that covered the heavens increased so rapidly that it was with difficulty he could guide his steps. The flower-wreathed columns seemed to reel and tremble; and with every instant he heard the ashes fall cranchingly into the roofless peristyle. He ascended to the upper rooms—breathless he paced along, shouting out aloud the name of Ione; and at length he heard, at the end of a gallery, a voice—*her* voice, in wondering reply! To rush forward—to shatter the door —to seize Ione in his arms—to hurry from the mansion—seemed to him the work of an instant! Scarce had he gained the spot where Nydia was, than he heard steps advancing towards the house, and recognised the voice of Arbaces, who had returned to seek his wealth and Ione ere he fled from the doomed Pompeii. But so dense was already the reeking atmosphere, that the foes saw not each other, though so near,—save that, dimly in the gloom, Glaucus caught the moving outline of the snowy robes of the Egyptian.

THE ROMAN YEAR

The ancient year was made up of 355 days. To keep in step with the sun's course, the Romans had to use a very complicated system. At various times they got badly out of step. This was largely because the regulation of the calendar was in the hands of a group of public servants, who were sometimes incompetent, sometimes merely lazy, and often corrupt. (Tax collectors liked long years; those away from Rome short years.)

These irregularities were abolished in 45BC by Julius Caesar, who introduced a new calendar which is basically the same as the western calendar today.

The Kalends were the first day of each month; the Nones fell on the fifth day in short months and the seventh day in long months; the Ides fell on the thirteenth day in short months and the fifteenth day in long months (March, May, July and October).

The farmer, before the new calendar, had to rely on his own experience and devised his own form of calendar made up of the twelve months marked by the signs of the zodiac, the number of days within the months, hours of light and dark, planting and harvest times and much more. One of these had been found at Pompeii and two more in Rome.

The Romans generally worked an eight-day week and had a market day on the ninth. But by the middle of the 1st century AD, a seven-day week was universal in the Roman world.

There was a full calendar of fixed festivals and games. Extra feast days were inserted for the birthdays, and special achievements of the emperors.

GRAPHITO FROM POMPEII. USED TO CALCULATE MARKET DAYS IN LOCAL TOWNS.

STONE SUNDIAL: THERE WAS A DIFFERENCE IN THE LENGTH OF HOURS IN THE ROMAN DAY, AS THEY HAD 12 HOURS OF DARKNESS & 12 OF LIGHT

FARMERS CALENDAR FOUND IN POMPEII

PART OF THE CALENDAR OF ROMAN FEASTS. BASED VERY MUCH ON THE AGRICULTURAL YEAR. APRIL TO THE FERTILITY GODS. NOT MANY FEASTS IN JUNE, SEPTEMBER OR NOVEMBER WHEN MEN WERE IN THE FIELDS. A LOT IN AUGUST WHEN IT WAS TOO HOT TO WORK. THIS DOES NOT MEAN THAT EVERY FEAST DAY WAS OBSERVED, MOST PEOPLE WORKED ONLY CEASING WHEN A PROCESSION OF PRIESTS CAME INTO SIGHT.

JANUARY
9TH TO JANUS
11TH 15TH TO CARMENTIS
13TH IDES, TO JUPITER
FEBRUARY
13TH IDES, TO JUPITER
15TH TO LUPERCUS
17TH TO QUIRINUS
21ST TO NETHER GODS
23RD TO TERMINUS
24TH TO JUPITER
27TH TO MARS CHARIOT RACE
MARCH
1ST KALENDS, TO MARS
15TH IDES, TO JUPITER
17TH TO LIBER & MARS
19TH TO MARS & MINERVA
23RD TO MARS
APRIL
4TH 10TH LUDI MEGALENSES
12TH 19TH LUDI CERIALES
13TH IDES, JUPITER
15TH TO TELLUS
19TH TO CERES, LIBER
21ST BIRTHDAY OF ROME
23RD TO JUPITER & VENUS
25TH TO ROBIGUS
28TH LUDI FLORALES
MAY
9 11 13TH TO LEMURES
15TH TO JUPITER
21ST TO VEDIOVIS
23RD TO VULCAN
JUNE
9TH TO VESTA
11TH TO MATER MATUTA
13TH IDES, TO JUPITER
JULY
5TH TO JUPITER
6TH 11TH LUDI APOLLINARES
15TH IDES, TO JUPITER
19TH 21ST TO LUCARIA
20TH 30TH LUDI VICTORIAE
23RD TO NEPTUNE
25TH TO FURRINA

SIMPLE ROMAN HOUSE (BELOW)
BASED ON GREEK PLAN WITH
ROMAN ADDITIONS.
1 VESTIBULUM (PORCH) 2 FAUCES
(PASSAGE) 3 ATRIUM (COURT) 4 TABLINUM
(RECEPTION) 5 PERISTYLIUM (COURT)
6 TRICLINIUM (DINING) 7 KITCHEN
OTHER ROOMS USED FOR BEDS, STORES.

PLAN OF TYPICAL BLOCK OF HOUSES,

OSCILLA: HUNG
BETWEEN PILLARS
TO REFLECT
SUNLIGHT

SHOPS & WORKSHOPS. INDUSTRY
AND THE POPULACE COEXISTED IN
CLOSE COMMUNITY
1 HOUSES 2 FULLERS (CLOTH
CLEANERS) 3 SHOPS & TAVERNS

THE HOUSE OF PANSA
SHOPS AND HOUSES HAVE BEEN BUILT AROUND IT.
AT THE BACK IS A LARGE GARDEN, FORMALLY LAID
OUT. ONLY THE GROUND FLOOR REMAINS SO THE
FIRST FLOOR IS CONJECTURAL. THE WALLS
WOULD HAVE BEEN RICHLY PAINTED.
1 ATRIUM 2 TABLINUM 3 PERISTYLIUM 4 OECUS
(RECEPTION ROOM) 5 COLONNADE 6 KITCHEN
7 TRICLINIUM 8 WINTER TRICLINIUM 9 GARDEN
10 BEDROOMS 11 SEPARATE HOUSES 12 SHOPS

FACADE OF THE HOUSE OF THE FAUN
A TYPICAL POMPEIIAN FACADE, WITH FRONT
DOOR, AND BALCONIED SHOPS.

LEFT
SUBURBAN VILLA OF DIOMEDES
1 ENTRANCE 2 PERISTYLIUM
3 DINING ROOM 4 KITCHEN 5 BATHS
6 SWIMMING POOL 7 GARDEN
RIGHT
COUNTRY VILLA, BOSCOREALE
1 COURT WITH TROUGHS 2 KITCHEN
3 BATHS 4 STABLES 5 TOOL ROOM
6 DINING ROOM 7 BAKERY 8 BEDROOMS
9 WINE PRESS ROOM 10 WINE FER-
MENTATION JARS CEMENTED
INTO COURT - TOPS OPEN SO
THAT THE ELEMENTS COULD WORK
ON THE WINE.

ANTEFIXA

WATERSPOUT

TILES MADE TO OVERLAP, 'IMBRICES'
FITTED OVER JOINTS. 'ANTEFIXAE'
ORNAMENTAL TERRACOTTAS, FITTED
THE ROOF TILES AT EAVES' ENDS.

THE ROMANS GROUPED THEIR
HOUSES INTO TOWN, SUBURBAN
& COUNTRY

VOLCANOES

There are many kinds of volcanoes. On the right the main types are illustrated. Basically they all have a tube which passes from the magma (reservoir of rock heated to melting point deep in the Earth's core). There are many theories on the reasons why volcanoes erupt. Some say that they erupt because of weak fault lines in the Earth's crust; others that radioactive 'mineral' pockets heat rocks to melting point and that the consequent pressure forces the magma to the surface. As yet there is no definitive answer.

1 MAGMA RESERVOIR 2 PIPE 3 DYKE
4 SILL 5 VOLCANOE CONE

CROSS SECTION OF VESUVIUS TODAY

VESUVIAN OR PLINEAN
LAVA & GAS BLOWN TO GREAT HEIGHT.
SHOWERS OF ASH AND WATER FALL.

VULCANIAN
LAVA SOLIDIFIES BETWEEN ERUPTIONS
AND BLOWN OUT AT HIGH PRESSURE.

STROMBOLIAN
GAS TRAPPED UNDER PRESSURE BLOWS
OUT LAVA AND ASH.

PELEAN
CLOUDS OF GLOWING LAVA AND HIGHLY
POISONOUS GAS ROLL DOWN SIDE.

HAWAIIAN
LITTLE PRESSURE, LAVA MAKES LAKE.
SPRAYS OF LAVA OCCASIONALLY SPOUTS.

ICELANDIC OR FISSURE
NOT VIOLENT, BUT LARGE VOLUMES
OF LAVA CREEP OVER THE SURFACE

AREAS OF VOLCANIC ACTIVITY

They hastened onward—those three: Alas! whither? They now saw not a step before them—the blackness became utter. They were encompassed with doubt and horror!—and the death he had escaped seemed to Glaucus only to have changed its form and augmented its victims.

CALENUS AND BURBO

The sudden catastrophe which had, as it were, riven the very bonds of society, and left prisoner and jailer alike free, had soon rid Calenus of the guards to whose care the prætor had consigned him. And when the darkness and the crowd separated the priest from his attendants, he hastened with trembling steps towards the temple of his goddess. As he crept along, and ere the darkness was complete, he felt himself suddenly caught by the robe, and a voice muttered in his ear,—

'Hist!—Calenus!—an awful hour!'

'Ay! by my father's head! Who art thou?—thy face is dim, and thy voice is strange!'

'Not know thy Burbo?—fie! Listen! Thy temple is full of gold and precious mummeries!—let us load ourselves with them, and then hasten to the sea and embark! None will ever ask an account of the doings of this day.'

'Burbo, thou art right! Hush, and follow me into the temple. Who cares now—who sees now—whether thou art a priest or not? Follow, and we will share.'

In the precincts of the temple were many priests gathered around the altars, praying, weeping, grovelling in the dust. Imposters in safety, they were not the less superstitious in danger! Calenus passed them. Burbo followed him—the priest struck a light. Wine and viands strewed the table; the remains of a sacrificial feast.

'A man who has hungered forty-eight hours,' muttered Calenus, 'has an appetite even in such a time.' He seized on the food, and devoured it greedily.

'Wilt thou never have done?' said Burbo, impatiently; 'thy face purples and thine eyes start already.'

'It is not every day one has such a right to be hungry. Oh, Jupiter! what sound is that?—the hissing of fiery water! What! does the cloud give rain as well as flame! Ha!—what! shrieks? And, Burbo, how silent all is now! Look forth!'

Amidst the other horrors, the mighty mountain now cast up columns of boiling water. Blent and kneaded with the half-burning ashes, the streams fell like seething mud over the streets in frequent intervals. And full, where the priests of Isis had now cowered around the altars, on which they had vainly sought to kindle fires and pour incense, one of the fiercest of those deadly torrents, mingled with immense fragments of scoria, had poured its rage. Over the bended forms of the priests it dashed: that cry had been of death—that silence had been of eternity! The ashes—the pitchy stream—sprinkled the altars, covered the pavement, and half concealed the quivering corpses of the priests!

'They are dead,' said Burbo, terrified for the first time, and hurrying back into the cell. 'I thought not the danger was so near and fatal.'

The two wretches stood staring at each other—you might have heard their hearts beat! Calenus, the less bold by nature, but the more griping, recovered first.

'We must to our task, and away!' he said, in a low whisper, frightened at his own voice. He stepped to the threshold, paused, crossed over the heated floor and his dead brethren to the sacred chapel, and called to Burbo to follow. But the gladiator quaked, and drew back.

'So much the better,' thought Calenus; 'the more will be *my* booty.' Hastily he loaded himself with the more portable treasures of the temple; and thinking no more of his comrade, hurried from the sacred place. A sudden flash of lightning from the mount showed to Burbo, who stood motionless at the threshold, the flying and laden form of the priest. He took heart; he stepped forth to join him, when a tremendous shower of ashes fell right before his feet. The gladiator shrank back once more. Darkness closed him in. But the shower continued fast—fast; its heaps rose high and suffocatingly—deathly vapours steamed from them. The wretch gasped for breath—he sought in despair again to fly—the ashes had blocked up the threshold—he shrieked as his feet shrank from the boiling fluid. How could he escape? he could not climb to the open space; nay, were he able, he could not brave its horrors. It were best to remain in the cell, protected, at least, from the fatal air. He sat down and clenched his teeth. By degrees, the atmosphere from without—stifling and venomous—crept into the chamber. He could endure it no longer. His eyes, glaring round, rested on a sacrificial axe, which some priest had left in the chamber: he seized it. With the desperate strength of his gigantic arm, he attempted to hew his way through the walls.

Meanwhile, the streets were already thinned; the crowd had hastened to disperse itself under shelter; the ashes began to fill up the lower parts of the town; but, here and there, you heard the steps of fugitives cranching them warily, or saw their pale and haggard faces by the blue glare of the lightning, or the more unsteady glare of torches, by which they endeavoured to steer their steps. But ever and anon, the boiling water, or the straggling ashes, mysterious and gusty winds, rising and dying in a breath, extinguished these wandering lights, and with them the last living hope of those who bore them.

In the street that leads to the gate of Herculaneum, Clodius now bent his perplexed and doubtful way. 'If I can gain the open country,' thought he, 'doubtless there will be various vehicles beyond the gate, and Herculaneum is not far distant. Thank Mercury! I have little to lose, and that little is about me!'

CASTS OF CORPSES
FOUND DURING EXCAVATIONS

'Holla!—help there—help!' cried a querulous and frightened voice. 'I have fallen down—my torch has gone out—my slaves have deserted me. I am Diomed—the rich Diomed;—ten thousand sesterces to him who helps me!'

At the same moment, Clodius felt himself caught by the feet. 'Ill fortune to thee,—let me go, fool,' said the gambler.

'Oh, help me up!—give me thy hand!'

'There—rise!'

'Is this Clodius? I know the voice! Whither fliest thou?'

'Towards Herculaneum.'

'Blessed be the gods! our way is the same, then, as far as the gate. Why not take refuge in my villa? Thou knowest the long range of subterranean cellars beneath the basement—that shelter, what shower can penetrate?'

'You speak well,' said Clodius musingly. 'And by storing the cellar with food, we can remain there even some days, should these wondrous storms endure so long.'

TERRACOTTA POT

The air was now still for a few minutes: the lamp from the gate streamed out far and clear: the fugitives hurried on—they gained the gate—they passed by the Roman sentry; the lightning flashed over his livid face and polished helmet, but his stern features were composed even in their awe! He remained erect and motionless at his post. That hour itself had not animated the machine of the ruthless majesty of Rome into the reasoning and self-acting man. There he stood, amidst the crashing elements: he had not received the permission to desert his station and escape.

They hurried on—they arrived at the house of Diomed—they laughed aloud as they crossed the threshold, for they deemed the danger over.

Diomed ordered his slaves to carry down into the subterranean gallery, before described, a profusion of food and oil for lights; and there Julia, Clodius, the greater part of the slaves, and some frightened visitors and clients of the neighbourhood, sought their shelter.

GLASS JUG

'Oh, blessed be he who invented gates to a city!' cried Diomed. 'See!—they have placed a light within yon arch: by that let us guide our steps.'

BRONZE POT

THE PROGRESS OF THE DESTRUCTION

The cloud, which had scattered so deep a murkiness over the day, had now settled into a solid and impenetrable mass. It resembled less even the thickest gloom of a night in the open air than the close and blind darkness of some narrow room. But in proportion as the blackness gathered, did the lightnings around Vesuvius increase in their vivid and scorching glare. Nor was their horrible beauty confined to the usual hues of fire; no rainbow ever rivalled their varying and prodigal dyes. Now brightly blue as the most azure depth of a southern sky—now of a livid and snakelike green, darting restlessly to and fro as the folds of an enormous serpent—now of a lurid and intolerable crimson, gushing forth through the columns of smoke, far and wide, and lighting up the whole city from arch to arch,—then suddenly dying into a sickly paleness, like the ghost of their own life!

In the pauses of the showers, you heard the rumbling of the earth beneath, and the groaning waves of the tortured sea; or, lower still, and audible but to the watch of intensest fear, the grinding and hissing murmur of the escaping gases through the chasms of the distant mountain. Sometimes the cloud appeared to break from its solid mass, and, by the lightning, to assume quaint and vast mimicries of human or of monster shapes, striding across the gloom, hurtling one upon the other, and vanishing swiftly into the turbulent abyss of shade.

The ashes in many places were already knee-deep; and the boiling showers which came from the steaming breath of the volcano forced their way into the houses, bearing with them a strong and suffocating vapour. In some places, immense fragments of rock, hurled upon the house roofs, bore down along the streets masses of confused ruin, which yet more and more, with every hour, obstructed the way; and, as the day advanced, the motion of the earth was more sensibly felt—the footing seemed to slide and creep—nor could chariot or litter be kept steady, even on the most level ground.

Sometimes the huger stones striking against each other as they fell, broke into countless fragments, emitting sparks of fire, which caught whatever was combustible within their reach; and along the plains beyond the city the darkness was now terribly relieved; for several houses, and even vineyards, had been set on flames; and at various intervals the fires rose suddenly and fiercely against the solid gloom. To add to this partial relief of the darkness, the citizens had, here and there, in the more public places, such as the porticos of temples and the entrances to the forum, endeavoured to place rows of torches; but these rarely continued long; the showers and the winds extinguished them, and the sudden darkness into which their sudden birth was converted had something in it doubly terrible and doubly impressing on the impotence of human hopes, the lesson of despair.

Frequently, by the momentary light of these torches, parties of fugitives encountered each other, some hurrying towards the sea, others flying from the sea back to the land, for the ocean had retreated rapidly from the shore—an utter darkness lay over it, and upon its groaning and tossing waves the storm of cinders and rock fell without the protection which the streets and roofs afforded to the land.

Through this awful scene did the Athenian wade his way, accompanied by Ione and the blind girl. Suddenly, a rush of hundreds, in their path to the sea, swept by them. Nydia was torn from the side of Glaucus, who, with Ione, was borne rapidly onward; and when the crowd (whose forms they saw not, so thick was the gloom) were gone, Nydia was

still separated from their side. Glaucus shouted her name. No answer came. They retraced their steps—in vain: they could not discover her—it was evident she had been swept along some opposite direction by the human current. Their friend, their preserver, was lost! And hitherto Nydia had been their guide. *Her blindness rendered the scene familiar*

to her alone. Accustomed, through a perpetual night, to thread the windings of the city, she had led them unerringly towards the sea-shore, by which they had resolved to hazard an escape. Now, which way could they wend? all was rayless to them—a maze without a clue. Wearied, despondent, bewildered, they, however, passed along, the ashes falling upon their heads, the fragmentary stones dashing up in sparkles before their feet.

'Alas! alas!' murmured Ione, 'I can go no farther, my steps sink among the scorching cinders. Fly, dearest!—beloved, fly! and leave me to my fate!'

'Hush, my betrothed! my bride! Death with thee is sweeter than life without thee! Yet, whither—oh! whither, can we direct ourselves through the gloom? Already it seems that we have made but a circle, and are in the very spot which we quitted an hour ago.'

'O gods! yon rock—see, it hath riven the roof before us! It is death to move through the streets!'

'Blessed lightning! See, Ione—see! the portico of the Temple of Fortune is before us. Let us creep beneath it; it will protect us from the showers.'

MOULDS OF CORPSES FOUND IN EXCAVATIONS

He caught his beloved in his arms, and with difficulty and labour gained the temple. He bore her to the remoter and more sheltered part of the portico, and leaned over her, that he might shield her, with his own form, from the lightning and the showers! The beauty and the unselfishness of love could hallow even that dismal time!

'Who is there?' said the trembling and hollow voice of one who had preceded them in their place of refuge. 'Yet, what matters?—the crush of the ruined world forbids to us friends or foes.'

Ione turned at the sound of the voice, and, with a faint shriek, cowered again beneath the arms of Glaucus: and he, looking in the direction of the voice, beheld the cause of her alarm. Through the darkness glared forth two burning eyes—the lightning flashed and lingered athwart the temple—and Glaucus, with a shudder, perceived the lion to which he had been doomed couched beneath the pillars; —and, close beside it, unwitting of the vicinity, lay the giant form of him who had accosted them—the wounded gladiator, Niger.

That lightning had revealed to each other the form of beast and man; yet the instinct of both was quelled. Nay, the lion crept nearer and nearer to the gladiator, as for companionship; and the gladiator did not recede or tremble. The revolution of Nature had dissolved her lighter terrors as well as her wonted ties.

While they were thus terribly protected, a group of men and women, bearing torches, passed by the temple. They were of the congregation of the Nazarenes; and a sublime and unearthly emotion had not, indeed, quelled their awe, but it had robbed awe of fear. They had long believed, according to the error of the early Christians, that the Last Day was at hand; they imagined now that the Day had come.

The Nazarenes paced slowly on, their torches still flickering in the storm, their voices still raised in menace and solemn warning, till, lost amid the windings in the streets, the darkness of the atmosphere and the silence of death again fell over the scene.

There was one of the frequent pauses in the showers, and Glaucus encouraged Ione once more to proceed. Just as they stood, hesitating, on the last step of the portico, an old man, with a bag in his right hand and leaning upon a youth, tottered by. The youth bore a torch. Glaucus recognised the two as father and son—miser and prodigal.

'Father,' said the youth, 'if you cannot move more swiftly, I must leave you, or we *both* perish!'

'Fly, boy, then, and leave thy sire!'

'But I cannot fly to starve; give me thy bag of gold!' And the youth snatched at it.

'Wretch! wouldst thou rob thy father?'

'Ay! who can tell the tale in this hour? Miser, perish!'

The boy struck the old man to the ground, plucked the bag from his relaxing hand, and fled onward with a shrill yell.

'Ye gods!' cried Glaucus: 'are ye blind, then, even in the dark? Such crimes may well confound the guiltless with the guilty in one common ruin. Ione, on!—on!'

CORINTHIAN COLUMN

ARBACES ENCOUNTERS GLAUCUS AND IONE

Advancing, as men grope for escape in a dungeon, Ione and her lover continued their uncertain way. At the moments when the volcanic lightnings lingered over the streets, they were enabled, by that awful light, to steer and guide their progress: yet, little did the view it presented to them cheer or encourage their path. In parts, where the ashes lay dry and uncommixed with the boiling torrents, cast upward from the mountain at capricious intervals, the surface of the earth presented a leprous and ghastly white. In other places, cinder and rock lay matted in heaps, from beneath which emerged the half-hid limbs of some crushed and mangled fugitive. The groans of the dying were broken by wild shrieks of women's terror—now near, now distant—which, when heard in the utter darkness, were rendered doubly appalling by the crushing sense of helplessness and the uncertainty of the perils around.

'Oh, Glaucus! my beloved! my own!—take me to thy arms! One embrace! let me feel thy arms around me—and in that embrace let me die—I can no more!'

'For my sake, for my life—courage, yet, sweet Ione—my life is linked with thine: and see—torches—this way! Lo! how they brave the wind! Ha! they live through the storm—doubtless, fugitives to the sea! we will join them.'

As if to aid and reanimate the lovers, the winds and showers came to a sudden pause; the atmosphere was profoundly still—the mountain seemed at rest, gathering, perhaps, fresh fury for its next burst; the torch-bearers moved quickly on. 'We are nearing the sea,' said, in a calm voice, the person at their head. 'Liberty and wealth to each slave who survives this day! Courage! I tell you that the gods themselves have assured me of deliverance—On!'

Redly and steadily the torches flashed full on the eyes of Glaucus and Ione, who lay trembling and exhausted on his bosom. Several slaves were bearing, by the light, panniers and coffers, heavily laden; in front of them,—a drawn sword in his hand,—towered the lofty form of Arbaces.

'By my fathers!' cried the Egyptian, 'Fate smiles upon me even through these horrors, and, amidst the dreadest aspects of woe and death, bodes me happiness and love. Away, Greek! I claim my ward, Ione!'

'Traitor and murderer!' cried Glaucus, glaring upon his foe, 'Nemesis hath guided thee to my revenge!—a just sacrifice to the shades of Hades, that now seem loosed on earth. Approach—touch but the hand of Ione, and thy weapon shall be as a reed—I will tear thee limb from limb!'

Suddenly, as he spoke, the place became lighted with an intense and lurid glow. Bright and gigantic through the darkness, which closed around it like the walls of hell, the mountain shone—a pile of fire! Its summit seemed riven in two; or rather, above its surface there seemed to rise two monster shapes, each confronting each, as Demons contending for a World. These were of one deep blood-red hue of fire, which lighted up the whole atmosphere far and wide; but, *below*, the nether part of the mountain was still dark and shrouded, save in three places, adown which flowed, serpentine and irregular, rivers of the molten lava. Darkly red through the profound gloom of their banks, they flowed slowly on, as towards the devoted city. Over the broadest there seemed to spring a cragged and stupendous arch, from which, as from the jaws of hell, gushed the sources of the sudden Phlegethon. And through the still air was heard the rattling of the fragments of rock, hurtling one upon another as they were borne down the fiery cataracts—darkening, for one instant, the spot where they fell, and suffused the next, in the burnished hues of the flood along which they floated!

The slaves shrieked aloud, and, cowering, hid their faces. The Egyptian himself stood transfixed to the spot, the glow lighting up his commanding features and jewelled robes. High behind him rose a tall column that supported the bronze statue of Augustus; and the imperial image seemed changed to a shape of fire!

With his left hand circled round the form of Ione—with his right arm raised in menace, and grasping the stilus which was to have been his weapon in the arena, and which he still fortunately bore about him, with his brow knit, his lips apart, the wrath and menace of human passions arrested as by a charm, upon his features, Glaucus fronted the Egyptian!

Arbaces turned his eyes from the mountain —they rested on the form of Glaucus!

He advanced one step—it was his last on earth! The ground shook beneath him with a convulsion that cast all around upon its surface. A simultaneous crash resounded through the city, as down toppled many a roof and pillar!—the lightning, as if caught by the metal, lingered an instant on the Imperial Statue—then shivered bronze and column! Down fell the ruin, echoing along the street, and riving the solid pavement where it crashed!—The prophecy of the stars was fulfilled!

The sound—the shock, stunned the Athenian for several moments. When he

STATUE OF THE EMPEROR AUGUSTUS

recovered, the light still illuminated the scene—the earth still slid and trembled beneath! Ione lay senseless on the ground; but he saw her not yet—his eyes were fixed upon a ghastly face that seemed to emerge, without limbs or trunk, from the huge fragments of the shattered column—a face of unutterable pain, agony, and despair! The eyes shut and opened rapidly, as if sense were not yet fled; the lips quivered and grinned—then sudden stillness and darkness fell over the features, yet retaining that aspect of horror never to be forgotten!

So perished the wise Magician—the great Arbaces—the Hermes of the Burning Belt— the last of the royalty of Egypt!

THE DESPAIR OF THE LOVERS

Glaucus turned in gratitude but in awe, caught Ione once more in his arms, and fled along the street, that was yet intensely luminous. But suddenly a duller shade fell over the air. Instinctively he turned to the mountain, and beheld! one of the two gigantic crests, into which the summit had been divided, rocked and wavered to and fro; and then, with a sound, the mightiness of which no language can describe, it fell from its burning base, and rushed, an avalanche of fire, down the sides of the mountain! At the same instant gushed forth a volume of blackest smoke—rolling on, over air, sea, and earth.

Another—and another—and another shower of ashes, far more profuse than before, scattered fresh desolation along the streets. Darkness once more wrapped them as a veil; and Glaucus, his bold heart at last quelled and despairing, sank beneath the cover of an arch, and, clasping Ione to his heart—a bride on that couch of ruin—resigned himself to die.

Meanwhile Nydia, when separated by the throng from Glaucus and Ione, had in vain endeavoured to regain them. In vain she raised that plaintive cry so peculiar to the blind; it was lost amidst a thousand shrieks of more selfish terror. Again and again she returned to the spot where they had been divided—to find her companions gone, to seize every fugitive—to inquire of Glaucus— to be dashed aside in the impatience of distraction.

Poor girl!—her courage was beautiful to behold!—and Fate seemed to favour one so helpless! The boiling torrents touched her not, save by the general rain which accompanied them; the huge fragments of scoria shivered the pavement before and beside her, but spared that frail form: and when the lesser ashes fell over her, she shook them away with a slight tremor, and dauntlessly resumed her course.

Weak, exposed, yet fearless, supported but by one wish, she was a very emblem of Psyche in her wanderings; of Hope, walking through the Valley of the Shadow; of the Soul itself—lone but undaunted, amidst the dangers and the snares of life!

Her path was, however, constantly impeded by the crowds that now groped amidst the gloom, now fled in the temporary glare of the lightnings across the scene; and, at length, a group of torch-bearers rushing full against her, she was thrown down with some violence.

'What!' said the voice of one of the party, 'is this the brave blind girl! By Bacchus, she must not be left here to die! Up! my Thessalian! So—so. Are you hurt? That's well! Come along with us! we are for the shore!'

'O Sallust! it is thy voice! The gods be thanked! Glaucus! Glaucus! have ye seen him?'

'Not I. He is doubtless out of the city by this time. The gods who saved him from the lion will save him from the burning mountain.'

As the kindly epicure thus encouraged Nydia, he drew her along with him towards the sea, heeding not her passionate entreaties that he would linger yet awhile to search for Glaucus; and still, in the accent of despair, she continued to shriek out that beloved name, which, amidst all the roar of the convulsed elements, kept alive a music at her heart.

The sudden illumination, the bursts of the floods of lava, and the earthquake, which we have already described, chanced when Sallust and his party had just gained the direct path leading from the city to the port; and here they were arrested by an immense crowd, more than half the population of the city. They spread along the field without the walls, thousands upon thousands, uncertain whither to fly. The sea had retired far from the shore; and they who had fled to it had been so terrified by the agitation and preternatural shrinking of the element, the gasping forms of the uncouth sea things which the waves had left upon the sand, and by the sound of the huge stones cast from the mountain into the deep, that they had returned again to the land, as presenting the less frightful aspect of

the two. Thus the two streams of human beings, the one seaward, the other *from* the sea, had met together, feeling a sad comfort in numbers; arrested in despair and doubt.

'The world is to be destroyed by fire,' said an old man in long loose robes, a philosopher of the Stoic school: 'Stoic and Epicurean wisdom have alike agreed in this prediction: and the hour is come!'

'Yea; the hour is come!' cried a loud voice, solemn, but not fearful.

Those around turned in dismay. The voice came from above them. It was the voice of Olinthus, who, surrounded by his Christian friends, stood upon an abrupt eminence on which the old Greek colonists had raised a temple to Apollo, now timeworn and half in ruin.

And the crowd knew the face of him they had doomed to the fangs of the beast—*then* their victim—*now* their warner! and through the stillness again came his ominous voice—

'The hour is come!'

The Christians repeated the cry. It was caught up—it was echoed from side to side—woman and man, childhood and old age, repeated, not aloud, but in a smothered and dreary murmur—

'THE HOUR IS COME!'

At that moment, a wild yell burst through the air;—and, thinking only of escape, whither it knew not, the terrible tiger of the desert leaped amongst the throng, and hurried through its parted streams. And so came the earthquake—and so darkness once more fell over the earth!

And now new fugitives arrived. Grasping the treasures no longer destined for their

lord, the slaves of Arbaces joined the throng. One only of all their torches yet flickered on. It was borne by Sosia; and its light falling on the face of Nydia, he recognised the Thessalian.

'What avails thy liberty now, blind girl?' said the slave.

'Who art thou? canst thou tell me of Glaucus?'

'Ay; I saw him but a few minutes since.'

'Blessed be thy head! where?'

'Couched beneath the arch of the forum—dead or dying!—gone to rejoin Arbaces, who is no more!'

Nydia uttered not a word, she slid from the side of Sallust; silently she glided through those behind her, and retraced her steps to the city. She gained the forum—the arch; she stooped down—she felt around—she called on the name of Glaucus.

A weak voice answered—'Who calls on me? Is it the voice of the Shades? Lo! I am prepared!'

'Arise! follow me! Take my hand! Glaucus, thou shalt be saved!'

In wonder and sudden hope, Glaucus arose—'Nydia still? Ah! thou, then, art safe!'

The tender joy of his voice pierced the heart of the poor Thessalian, and she blessed him for his thought of her.

Half leading, half carrying Ione, Glaucus followed his guide. With admirable discretion, she avoided the path which led to the crowd she had just quitted, and, by another route, sought the shore.

After many pauses and incredible perseverance, they gained the sea, and joined a group, who, bolder than the rest, resolved to hazard any peril rather than continue in such a scene. In darkness they put forth to sea; but, as they cleared the land and caught new aspects of the mountain, its channels of molten fire threw a partial redness over the waves.

Utterly exhausted and worn out, Ione slept on the breast of Glaucus, and Nydia lay at his feet. Meanwhile the showers of dust and ashes, still borne aloft, fell into the wave, and scattered their snows over the deck. Far and wide, borne by the winds, those showers descended upon the remotest climes, startling even the swarthy African; and whirled along the antique soil of Syria and of Egypt.

THE NEXT MORNING

And meekly, softly, beautifully, dawned at last the light over the trembling deep!—the winds were sinking into rest—the foam died from the glowing azure of that delicious sea. Around the east, thin mists caught gradually the rosy hues that heralded the morning; Light was about to resume her reign. Yet, still, dark and massive in the distance, lay the broken fragments of the destroying cloud, from which red streaks, burning dimlier and more dim, betrayed the yet rolling fires of the mountain of the 'Scorched Fields.' The white walls and gleaming columns that had adorned the lovely coasts were no more. Sullen and dull were the shores so lately crested by the cities of Herculaneum and Pompeii.

In the silence of the general sleep, Nydia rose gently. She bent over the face of Glaucus —she inhaled the deep breath of his heavy slumber,—timidly and sadly she kissed his brow—his lips; she felt for his hand—it was locked in that of Ione; she sighed deeply, and her face darkened. Again she kissed his brow, and with her hair wiped from it the damps of night. 'May the gods bless you, Athenian!' she murmured: 'may you be happy with your beloved one!—may you sometimes remember Nydia! Alas! she is of no further use on earth!'

With these words she turned away. Slowly she crept along by the *fori*, or platforms, to the farther side of the vessel, and, pausing, bent low over the deep; the cool spray dashed upward on her feverish brow. 'It is the kiss of death,' she said—'it is welcome.' The balmy air played through her waving tresses—she put them from her face, and raised those eyes—so tender, though so lightless—to the sky, whose soft face she had never seen!

'No, no!' she said, half aloud, and in a musing and thoughtful tone, 'I cannot endure it; this jealous, exacting love—it shatters my whole soul in madness! I might harm him again—wretch that I was! I have saved him— twice saved him—happy, happy thought: why not *die* happy?—it is the last glad thought I can ever know. Oh! sacred Sea! I hear the voice invitingly—it hath a freshening and joyous call. They say that in thy embrace is dishonour—that thy victims cross not the fatal Styx—be it so!—I would not meet him in the Shades, for I should meet him still with *her!* Rest—rest—rest! there is no other Elysium for a heart like mine!'

A sailor, half dozing on the deck, heard a slight splash on the waters. Drowsily he looked up, and behind, as the vessel merrily bounded on, he fancied he saw something white above the waves; but it vanished in an instant. He turned round again, and dreamed of his home and children.

When the lovers awoke, their first thought was of each other—their next of Nydia! She was not to be found—none had seen her since the night. Every crevice of the vessel was searched—there was no trace of her. Mysterious from first to last, the blind Thessalian had vanished for ever from the living world! They guessed her fate in silence: and Glaucus and Ione, while they drew nearer to each other (feeling each other the world itself) forgot their deliverance, and wept as for a departed sister.

ROMAN MERCHANT SHIP
1ST CENTURY A.D.

APPENDIX

POMPEII AND HERCULANEUM

A CHRONICLE OF CATASTROPHY AND EXCAVATION

Though the excavations were slow and not particularly scientifically carried out, large areas were uncovered, and these were later filled in.

In 1806 Napoleon Bonaparte began to take an interest, and the work progressed faster. New discoveries were made at regular intervals. In 1813 the basilica was uncovered. By 1825 the excavation of the forum had been completed. The 1848 revolution meant that no work was carried out. Work started again when Naples was absorbed into the Kingdom of Italy in 1859. Giuseppe Fiorelli was put in charge of the new excavations and brought in an improved and more scientific method. By the end of the 19th century half the town had been excavated. Since then work has progressed more slowly, because the attention paid to cataloguing and preserving finds has been greater, and also because labour and finance have been more difficult to procure.

Amedeo Mairuri was in charge during the 1920's and was responsible for keeping on the site as many of the finds as possible – rather than sending them to the Naples Museum.

During World War II, The Allies bombed Naples and destroyed the museum; but the bombing also brought to light a large house under the museum. The bombing also uncovered the Temple of Dionysus.

Since the war, the main efforts have been directed towards preservation, rather than excavation.

The first excavation of Pompeii was made just after the AD 79 destruction, with a view to recovering valuables. But it was not until Domenico Fontana was digging a water channel (1594-1600) that anyone disturbed the town. Fontana did not bother to excavate further.

The first proper excavations took place at Herculaneum in 1709. They were led by Count Elbeuf, whose only desire was to retrieve the statuary and marble. Little was recovered, The director of the dig, Rocco Gioacchino, inspected the water channel dug by Fontana and shortly afterwards work was switched from Herculaneum to Pompeii. Gioacchino thought that he was excavating Stabiae (where the elder Pliny had died in AD 79). In 1750 work was stopped, but was resumed in 1754 after work south of the town revealed the ruins of tombs.

GLOSSARY

Note : The editor has included only those instances which might cause puzzlement to the reader or which are in themselves of especial interest.

ædile – a kind of magistrate, among whose duties was the repression of open vice and public disorder. The office of ædile varied at different times and places during the Roman empire.

alea – basically any game of chance, but here meaning the dice. Gaming was generally frowned upon, except during the Saturnalia, the festival which began on 17 December, where general licence prevailed.

Anubis – Egyptian dog-headed god, whom the Romans worshipped from the later days of the Republic.

Apis – the Sacred Bull of Memphis, in Egypt, regarded as a god. When he died, public mourning was proclaimed until the priests found a suitable bull to replace him.

apodyterium – where people undressed in the baths.

Arcadian reed – the Arcadians, self-dubbed the oldest race in Greece, lived in the middle of the Peloponnese. They were addicted to music.

Argus – the 100-eyed giant whom Hermes killed but whose eyes were used by Hera to decorate the tail of the peacock.

Ate – the daughter of Strife, an ancient Greek goddess and the personification of infatuation.

atrium – the central hall in a Roman house, open in the centre to the sky.

Bacchus – the god of wine, also known as Dionysus. He was the son of Zeus and Semele, and Hera, Zeus' wife, showed her jealousy by making him mad. According to the legends, he then journeyed through Egypt, Syria and Asia, spreading civilization and knowledge of the cultivation of the vine.

Baiæ – a favourite watering place for wealthy Romans, on a small bay west of Naples.

bestiarii – those who fought wild beasts in the circus games.

Bromian god – Bacchus.

Cacus – a giant, the son of Vulcan, he was killed by Hercules after he had stolen part of Hercules' herd of cattle.

calix – a small drinking cup.

Campania – district of ancient Italy which includes the region round Naples. It has a good climate and was popular as a holidaying area for the wealthier Romans. It was the market garden of Italy.

canicula – or *canis*, the 'dog-throw', the lowest throw of a dice.

Castor and Pollux – heavenly brothers, worshipped at Rome from an early date. Pollux was a skilled boxer and Castor a fine trainer of horses; hence they were accepted as presidents of the public games – and Pollux was a natural hero for the gladiators to swear by.

cella – the interior part of a temple.

Cerberus – the watchdog of Hades, a fearsome creature with three heads and snakes twined round its neck.

cestus – the thongs of leather, often furnished with nails and knots, wound round the fists and forearms of pugilists in the public games. They were vicious weapons, sometimes lethal.

Chloris – the personification of Spring – the Greek Flora.

Cicero – the famous orator (106–43 BC). On the orders of Mark Antony he was beheaded for his vehement speeches directed against Mark Antony.

cithara – the cithara and the lyre were essentially the same stringed (and plucked) instrument. Normally no more than seven stringed, the cithara appears to have been lighter in tone than the lyre.

cœna – the main meal of the Roman day.

comissatio – a late night drinking session, usually undertaken with a minimum of food, with entertainments after the meal.

cyathus – a ladleful.

Cybele – ancient earth goddess. She was closely associated with Eastern worship, and the excesses which accompanied her worship would have been deeply repugnant to a Christian.

Cyprian Venus – Venus (or Aphrodite) was especially worshipped in Cyprus. Goddess of love and beauty, her worship mixed Eastern and Greek ritual.

Delphic oracle – in the centre of the temple of Apollo at Delphi, on the slopes of Mt Parnassus, was a small hole in the ground from which escaped foul vapours. Pythia, the priestess of Apollo, would pronounce the revelations of the god while seated on a tripod above this cleft. This was the oracle, whose meanings were seldom clear.

designator – master of ceremonies.

Doric architecture – the simplest of the three basic orders of classical architecture was characterized by simple tapering pillars with no base and an unadorned capital.

drachm – a Greek coin, and also a weight. Though the actual weight has been calculated by scholars, the word is often used as we might use the word 'ounce' as a general indication of weight.

Epimenides – a Cretan poet and prophet, whose life was partly mythical (he was supposed to have fallen asleep for many years in a cave) but who certainly cleansed Athens of a plague in about 596 BC. St Paul, in his Epistle to Titus, quotes a verse by Epimenides: 'The Cretians are always liars, evil beasts, slow bellies.'

Erebus – the darkness through which the shades travel on their way to Hades.

Falernian – wine produced at Falernus Ager in northern Campania was noted for its fine quality.

fane – a consecrated place.

fibula – originally a brooch used for fastening garments and consisting of a pin and a curved portion furnished with a hook. Many examples survive. Later the word was also used for a buckle.

flamen – a Roman priest whose duties were to serve a particular deity. Thus the Flamen Dialis was a Priest of Zeus (Juppiter).

forum – the market place, the main meeting place for the town.

freedman – (*libertus*) a slave who had been granted his freedom. Though Roman laws on the subject were extremely complicated, and while there were different classes of freedman, none possessed the full rights of citizenship. Their sons became *ingenui* (i.e. they were considered to have been born free), but even they could not claim the rights of a *gens* (patrician family). Descendants of freedmen were, like Diomed, sometimes taunted with their origins.

Graces – Charites in Greek, Gratiæ in Latin, were three daughters of Zeus – Euphrosyne, Thalia and Aglia. They lived with the nine Muses, in Olympus, and were particularly connected with poetry.

Hecate – a goddess who dispatched demons from the nether world. She was well versed in witchcraft.

Herculaneum – ancient city in Campania which was largely destroyed by the earthquake of AD 63 and then utterly buried by solidified mud during the great eruption of AD 79. It now lies some 100 feet below the surface of the ground. It was accidentally discovered in the late 17th century.

Hesperides – the guardians of the golden apples presented by Gæa to Hera.

Hesperus – the evening star.

Ilissus – a small river in Greece, rising in Mt Hymettus and flowing east of Athens.

Isis – wife of Osiris, mother of Horus (*see* Orus). In Roman Imperial times her worship became very popular.

lanista – gladiators were trained in special schools, where they were taught the skills by professional lanistæ. One lanista would train a whole group (*familia*) of gladiators, and he would also sometimes own and lease out gladiators for exhibitions.

Lares – protective deities who looked after individual houses.

larva – a spectre or ghost.

Leda – mother of Castor and Pollux; she was seduced by Zeus disguised as a swan.

lemures – as *larva*, spectres or ghosts.

Lethe – the underworld river of forgetfulness.

lictor – a public officer, often attendant on a magistrate, whose duties included the infliction of punishment and certain protective roles.

manes – kindly spirits of the underworld.

mappa – a small personal table-napkin, with which fingers were wiped (forks had not been invented). Curiously, this word is thought to be of African (Carthaginian) origin. A larger napkin, so large as to be used also as a table cloth, was called a *mantele*.

Misenum – promontory in Campania, one of the principal Roman ports.

murænæ – lampreys, small eel-like fish which were a favourite gourmet dish in Roman times.

musca – (literally a fly) unwelcome and uninvited guest.

Muses – the nine Muses (Clio, Euterpe, Thalia, Melpomene, Terpsichore, Erata, Polymnia, Urania, and Calliope) were goddesses of the arts. They lived in company with the Graces. Thalia appears both as a Muse and a Grace.

Nazarene – a follower of Jesus of Nazareth, a Christian.

Neapolis – Naples.

Nemesis – goddess of happiness and misery.

Nero – Roman emperor, adopted by the emperor Claudius AD 50. He died in AD 68.

ninth ide of August – 24 August.

Nox – daughter of Chaos and the representation of Night. She lived in the underworld.

Orcus – Pluto (Hades), god of the underworld.

ornatrix – a female slave, expert in the art of dressing her mistress' hair.

Orus – Horus, the son of Isis and Osiris. This Egyptian hawk-headed god was worshipped by the Romans and the Greeks (who called him Harpocrates).

Osiris – Egyptian god, husband of Isis.

palla – a wide cloak.

Pallas – Athena (Minerva), goddess of wisdom, the arts and science.

pallium – basically a rectangular piece of cloth, it was worn as a garment both before the adoption of the toga (*q.v.*) and, except by patricians and on ceremonial occasions, after the toga had had its day.

Paphos – a town in the west of Cyprus which was the centre of the worship of Aphrodite (Venus).

Parian marble – marble was the most famous produce of the Aegean island of Paros. Most of the stone was quarried from a hill named Marpessa.

peristyle – collonaded court surrounding a garden and with the main rooms leading off it.

'Persicos odi, puer, apparatus' – 'I hate the luxury of the Persians, my boy' (Horace *Odes* I xxxviii).

Phlegethon – a river of fire in the underworld.

Pindar – Greek poet (*c.* 522–442 BC) of splendid celebratory verse.

popularia – the third-class seats for the people (*populus*) in the amphitheatre.

prætor – a senior Roman magistrate, who assisted the consuls and looked after civil courts. The number of prætors varied at different periods, but their power was great, and they often became administrators of a province after discharging their prætorial duties.

Rameses – altogether there were eleven kings of Ancient Egypt named Rameses.

sacellum – a small roofless shrine, dedicated to a god. It was often built as a private place of worship.

saga – a wise woman or fortune-teller.

Sappho – the great female lyric poet of the 7th century BC.

scoria – fragments of cellular volcanic lava.

sesterces – there is a danger of confusion here in Roman money. A sesterce (*sestertius*) was the basic unit coin for accounting. It was small and silver (in the empire it was large and brass). *Sestertium* denoted 1000 sesterces, and was not a coin but a sum of money.

Silenus – a Satyr and companion of Bacchus. He was a fat, drunk, jolly old man, the son of either Hermes, Pan or Gæa, one of the goddesses of the underworld.

spoliarium – the place to which the killed or mortally wounded gladiators were dragged from the arena.

stilus and tablets – the stilus was a writing instrument, usually of iron, pointed at one end and rounded and flattened at the other, so that the surface of the waxed writing tablet could be smoothed over in case of error, or for re-use. It was about the size of a modern pencil. The tablets were commonly thin pieces of wood, on which wax was spread to receive messages. Tablets were often carried in pairs, the waxed surfaces facing each other and protected by raised ridges round their edges.

sybarite – a pleasure-lover, so named from the town of Sybaris, in southern Italy, whose ancient citizens were renowned for their luxurious living.

tablinum – reception room.

tepidarium – the warm chamber of the baths, where habitués often sat sweating with their clothes on before moving on to the *calidarium*.

thermæ – originally warm springs, they later also referred to the superb baths of the Empire, with all their luxury and facilities, in contrast to the simpler public *balneæ* of the Republic.

tibia – a reed pipe, not unlike a primitive oboe, and very popular, used both by the Greeks and the Romans, normally played in pairs.

Tibullus – Roman poet (*c.* 54-18 BC) of gentle elegiac verse.

Titus – Roman emperor, AD 79–81 (lived AD 40–81). It was he who completed the building of the Colosseum. Vesuvius erupted and destroyed Pompeii and Herculaneum in the first year of his reign. Son of the emperor Vespasian, he was unpopular in his early days, but in his brief period as emperor he strove for the happiness of his people.

toga – the outer gown, worn originally only in Rome itself. Later it was worn chiefly by the upper classes and for certain formal occasions (no longer by the time of this story).

Tyrian dye – The expensive purple dye obtained from the murex shellfish. Because of its cost, clothes dyed purple denoted the wearer's wealth.

ustrinum – place for burning the dead. The remains, after the cremation, were buried elsewhere.

Venus, girdle of – the girdle of Venus (*cestus*) was fashioned by Vulcan, Venus' husband. It fell off during a moment of dalliance with Mars, and was considered the symbol of irresistible attraction. (The word *cestus* was also the boxing glove used by gladiators.)

Vesta – the Roman goddess of the hearth – the point of assembly in a Roman home. Her priestesses, the Vestals, were virginal girls.

vestibule – entrance in front, the main door of a Roman house, surrounded on three sides by the house, and open on the fourth side to the street.

Vesuvius – Mt Vesuvius is today nearly 4000ft high, and still active. In recorded history, though it was known to be volcanic, there are no eruptions until AD 79 (the year in which this book is set), though in AD 63 earthquakes had severely damaged surrounding towns, such as Herculaneum.

viridarium – an ornamental garden.

Vulcanalia – a festival in honour of Vulcan, the Roman god of fire, held on 23 August. The day started with candle-light, in honour of the god.

ATRIUM OF THE
HOUSE OF PANSA

MUSEUMS FROM WHICH MATERIAL
WAS USED FOR REFERENCE

Museum of Roman Civilisation	Rome
Vatican Museum	Rome
National Roman Museum	Rome
Berlin Museum	Berlin
British Museum	London
National Archaeological Museum	Naples
Pompeii Museum	Pompeii

VIRIDARIUM OF THE
HOUSE OF VETTI

BOOKS FOR FURTHER READING AND WORKS OF REFERENCE

J. P. V. O. Balsdon, *Life and Leisure in Ancient Rome*. The Bodley Head, London 1969.

R. C. Bell, *Board and Table Games*. Oxford University Press, London 1960.

Marcel Brion, *Pompeii and Herculaneum*. Elek Books, London 1960.

Andre Cailleux, *Anatomy of the Earth*. World University Library, Weidenfeld & Nicolson, London 1968.

Paavo Castren, *Ordo Populusque Pompeianus*. Acta Instituti Romani Finlandiae, Vol. VIII. Rome 1975.

G. Clarke, *Pompeii*, Vol. II. Charles Knight, London 1832.

M. Della Corte, *Pompeii: The New Excavations*. Italy 1927.

Egon Caesar Conte Corti, *The Destruction and Resurrection of Pompeii and Herculaneum*. Routledge and Kegan Paul, London 1951.

Ch. Daremburg & E. Saglio, *Dictionnaire des antiquités grecques et romaines* Hachette, Paris 1877.

Joseph Jay Deiss, *Herculaneum* Thomas Y. Crowell, New York 1966

John Ferguson, *The Religions of the Roman Empire* Thames and Hudson, London 1970.

Barbara Flower and Elizabeth Rosenbaum, *The Roman Cookery Book*. George G. Harrap & Co., London 1958.

Giulio Giannelli, *The World of Ancient Rome*, Putnam, New York, 1967.

Michael Grant, *Cities of Vesuvius* Weidenfeld & Nicolson, 1971.

Pierre Gusman, *Pompeii – la Ville – les Moeurs – les Arts*. Emile Gaillard, Paris 1906.

August Man, translated by Francis W. Kelsey, *Pompeii – its Life and Art*. MacMillan & Co., London 1899.

J. F. Kirkaldy, *General Principles of Geology* Radus Books/Hutchinson, London 1966.

Dr Fritz Kretzschmer, *La Technique Romaine* U.D.I. Verlag, Dusseldorf 1958.

Wolfgang Leppman, *Pompeii in Fact and Fiction*. Elek Books, London 1968.

A. G. McKay, *Houses, Villas and Palaces in the Roman World*. Thames and Hudson, London 1975.

Amadeo Maiuri, *La Casa del Menandro*. La Libreria dello Stato, Rome 1933.

H. J. R. Murray, *A History of Board Games Other than Chess*. The Clarendon Press, Oxford 1962.

J. Overbeck, *Pompeii in Seinem Gebäuden*. Alterthümern und Kunstwerken, Verlag von Wilhelm Engelman, Leipzig 1866.

Ed. William Smith, *A Dictionary of Greek and Roman Antiquities*. London 1842.

Paul Vigneron, *Le Cheval dans L'Antiquité Greco-romaine*. Universite de Nancy, France 1968.

K. D. White, *Farm Equipment of the Roman World*. Cambridge University Press, 1975.

Lilian M. Wilson, *The Clothing of the Ancient Romans*. The John Hopkins Press, Baltimore 1938.